Magpie Genesis

MAGPIE GENESIS

The Magpie Odyssey III

A Novel

Lorretta Lynde

For Fred & Ellen
Le gach dea-ghui

Lorretta Lynde

iUniverse, Inc.
New York   Bloomington

Magpie Genesis
The Magpie Odyssey III

iUniverse books may be ordered through booksellers or by contacting:

iUniverse
1663 Liberty Drive
Bloomington, IN 47403
www.iuniverse.com
1-800-Authors (1-800-288-4677)

Because of the dynamic nature of the Internet, any Web addresses or links containe++d in this book may have changed since publication and may no longer be valid. The views expressed in this work are ++solely those of the author and do not necessarily reflect the views of the publisher, and the publisher hereby disclaims any responsibility for them.

ISBN: 978-1-4401-2349-8 (pbk)
ISBN: 978-1-4401-2350-4 (ebk)

Printed in the United States of America

iUniverse rev. date: 2/17/2009

*For my father and mother, Myron and Eleanor Lynde,
who always believed there was magic in their children.*

M O N T A N A

Magpie
Genesis
Country

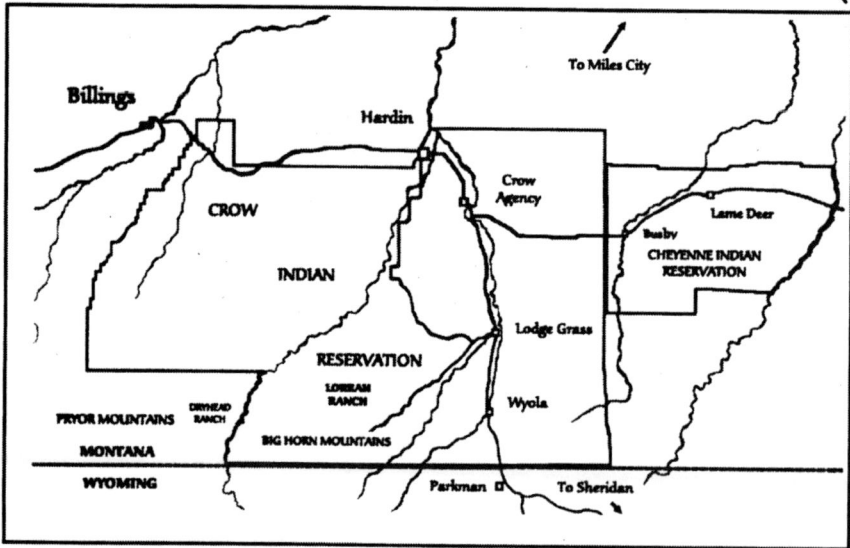

Billings

To Miles City

Hardin

CROW

Crow
Agency

Lame Deer

Busby

CHEYENNE INDIAN
RESERVATION

INDIAN

RESERVATION

Lodge Grass

LODMAN
RANCH

DRYHEAD
RANCH

Wyola

PRYOR MOUNTAINS

MONTANA

BIG HORN MOUNTAINS

WYOMING

Parkman

To Sheridan

Lorrah Family Tree

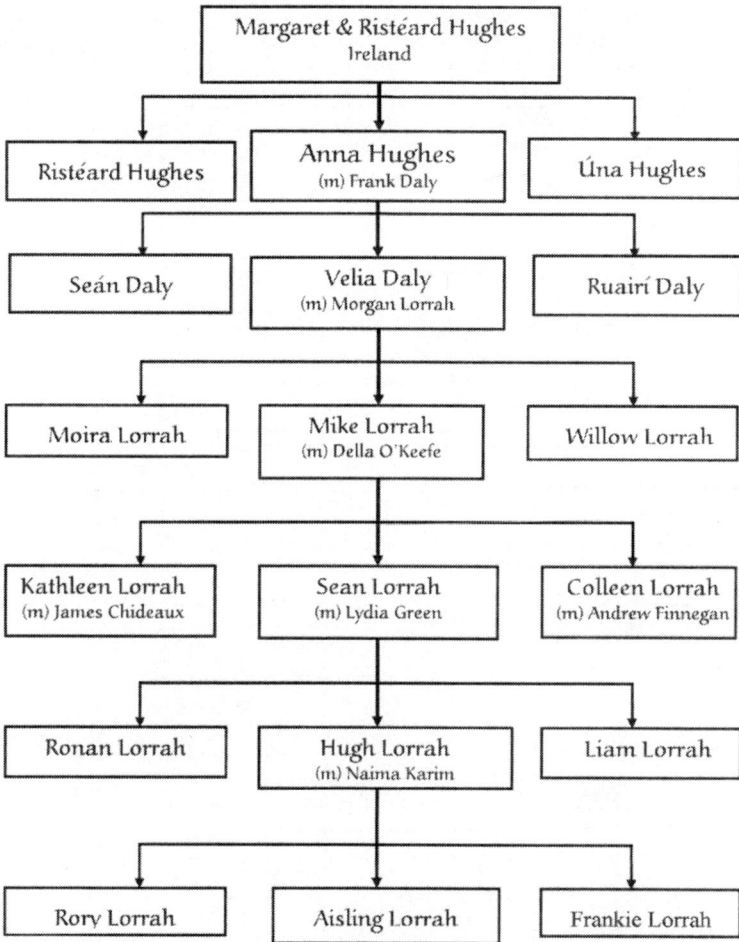

Margaret & Ristéard Hughes
Ireland

Ristéard Hughes

Anna Hughes
(m) Frank Daly

Úna Hughes

Seán Daly

Velia Daly
(m) Morgan Lorrah

Ruairí Daly

Moira Lorrah

Mike Lorrah
(m) Della O'Keefe

Willow Lorrah

Kathleen Lorrah
(m) James Chideaux

Sean Lorrah
(m) Lydia Green

Colleen Lorrah
(m) Andrew Finnegan

Ronan Lorrah

Hugh Lorrah
(m) Naima Karim

Liam Lorrah

Rory Lorrah

Aisling Lorrah

Frankie Lorrah

PROLOGUE

▼

Aisling rammed clothes into her backpack. She was getting ready just as she had each year since she was eight years old. Once her father put the finishing touches on the painting he was working on, he would load her things into his pickup truck. Then they would leave for the Clear Spring line camp. Aisling spent every summer there, and she had loved it -- when she was younger.

Now that she was a teenager, she was less enthusiastic. School was barely out for the summer. She would miss all the fun of vacation, sequestered away in the Big Horn Mountains with her Aunt Colleen and Uncle Andrew, seeing no one else for three whole months. She flung her hairbrush in on top of the jeans and t-shirts already in the pack, and sat down heavily on the bed with a theatrical sigh. Her mother, Naima, looked around the door to assess her progress.

"Are you almost packed, Aisling?" she asked. "Your dad will be ready in a few minutes, and he wants to make the trip up and down the mountain in daylight."

The girl looked at her pleadingly.

"Mom, do I *have* to go?"

The question hung in the air, floating on the hint of a whine.

Naima regarded her thirteen-year-old daughter. If you overlooked the sour expression on her face, she looked almost angelic. Her honey brown hair cascaded to her shoulders, framing the creamy skin of youth and startling cobalt blue eyes. How could this beautiful child, always so eager to please, suddenly turn into a rebellious teenager?

Naima's tone was matter-of-fact.

"Your aunt and uncle are expecting you. You have spent every summer with them since you were a little girl."

"But my friends are all here and I have to miss my whole summer with them!"

"They'll be here when you come back for school."

Aisling did not hide her annoyance.

"But they will have completely forgotten me!"

Naima suppressed a smile at the ridiculous statement.

"Then they aren't really very good friends, are they?"

"Oh, *Mom!*" This time the whine was overt. "You just don't understand!"

Naima's calm gaze rested steadily on her daughter until the girl dropped her glaring expression.

"You know you love the mountain. It's something none of your friends have the opportunity to do, and Aunt Colleen and Uncle Andrew have so much to share with you. Why would you want to miss that?"

Aisling did not have an answer for her mother's question. She just knew that her friends had many activities planned that she did not want to miss. But she had to go to the mountain instead. None of them had to do anything like this. It just wasn't fair.

Following the rules in place since the first time she made this trip, she had piled all the paraphernalia of her "civilized" teen-age world on her dresser…i-Pod, cell phone, video games. She knew from experience that she would not need them, nor would they work in the remote mountain location. They sat -- a mournful monument of all she would leave behind to go to what now seemed an exile far, far away. A mixture of resentment and loss churned in her heart. It was in this dejected pose that her father, Hugh Lorrah, found her. His slate-blue eyes surveyed the scene, and came to rest on his daughter's woeful face. Resisting the urge to chuckle at this adolescent funk, he put on an equally serious expression and sat down next to Aisling. Naima had already filled him in on her previous exchange with the girl, and Hugh measured his approach.

"Having a little trouble letting go of your summer months?" he asked.

Aisling gave him a sidelong glance.

"Nobody cares how *I* feel," she muttered.

Hugh knew better than to rise to this drama.

After a few quiet moments, he spoke again.

"We won't force you to go," he said. "But you have always looked forward to it. Last year, you were sitting in the truck waiting for *me*. But after your first summer up there, it has always been your choice."

Aisling's memory slid back to that day. The sun had been shining on the budding spring leaves, and she was excited to get to the mountain. She loved

2

her Aunt Colleen and Uncle Andrew, and the mountain's pine-fresh air and abundant wildlife energized her.

So what was different about this year?

For one thing, she was growing up. Feelings and emotions that had not existed a year ago rioted in her psyche. Over the past year in middle school, her friends and she had turned their attention to fashions, music and …yes, boys. A need to belong and conform to what her friends deemed important had all her focus.

Yet she knew she was different from her friends. It was internalized, but she occasionally caught herself thinking that her friends were superficial. The time she spent with her family and the summer months on the mountain had shown her that there were many things beyond most human experience. Now, her father was sitting here, and she did not know how to tell him about her inner turmoil at moving between the two worlds.

Hugh sensed what she felt, even though he did not know everything in her heart.

"I'll tell you what," he said, addressing her as an adult. "Let's take one more day to think about this. We don't have to leave today. Why don't you spend some time here at the house with your mom and your brothers and me? Clear your head. At least sleep on it tonight."

Aisling breathed a sigh of relief. It was not so much a feeling that she had been let off the hook, but rather that her parents believed she was mature enough to give her time for further thought. Nodding silently, she rose from where she sat, pulled off her jacket and laid it across her pack.

Hugh watched her carefully, remembering how he felt when he first discovered the ancestral powers and responsibilities of the Lorrah family. He had been just eight years old when he saw his grandfather charm an owl from its perch in the huge tree near the ranch house.

It was a cold night, illuminated by an almost-full moon. He and his parents were visiting the ranch, and he heard a sound that caused him to get up and go to the window. In the blue moonlight outside, he had seen his Grandfather Mike standing still in the snow. The moon illuminated the white sheepskin that lined the tall man's coat, and his eyes glinted like photos Hugh had seen of wolves.

As the boy watched with fascination, his grandfather moved his arm up high in front of his face and continued to stand there. Just when Hugh began to think Mike might have lost his mind, a flurry of motion was visible in the bare branches of the tree. In absolute silence, a gigantic white owl launched itself smoothly into the air and glided to Mike's waiting arm. Mike lowered his arm so that he and the huge bird were eye to eye. A current of recognition and communication ran between the man and the raptor, casting an aura of blue around them. The connection went on for what seemed a very long time, then the white wings spread wide and the owl sailed away in the crystal air.

At that moment, Hugh became conscious that his bare feet had become very cold as he stood by the window on the wood floor, and he crawled back under the big quilt. The next morning, he wondered if it had been a dream. But when he put his boots on and went out into the snow, he could see his grandfather's path to the very spot where he had seen him the night before. The tracks led to a tramped-down area where the man had stood, then the tracks turned and led back to the house. Hugh knew with certainty then that his memory was accurate.

Later in the day, he found his grandfather alone, doing paperwork in the ranch office. When Hugh hesitated at the door, Mike looked up, and motioned him into the room. Hugh took a seat in the big leather chair facing the desk.

"Grandpa," he began, "I saw something very interesting last night."

There was no surprise or curiosity in his grandfather's expression.

"I knew you were watching," Mike said. "You were supposed to see that. You are old enough now."

"Is that a tame owl?" Hugh asked.

"Not really," Mike replied. "It's a spirit animal. That means it is an animal that watches over me and helps me when I need it. There will be many more such contacts, and one of these years, you will meet your own spirit animal. Then you will understand."

As the years passed, and Hugh grew up, he had more and more encounters like this, and he came to understand that his was not an ordinary family. There were many mysteries and many secrets, connected directly or indirectly with its Irish heritage or the long-term friendship with the Crow Indian tribe.

Looking back, Hugh wondered why he had not felt it necessary to ask more questions at that time, but his grandfather's answer had satisfied him then. It was later, in the far mountain country, that he had found his own destiny within the family traditions. At least Aisling was being eased into this strange world, rather than having it suddenly appear as it had to him.

He turned back to his daughter.

"Does that sound okay to you?" he asked, looking directly into her eyes.

Aisling gave him a long look, suddenly wishing he would just say she did not have to go at all, or at least make the decision for her. Making it her responsibility was something she had not counted on. He did not waver. Dropping her gaze, she shrugged.

"Okay. I'll decide by tomorrow. But I'm sure I won't want to go this summer."

Hugh nodded.

"I don't want you to say what your decision is until tomorrow," he told her.

Aisling nodded her assent, and Hugh left the room. Once he was out of her sight, the girl made a move to unpack her things. If he said she didn't have to, then she wasn't going. But something made her pause. Thinking of her aunt and uncle, she recalled how much she fell into the rhythm of the mountain and the forest when she was with them. Their presence calmed her, and she seemed to have far fewer crises than her school friends did. Something about her demeanor discouraged those friends from questioning or ridiculing her for the different way she spent her summer. Still, she felt at odds about going away.

Shrugging on a light jacket, she told her mother she was going out, and she ran down the street to where her best friend, Jessica, lived. As soon as her friend's mother answered the door, she could hear the giggling of voices coming from Jessica's room. The familiar hallway welcomed her as she made her way toward the sound.

"Hi," she said, poking her head into the room.

"Omi*gawwd*!" squealed Jessica and another friend, Amy. "You didn't go today! Come look at this great nail color we got!"

Both girls flashed fluorescent green fingertips at her.

"Want to try it, too?"

"Not today," Aisling replied. "I just did mine in this bronze-y color and put on these little appliqués. What do you think?"

Both girls grasped her hands and peered at her work. She wished she had not cut her nails so short, but on the mountain, she knew longer nails would not survive.

The girls continued to examine the artful nails she had spent so much time creating, but they soon lost interest, and began to chatter about their most recent trip to the shopping center.

"We're going to go every day all summer and just hang out!" Jessica exclaimed. "Isn't that just the *best* thing?"

Suddenly, the thought spending the entire summer on such activities made Aisling think she might prefer to be on the mountain.

Jessica asked her, "So, do you get to stay home, or do you have to go up there and spend the *whole* summer with those *old* people?"

The question stung. Aisling had never thought of Colleen and Andrew as old. They were more fit and energetic than she was. They knew everything about the wild plants and animals that lived in their environs, and they taught her about them when she came for the summer. They never bored her. Her mind was ravenous for such knowledge, and it was beginning to occur to her that it might be better to spend her summer with them. Then there were the other feelings she did not really understand about the changes that were coming over her body. Confusion swirled in her thoughts. Why had she told her friends anything about Colleen and Andrew? They could never know what it was like to be with them.

She shrugged.

"They are old, I guess. But they are pretty interesting. And the mountain is so beautiful."

Her friends looked at her like she had announced that a UFO had landed on the front lawn. They would never understand, and she knew it. In the midst of this discussion, some part of her made the decision to go.

Smiling apologetically at her friends, she sighed.

"I really wish I could stay here for the summer, but this is something my parents want me to do. I'm not quite sure why, but it is really important to them. And at least I get away from my little brothers for a while."

Her friends nodded in unison. Aisling's little brothers were mischievous to be sure, and they had pestered the girls on many occasions. This comment made sense to them.

"We'll keep diaries, and tell you everything that went on this summer. The boys will miss you for sure…but they'll probably pay more attention to us if you're not here!" Jessica giggled.

Both girls had always declared Aisling to be the most beautiful of the three. Aisling shook her head, her silky hair flowing with the motion.

"They won't even notice I'm gone!"

She listened to her friends for a little longer, then returned home. She found her parents sitting at the kitchen table, drinking tea.

"Okay," she said with a dramatic sigh. "I guess I'll go to the mountain. But I probably won't enjoy it."

CHAPTER 1

▼

Hugh rose very early the next morning, dressed, and carefully placed his grandfather's hat on his head. The Stetson was a prized possession and it always made him feel that Mike Lorrah was with him when he went into the mountains. He had packed the pickup with gear and snacks the night before. He secured the groceries his Aunt Kathleen had dropped off for him to deliver as well. It was her mission to make sure her younger sister and her brother in law had a few homemade food items whenever someone went to see them. Leaning against the old truck, he waited, gazing at Aisling as she made her appearance. One hand carried her duffle and she wore her usual mountain wardrobe – sturdy jeans and a flannel shirt. She carried her jacket and an extra pair of hiking boots. Without a word, she climbed into the passenger seat, and the two of them set off.

The first stop would be at the family ranch, where Aisling's grandparents now lived. Sean and Lydia Lorrah had moved to the ranch at the foot of the Big Horn Mountains after a fire destroyed their home in Billings. It was the perfect place for Sean to write, and Lydia enjoyed the peace and beauty of the country. She handled the business of the ranch with her calm efficiency, and indulged herself in long walks. Aisling knew her grandparents would be very happy to see her and Hugh, and she looked forward to seeing them, too.

A long ride on the Interstate took them onto the Crow Indian Reservation, and to the interchange that led into the tiny town of Lodge Grass. This community had suffered the fate of many Montana towns bypassed by the major highway, and parts of it looked shabby. There was one Co-op gas station, a lone grocery store with no windows and a single entry door, a post office, three or four churches, and a few little businesses. Most people did their shopping in Billings or Hardin now and there was little need for other stores. Many of the homes were small and poor, and there were empty lots where buildings once stood. There had been some funding for streets and curbing, so it was easy enough to drive around, but the town wasn't a very inviting place. Aisling was glad that she had not grown up here.

Hugh turned the truck up Lodge Grass Creek Road and they drove in silence for the ten miles it took to reach the ranch. Every mile took them closer to the Big Horn Mountains, splendid in hazy elevation. Lodge Grass Creek meandered from side to side of the valley, and the fields were lush and green with new grass and alfalfa. Cattle and sheep dotted the fields and wildflowers reveled in a dozen colors at the side of the road. Redwing blackbirds chirruped from the cattail slough, and occasionally a meadowlark sounded its unique call. In the misty distance, the Bighorn Mountains reared their blue immensity. Aisling felt a sense of wonder as peace began to settle over her. These sights were familiar and new at the same time…how could that be?

At the entry gate to the ranch, they were greeted by the antics of the new lambs. The bold little critters scampered over ditch banks and bounced on stiff legs with tails wriggling. Laughter seemed to break a little of the tension between father and daughter, and Aisling turned to Hugh with her eyes shining.

"Do Grandma and Grandpa know we are coming?"

"Of course."

The truck negotiated the curved lane as it swept around to deliver them to the front of the grand old log ranch house. Sean and Lydia Lorrah sat in the homey wood rockers on the vine-covered porch that extended all the way across the front of the big house. Before the pickup stopped rolling, Aisling leapt out of the passenger side, and raced up the stairs to throw herself into the arms of her grandfather.

"Hi, granddaughter," Sean laughed. "On your way to the mountain?"

Aisling was serious for a moment and then the truth slid from her mouth.

"Yes. I wasn't sure I wanted to come this summer, but here I am, I guess."

Lydia looked carefully at her granddaughter. She recognized the changes in the girl, noting that she had grown several inches over the winter, and womanhood was blossoming on her body.

"Was it hard to leave your friends for the summer?' Lydia asked.

"At first," Aisling replied. "But then I really didn't want to spend the whole summer hanging out at the mall, either."

"Lesser of two evils, I guess...or maybe the greater of two goods!" Lydia said.

They spent the night at the ranch house. Aisling loved her grandparents, and this time spent with them made the prospect of the summer at Clear Spring more palatable. Her Grandfather Sean had many stories about trailing bands of sheep to the high country with her great grandfather Mike, and he spoke of the beauty of the place and how fortunate the family was to have access to the grazing ranges on and off the Crow Indian Reservation.

The ride to the mountain the next day was long and rough. The four-wheel-drive crawled over stones and washouts in the seldom-used track that passed for a road. Magnificent scenery rolled by slowly, cliffs and trees framing the view. The further they ascended into this remote area, the more spectacular the forests and canyons became. They edged along a rocky rim so high that they were above the wisps of clouds parading between the canyon walls. Aisling gazed out the passenger side window, an impassive expression on her face. Hugh made a couple of stabs at conversation, but his daughter only gave the briefest responses, going back to staring out the window after each one. Finally, he gave up and just drove. He allowed his mind to roam back to his time of discovery in the mountains and along the streams with his father.

The beginning was when he and Sean were getting the campsite ready for his brothers and his mother near Wolfclaw Lake. Sean was teaching him to set up a Crow teepee, which they had always used for camping. It was an eighteen-footer, large enough to house Sean, Lydia and the three boys comfortably. Sean had insisted that he and Hugh come ahead of time to prepare the place.

"I wanted some time with you, Hugh, just you and me. It is time for you to begin to understand your connection to Nature and to our family legacy," Sean told Hugh. "Until now, you have been learning to identify plants and animals, but you did not understand how you are tied to everything that surrounds you."

They bound the four strongest lodgepole pine poles together with rope, about fifteen or sixteen feet from the bottom.

Sean continued, "Many tribes use three poles as the base, but the Crow use four, to represent the seasons of the year."

They stood the poles up and walking under them, they extended them like a tripod, albeit one with four legs. Sean insisted that they set the poles exactly at points located at the northeast, the southwest, the southeast and the northwest. He placed them himself, without directional assistance, and explained that these corresponded to the four seasons. The opening would face precisely east.

Hugh pulled out the compass his grandfather had given him, and discovered to his amazement that his father's location of the poles was dead on. Before he could ask how his father was able to do that, Sean showed him how to stack the remaining fifteen poles at even intervals against the four base poles leaning them in forming a circular framework.

"This creates a shelter that the Crow call 'Our Second Mother,'" Sean said. "They believe the first mother is Mother Nature, and the third mother is Mother Earth. But they look at the teepee as a womb from which we get to be reborn every day. Their legends say the design for the teepee was given to them by the Great White Owl, and that is why the covers of their lodges are always white."

They unfolded the brilliant white teepee cover and laid it out flat on the clean grass. They used two poles to raise it onto their framework.

When they finished, Sean walked Hugh around the teepee, telling him, "Here on the east side, the two door poles represent the spirit of the Mountain Lion on the right and the Wolf on the left. These are considered ferocious animals who will not allow evil to enter this lodge. The Crow believe that the Grizzly Bear guards the door and scares evil away. The smoke flaps on top are the Coyote, who watches over the lodge during the day and the Owl, who watches over it during the night…both to warn the people inside when danger is coming."

Sean continued, "So you can see that this lodge represents harmony with nature. When your gift, your special skills come to you, this will unite you with what surrounds you."

As they stood back to admire their work, a huge white owl glided in and perched at the spot where all the poles were tied together. It examined the structure, hooted in a low tone of approval, then lifted off in total silence to soar toward the trees. Before it reached them, it vanished from their sight.

Hugh turned excitedly to Sean.

"Dad!" he whispered, "Did you see that?"

"Yes,' Sean replied. "It happened when my father and his friend Black Bird Shows taught me what I am teaching you today."

This memory helped the trip to speed by for Hugh, as he transported Aisling to her date with the family destiny. Before he knew it, they were pulling up in the flat area by the line camp cabin that served as year-round home to his aunt and uncle. At first, it seemed no one was there. Then the trees next to the cabin began to shimmer and undulate like a curtain. Materializing through this mirage, Colleen and Andrew appeared directly in front of them. He could not be sure if they had been standing there all along, or if they had suddenly become visible from thin air.

Whatever the case, there they were.

They were a striking vision of good health and serenity. Living year round on the mountain, despite extremes of weather and season, obviously agreed with them. Colleen's rich dark tresses tumbled loose to her waist, framing a face without lines. Hugh noticed for the first time that there were many silver strands in her hair. A few small laugh lines creased the smooth skin around her arresting blue eyes, but her posture was straight and strong. Andrew's thick hair had gone almost completely white, but he looked healthy and fit. His green eyes reflected sunlight as he gazed at his guests. Considering the injuries his Irish uncle had sustained in the Omagh bombing, Hugh found his condition remarkable. The oddest thing was that they both appeared to be smaller than he remembered. Was it because they were aging? They were in their sixties, after all. So many older people lost height, but this seemed to be more than that. Andrew, who had stood as tall as Hugh when they first met, was a good two inches shorter than he, and Colleen was smaller than he knew she had been the last time he had seen her. The presence of these two people was still so potent that their physical size did not initially strike the observer. They radiated knowledge and power that made them seem much taller and stronger.

Colleen wore jeans and a cable-knit Aran sweater. On her feet were the intensely beautiful moccasins that had been a gift of her friend, Thomas Skyhorse. The doeskin they were made of was so white that they appeared to glow. Beaded on the front of each tall legging was a single magpie, and the beads glittered in the sun. Andrew wore a leather shirt, fashioned in the old Crow Indian style, and he wore his plain moccasins like a second skin. Hugh grinned, and the two older people each raised one hand in greeting.

This period was one of the rare times that Colleen and Andrew were actually in day to day residence at the camp, primarily to be ready to receive Aisling for the summer. You couldn't say they lived there in any permanent fashion, since they usually slept under the stars in the music of the Big Horn Mountain forest, and spent most of their time ranging through the canyons and meadows. The only time they slept inside the place on a regular basis was during the raging snow storms that often visited the mountain during the winter. Otherwise, they lived like wild things, eating what nature provided, and drinking the water of the cold spring for which the place was named. Once in a while, hungry for a more "civilized" meal, they would cook on the wood stove that heated the place. Today the fare was a rich soup of rabbit, along with many wild plants they had harvested.

Aisling hugged each of them warmly, then strode off into the meadow, removing herself from the discussion. Andrew followed her, catching up as the girl was settling herself among the wildflowers. Hugh turned to his aunt.

"I feel helpless," he said. "She really struggled with whether or not she had to come this year. I know we agreed that she could choose, but I'm afraid she will miss her chance to understand everything, if she does not learn it from you."

Colleen's brilliant eyes rested on his face. Memories of her own early encounters with the family mysteries swirled in her mind, and love for this nephew warmed her heart. They had shared much, this young man and his aunt, and she knew he felt responsible and committed to his daughter's education.

At last, she spoke.

"Was it ultimately her choice to come or did you have to order it?"

"Hers," Hugh replied. "But it took her an entire day to decide, and she still doesn't seem too happy about it."

"Let's tell her that she can choose to leave the mountain if she remains unhappy after a week. That will give her a chance to decide if the time has come to take a break from all this. Stay for some soup, and let's talk a bit more before you go back down."

Hugh stayed and while helping Colleen dish up the food, marveled as he always did at the richness of these surroundings. At Aisling's age, he had spent many days in the Big Horns with his father. Sean had introduced him to the symphony of sounds, smells, and feelings this remote place had to offer, and he had found his gift here. Hugh had the ability to translate sight to canvas with ease, and it had come directly with his connection to the place.

After they finished lunch and Hugh left, Colleen went outside. Aisling and Andrew were already back in the meadow. The day was splendid. The crystalline sky arched over the mountain, illuminating every blade of grass and every green pine needle. Flowers were rampant and butterflies flitted from one to another with abandon.

As Colleen approached Andrew and Aisling, she took a long look at her great-niece. The aura of dawning womanhood wrapped around the girl like a gossamer shawl. The change from the previous summer was amazing and not just a little disquieting. Then she had still been a child. Now the woman she was to become was clearly visible.

In the following days, Colleen took Aisling out, ranging through the meadows and forests, hiking the narrow deer trails into the canyons, and refreshing the lessons on plants and animals from the previous years. Aisling liked being with this woman, who treated her as an equal in many ways, and who always respected her questions and observations. When Colleen picked up the pace and moved out at a fast trot, Aisling found herself thankful that she had participated in cross-country track at her school during the year. It was amazing how much strength and endurance her great-aunt had. Andrew accompanied them on some of these journeys, but often he went off into the wilderness on treks alone. Since coming from Ireland to live with Colleen in the mountains, Andrew had made them his own. Like Colleen, he was at ease in the wild, and at peace with their life together. While they both enjoyed their occasional visits with her brother Sean and her sister Kathleen, they preferred the deep serenity of the forest and mountain grasslands.

When Colleen was satisfied that Aisling was current with her knowledge, she took the next step, allowing Aisling to see something she had never witnessed on previous stays. Giving the girl a place to stand at the edge of a clump of spruce trees, Colleen moved without speaking into the center of an open grassy swale and stood very still. As if in response to a silent call from her, an entire herd of elk entered the expanse and surrounded her. Aisling was afraid of what the huge animals might do, but they merely walked around Colleen until she could not be seen. Seemingly on cue, the herd parted, forming a corridor from the outside to Colleen. A magnificent bull elk, his gigantic antlers in the velvet of summer, ambled into the area, and strode up this opening, head held high and back, balancing the weight of those antlers. When he was face to face with the woman, he extended his nose to her, breathing easily. Above Colleen and the elk, a trio of glistening magpies wheeled in the air, and finally they settled onto the horns of this monarch. This tableau played out for several minutes. Then the magpies launched into flight one by one, circling in lazy spirals higher and higher into the sky. The bull elk bowed his head, turned and walked elegantly into the forest. It was then that Aisling exhaled, realizing that she had been holding her breath throughout this display.

Colleen came back to where she had left Aisling, and the girl could barely get her thoughts out.

"How did you do that? That was the most amazing thing I have ever seen!"

"It's a gift," Colleen replied. "You come from a family with many gifts. Some of these start out slowly, and build upon themselves. When I was a child, the first gift I received was the three magpies who have been my companions almost all my life. They serve as guides to show me the way when I need it. Communication with animals like what you just witnessed came much later, after I returned to the mountains for solace five years ago. Your great-grandfather could always do this."

"What other gifts do you have?" Aisling whispered the question, eyes wide with wonder.

"I was given the herbal book your great-great-great grandmother used. It is a collection of potions, medicines, teas, and salves that go back many years and at least four or five generations in our family. She and her mother-in-law, a frontier doctor, collected formulas from many places, old Irish recipes, Crow and Sioux Indian medicine mixtures, and other sources. They wrote them down in detail. I had to learn how to use these things, but your great Uncle Andrew had vast knowledge of natural remedies and potions, too, and he taught me a great deal."

Aisling was silent. It was just too much to take in all at once, and she did not know what to make of it. Part of her mind wondered if this was just a fairy tale she was being told to make the visit to the mountain more interesting. If she had not seen the strange sight of the elk communing with Colleen, she might have dismissed what she was hearing. But she had seen those magnificent wild beasts giving deference to this woman. She needed time to decide what she really felt about this.

After several more days with Aisling, Colleen felt compelled to ask about what she was observing in her. Seeing her so quiet and removed, and sensing a tension that had never been there before, Colleen chose the direct question.

"Aisling," she said, "I can't help noticing changes in you. On your last visit, you were still a kid. Now you're becoming a woman. You used to look forward all year to coming here to the mountain for the summer. Now I wonder if you would prefer to be elsewhere."

Aisling was stunned to have her great aunt sum up her feelings so simply. She thought she had hidden them pretty well, but Colleen was describing exactly how she felt before coming to the mountain. Caught in Colleen's steady gaze, Aisling's defenses crumbled.

"Everything's different," she sighed. "I miss my friends at home and all the fun they're having."

Colleen was silent for a moment.

"Anything else?" she asked.

"I just really don't know why I have to be here. You've taught me a lot about plants and animals, and seeing you with the elk was awesome. You and Uncle Andrew are great. My dad has his stories about the family, too. But I've been here for four summers – this'll be my fifth. I just don't see what all this has to do with me."

"I know it's hard to understand. There's no doubt that we owe you a good explanation," Colleen said thoughtfully. "But I'm going to need help to give it to you. Give me a day or so."

Aisling moved her shoulders in her teen-age shrug, and the conversation was over. She went to sit with Andrew, where they watched the antics of a tiny ground squirrel.

Colleen was uncertain how to help her great-niece move forward in her destiny. It had to begin with the history of the legacy the family carried. Did she have the ability to explain it to Aisling? All of this had just been part of her own life since she was born, and even with that, there was much she did not know or felt she could not explain. Now it was two generations removed, and there was only one person who could give the girl the detail she needed.

A few steps from the cabin took Colleen to the edge of the forest. A flash of black and white exploded from the branches of a big pine tree, and a brilliant magpie glided toward where she stood, settling onto another branch just above her head. It caught Andrew's and Aisling's attention and as they watched, Colleen raised her hands in some form of silent communication between her and the bird. The magpie lifted off and spiraled straight up into the clear blue sky above the woods. Then it wheeled around and headed east, wings flashing kaleidoscope black, white, and iridescent blue, purple and green in flight.

Colleen waited. In a short time, the bird returned, made a joyful swooping flight around her, then disappeared back into the trees. The message had been delivered.

The next day, a man appeared at the edge of the woods on the far side of the meadow, just as Colleen, Andrew and Aisling were enjoying the early morning sun. His silhouette was familiar, yet there were some aspects that Colleen did not recognize. It was Black Bird Shows, to be sure, but he seemed smaller and more shadowy than she remembered.

She turned to Andrew.

"Do you see him?" she whispered.

Nodding thoughtfully, Andrew kept his eyes on the old Crow medicine man as he came toward the camp.

Andrew was fascinated with Black Bird Shows. During the years he was growing up in the troubles of Northern Ireland, Andrew had encountered magic of a different, although similar, kind. When he met this man after he and Colleen were together, he was amazed at what he experienced in his presence.

They watched. It was always intriguing to observe Black Bird's approach. First, he would appear at the edge of the trees, then seem to materialize in stages a hundred feet closer each time. His straight back and thick white hair, worn in three braids in the old Crow way, gave him an ethereal appearance. Sometimes he came on horseback, but most often on foot, always without a sound.

Colleen never failed to feel excitement over his visits. He had been part of her world since she was born, a long-time friend of her father's, and her teacher when it came to Crow Indian mysticism. He was the link to her father, now dead for many years. The two men had been childhood friends, although she knew very little about how this relationship had formed and lasted. She only knew that Black Bird was always there when she needed him, and that he always brought magic with him.

In the time it took for these brief thoughts to dart through her mind, Black Bird was directly in front of her, Andrew and Aisling. The mountain breeze stirred little strands of his hair around the leathery skin of his face, and his outline seemed to shimmer in the early morning sun. The glistening black of his eyes harbored warmth and mystery. He barely came up to her shoulder now, although she thought of him as a giant.

"*Ka-hay, Sho'o Daa' Chi,* Mike's daughter," Black Bird said. "and my friend, Andrew. It is good to see you, too, Mike's great-granddaughter."

Aisling smiled. She had seen this man a number of times on her trips to the mountain.

"Hello, Black Bird," Colleen replied. "It is good to see you. What brings you to our cabin?"

His look was quizzical.

"You know I was called. The young one has questions," he said, indicating Aisling. Then to Colleen, "And so do you."

"How will you know what to tell?"

"You must ask the things you want to know. Ask everything now. One day I will no longer be here, and I must tell you all you ask, now."

A shiver ran through Colleen. She could not imagine her world without Black Bird Shows.

"Eat with us," she said.

It was apparent that this would be one of Black Bird's longer visits. He unshouldered the bundle he carried and set it against the outside wall of the cabin. It was a roll of blankets, and from previous experience, Colleen knew the old man intended to sleep nearby.

Once Black Bird settled in his customary way on the grass, with Andrew and Aisling sitting facing him, Colleen brought them enamelware bowls of venison soup. Black Bird received his with both hands, inhaled the savory aroma, and nodded with approval. All four of them ate in companionable silence, accompanied by the sound of their spoons against the metal of the bowls.

When they finished, Black Bird leaned back and lit an old clay pipe he had smoked for as long as Colleen could remember. It always struck her as a little odd, since it looked more like pipes she had seen her Irish great grandfather holding in old pictures than anything she had ever known Crow elders to use.

Finally he spoke.

"I know you have many questions," he said. "Now you will have the answers."

There was no doubt about the need for answers. While Colleen had accepted all the strange and magical things that had happened to her in the previous few years, Aisling's need was deeper. The Irish legacy inherited by Colleen from her father and her aunts, and her grandparents and great-grandparents before them, seemed natural to her. It was these things that had led her to Ireland, where she found the love of her life, Andrew. The sequence of events that caused her to lose him, then find him again were otherworldly. Colleen understood this, but she knew it was now time to teach the next generations of the Lorrah family about this history, and she felt ill prepared. Aisling had questions …even if she did not fully recognize the fact.

Black Bird Shows reached inside his shirt and brought out a small rawhide packet. He handed it to Colleen. She opened it and looked at the pungent mixture of crushed leaves, seeds and dried berries, all mixed together.

Black Bird spoke again.

"Look in the herb journal. There's a page called 'Dreaming the Past.' It will tell you what to do. Bring a cup for each of you."

Colleen rose and went into the cabin. One of the family's most treasured possessions lay in its place on a small table in the corner. It was the herbal journal created by her great-great grandmother, frontier doctor Flora Daly. Dr. Flora had left it to Anna Hughes, who was Colleen's great-grandmother. Anna had added her own pages to it, with the help of several Crow Indian medicine men over the years. The rich, soft leather of its cover glowed in the beam of morning sunlight. The book had a life of its own, and pulsated in her hand. At her touch, the herbal opened, its rich paper making a sound like heavy satin. She ran her fingers along the edge of the book, and the pages parted to the one Black Bird had named. It had exquisite drawings and elegantly hand-printed descriptions of ingredients for the tea, and she saw that they included the items he had given her, along with a few others.

Following the instructions in the herbal precisely, she set the blackened old tea kettle on the wood-burning camp stove and filled it with pure water from Clear Spring. Then she reached into a recess in the log wall, and pulled out a worn, fringed buckskin bag. Inside it was a selection of neat little bundles. Some were dried leaves and flowers and some were wild berries, still on the twigs that had borne them. Carefully, she selected several of the fragrant leaves and a few of the flowers. They were so perfectly dried that their color and aroma made them seem freshly picked.

When the water had boiled, she dropped Black Bird's ingredients and her own plant mixture into it. When the brew had steeped for exactly the right amount of time, she poured three cups and brought them outside. While she was gone, Andrew had built a small campfire to take the edge off the cool air.

"Each of you, drink the whole cup," Black Bird instructed. "You all will dream the past as if you were there. You will each become one of the trees that watch everything. Your dreams will tell you all you wish to know about Mike Lorrah."

It did not occur to Andrew and Colleen to question Black Bird Shows, but Aisling hesitated for a moment.

"Is this some kind of drug?" she asked. "Mom and Dad wouldn't like it if it was a drug."

Colleen smiled.

"This is a tea your father drank when he was about your age," she said. "It helped him to understand the family's role in the magic of time."

Aisling was silent. She was not sure, but her aunt and uncle had never led her astray.

Andrew rose from his place by the fire, and went into the cabin. He brought out blankets to make them all more comfortable sitting on the ground. He had learned that there was a purpose to everything Black Bird said and did.

With Black Bird looking on, each of them drank their cup of tea. For a few moments, they held the earthy mixture in their mouths, not swallowing. As they did so, the mixture melted with their saliva, and all the solid parts of it vanished, leaving only a flavorful taste on their tongues. As time passed, they relaxed.

Then Black Bird Shows began to sing. It was an eerie sound, unearthly in tone, and as he sang, the air began to shimmer. The sounds of nature went silent, and they crossed a boundary of time and space. The present became the past, and the past became the present. Somewhere in the air, blended with the Indian songs, came the thrumming of a bodhran, an Irish drum, and then flutes, both Indian and Irish sang an ancient melody.

In their shared dream, the two older people and the girl found themselves becoming trees, exactly as Black Bird had said. They grew and grew, branches reaching toward the sky, and roots sinking deep into the earth. They found themselves watching the original house on the Lorrah ranch from high above it. The time was just before sunrise, and a beautiful woman stepped out onto the east porch. Colleen recognized her from old family photographs. It was her grandmother Velia.

CHAPTER 2

▼

Velia Lorrah watched as daylight began to grow behind the distant Wolf Mountains. Rising before sunrise was not her preference, but the cowboys had to be fed breakfast. As they rode off, she stood on the sweeping veranda-style porch of the two-story log house absently wiping her hands on her white, ankle-length apron. She spread her arms to luxuriate in the beauty of the early Montana dawn. A mourning dove called from the majestic cottonwoods lining the banks of Lodge Grass Creek, and a meadowlark sang its aria to the rising sun. Her mother and her grandmother had taught her to greet each day in this ceremonial manner. Facing east, she allowed the first beams of light to touch her face and she felt synchronization with all of nature and the earth itself. The rays moved across the valley floor and painted the logs of the house a rich dark gold, sparkling off the dew on the grass and warming the stones of the walkway.

Her reverie was short-lived. The lusty cry of her two-year-old daughter, Willow, pierced her thoughts, and she stepped in from the porch to tend to the demanding toddler. As she passed through the kitchen, she glanced at five-year-old Moira, who was concentrating on her beautiful wooden doll. The child was so serious and intense that Velia sometimes worried about her, but she seemed content enough with her play. She loved that doll that her grandfather had so artfully carved for her. It was amazing how she could shut out the din coming from the newest member of the family.

Entering the toddler's room, Velia saw ten-year-old Mike. He was earnestly dancing a rag doll in front of little Willow, but to absolutely no avail. The tiny child took a huge breath when she saw her mother cross the threshold, but it was only to refuel her protest with a wail that seemed to shake the leaves of the mountain ash tree outside the open window. Mike winced at the penetrating pitch of his tiny sister's shrieks, but kept trying to entertain her despite his obvious discomfort.

Velia's blue eyes rested on her son. He was a perceptive and devoted boy, intent upon trying to help his mother with this squalling tot, but she knew his father would soon be demanding that he take on more ranch work. Morgan Lorrah was an old-school cowboy, showing little affection toward their son, and talking already about "making a man of the boy." If her mother, his grandmother, Anna, were not there to insert herself between Mike and his father, it probably would have started much earlier. Anna had guided the development of Mike's empathetic senses, and had reached deep into his spirit to teach him how to connect with every living thing around him. Velia wondered how much of this teaching would be lost when Morgan began to accelerate his demands on him.

And the demands were growing. Morgan was hammering his ranch holdings together with drive and fury, sometimes crossing the line of both. There was a dark side to his actions, but he had his softer side, too. He adored Velia, whose beauty had bewitched him from the first time they met. He was working the cattle herds in Wyoming on the fateful day he entered the café at Arvada. It was a shipping point, and the one place for a meal was the ramshackle hotel that served the cattle yards there. Velia was cooking and serving there, and every cowpuncher who saw her was smitten by her black hair, creamy skin, and slim figure. There always seemed to be an air of mystery and allure about her that could not be defined. Morgan was tall, handsome and fearless. Some part of Velia recognized a match for her own passion, and they were married just a few months later.

So Morgan triumphed, but he had not reckoned with the history of Velia's family. Her mother, Anna, was never far from her daughter, and made it her mission to instruct her grandchildren about the traditions of her parents and grandparents. Velia's father, Frank Daly, was short, strong, and quiet. He understood his wife with telepathic clarity, and loved his family with all his being. Everything about him was Irish. He had been born on the boat in passage from the famine-ridden Old Country, and made sure that Ireland was always with them in "Mericay". He never knew his father, but his mother, Flora Daly, had translated her American dream into the unlikely achievement of becoming a doctor. She had brought her skills to Deadwood, South Dakota, and built a practice there that made her a beloved legend among the locals.

Frank grew up to work on the railroads that were spinning a web of transportation all over the west and Midwest in the late nineteenth century. His travels brought him to Iowa, where he met Anna Hughes. They were married first in an ancient ceremony of the Old Religion of Ireland, then again in the Catholic Church, primarily to allay the judgments of the community. Their marriage produced two sons, Seán and Ruairí, and a daughter, Velia. The two sons had worked on ships, but eventually followed in Frank's footsteps to join the railroad. This work periodically brought them through the Lodge Grass area. These visits were always special occasions of music and laughter.

The sons of Anna and Frank Daly played fiddle and whistle with supernatural skill and no one could resist singing and dancing to their tunes. They had been to Ireland several times, working on ships when they were very young. Now, they sometimes brought visiting or immigrating "cousins" from the Old Country and the lilt of Irish brogues would fill the house. Storytelling, songs and news of relatives in Ireland were particular favorites. Neighbors came from everywhere to join in and the festivities generally went on until the early morning hours. Mike loved the visits from his uncles, and he always hated to see them leave. They were much more fun than his father seemed to be. Warm and humorous, they would tease his mother and her blushing laughter would raise the image of the girl she had been. Their guests made Ireland seem real and close, just as his grandmother's stories did.

His grandmother Anna encouraged his relationship with them. She wanted to be certain he had the chance to hear about Ireland from people who had walked the land of their ancestry. At this point, Mike was the only one she deemed ready to understand what she had to teach. Because of this, Anna intervened in the style of generations of Irish mothers and grandmothers before her.

When Morgan wanted to push Mike into responsibilities too heavy for his young age, Anna stiffened her solid frame and fixed her icy blue eyes on the man. The force of that gaze was enough to cower most people, but Morgan was stubbornly determined not to shrink from her. He made every effort not to show the discomfort she made him feel, but she knew it was there.

"Now Morgan," she would say. "He's just a lad. I know y' want him to grow up fast, but y' should be givin' him a chance to be a child first."

Morgan knew better than to challenge her. She had seen more than most, working as a nurse and midwife with her mother-in-law in Deadwood. They had treated cowboys, gunfighters, Indians, prostitutes, Chinese, miners, and drifters. It was common that any woman doctor in gold camps got the undesirables as their patients. Dr. Flora treated all comers, and when Anna and Frank Daly arrived there, Anna did not question this. Unafraid, she merely rolled up her sleeves and took on the task of caring for those who needed her. Anna brought her own mother's folk medicines and magic to Dr. Flora, who already had compiled a vast array of practices and natural remedies of her own. She kept a meticulous journal of the herbs and other plants and potions. The two women provided care to the locals, and learned even more from the fierce Sioux Indians who lived in the vicinity. After all that, her son-in-law could not hope to intimidate her, but it was an uneasy truce for both of them. When Dr. Flora died, Anna and Frank came to the Lodge Grass Creek valley, the place the Crow Indians called the Valley of the Chiefs, to live near their daughter and her family. Anna brought the journal and experience that made her a welcome addition to the population of the community.

For her part, Anna knew she could not hold off Morgan's expectations for Mike much longer. Many of his contemporaries' sons were already helping to round up and break wild horses, ride on long cattle drives, and hunt wolves. Morgan's pride would not allow him to suffer ridicule from the fathers of these boys. While he knew she was right about allowing the child to grow up a little more, he would only wait so long. Anna knew he was a hard man who had his own definition of what made a man, and that he would stop at nothing to have his way. When the time came, childhood would end for Mike. For now, Morgan chose his demands carefully. The boy worked in the garden, and he milked the ranch cow, so there was a supply for the household. And he took care of the horses, giving them grain and water in the summer, and pitching hay to them in the winter. Morgan also demanded that he keep the big horse-barn spotlessly clean. It wasn't as much as Morgan wanted, but Mike's mother and grandmother were able to live with it.

Velia scooped up the crying child. Even her embrace did not comfort the screaming girl. A check of diapers revealed this little one was dry, and Velia had just fed her an hour before, so hunger was not the problem, either. Mike watched helplessly. He had done all he could, but it was not enough for Willow.

Velia began to pace about the house with Willow. The baby squirmed and continued to scream. As her mother walked through the kitchen, Moira finally looked up. Gazing with annoyance at the baby, the girl spoke.

"Mama," her exasperated voice was low. "Take her outside. She doesn't want to be in the house any more."

In desperation, Velia opened the screen door and stepped out onto the long porch. Willow continued her screeching. Down the steps they went, into the shaded yard. As soon as they left confines of the house and porch, Willow transformed. She scanned the lawn and the trees, and then broke into a sunny smile. She reached out a pudgy hand toward the branches overhead, cocked her head to listen to the singing birds, and fidgeted to get down.

A blanket should be put down on the grass for the child, but previous experience had demonstrated that Willow would not stay on it. Velia set her down.

Willow giggled. She sat upright on the grass, and waved her arms about. As she did so, a pair of mountain bluebirds lit nearby, completely unafraid of her. A huge monarch butterfly flitted up close, then landed on her copper penny curls like a fragile, living orange bow.

Velia shook her head. Raising this child would be a challenge. As young as she was, it was apparent that she was not at all like her brother or her sister. She was most definitely a child of the outdoors, and nature responded to her as if she was a wild thing, not a human child.

Velia's mother, Anna, frequently told her that Willow was "special," destined for great deeds. When she heard these things, Velia felt a chill down her spine. The thinly veiled reference was to the ancient Irish beliefs handed down through generations of the family, and Velia had hoped none of her children would be fey or otherworldly. She knew their lives would be much easier if such abilities were not visited upon them. But Willow showed obvious signs, like those attributed to her great grandmother.

Once his mother had taken Willow outdoors, Mike breathed a huge sigh of big-brother relief. He loved his sisters, but Willow confounded him at every turn. He sauntered into the kitchen to see what Moira was doing. She was deep in her imaginary world again, moving her doll about, and playing with the ribbons on its dress. She was so solemn. Mike knew better than to try to intrude on her game. She would play with him when she wanted to, but not now.

While he loved living this far out of town on the ranch, there were times when he wished his friends lived a little closer. Moira was not much fun most of the time, and he longed for a boy his own age to share his adventures. School provided opportunities to meet and befriend other children, but he seldom saw them outside of the academic year. His father did not believe in boys playing too much.

It looked like as good a time as any to go outside where his mother had taken a seat in the grass beside the baby. The sun touched his mother's raven-wing hair with a halo of blue-black highlights, and he paused to look at her before she could realize that he had come out of the house. He was so proud of her. When they went into town, people looked at her with such admiration. At the general store, he had heard some other ladies comment on how beautiful they thought Velia was. And it was true. Her fair skin and hair and slim figure accented by the long dresses she wore were always perfect. Her unfathomable eyes glowed with blue inner fire, suggesting a mystery held deep within. Absently, she reached into the grass, and without looking, retrieved a four-leaf clover, an act that fascinated anyone who saw her do it. Mike had tried repeatedly to find the four-leafed clovers among the three-leafed ones that grew throughout the lawn, and he had never been able to do so.

After several seconds, he spoke.

"Mother," he said, using the formal word that his grandmother insisted upon. "I've finished filling the wood box, and hauled the water in. Do you think I could go fishing for a while?"

Velia turned and smiled, a dazzling sight that he never tired of seeing.

"Of course," she replied. "But don't be gone too long. Your father will be back for the other horses, and he will want you to catch them for him."

Mike's bond with horses was extraordinary. The cowboys had to chase and lasso them. But when Mike went into the horse pasture, the horses focused on him, ears pricked as they sauntered right up to him. He would turn and walk to the barn lot, horses behind him in Pied Piper formation, and they would enter the corrals together. Once the gates were closed, the horses were in tighter quarters, ready for Morgan and the cowboys to catch and saddle. Mike's only caveat was that he would not catch each horse for each man. In the event that one of the riders was unkind, Mike did not want to be the person who turned the horse directly over to him. Morgan tried to force him do this, but when Mike stood up to him, he relented, relieved to see some sign of backbone in the boy. They had a tacit agreement. Much as he disliked the idea, Mike would catch and saddle Morgan's horses, but not those of the other men.

Mike settled in on the lush grasses of the creek bank. He pulled out the fishing rod his grandfather had made for him, and threaded a wriggling earthworm onto the hook. When all was ready, he cast his line into a pool just past the ripples of a small eddy in the water. The sun made him feel a little drowsy, and he leaned his back against one of the sturdy cottonwood trees that grew in this place. Cicadas buzzed and their sound merged with the gurgle of the creek as it made its way. Eyelids heavy, he was almost asleep when something changed in the air around him. Suddenly, he was certain that he was not alone. There was no sound, no movement of the chokecherry bushes that lined the creek, but something set off alarms in his head.

Was it his father? There would be hell to pay if Morgan caught him sleeping when he should have been ready to corral the horses. If that happened, he would not wait to scold him for his neglect. On similar occasions, Morgan had even snapped his horse quirt at the boy, leaving a stinging reminder of what to expect if he shirked his duties. Mike wanted to please his father, so he had learned to be quick in his responses. But this was different.

He waited, listening. Although he was motionless, his eyes darted about, searching for what it was that he was sensing.

It most definitely was not Morgan. His father's arrival was always with a thunder of hooves and creaking of leather tack. The cicadas had become silent, and even the sounds of the creek were muffled. The atmosphere seemed to have shifted, although everything looked the same. Mike had an undeniable sense that someone was watching him. Finally, he sat up straight and called out.

"Who's there?"

Silence.

"I know you're there. Come out where I can see you."

Still no answer.

Mike suddenly knew where the intruder was. In the thickest chokecherry bushes, a few leaves moved imperceptibly, as if stirred by breathing. Mike's sharp hearing told him whoever or whatever was in the brush was trying not to be detected. But Mike was blessed with extra senses. His Irish grandmother told him it was inherited, that he was "fey." It was that extraordinary ability that had caused him to first sense the presence of his visitor, and now he was alert and focused.

"Who's there?"

No answer.

"I know you're in the chokecherries. Come on out."

Nothing.

Mike rose, and laying his fishing pole carefully aside, walked with purpose toward the trembling leaves.

When he got up to the bush, he reached out and parted the branches with both his hands. He found himself staring into the deep brown eyes of an Indian boy who appeared to be a few years older than he was. It was hard to tell who was most surprised.

The Indian boy moved as if he was about to run, but Mike reached out and grabbed his arm.

"What are you doing here?"

The boy just stared at Mike, defiant, yet frightened, too.

"Do you speak English?"

The boy did not answer for a moment, then he nodded slightly.

"You do? What are you doing here?"

Mike had spent a great deal of time with Crow Indian children, but he did not recall this one. Any instinct to fear the young intruder was tempered by the misery in the dark depths of his gaze. A black eye and several cuts marked the boy's face. Despite the frayed white man's clothes two sizes too big for him, the ragged haircut, and the old and dirty moccasins on his feet, there was a presence of strength. This boy was not afraid of Mike, but there was a haunted look on his face.

Mike's instincts, which never failed him, told him that this boy deserved concern, not fear or suspicion.

"Look," Mike said. "I'm not going to hurt you. What are you doing here?"

The boy looked at the ground and mumbled something that Mike could not understand.

"What? You have to speak up. I can't understand you."

Finally the boy looked up.

"I got to go," he said, trying to free his arm from Mike's grasp.

"Where?"

"My uncle's place."

"Who's your uncle?" Mike did not remember ever seeing this boy, and was sure he would have known him if his uncle lived anyplace close by.

The boy's eyes softened, and took on a peaceful glow.

"Takes the Hawk."

Mike found this curious. Takes the Hawk was a very old Indian who lived just a short distance away along the creek. He had built himself a nice house of logs, and while he occasionally came by the ranch house, he did not socialize much. Mike had never known he had any relatives.

"He's your uncle? So his brother or his sister is one of your parents?"

The boy gazed at him as if he had said something foolish, then he shrugged.

"No. He's my clan uncle." He hesitated and then added, "My mother and father are dead."

Mike was not sure what the designation of 'clan uncle' meant, although he had heard some of his Crow Indian playmates use the term. It was apparent that these relationships did not mean the same thing to tribal people as they did to him. He dropped this line of questioning.

"How long have you been hiding here?' he asked.

"Couple a' days. They're trying to catch me."

"Who?"

"The school people."

"You mean from the grade school in Lodge Grass?"

"No. The boarding school at Crow."

The boy spat the words like dirt from his mouth.

Mike had heard stories of Indian boarding schools, including the one at the Crow Agency. His Crow playmates said they were the lucky ones, because they had not been forced to go away to these schools. They were allowed to attend to the missionary school or even public school right there and they went home to their families each night. Several of them had cousins or even older brothers and sisters who had been sent off to these boarding schools to "learn the White ways." They related nightmarish stories of the abuse suffered at the hands of the schools' staff in their pursuit of eliminating "everything Indian" in the children. Their braids were cut, their clothing was taken away and destroyed, and they were made to wear only white people's garments. Their living conditions were sparse, and the children were often hungry. The greatest punishments were handed out for speaking the Crow language and for trying to keep anything related to their culture.

When Mike told his grandmother what he had heard from these children, she clucked her tongue.

"T'is like the stories m' ma told me of the Irish, when the English came," she said, shaking her head. "Our language was a mark of shame, and the English wanted us to stop bein' Irish. It is so wrong."

Mike asked her how it was that she had been able to learn to speak the Irish language.

"T'was m' ma," she said. "She and Da' got away and came to Mericay, where they could be with other Irish and try to be free. They weren't treated a lot better than they had been in Ireland at first, but when they came north and got away from the cities, they were able to keep their language and their beliefs. Every day, they taught us about them, and m' ma said we had to learn, so these things would not be lost."

Remembering now what his grandmother had said, Mike instantly understood what this Indian boy was running away from. His heart went out to him. He released his hold on the boy's arm, and stepped back to try to make him feel less threatened.

"Listen," Mike said, "I'm the only one who knows you are here. Takes the Hawk lives a ways on up the creek and you look like you need some rest. Are you hungry? When did you last have something to eat?"

The Indian boy drew himself up proudly.

"I don't need white peoples' scraps," he declared.

Mike caught the meaning. This boy did not want charity.

"It won't be scraps," Mike said. "I'm kind of hungry, too, and I know how to make my own sandwiches. Just wait here."

Mike turned and ran to the house, where his mother still sat on the grass with Willow.

"I got hungry, Mother," he explained to her puzzled expression. "I'll just make myself a sandwich to take down where I'm fishing."

Velia nodded, a little dreamily. She was enjoying the morning sun, and was glad that Mike had reached an age where he was so self-sufficient.

In the kitchen, Mike pulled the remainder of a loaf of his mother's homemade bread out of the breadbox. Cutting several thick slices, he slathered them in fresh butter, and spread glistening purple gobs of chokecherry jelly. Once he had made two sandwiches, he wrapped them in a dishtowel, and went back out the door. If his mother noticed that his bundle was too large for just one sandwich, she said nothing.

When he got back to his spot by the creek, there was no sign of the Indian boy.

Mike spoke quietly.

"I did not tell anyone you are here," he said, speaking into the air, "But I have a sandwich for each of us, if you want one. It is not scraps, these are fresh-made. We'll eat together."

He held one of the sandwiches out in the direction of the stand of chokecherries.

His guest hesitated warily, but his hunger won the battle with caution, and he stepped out of the brush and snatched the sandwich from Mike's hand. He settled down, back tight against the chokecherry thicket. Mike sat down facing him, and took a bite from his own sandwich. The Indian boy wolfed his food, almost seeming not to chew it. He stared at Mike as he ate, taking measure of him.

Mike tore off the biggest piece of his own sandwich and offered it.

"Here," he said. "I'm not as hungry as I thought I was."

This offering vanished as quickly as the first.

At the tattoo of approaching hoofs, Mike put his finger to his lips and gestured for the boy to conceal himself.

"That's my dad," Mike said. "He won't like it if he finds you here. Just stay hidden, and I'll come back as soon as I can."

Mike gathered his fishing rod, and climbed up the bank to the road. Just as he put his foot on the surface of it, Morgan rounded the corner on his big bay horse, tack jingling. He was an imposing figure on horseback. He was tall, and rode with a straight back, hat jammed down on his head, shadowing his features and his hard eyes. His boots were adorned with a pair of silver Mexican spurs with large, cruel, ten-point rowels, nearly three inches in diameter. The mountings were engraved with snakes and scorpions, and Morgan had once said he won them in a poker game from a Mexican cowboy. Mike hated the spurs and quirt that his father used. It was wrong to use such cruel means to get a horse to do what a man wanted.

"Mike!" Morgan shouted. "Put this horse away and saddle another one. C'mon, boy! You can't fish all day."

Morgan's horse was dusty and wet with sweat. The big gelding had been ridden hard and he was blowing loudly from the exertion. Mike walked behind Morgan and the horse until his father dismounted at the gate to the house. He noted how his father's eyes lit up at the sight of his mother and Willow in the grass, and he took the reins of the gelding to lead him to the barn. He would be expected to unsaddle this horse, brush him down, and give him grain and water. Then he would catch another mount and ready it for the next ride. Mike did not know where Morgan went or what he did, since he did not talk about it, and no one else seemed to know either. Often times, he and a group of men rode out in the dark of night, and came back just before dawn. Those rides were never discussed, and the men who rode with him on those journeys were not the same men who worked the cattle on the ranch.

Mike knew he would have some time, because his father would spend a few moments with Velia before riding off again. He could think about how to help the Indian boy while he got the horse ready.

The hayloft of the barn offered a good possibility for a secure hiding place. The boy would be safe and warm, and there were two ways to reach it, which would offer him a clean escape if someone should decide to climb to the second level. A few small piles of leftover hay and straw were stored in the loft, but no one went up there in the summer. The horses were all out in the pastures at this time of the year, and there was no need to ascend the steep ladder for anything. Even when Morgan and his men brought new horses to the main corral, they did not give so much as a glance to the upper floor of the immense log building. That area was used only in the winter, and even though the barn itself was big enough to stable upwards of thirty horses, only a few stalls were occupied in spring and summer. Mike knew every niche and corner of the building by heart. He had cleaned the place to a pristine level when spring arrived, and it glowed with the warmth of well-worn wood.

As he led the horse down the hill from the house toward the barn, he stopped at the chokecherries. The boy peered out from his shelter after a brief hesitation, and Mike spoke to him.

"You're going to be a lot safer if you wait here a day or two, then move on in the dark," Mike said. "If they come looking for you here, no one will think of the place I have for you to hide. Stay hidden here until my father leaves, and I'll show it to you. If you don't like it, you don't have to use it, but it would be a lot warmer and more comfortable than this."

The boy stared at him for a moment.

"Why you doin' this?" he asked.

"You look like you have a good reason for wanting to get to your uncle," Mike replied. "If it was me, I'd want some help. You think about it, and I'll be back later tonight."

Mike turned and walked the tired horse to the barn. Inside one of the stalls, he quickly unbuckled the cinch, slid the saddle from the wet back of the animal, and removed the bridle. The horse made a couple of chewing motions, relieved to have the bit out of his mouth. Mike ran an old blanket over the horse, wiping the sweat from its back and flanks. He went to the hand pump, drew a bucket of water, and placed it in front of the animal, watching to make sure it did not drink too quickly. A scoop of oats in the feeder, and he closed the gate, leaving the horse to rest.

Carrying the saddle to the side of the corral that was attached to the barn, Mike whistled. From the far side of the enclosure, another horse raised its head, spotted the boy, and trotted to where he stood. Mike put the bridle on him, and stepped back into the barn to get a dry saddle blanket from the tack room. When he emerged, the Indian boy was standing in the open area outside the stalls. Tiny motes of dust danced about him in what sunlight crept in through small cracks around the slatted windows and doors. Out of the brushy hiding place, he looked even more proud, and his clothes looked even more shabby. Mike couldn't help scolding him.

"You should be more careful!"

The Indian boy's eyes were calm.

"No one saw me," he said.

"Why did you follow me?'

"To hear how you think you can help me."

Mike pointed silently to the ladder to the hayloft. The boy scaled it as easily as a squirrel might climb trunk of a cottonwood. Mike watched him go to the top, pause there and look through the opening at the spacious area above. For a few heartbeats, the only sound was that of pigeons cooing from their niches in the structure.

"I could stay here?" the boy called down through the opening.

"No one would look for you," Mike replied. "I can bring you food."

There was a long silence then.

Finally the boy spoke again.

"I will do it," he said.

So it began. The first day, Mike left the house to do his morning tasks. Since he had always gone to the barn to care for Morgan's horses, neither his father nor his mother saw any real difference in his routine. He ate his breakfast quickly, and the fact that he was eating more pleased his mother. She had worried about him because he never seemed to eat as much as other boys his age. Now he loaded up his plate with biscuits, bacon and fried potatoes. Moira sat at the table, continuing to play with her dolls and not looking at him at all. As his mother rose periodically from her seat to tend to Willow, and when Morgan stepped aside for his morning smoke, Mike slid a sheet of newspaper from a pocket and scraped half his breakfast into it, folding it carefully and pushing inside his shirt. It sat against his skin, warm and a little greasy, but completely inconspicuous. Mike had long ago realized that no one ever looked at him very closely, and this confirmed it. Then he took his plate to the counter of the kitchen, called to his mother to tell her he was off to the barn, and left the house. When he got outside, Morgan was there, smoking his rolled cigarette and scribbling some figures on a small sheet of paper as Mike passed him.

"Get that horse up here, boy," Morgan said without looking up.

"Yes sir!"

Mike trotted down the dusty road that curved away from the house and to the bridge that crossed Lodge Grass Creek into the barn lot. He breathed a big sigh of relief, thankful for the first time that he was not the center of attention. Once out of sight of the house, he broke into a run. When he reached the barn, he entered the big door, then stood, listening. There was no sound, except for the cooing of pigeons. A few errant flakes of straw sifted silently down through the splits in the floorboards of the hayloft. Mike knew it took something moving around up there to cause that to happen.

Quickly, he ascended the ladder and turned to look around the big empty upper space. At first he thought there was no one there. Then the Indian boy stood up from behind a straw pile. Mike eased his newspaper-wrapped package from inside his shirt, and balancing it on one hand, unwrapped it carefully. The Indian boy's eyes widened when he saw how much food it contained. Mike held it out to him. The boy snatched it and gulped it down.

"I don't have much time right now," Mike said. "I'm supposed to get my father's horse for him. Once he's gone, I'll come back with some water for you."

The boy nodded.

Mike paused.

"You know, you still haven't told me your name."

The boy grunted.

"They called me Joseph Black at the school." he said. "But I never want to hear that name again in my life. My Crow name is Black Bird Shows."

Mike held out his hand.

"I'm Mike Lorrah. Glad to meet you, Black Bird Shows."

Black Bird Shows stared at Mike's hand. Then he shrugged. He couldn't expect Mike to recognize that the gesture was entirely of the white man's world. He extended his own hand and grasped that of this white boy.

"Mike Lorrah," he repeated, as if memorizing the name.

For the next several days, these meetings became routine. Mike had numerous chores to do around the barn area, so nothing about his frequent trips there attracted attention. He was able to smuggle enough food to keep his new friend comfortable, and Black Bird Shows would slip down to the creek after dark or before sunrise to get the water he needed.

The two fell into conversation during these stolen visits. Mike learned that the obvious injuries he had observed on Black Bird Shows had been inflicted by one of the employees of the boarding school. The man's name was Bart Knight, and he considered it his mission to punish any "Indian" behaviors he witnessed in the children.

"Some of the younger kids were playing hoops," Black Bird told him. "Knight didn't like it, so he started whipping 'em. I told him to stop, that the kids were too young to understand they weren't supposed to do that."

"What did he do?" Mike asked.

"No one talks back to him. He attacked me with his whip and then with his fists. That's how I got this and these," Black Bird said, indicating the fading black eye and the cuts on his face.

He paused, remembering, then continued, "I pushed back, and he fell. He hit his head and it knocked him out. I knew I had to run then, or he would punish me in a big way when he woke up. I knew a way out of the boarding school where I wouldn't be seen, and with him out cold, it was my chance. I felt bad for the little ones, but I wouldn't be any good to them if Knight killed me."

Mike was shocked.

"Do you really think he would have killed you?" he asked.

"Don't know. But a couple of other Crow kids who resisted him disappeared, and I never knew what happened to 'em. He's a bad one."

"How did you get here from Crow Agency?" Mike asked.

"Sneaked onto a freight car on the night train that stops for water in Crow. It was still dark when it got to Lodge Grass, so no one saw me jump off. Then I walked from town up Lodge Grass Creek because I know my uncle lives on the creek."

Mike kept all this to himself. He had trouble keeping his secret from his grandmother, however. Her keen Irish intuition perceived that he was hiding something. He spent a great deal of time with her by agreement with his mother. When she and his grandfather came to live with them on the ranch, it was a special time. She continued to treat people with her mother-in-law's herbal remedies, and he liked the way she seemed to respect him. She never talked down to him, and spent as much time as she could teaching him the secrets of the plants in her garden.

Eventually, she engaged him in conversation as the two of them worked.

"Michael" she said, giving it the Irish pronunciation *'Mee-hall'*. "I know y' have something y' are not telling me about. Are y' in some kind of trouble?"

Mike stopped hoeing the row of onions. For a moment, he felt like a rabbit caught in a snare. He never could lie to his Grandmother Anna, not when she asked a direct question. He turned to her and spoke quietly.

"It's not me who is in trouble, Grandmother," he said. "Well, I might be, but not like you're thinking…"

She waited.

"I found a boy hiding in the chokecherry brush – a Crow Indian boy."

"What was he hidin' from?"

"He ran away from the boarding school. He knows they're hunting for him."

"Where is he now?"

Mike took a deep breath. Finally, knowing he could trust his grandmother completely, he blurted out his reply.

"I hid him in the hayloft of the barn."

He watched his grandmother with pleading eyes as she gazed levelly at him. In his heart, he knew she loved him even more than she had loved her own children. She had given him much of her time, since his mother was so busy with the two girls. They had become very close. But this was a serious matter, and he hoped she understood how much courage it had taken for him to shelter a runaway, especially an Indian.

"Michael," she said, her tone indicating that she recognized the gravity of this matter. "Where is this boy planning to go?"

"His uncle is Takes the Hawk. He lives on up Lodge Grass Creek, and if Black Bird Shows – that's the boy's name – can get there, he will be safe. I want to help him get there, but I don't know how to do it without my dad finding out. I've been taking him food, and we talk. I know he's a good boy; he just doesn't want to be in the boarding school where they are trying to make him not be Indian any more. And if they catch him, they'll punish him bad, I know they will!"

He stopped to catch his breath, having poured out emotions along with words. His eyes implored Anna to understand.

Anna was silent for a moment, thinking. Her grandson was an extraordinary young man, and she formulated her answer carefully.

"I know Takes the Hawk. He is a spiritual man, and he helped me when I was tendin' to some sick people," she said. "'Tis little wonder that this boy wants t' be with him. I'll call on him, and he'll decide what t' do. Get the buggy for me."

Mike raced back down the road to the barn lot. He was not surprised to learn that his grandmother knew Takes the Hawk. Her unorthodox medical practices put her in contact with many unusual people. Once, a band of tinkers had stopped by the ranch, asking for her help. They were gypsies, usually engaged in small repairs and kitchen trade. When they came, he heard his grandmother speaking Irish with them, and she later explained that they were "Travelers."

"There were many of them in Ireland," she told him later. "They fled the Hunger, same as m' ma and da'. Their baby was sick, and they knew about Dr. Flora's medicines."

"Did they pay you?" Mike asked.

"Better than that," she replied. "They added things to m' collection of herbs and tonics. It will help many people here."

She indicated a carefully laid out a mysterious collection of dried plants, rock crystals, packets of powders, and several oddly shaped bottles of liquid that seemed to have a life of their own. Mike stared at them, and finally he asked, "How do you know what to do with all those things?"

"M' ma taught me all her secrets. She was very powerful, and knew much about the Otherworld."

Mike prodded, "Tell me more about her, Grandmother."

He loved her stories about Margaret and Ristéard Hughes, her mother and father.

Anna's eyes took on a faraway look.

"Yer great grandmother had to flee from Ireland during the Great Hunger," she said. "Fer her, 'twas not because of the lack of food. She knew how to make the smallest plant give up its food to her. 'Twas the persecution. Because she and my father were of the Old Religion, they could find no safe harbor. No one would protect them or help them. They were accused of heresy by Protestant and Catholic alike. So they went down to the port, and when they found a ship returning to 'Merica after delivering cotton to the Sasanach." She hissed the syllables of the Irish word for English. "The ship needed weight in the bottom for ballast, so they took starving Irish into the hold for that purpose."

"M' ma and da' slipped aboard, and hunkered down in the darkness of the hold, eating what little they could scavenge. Many of the people shared what little they had. Some of the passengers lived, and some died, but nearly all were terribly sick on the voyage. When the ship docked in New Orleans, me ma 'n da', stayed on while all the others left the ship, then crept off when night came, avoiding the captain's head count of surviving passengers. They tried to live in New Orleans, but they weren't made for the city. So they went north up the Mississippi, and finally came into Iowa farm country."

Remembering this conversation now, Mike began to understand that his grandmother put her patients first. If the best treatments and medicines were from modern medicine, Tinkers wagons, or herbs and powders from Crow Indians, she would not hesitate to learn about them. She must truly trust Takes the Hawk, to have worked so closely with him.

He readied the buggy, and harnessed the horse. It was a smart little Parry Storm Buggy that Anna had inherited from Dr. Flora. Mike ran his hands over the fine gold stripe that graced the smooth dark bottle green body, and admired the welted leather upholstery. He loved it when his grandmother had him get it ready for her use. It meant he could drive it up the hill from the barn lot, behind her grey horse, Doc. When Mike pulled up to the house, his grandmother was ready to go. She had changed from her gardening clothes into traveling attire, and she easily stepped up on the mounting block and swung herself into the buggy. Looking intently at Mike, she smiled.

"I'll be after solvin' this little problem, Michael. Just be at peace," she said.

Anna moved the reins slightly and Doc moved out calmly, setting off up Lodge Grass Creek. Mike admired his grandmother's way with animals, and had always tried to emulate it. It almost seemed she could read their minds, whether it was dogs, horses, or the wild things that inhabited the area around the little white clapboard house she occupied with his grandfather. He was glad they lived so close.

Shortly after her departure, Mike looked up from the row he was hoeing to see three strangers ride up to the house. Velia met them at the end of the path. They appeared to be questioning her and he could see her shaking her head. They engaged her in conversation for a few moments. The apparent leader of the group was a tall, too-thin man in black, whose narrow eyes glittered in the shadow of his hat brim. His mouth was a pencil line slash across the lower part of his pale, pock-marked face, and everything about his carriage telegraphed the tension and anger. From where Mike stood, he could tell the man was the one asking his mother questions, and each answer she gave came with another negative shake of her head. Mike felt an instinctive fear for his mother. But she favored the men with one of her brilliant smiles, and the leader tipped his hat to her respectfully. The motion revealed a flash of stringy, rusty red hair as he reined his horse around, and the group trotted off to the main road.

Mike watched as the men turned back toward Lodge Grass. Relief flowed over him when they went in the opposite direction from the way his grandmother had gone.

Velia came toward him, a thoughtful expression on her face. She gazed at her son.

"Those men were from the boarding school at Crow Agency," she said. "They are looking for a runaway. It seems a boy left the school about a week ago. I asked them why they were looking here, and they said they'd been all over the reservation. Apparently he completely disappeared. You haven't seen an Indian boy passing through the ranch, have you?"

Mike's throat was dry as he formulated his answer. He did not want to deceive his mother. But he had to protect his new friend. He compromised.

"No," he said, thinking of Black Bird ensconced in the barn loft. "No boy passing through."

Morgan was back from his travels, and Mike had cooled down the horse he had used, watering it and giving it oats. He had found it necessary to take a bucket of cool water and wash down the sweat that lathered the animal's body. It was obvious that the tall, sturdy roan had been ridden very hard. Morgan viewed his mounts as a means to an end, pushing them to the edge of their endurance but not to the point of permanent damage. It was so different from the way Mike saw the big hearted creatures. He murmured quietly to the roan as he bathed the gashes left by his father's spurs, and when he finished, he spent some extra moments stroking the big horse's neck. It was the best he could do in the way of an apology. The fact that he was the one who caught whatever horse Morgan rode, and turned it over to the man who had so little regard for his mount was hateful to him, but there was no way to escape that duty. He could only try to make it up to the horse at the end of the day.

Mike knew that Black Bird Shows observed him from the loft, but he gave no acknowledgement that he was aware of it. It was important to err on the side of caution in this matter.

The rattle of hooves on the bridge to the barn lot signaled his grandmother's return, and Mike stepped up to take Doc's reins. The difference in condition of the two horses was glaringly obvious. Doc looked as fresh as he had when he departed and he gave a low whinny at the sight of Mike. Laying down the reins, Mike stepped up to the side of the buggy to help his grandmother step down.

As did so, he whispered urgently, "Three men came here from the school today. They were looking for Black Bird Shows. We *have* to get him out of here!"

"Don't be worryin' about it. I have a plan," his grandmother replied. She smiled, and continued, "Takes the Hawk was happy t' hear my news. He's looking forward t' the medicines I will bring him tomorrow. Of course, I'll need you to help me load them."

She winked at Mike.

He grinned back at her.

"I'll be ready," he said.

Anna patted his shoulder and walked up the hill toward the houses.

Mike parked the buggy, and released Doc from his harness. He had already set out water and grain for the horse, and when he was sure Doc was enjoying his meal, he hung the harness up in the tack room. In the lengthening shadows, he spoke to the ceiling.

"Did you hear that, Black Bird? It looks like your journey will be over tomorrow."

A quiet voice drifted down from above, breaking slightly.

"I will be ready, too. Thank you, Mike Lorrah."

It was the second time Black Bird Shows had spoken his name.

CHAPTER 3

▼

At dinner that evening, the entire family ate together. Mike's grandfather, who worked in town, taking care of the school building and helping with the mail at the railroad depot, was home. He carried on a conversation with Velia about a gate he was building for the front walk of the ranch house. Morgan sat sternly at the head of the table, watching out the front windows as if he were expecting someone. He was obviously distracted, and the entire family knew better than to interrupt his thoughts with a question or conversation.

Moira sat primly, eating her dinner and watching all the adults with great serious looks. She adored her grandfather, and she looked at him often. Occasionally, Frank would look back at her, and wink, causing her to smile. His warmth and care made his attention something she craved, as opposed to Morgan's cool distance from his children. Her father frightened her a little, and she avoided looking at him, since he had scolded her for staring at him a number of times in the past.

Willow was already sleeping, having exhausted herself playing in the grass all afternoon.

Anna bustled to and fro, setting additional food on the table, and helping Velia with dinner tasks so her daughter could have a few moments to sit and relax.

Toward the end of the meal, Anna spoke.

"I will be goin' up Lodge Grass Creek tomorrow. Mrs. Winston is very sick, and I promised I'd be lookin' in on her. I'll be takin' a few supplies to the family, too. After that, I'm going to stop and see old Takes the Hawk."

Mike sneaked a look at his father's face. Morgan did not like Anna tending to poor farm families or to Crow people either, even though he did business with many of them on a regular basis. If Morgan heard Anna, he made no indication. As soon as the meal ended, Morgan pushed back his chair, rose, and walked back to the room that served as his office. The family knew they would not see or hear from him again that night.

Before going to bed, Mike helped his grandmother package up food and other supplies like her homemade soap and several packets of medicine. They put them in wooden apple crates and Mike made several trips to the barn to place them in the buggy.

On one of his returns from the barn, he overheard his mother and Anna talking as they stood on the porch, enjoying the evening air.

"Three men were here today looking for a runaway boy from the Crow boarding school," Velia said. "The leader was a red-haired man named Bart Knight. All my senses told me he is a very bad person, and I didn't like the way he looked at me."

"Did y' say he was called Bart Knight?" Anna asked, sounding surprised and concerned.

"Yes. He asked if the boy had passed through the ranch, and he demanded that we tell him if the boy did show up here."

There was a long silence, and then Anna said, "I know who he is. In Deadwood with Dr. Flora, we took care of all comers. A young Sioux Indian girl came t' us once to have her baby. She was no more than fourteen, and she had been raped by a white fellow who'd come to the area lookin' fer gold. Her brothers found out and killed the man, and the girl was scared to tell them about the baby. She had been hidin' out until time fer the birth, then she came t' us. The babe was sweet, but he did not look at all Indian. Had red hair, in fact. She made us swear that we would never tell, and she stayed off the reservation with the babe. She was too ashamed to go back t' her family, and she tried t' make a livin' workin' fer whites. There was very little work fer her, and then, when the boy was about eight, she died of pneumonia. Don't know if she told the boy his history, but he always seemed like a very angry lad. Got in a lot of trouble, stealin' and gettin' in fights with whites and with Indians, and he had trouble stayin' in school. People who knew him said he was mean. I patched up a few of his more serious injuries on a couple of occasions, and tried to talk to him. 'Twas a shame, so young for so much anger. Last I heard of him, a missionary managed t' get him educated, and he left the Black Hills. 'Twas said he changed his name from Bartholomew Kills in the Night to Bart Knight. He wanted to pass as white, and knew he could not in Deadwood, since everyone knew his history. So *this* must be where he went. He always hated both Indians and whites, and I'm sure he still does. Surely doesn't like himself much, either. Hope that poor runaway Crow boy gets far, far away from where he can find him."

The next morning, Morgan and his men were off in the pre-dawn half-light, long before the sun cleared the mountains. Mike held Morgan's horse while he mounted, and struggled not to wince when Morgan dug his spurs into the animal's sides. He wondered where his father and these men rode off to, and he knew the day would come when he would be expected to ride with them. They were tight-lipped about these journeys.

But today, he was relieved to have them go. After saddling his father's horse and seeing him off, it was his job to be sure the horses from the previous day's ride were given oats and water. He moved methodically from one task to the next, making sure there would be nothing for Morgan to criticize when he returned that night. With every motion, he thought about Black Bird Shows. What was the boy feeling? Did he worry that Mike and his grandmother might not help him, even though they had promised to do so? Mike wondered what it would be like to be pursued and punished as Black Bird Shows had been at the boarding school.

Suddenly, Doc whinnied from his place at the feeder. Mike looked up toward the house, and saw Anna striding down the road toward him.

"Michael," she called out. "Is m' buggy ready? It's a lot of ground I have t' cover today."

He turned to catch Doc, but need not have bothered. The big gray was already trotting up to the fence to greet his mistress, and his friendly neigh revealed how much he loved her. Mike went inside, pulled the bridle off its hook and came out to put it on the horse. Then he put the harness on and attached the horse to the buggy where it sat in the barn. When all was ready, Anna, who had been watching him work, nodded.

She looked up at the floor of the loft above her, and spoke softly.

"Black Bird Shows," she said, "Come down now."

There was a long moment with no sound, then the Crow boy's two feet appeared on the ladder. He shinnied down quickly, looking around fearfully in every direction.

"Y're safe enough," Anna said. "But you must do exactly as I say. Get into the buggy there, behind the seat and lay flat on the floor. Michael, put the horse blanket over him, make it look like he's a bundle of supplies. Black Bird, y'll be lyin' very still 'til I tell y' it's safe t' move. Do y' understand?"

Black Bird Shows wavered a moment, as if still weighing whether he could trust this little old white woman. Like so many other people, her voice told him all he needed to know. He climbed up into the buggy, rolled himself over the leather seat, and dropped into the small back space on his hands and knees. Then he lay down and curled his legs up to his chest as Mike arranged the horse blanket over him, and tucked it under. When Anna and Mike looked at this piece of handiwork, they weren't satisfied.

40

"It looks like a blanket over a boy," Anna said. "T'won't do."

Mike nodded and tucked the apple boxes up tight against the boy's prostrate body. He put one by Black Bird's head and one near his feet, then pulled the horse blanket tight and the cargo in the back of the buggy looked much less like a person. Anna placed her medical bags around the boy and stepped back to see how everything looked with these adjustments.

Satisfied, she moved to get into the buggy. Mike hurried to help her up, and stepped back.

"Nay, Michael," she admonished. "Y'll be comin' with me. I already told yer ma and da' I needed your help."

Mike was surprised. He had not expected to go along on this journey. But he did not have to be asked twice. He swung in and sat next to Anna as Doc strode out of the barn. They climbed the short stretch to the house and Anna waved at Velia.

"We'll be back before dark," she called out, and Velia nodded.

Mike was always delighted when his grandmother had him accompany her on calls. It was not a frequent occurrence, but there were times when she needed an extra set of hands, to load and unload supplies, or to babysit with other children in a family when she was delivering a baby. He loved sitting next to her in the buggy seat, watching the countryside flow by as she drove. Their human cargo lay still, completely concealed from curious eyes should they meet other travelers.

They took the road up Lodge Grass Creek, and after about six miles, she turned off onto a small lane that was barely more than a path through the grasses. They dropped down into a wooded area and approached the banks of the creek. When they entered the shade of the cottonwoods that lined the stream, the air changed. Sounds were muffled, and the light was dappled with the shade pattern of the leaves of the huge old trees. It was much cooler in this place, and it seemed very far from the rest of the world. The horse's footfalls made no sound, and the wheels of the carriage seemed to float above the ground. The air was crystalline, and it had a depth that Mike had never experienced.

They rounded a cluster of wild plum bushes and an opening appeared, revealing a shallow crossing in the creek, and a tidy house of graying logs that manifested itself on the other side. Doc's ears pricked and he let out a low sound as he splashed into the water, bringing his mistress to the house. When they arrived, a small wizened Crow Indian man stepped out of the front door. Takes the Hawk was only slightly taller than Mike, and he had three thick white braids of hair that framed his dark brown face and reached below his waist. A tall black reservation hat with an eagle feather in the band sat on his head. He raised one hand, palm forward, in greeting, and this gesture was mirrored by Anna.

She dismounted before the buggy stopped completely, and motioned for Mike to do the same. As he came around from his side, he saw that Anna and Takes the Hawk were already engaged in conversation, spoken in Crow and animated sign language. Mike was astonished. He had no idea that his Irish grandmother had knowledge of these two languages. She stepped up to the buggy and reached behind the seat to remove the blanket that covered Black Bird Shows. The boy blinked at the sudden light and sat up. He was a bit disoriented at first, but his eyes immediately turned to the old man. His face lit up, and he leapt from his hiding place. Once he stood before Takes the Hawk, he averted his eyes in respect, and waited for his uncle to speak.

Takes the Hawk looked at him for a long time, as if sizing him up. Then he spoke to his nephew, a long stream of words in Crow that Mike did not understand. If his grandmother did, she did not react. Black Bird Shows was silent. Finally he nodded, and then he looked at Anna and Mike.

In English, he said, "I am grateful to you. My uncle says I must never forget what you have done, and I promise I will not."

Anna smiled.

"Black Bird Shows," she said. "The only thing we want is that y' live a good life, and learn everythin' y' can from yer uncle. His knowledge is vast, and he has much t' teach. Let us know how you are doing from time t' time."

Black Bird Shows nodded in understanding. Then he spoke to Mike.

"You saved my life, Mike Lorrah," he said. "I will see you again one day."

Mike held out his hand, and Black Bird Shows glanced at his uncle for direction. Takes the Hawk said something in Crow, and Black Bird Shows took Mike's hand, shaking it in the white man's way.

Mike said, "I hope it will be soon."

Takes the Hawk smiled at Anna. He spoke rapidly to her in Crow, and Anna replied in the same tongue. She turned and put a hand on Mike's shoulder.

"He says y're a good boy and that y'll become a good man. I told him t'was true, and that I already knew it."

"Does he speak English?" Mike asked.

"He does, but he said English does not have the right words for somethin' this important. So he said it in Crow."

Takes the Hawk held up his hand, and hurried into his house, leaving all three of them standing there. When he emerged from the door, he had a bundle in his hands. He motioned for them to sit down in the grass, and he began to spread out the items. In what seemed to be an almost formal manner, he made a small pile in front of each of them. For Anna, there were numerous rawhide packets and deerskin bags of what Mike could only guess were medicines and herbs. For Black Bird Shows, there were new clothes perfectly sized for him, including a new pair of moccasins. For Mike, there was a buttery soft deerskin vest, finely worked and big enough that it would fit him for a long time to come.

Mike looked from Takes the Hawk back to his grandmother, trying to determine what he should say or do.

"Put it on," Anna said. "And thank him – in English. He'll understand y' perfectly."

Mike ran his hands over the extraordinary gift, then hurried to pull it on over his plain shirt. It felt like a second skin, and he could not remember ever having anything as magnificent. He looked into Takes the Hawk's face, his eyes shining with excitement.

"Thank you very much, sir," he said. "It is very handsome. I'm proud to wear it."

The old man allowed the hint of a smile to play across his lips at this earnest proclamation. He gave a small nod to Mike, then moved his attention to Anna.

More words in Crow were exchanged. Then Anna went to the carriage and reached for one of the boxes. Mike was at her side instantly, and he unloaded it for her.

"Put it on the step, there," she said, indicating the small stoop at the door of the log house.

Once he placed it, she pulled away the towel she had used to cover it. Not only were there homemade bread, freshly churned butter and some cheese, but there were eggs, a slab of bacon, and several jars of jellies, and jars of canned fruits and vegetables. She spoke again in Crow to Takes the Hawk, who laughed aloud. Knowing that Mike was very curious about what she had said, she turned to him.

"I just told him that he is not used to having a growin' boy in his house and that he'll need much more food to get started!"

Rustling around in the bottom of the crate with her hand, she came up with several packets wrapped in white paper. Mike knew what these were. They were mixtures of herbs, leaves, seeds and grasses from Dr. Flora's fascinating handwritten journal for various kinds of treatments and cures. She had allowed him to watch her make up these medicinal mixtures many times, and they were in great demand in the area. She handed the packets to Takes the Hawk, who received them reverently with both hands. It was almost like a state ceremony, watching these two old people passing magic between them. Once Anna was satisfied that all her cargo was delivered, she bowed her head to Takes the Hawk. Beckoning Mike, she mounted the step of her buggy. He hurried to take his seat beside her, and waving back at the boy and the old man, they took their leave.

When they were out of sight of the house, Mike turned to Anna.

"Will he be all right, Grandmother?"

"He'll be better than all right, Michael," she replied with a knowing smile.

C H A P T E R 4

▼

The days raced by as Mike busied himself with all his assigned chores. His father and the men continued to leave before dawn and return after dark. Sometimes, there were strange horses in the corral after they unsaddled their mounts. Mike wondered if he was the only one in the family who noticed this as he continued to care for the ranch's horses. It was odd the way these other animals appeared and disappeared. Some of Morgan's men came in even later than the rest, and they were the ones who delivered these new horses to the enclosure and took them away again. The horses had a variety of brands on them, and Mike did not recognize most of them. It was part of the secret life his father lived, and Mike knew better than to ask questions.

It was a relief to know Black Bird Shows was safely away from the ranch, but Mike missed him. A good friendship had begun to develop between them, and he wished he could see Black Bird again. There had been no further appearances of men from the boarding school, so it could be assumed the administrators had decided it was not worth trying to find the escaped student in the vastness of the reservation. Mike and Anna did not discuss the matter, and it remained a secret between them. In the only exception during the weeks following their delivery to Takes the Hawk, Anna had driven off to check on the old man and the boy. She took Mike aside upon her return and assured him that Black Bird Shows was doing well at his uncle's home.

"Grandmother," he said. "I miss Black Bird. It was good having a friend right here on the ranch. Do you think I'll see him again?"

Anna smiled at her sincere grandson.

"I'm sure y' will," she said. "I just don't think 'tis a good idea for y' t' take the chance right now that your father will find out. He wouldn't understand."

Mike was absolutely certain this was true. His father did not like to be too friendly with the Indians, and he did not want the family to be friendly with them either. It was the reason Mike had taken extra care to make sure the barn loft was spotless after Black Bird left. He did not want any trace of the boy's presence to trigger suspicion on his father's part. It was unlikely that Morgan would go up into the loft, but there was no use taking chances.

Morgan was increasing the pressure to take Mike on one of the rides with him and the men. The day finally came when there was no further way to avoid it.

One evening at dinner, Morgan interrupted the usual conversation at the table.

"Mike," he said, his cool gaze leveled on his son. "You'll ride with us in the morning."

Mike was silent, waiting for his mother or his grandmother to object. But both of them looked down at their plates and did not say anything. His grandfather looked solemn, but held his silence, as well. It was apparent that this subject had been discussed and decided.

"Well?" Morgan's voice was hard.

"What will I be doing?" Mike asked.

"You'll see."

Morgan bit off the words, and past experience had taught Mike not to ask any further questions.

Before the sun was up in the morning, Mike had Morgan's mount ready. He also had saddled a horse for himself. It was a sturdy sorrel with white socks all around, named Pal. Mike liked to think of this horse as his own, but he had learned early on that Morgan might sell any animal if someone offered enough money for it. Mike had ridden this horse often when gathering up the milk cows or going into Lodge Grass to school, and the two of them had a solid rapport. The sorrel was reliable and strong, and very much attached to Mike.

The air was crisp, but Mike had a hat on, ready for the harsh sunshine that was sure to come later in the day. He handed Morgan's reins to him, then stepped up into his own saddle.

Morgan gave a curt nod, and they were off.

Riding through the pre-dawn half light, Mike felt some pride in being included with the men. Twinned with the pride was apprehension, since he did not know what their mission was. He marveled at the total silence the men kept. It seemed to him that even the usual sounds of tack and spurs were muffled as this collection of tough men rode.

They traveled hard and fast for most of the day, the men pushing their mounts at a pace that demanded much of their strength. In a place south of Wyola, they turned up a trail that led toward the foothills of the Big Horn Mountains and into a remote, hidden ravine. There, in a brush corral, was a group of twenty horses. The animals had apparently been confined there on the previous day.

They stopped next to the enclosure, and waited out the rest of the day. Most of the men found what shade they could, and stretched out on the ground for a little sleep. When the sun began to set, several of the men removed the brush that blocked the end of the ravine. The horses began to move out. Morgan sat rigid in his saddle, watching the herd. Mike sat on his horse, looking at him for any indication of what he should do. His father ignored him and observed the men moving the horses. He was not satisfied with the speed of the wrangling, and suddenly, he spurred his horse toward one of the cowboys who was not moving quickly enough for him. He shouted several expletives and slashed at the man's horse with his quirt. The horse bolted forward to escape the stinging attack, and nearly unseated his rider. Morgan yelled several commands, and the man jerked on the reins to comply.

Meanwhile, the herd of grunting, gasping horses sped up to a flat-out gallop as the drivers whooped and slapped their lariats to push them. The sounds were thunderous.

Morgan yelled for Mike to join him at the back of the herd.

"C'mon, boy," Morgan shouted. "Keep 'em together. We have to move fast."

Cringing, but glad for activity, Mike urged his horse to the side of the herd, watching for any straggling horses as they moved at a furious pace. He was horrified to see how relentlessly they were driving the animals, and wondered how far they were going to travel. Some of the horses were stumbling; many showed the whites of their eyes in fear and exhaustion. Mike had never driven any animals like this, and he was tortured by the pain he could sense from them.

The drivers turned the horses into a shallow portion of the Little Big Horn River, and pushed them along for a quarter mile. It occurred to Mike that the intent was to cover some distance without leaving tracks. After that the men divided the horses into smaller groups, and split off in several different directions. By now, there was no question that this was an illegal operation. Mike wondered where the horses came from, but asking his father was not an option. He just put his head down and did as he was told. Morgan watched the men go, and then turned his horse toward the home ranch, his son silent at his side.

When they reached the house, it was completely dark outside. Mike slid off his horse, and took Morgan's reins. His father strode toward the front door, spurs ringing against the plank walkway. Mike walked from the house down to the barn lot, and unsaddled the exhausted animals. He brushed both horses, rinsed their coats and gave them oats and water. All the time he worked, he murmured apologies again and again for the merciless ride. He despaired at what he had seen, and he knew this would now become a part of his life for as long as Morgan ordered it to be.

When he finished, he trudged back to the house. On the porch, he removed his dusty boots and hat before entering. His mother watched him carefully as he rinsed his hands and face in the basin she kept in the alcove of the kitchen.

"Mike," she said, "I made you some sandwiches. I'm sorry I don't have a hot dinner for you, but your father ate while you were taking care of the horses."

"Thank you, Mother," he replied. "I'm not very hungry. A sandwich will be just fine."

Velia was quiet. She wondered what had happened to her son's appetite. He had been such a hearty eater for several weeks, and now it seemed he was not eating much at all. She did not know how to ask him about the day. That was between him and his father.

Mike took a few bites from the sandwich, drank a glass of milk, and tried to edge his way through the living room to his bedroom. Morgan saw his furtive attempt, and spoke to him in a low voice.

"Well, son," he said slowly. "You did all right today. You know, of course, that you won't be discussing these rides with anyone, don't you?"

"Yes, sir."

"Get some sleep, boy. You'll be helping your grandmother with the garden tomorrow. We won't be ridin' again for a while."

Mike hurried to his room, relieved that the conversation had not been longer. He pulled off his clothes and sat down on the edge of his bed. With the door closed, he allowed the tears to come, weeping for the cruelty he had witnessed that day, and for the loss of his youth.

He finally lay down, but he was not able to sleep. Each time he closed his eyes, he saw the beautiful horses struggling to continue running from the men, and he felt their fear and pain. It was the worst thing he could remember ever seeing.

Very late in the night, he heard the rumble of hoofs outside the house. The night riders were returning, and they rode past the main house to the corrals. He knew he would find all their horses, worn out and crusted with sweat in the morning. The men would sleep late in the bunkhouse. He'd seen them do that before, but now he understood the reasons. He wept again as he tossed on his bed.

The next morning, Mike plodded through his chores, washing down the horses and giving them food and water. A couple of them were more than exhausted. A buckskin gelding stood in the far corner of the corral, displaying no interest in water or grain. His head hung down and his eyes were dull. Flies buzzed around his face, and he made no effort to shake them away.

Mike carried water to the horse, and brushed him where he stood. Then he brought oats in a bucket, but the animal made no effort to eat. Mike felt like his heart would break. Such abuse was outside his understanding. He loved each of these grand animals. They gave their all to their riders, only to be used hard and tossed aside for fresh mounts with no care about their condition. Tears sat in Mike's throat as he stroked the horse's neck.

"It's all right, boy," he whispered to the big buckskin. "At least you won't have to work today, and I'll be back to check on you later."

He couldn't help identifying with the animal. He was relieved that neither of them had to go out with the men that day. Working with his grandmother would be an escape for him, and he wanted to talk to her about what he had seen. When he finished caring for the horses, he trudged up the hill to the garden.

Anna was already out among the plants. The garden spread out around her sturdy form in verdant splendor. Every vegetable and flower was flawless, bigger than any others grown in the entire valley. There was not a single weed to be seen, and the soil was black with nutrients. Mike's task was to carry buckets of water from the hand pump to the garden and carefully pour it into little ditches and wells that his grandmother had made around each plant. He loved these times with Anna. And he could swear the plants trembled with delight at the fresh water cooling their roots.

Anna looked up as he brought the first bucketful to her. She scanned his face and frowned at what she saw there. Mike looked like he had aged overnight. Weariness overlaid his expression, and there were dark circles under his eyes. In those eyes, she read a great sadness.

She waited for him to speak.

He paused, then plunged right in.

"Grandmother," he said, "Father told me not to talk about it, but I hated going with the men yesterday. They had captured horses, and they drove them so hard. The ones they rode were run until they could hardly stand up any more. It was awful, and I don't want to go again!"

"Oh, Michael," she said. "There's no stoppin' yer da'. I held off his effort t' take you along for this entire year. Now he's had you once he won't be stopped."

"I'll run away!"

"Doin' that would be breakin' your mother's heart."

It was an argument he could not counter. He would never do anything he thought might hurt his mother. He idolized her, and avoided disappointing her at all costs. This was the first time he had been so torn by circumstance. Seeing the horses in the corral, nearly broken down by their callous use was horrible. His father was a hard man, and Mike knew he would never meet his expectations. Tears brimmed in his eyes again and threatened to spill over.

Anna could not bear to see her grandson in such turmoil, but she wasn't sure what to do for him, either. Perhaps his grandfather would have some idea when he returned home from work at the school. Frank Stanford was a good grandfather to the Lorrah children, gentle and kind. Anna hoped he would have an idea for a solution to this quandary. He understood that Morgan was distant and separate from his children in many ways. The warmth, humor, and love they sought in a father figure came from him. He was devoted to all three, but particularly to Moira, who seemed to need him most. Anna knew he would help Mike, if he could.

Mike and Anna worked in silence for the rest of the afternoon. When they finished, she gave him a handful of the biggest strawberries he had ever seen as a reward. He ate them to satisfy her, but could not really enjoy the luscious taste, thinking of the horses.

"Grandmother," he said, "May I have some of the carrots for those poor horses? They deserve something for all their suffering."

Anna gave him a small smile. Her grandson was so compassionate. Small wonder the animals all loved and trusted him. It was as if he could read their minds.

"Of course y' can," she said. "But don't be lettin' yer father see. He doesn't like it when we take things from the garden t' give t' the livestock. He believes that everything we grow is for people, not for animals."

Mike nodded. He felt so tired and hopeless. Anna pulled up several of the largest carrots and placed them in his hands, then turned back as if to look at the flowers that grew along the edge of the garden. She did not want him to see her cry.

CHAPTER 5

▼

Mike had a brief respite from his father's demands for a couple of weeks, but one Sunday, it was over.

That evening, Morgan returned after dark, as usual.

As he removed his spurs and his jacket, he told Mike that they would leave at three o'clock the following morning. Mike stared downward, examining his father's spurs.

"Look at me, boy! We're going for horses up toward Miles City tomorrow. Bring what you need for three days," Morgan said. "And have my horse ready."

Mike nodded in understanding, feeling cold inside. If one day's ride was bad, what would three days be like?

He went to bed early, but sleep eluded him. He tossed and turned until he heard his mother in the kitchen, preparing breakfast and no doubt, food for them to take along on the ride. Dragging his body from the warm blankets, he danced on one foot and then the other as the icy floor sent tiny shocks of cold into the soles of his feet. He tugged on his socks and his boots, and walked through the kitchen toward the door. He picked up a kerosene lantern to help him see where he was going.

Velia looked up from the stove.

"Mike, you must have something to eat. It's going to be a long day," she said.

His stomach was in a knot, and he could not imagine putting anything in it at that moment. He shook his head.

"I have to get the horses ready," he replied. "I'll bring them up here, and I'll eat then, if there's time."

At the corral, he enticed the big black with a handful of oats, and quickly saddled him. Once the horse finished munching on the grain, Mike slipped the bit into his mouth and buckled the bridle on. The horse was a big, tough mixture of Indian pony, thoroughbred and quarter horse, deliberately bred for speed and endurance. He was a big-hearted animal, too. He always allowed Mike to catch him, even though he knew it would lead to a very hard day of work. It was as if he understood that Mike had nothing to do with how he was treated. Morgan never called his horses by name, but Mike had named this one. He called him Prince, for his regal appearance and his dignity.

Mike's horse nickered as he came from the corner of the corral, jealous of the attention the black was getting. Soon Pal's soft muzzle was checking to see if Mike's pockets held any treats. He was never disappointed. Mike fished into his shirt and pulled out a contraband lump of sugar, taken from the previous night's dinner table. Then he saddled the little sorrel and put his bridle on. The act of putting the bit into the horses' mouths was done first by most horsemen, but Mike preferred to allow them to go as long as possible without the hard metal bar against their tongues. They never tried to move away from him when he saddled them, so it was his style to give them that small amount of extra time.

He swung up into his saddle, leading the big black with the reins. In front of the house, he tied both mounts to the log hitching rail his grandfather had installed there. Then he went inside, where Morgan had already finished eating.

"Grab a biscuit, boy," his father said. "You can't be here at the table, then you won't get much to eat."

Velia hurried to hand him a cloth bag, knotted at the top. It held the food he would eat during the long journey they were making. As the big railroad clock on the wall struck three, Mike stuffed two biscuits into his jacket, trying not to think of what else had been in his pockets before. At least the baking powder concoction would take the edge off his hunger. He followed his father out the door, while Velia watched with a worried expression on her face. She knew her son had to grow up sometime, but this seemed so early... and so harsh.

Morgan mounted his horse with uncanny grace, and the black twitched his skin in the area where the spurs jingled next to his side. But the horse was calm and rested, ready for the tough trip ahead.

Mike grabbed the saddle horn and swung onto the sorrel's back without putting his foot into the stirrup, the same way he did when he rode bareback. The sturdy little horse stood very still, but once his rider was seated, he shuffled his feet, ready to go. Morgan turned for a long look at Velia, standing in the lighted doorway, then checked his lariat and his bedroll. Even though Mike had secured them to his saddle, the double check was elaborate, indicating that he did not necessarily trust his son's work. Digging the rowels of those cruel Mexican spurs into the side of his horse, he set off at a fast trot, Mike right behind him.

They rode for several miles along Lodge Grass Creek, and suddenly six riders joined them. It was still dark, but Mike knew they were the same men as before. Few words were exchanged, and all the men seemed intently focused.

They continued north, riding hard, even as the sun began to beat down on them. Morgan was now in the lead, and Mike had dropped back. Dust swirled up from the hoofs of those in front, and surrounded the riders behind. Several pulled their bandanas up around their faces in an effort to screen the air they breathed. The day passed in a blur for Mike, who only wanted to stop and get down off his mount for a rest. He was used to riding along on cattle roundups and other ranch tasks, but this was very different. After many miles, they approached a river. Morgan held up a hand, and they stopped for the horses to drink, and for the men to splash a little water on dirty faces. Several of the men dug into their saddlebags and retrieved some item of food, wolfing it down as fast as they could. Mike got off and stretched his tight muscles, only to scramble for his mount as the men quickly climbed back onto their horses and took off again.

They rode at a trot all day, stopping for a few other short breaks, but not enough to rest. These were rugged men, and Mike felt himself struggling to keep up. There was no choice. Either keep up, or face Morgan's wrath. He detested pushing his horse like this, but that sentiment was not shared by his father or the rest of the gang.

When darkness fell, the group found a spot in the shelter of some trees alongside another stream. They stopped, dismounted, and allowed their horses to graze while they ate a bigger share of the food they carried. Mike drank some water, but he was too tired to eat. In the light of the small fire they lit, he looked at the faces of the men. All were dusty, and most looked as if they had not shaved in several days. Their eyes glinted in the reflected flames, and they continued to be silent and grim. All gave deference to Morgan, who was obviously the principal of this endeavor.

Mike followed the others and did not unsaddle his horse. He only pulled off the bridle, hung it on the saddle horn, and put a lead-rope on Pal so he was not hindered in his grazing. He wondered when they would pull down their bedrolls from the backs of their saddles and make camp. The fire burned down to embers, but no one made a move to settle for the night.

As if by some unseen signal, one of the men kicked dirt onto the fire, and everyone mounted up. Mike rushed to re-bridle his horse, and got on quickly. To his dismay, they set off again, and there was a sense that this would be a long ride into the night.

Sometime around midnight, they crested a rise, and looked down on a pasture where they could see more than thirty horses scattered out in the moonlight. The ranch house, some one hundred yards from the area, was dark. Moving as silently as mountain lions, two of the men dismounted, and crept down into the field, quietly bunching all the horses, and moving them toward an opening the others had made in the primitive split-rail fence. The rest of the men waited until the horses passed where they stood, and then began to move them quietly up into a draw. The two who had walked them out remounted and helped keep them moving. This silent herding continued until the animals were out of earshot of the house. Then the group started pushing their captives harder, until they were at a full gallop.

Mike worried for his own horse, and hoped that Pal could see better than he could. The terrain was rough and rocky, filled with sagebrush and scrub trees. There probably were prairie dog holes out here, too. None of this slowed the pace, and they ran the horses for an hour or so, staying on rocky ground to help obscure their tracks.

At last, they came to a hidden enclosure similar to the one he had seen on his first ride with them. They pushed the horses into it, and barricaded the opening with brush and branches to conceal its location. When they finished, the first light of dawn was breaking.

They mounted up again and rode a few miles to another cluster of trees along a small creek, and made camp. Mike now understood that they would camp during the day and move only at night, and he was sick and sad about what this told him. Pal was covered with dust and sweat when the saddle was removed, and Mike wished he had something to give him for a treat. He seemed to look at Mike with reproach, and the boy could only stand with him and stroke his neck for comfort.

Finally, the horse went to sleep where he stood, and Mike rolled out his bedroll next to him. Sleep was slow in coming. This was against all the lessons he had learned from his grandmother and his mother. Morgan was making him do something he knew was wrong, and he could see no way out of it. At last, he slept.

He woke when he heard the others moving around, and he sat up when he smelled coffee cooking over the small fire. Every muscle in his body hurt, and he wished he was home, eating one of his mother's excellent breakfasts. One of the men came over to him.

"Want some coffee, boy?" he asked.

Nodding, Mike looked at the man carefully. He was a grizzled, older man, with a huge scar running up his left cheek. Despite his ferocious appearance, he seemed to be concerned about the boy who rode with them.

"Yer Morgan's son, ain't ya'?

Mike nodded again, taking the cup from the man's hand.

"Damn shame, if you ask me, making a kid like you ride with us."

The man fumbled in the pocket of the coat he wore, and pulled out a small flask. He poured some of the tawny liquid it contained into Mike's coffee.

"Here, boy. This'll help with yer aches and pains," he said.

Mike knew it was whiskey, but he did not want to seem like a child, so he took a sip of the coffee. The combination of the coffee and the alcohol made him cough violently with the first swallow, and the man shushed him.

"Take another drink," he hissed. "It'll get better as ya' go along."

Mike obeyed, and discovered that what the man said was true. His throat did not rebel against the fiery liquid the second time. His muscles started to feel better, and the liquor partially soothed his distress about what Morgan was ordering him to do. He stood up, and began to care for his own horse, leading him down to the stream for a drink.

Morgan motioned him over to where he was sitting with several of the other men.

"Take care of the other horses, while you're at it," he said.

Mike took each horse to the river, and with a spare saddle blanket, washed the dust and crusted sweat off their backs. The horses looked somewhat rested, and seemed to have recovered from the difficult ride of the previous night. Of all of them, Pal looked the worst. He was not hardened to this kind of grueling work.

The day wore on, and the men spent time playing cards with a grimy, tattered deck. Mike watched them, but kept to himself, staying on the fringes. Bits of conversation drifted his way, and all confirmed what he knew already. This was a ring of horse thieves, and his father was deeply involved in the operations.

When the light of day faded, they resumed their ride, returning to the place where they had hidden the horses. Releasing them, they set out in the half-light, riding at a relentless pace, then repeated the maneuver of running them along in a stream bed to throw off anyone who might be trying to track them. When they reached a point where the river became deep, they swam the animals for some distance, then headed them for the bank and urged them up out of the water. Once again, they pushed them into a flat-out run and headed south across the rolling hills.

Suddenly, one of the horses lost its footing in a ravine and stumbled to its knees in the twilight. The other horses ran blindly, first past it, then over it. Morgan cursed and rode over to where the animal lay on its side, kicking in an effort to get back on its feet. He looked down for a moment, then pulled out his pistol and shot the horse in the head.

Mike felt nauseous. He was grateful for the bandana that would keep his father from seeing how upset he was.

The cruelty did not end there. One of the men pulled a bull whip from where he had it tied on his saddle, and began to crack it at the horses that were running more slowly. One little bay mare was particularly far behind, and at last, Morgan pulled out his lasso and roped her around the neck. He pulled her off toward a pile of brush and when Mike could no longer see where he went with her, he heard another gun shot.

Morgan emerged from the thicket and rejoined the drive. On they ran, until it seemed like they would gallop through eternity. Mike's senses had shut down after the shooting of the mare, and he just rode. If he allowed himself to think about what he had seen and heard, he would be unable to stay on his horse.

At last, the surrounding country started to look familiar. They came to the location where they had divided the horses before, and the action was repeated. The men vanished into the night with their booty, and Morgan and Mike turned toward home.

They came to the corrals just after midnight, and Morgan rode up to the gate of the yard, sliding off and handing Mike the reins. Mike led the big black to the corrals, where he unsaddled Pal and Prince, giving each an extra measure of oats. He rubbed them down by the light of oncoming dawn, placed the saddles in the barn, and crawled up into the loft where he collapsed on the pile of straw and sobbed, his heart broken for the useless deaths of the two horses who were only trying to keep up with the herd.

Finally, when he had no more tears, he descended, washed his face off in the water trough, and walked back up to the house. Morgan was sitting in the parlor with Velia, and they were so wrapped up in each other that they did not notice when he walked by. He looked around for his grandmother, but she was probably at her house making breakfast for his grandfather. It was just as well. He really did not want to see any of them. He went to his room, threw himself on his bed and drifted off into an exhausted sleep.

CHAPTER 6

▼

It was six o'clock when he awoke the next morning. He could smell coffee brewing and knew his mother and father would be at the table. It was difficult for him to go to the kitchen, because he dreaded looking into Morgan's face. But if he did not get up, the punishment he would receive would be worse than a face-to-face encounter under his own terms.

Pulling on his clothes, he hurried to take his place with the rest of the family. Morgan looked at him intently, assessing him in a way Mike had not experienced before. It made him squirm. He loved his father and wanted to please him, but this business with the horses was just wrong. Nothing was said as he slid into his chair and took a drink of the milk his mother had placed at his plate. Moira had a bowl of porridge in front of her, and baby Willow sat in her high chair, staring raptly at her parents.

Velia spoke first.

"How are you this morning, Michael?"

"I'm all right, Mother."

She could see that he wasn't.

"Do you want to talk about anything?"

The shake of his head told her she would not hear what was upsetting him. He picked at his food in silence, while his parents chatted about people they knew, about what work was being done on the fencing for the ranch, and a multitude of other superficial subjects. Moira ate carefully, doing her best to imitate adult table manners.

After what seemed an eternity, Morgan rose from the table. Mike watched as his mother tipped her face up for her husband's kiss, and then waited for his father to go to his office at the back of the house.

"May I be excused, Mother?" he asked.

"Michael, you hardly ate anything. Are you sure you feel all right?"

"I'm fine, Mother," he said. "May I go to see if Grandmother needs any help today?

"Of course. That's very good of you."

Mike picked up his plate and silverware and took it to the counter where his mother could wash it. He mussed Moira's hair, much to her annoyance, and planted a kiss on the top of baby Willow's burnished red hair. She giggled with delight at her big brother's attention.

Once out the door, he walked the hundred yards to his grandparents' house. He knocked at the door, and his grandmother called for him to enter. She was in the kitchen, preparing rhubarb pies, something she often did in the early part of the day to beat the heat. One look at Mike's face told her something was wrong, and she wiped her hands on her apron.

"Sit down, Michael," she said. "You look very unhappy."

Despite his resolve to be mature about this, Mike could not contain his emotion. He sat down, and tears streamed silently down his face. When he had wept himself dry, he told her what he had seen. Knowing his love for all animals, Anna understood that he was sick at heart.

"I don't know what I can do for you with yer da'," she said. "He will be angry if he knows y' told me all this. Let me talk to your ma."

Mike looked at her with alarm.

He loved his mother and did not wish to upset her.

"No, grandmother," he said. "I think I just needed to talk about it. Let me handle it for myself."

Anna looked deeply into his face. It took courage for him to take on this burden, particularly in light of the demands of his father. It was a heavy load for someone so young. She would let him do this for now, but she would watch closely to make sure he had the support he needed.

"Now," he said. "What I really came for was to see if you needed any help in the garden. Is there something I can do?"

Smiling at him, she replied, "Y' can be carryin' water to the tomatoes. Once m' pies are done, I'll be joinin' y' out there."

Mike rose, went to the door, and turned to face her.

"Thank you for listening, grandmother."

As he left her house, he noticed a rider coming toward his parents' home at a full gallop. The man swung down and rushed to the door of the house, where he was admitted by Velia. Mike hoped it was not another of the school authorities who had come looking for Black Bird Shows, but he knew the boy's secret was safe. His parents did not know about him, and his grandmother would never discuss such things with anyone.

Once in the garden, Mike went to the hand pump and began carrying buckets of water to the tomatoes. Later the entire garden would be irrigated with a series of ditches he had dug under his grandmother's direction. But for today, the little plants needed more individualized watering.

Suddenly, his father emerged from the house with the man.

"Mike!"

"Yes sir?"

"Get my horse and saddle him up. I have to go to town!"

Mike jumped to obey the command. He jogged down to the barn and caught the big black. He marveled at how well rested Prince appeared to be. Mike swung the saddle onto the big horse's back and cinched it down securely. Then he put the bridle on, and stepped up onto the horse, trotting him to the house for his father.

Morgan took the reins as Mike slid off, and mounted.

"I'm going to be overnight. I've told your mother to pack some things for me and give it to you to bring to town. You can find me at the livery stable."

Mike nodded, and watched his father and the man ride off. Something was different with his father. He wondered why he was not wearing his spurs this morning. Perhaps they would be in the things his mother packed.

Velia gathered some clothing together for Morgan, while Mike ran next door to tell his grandmother that he would not be able to finish his garden tasks. Then he hurried back to the barn to catch his own horse. Pal was not as refreshed as Prince had been, but he came willingly when Mike whistled for him.

"Sorry, Pal," Mike said. "I wish I could have given you a day to rest, but I have to deliver these things to my father."

The horse munched the carrot his master had brought him, and gazed placidly at the boy. Mike chose to ride him bareback and with a halter instead of putting a bridle bit into his mouth.

"At least I can give you a break from that much," he said to the sorrel.

When he rode up to the gate, his mother came out with a satchel. He took it from her, set it in front of him, grasping its handle, and set off at an easy trot for Lodge Grass.

The town was buzzing with excitement. A horse rustler had been shot by a rancher from up Miles City way. The rancher had tracked the man to a place near Lodge Grass and surprised him with his stolen horses. The body of the man was laid out at the livery barn, and an inquest would be performed there. Every adult was headed toward the scene, since this was the most excitement the town had had in a while. Mike proceeded that way, too, since he was sure that was where he would find his father.

He saw Prince hitched to a post near the livery barn, and he secured the satchel to his father's saddle. Then he went in search of Morgan. He was with several other men, standing around the plank-and-wooden sawhorse platform where the body of the rustler was laid out. The dead man was fully clothed, and his head had been covered with a sheet. There were spots of blood on the white material. Mike could not see the entire body, since there were so many people standing close to where it was laid out. He was very curious. It was the first time he had ever seen a dead person, and this was made all the more exciting because of the way in which the man had died.

Several adults spotted young Mike and tried to shoo him from the barn, but he assured them he was there at his father's order, and they let him pass. When he squeezed through the crowd to get close to where Morgan stood, he stopped abruptly when he saw the dead outlaw's feet. There, on the scuffed pair of boots, were his father's Mexican silver spurs.

Someone pulled the sheet off the man's face. It was one of the men who had ridden with his father on the two rides Mike had been on. Fear grabbed at Mike. What would happen now? Many people had seen Morgan in those spurs. Would he be arrested? Would people know that Morgan had been part of all this, too?

Then he heard his father say, "I wondered what happened to my spurs. They were stolen out of the barn at the ranch about two weeks ago."

Mike cringed at the lie. He had seen Morgan in those spurs just two days before. Had anyone else seen him? Mike was suddenly very afraid.

Morgan saw Mike standing there, and he studied the boy's expression. He called him over, and Mike told him he had brought his things. Morgan stared intensely into his son's eyes.

"Well, son," he said. "I think you should be on your way home, then, don't you?"

Mike swallowed hard, and nodded. Then he stumbled out of the barn and found his way to his horse.

When he got home, he rubbed Pal down, and gave him even more oats. Returning to the garden, he found his grandmother weeding the rows. He told her what he had seen, and resumed watering the tomatoes. His grandmother watched him working for a few minutes, then set her hoe against the fence and walked resolutely to her daughter's house.

Morgan came home late that evening. As usual, Mike gave his father's horse the care it needed. When he walked back toward the door of the house, the conversation between his mother and father was drifting out of the open kitchen windows. Rather than walk in and interrupt, he remained outside and listened from below.

"You have to stop whatever it is that you do with those men at night, Morgan," Velia was saying.

"It's made us plenty of money," Morgan replied.

"Money is not as important as your family. You cannot take Mike with you on those rides any more."

"Why? What did he say to you?"

"Nothing. But my father was in town today during that horse thief's inquest. He recognized your spurs on the man. It didn't take much for him to put the pieces together. As Mike's grandfather and my father, he told me that Mike must not ride with you again."

"What am I supposed to do? This ranch doesn't support us yet," Morgan's retort was abrupt, but the undercurrent of pleading revealed how much he hated to argue with Velia.

"Find something."

Velia's stony tone left no doubt that this was her final word.

Mike opened the door and walked into the house. Neither of his parents spoke to him, but the tension in the air was thick.

He went into the living room. Moira was looking at pictures, and Willow was testing her patience, tugging at her dress and reaching for the book she held in her lap. Mike leaned over and swept his baby sister up in his arms. She gurgled at her big brother's action, pleased to have some attention. Sweeping her arms wide, she hugged him, and then made her usual plea.

"Outside," she said.

Mike turned and carried her out into the yard, once again passing his parents who were still looking at each other, each waiting for the other to speak. He was glad to remove himself from the area. It was starting to get dark, and the night birds were just beginning their songs. Willow begged to be put down in the grass, and when he deposited her on her little bare feet, she twirled about, curls bouncing, and eyes sparkling.

All of a sudden, a red fox kit appeared out of the gathering darkness, and circled where the child was dancing. It sniffed the air, tilted its head in some kind of greeting and began to dance with her. Mike stood absolutely still, unable to believe what he was seeing. There was a kind of silent communication between the girl and the little fox. It stood on its hind legs when she opened up her arms, and dropped to all four when she closed them. There was no fear on the part of either one of them.

As it grew darker and darker, the fox took on a rosy iridescence that gave it a ghostly appearance, but still it continued to mimic the girl. Willow was silent, too, but there was a huge smile on her face, and she seemed to recognize the animal. Finally, the kit reared up one last time, and began to dissolve into mist. It circled the child several times, and vanished into the night.

How much time had passed? He picked up Willow, whose drooping eyes were about to close for the night. As they entered the house, he saw that his grandfather and grandmother were now in the kitchen with his mother and father. They were all speaking in low voices, and appeared surprised when he carried his sleepy burden past them. It was the first time in his life that he had seen his grandfather look so stern, and he wondered where the conversation had led.

He stole a look at his father.

Morgan was angry. Mike had seen that expression before. He looked frustrated, and Mike wondered what he would do, now that the family had confronted him. Morgan was strong-willed, and not used to being questioned. On the other hand, he could not deny Velia anything.

Several weeks passed, and tensions continued to run high in the family. Mike kept his head down and did his chores, staying out of everyone's way, except for his sisters. He took every opportunity to get them out of the house and take them on adventures. Moira and Willow both liked to walk through the fields and into the hills. They loved picking wildflowers, and for days, the house overflowed with bouquets they brought back for their mother and grandmother. Moira always kept one flower out to put into her grandfather's shirt buttonhole when he came home. Both women exclaimed over these offerings, which only encouraged the girls to bring back more. The sweet scent wafted out the door each time it opened, and the colors brought some cheer to the strained atmosphere.

Finally, Morgan made his announcement. The family was seated at the dinner table, silent except for requests to pass the potatoes or the salt, when he cleared his throat.

"Well, I've decided," he said.

Every set of eyes turned toward him.

"I talked to Bob Sloan. I'm going to buy the livery barn in town. There's plenty of call for stabling horses with the passenger trains running regularly, and I can sell some hay and straw on the side. I'm also going to trade horses – and that means I'll have t' do some travelin'."

Velia raised an eyebrow when she heard the horse trading remark, and he noticed immediately.

"Now, Velia. It is legitimate. I might buy and sell a few horses, but that's it. Bob doesn't want much for the place, and it's what I know how to do."

Velia was quiet for a moment, then she spoke.

"It sounds like a good solution, Morgan. As long as you don't do any business with the kinds of men you have been dealing with. Can you really separate that?"

"I said I could, didn't I?"

There was an edge to Morgan's voice that made Mike wonder if he really could stay away from his previous business partners.

Finally Frank spoke. He was a quiet man, usually content just to be Velia's father, Anna's husband, and the children's grandfather. But he was a thoughtful, sensible person, too.

"I'll help y' any way I can, Morgan," he said. "It sounds like good work for Michael, too. A lot better than ridin' with those men."

Morgan nodded brusquely, his irritation apparent.

"Yep, the boy can work there, and there'll be times he can help break the green stock. Bustin' a few broncs will make a man of him soon enough."

There was a sharp intake of breath from Velia and Anna.

This time, it was Anna who had her say.

"No harm better be comin' to that boy, Morgan. He's still a child, and you must not forget that."

Morgan just smiled, a tight grin that was more grimace than pleasantry. It was apparent that this was not the solution he preferred, but he had to do something or risk a wholesale mutiny on the part of the family. And he could not bear Velia's anger.

The dreaming faded. Colleen, Andrew, and Aisling awoke slowly. They had no idea how much time had passed, but the sun had gone down and night sat softly on the area. The fire still burned brightly, and Black Bird Shows sat watching the three of them, a tiny smile playing around his mouth.

Looking at Andrew and Aisling, Colleen spoke.

"Did both of you dream? About the Lorrahs and the Hughes?"

At the affirmative nods, she stared at Black Bird Shows.

"Black Bird? Was that boy you?"

"Yes," he responded. "The tea has done its work."

"What now?" Andrew asked.

"Get up, move around," Black Bird said. "Use your body. Then Colleen will make more tea, and you will dream again."

Aisling looked at the adults, one at a time. A small line formed in her forehead.

"Aunt Colleen, that was an amazing experience. But what were we supposed to get out of it?"

"Black Bird is making our family history real to us, Aisling. I'm learning as much as you are. For me, it is filling in things I wondered about but never knew. For you, it is answering your questions about why it is important for you to spend time on the mountain."

"What about Uncle Andrew?"

"He wants to know, because he loves us and Black Bird."

Andrew grinned at Aisling.

"Come with me, little one. Let's get some more wood for the fire! This is fun!"

Aisling could not resist his enthusiasm.

"Okay, but you have to carry the heavy pieces!" she said.

When they had walked away to the stack of firewood, Colleen turned to Black Bird Shows.

"Thank you for helping us," she said. "What can I get for you?"

"Old men don't need much, Mike's daughter," he said. "If you could give me more time, that would be a gift. But we only get so much time, so let us use it well."

It was unsettling to hear him repeat the thought he had stated earlier. Colleen loved this medicine man, who had filled some of the vacuum left by her father's death. What would she do if a time came when he was not there to advise her? She brushed the thought aside and went in to brew more of the Dreaming Tea. A fourth cup was filled with coffee for Black Bird.

After a little more moving about, they took their seats again.

"Are you ready, Aisling?" Colleen asked.

There was a moment of hesitation on the girl's part. Without a word, she reached out her hand. Cradling the warm cups, they all sipped, then drank the contents down and settled back to listen to Black Bird's songs. The dreaming came on more quickly this time. They returned to see that Morgan's purchase of the livery barn was bringing big changes to the family.

C H A P T E R 7

▼

Mike and his father rode the ten miles into Lodge Grass early each morning, and returned late every evening. There was a hired man to watch over the horses and the business most nights. Even though a few of the local people had acquired automobiles, horses were still the major means of transportation. The livery business had a good future, and it was a respectable venture that none of the townspeople would have reason to question.

Mike's grandparents had bought a small house in town and moved from the ranch. Frank said it was to be closer to his work at the school, but Mike suspected that the confrontation with Morgan had created a rift in the family, and the distance was intended to try to soften any hostility. Moira was upset at the announcement of her grandparents' move.

She threw her arms around her grandfather, and, sobbing, declared, "I'm going with you!"

Frank patted her dark hair. There was a special bond between him and this girl.

"Yer mother is goin' to be needin' your help, Moira," he told her. "You'd break her heart if y' came t' live with us."

"But I won't see you any more!"

"Yes, y' will. I already talked t' yer mother, and y' can stay with us on Saturday nights, so y' can go t' church with us on Sunday mornings. How do y' feel about that?"

Moira sniffed back her tears, looking into her grandfather's face to be sure she had heard him correctly.

"Truly?"

"Yes."

Moira nodded sadly, and sighed.

"I guess that will have to do."

This decision worked out well for Mike on the nights that he had to stay in town because customers were coming in late. His grandmother always welcomed him and it was a relief to be with her and his grandfather, where there was no pressure to be anyone other than himself. Morgan always went home for supper with Velia. Mike liked the occasional chance to visit with his grandparents; most days, however, he rode back out to the ranch with Morgan. These rides were companionable, but not conversational. Morgan usually seemed lost in thought, and Mike knew from experience not to interrupt his reverie.

At the beginning, Mike's assignments were the stablehand tasks, but as time went on, Morgan insisted he work with a number of of the worst horses. Some of the animals were young and needed gentling, but occasionally there were very rough broncs. Mike was thrown many times, and felt lucky not to suffer any major injuries. If he was too battered, Morgan would order him to stay overnight at the livery barn and "not bother your mother or your grandmother with the sight of those bruises." Morgan believed this was the way to "make a man" of Mike, and it gave him added leverage to be able to tell potential buyers that these horses were "gentle enough a kid can ride 'em."

Summer ground its way into fall, and when school started, Mike worked his chores around his classes. He was bright student, loved school and found it easy to do both his studies and his livery work. He brought his books to the stable, and when he finished his chores, he often sat on a bale of hay and did his homework. As a side diversion, he loved listening to the cowboys, as they spent idle times at the stable. It was a good place for conversation, companionship, a sip or two of whiskey, and the frequent poker games. The cowboys were a varied lot, and some of them knew the time was coming when they would be off to fight in the Great War, World War I. News came every day that made it more and more apparent that this would be the direction the younger of these men would go.

While he enjoyed visiting with his grandparents, he preferred not stay overnight there or at the stable. He loved going home to the ranch. The land it was situated on held a special place in his heart, and he wanted to be there as much as he could. He missed his sisters and his mother when he was away from them for too long.

Life developed a routine, and time passed quickly. Mike entered his teens with little trouble, other than an insatiable quest to please his father, a goal he usually felt he failed to achieve.

A night came when he was studying at the livery while his father played cards with the night man and several other men from the community. The door opened and Anna stood in the lantern light.

"Morgan," she said. "I'm needin' m' buggy rigged, and Michael t' go with me. I'll be goin' up Lodge Grass Creek t' see a sick man, and I 'll be wantin' Michael's help."

Mike looked from her to his father.

"Get your grandmother's rig ready, boy!" Morgan barked, making it clear to his fellow card players that he was in charge.

"Should I go with her?"

"She asked fer y' to, didn't she? Get movin'!"

Mike harnessed Doc, who now lived at the stable. Then he hitched up the big grey to the buggy, and brought it around to the front of the building. Anna was waiting outside.

The two of them climbed in, and they were off, Anna driving Doc at a fast trot. Once they were out of earshot of the livery, she spoke to Mike.

"Takes the Hawk is plannin' to leave this world. He needs me there with him, and you must be with Black Bird Shows."

Mike was shocked. He had often thought of the brave Indian boy he had helped escape from boarding school, but he had not seen him since they delivered him to his clan uncle.

"Is Takes the Hawk sick, Grandmother?"

"'Tis not clear," she replied. "A Crow woman named Bright Bird came t' m' house a few minutes ago and told me what I just told you."

The ride up Lodge Grass Creek seemed to take forever. Mike had a foreboding feeling that made his chest feel tight, and his grandmother added to it by saying very little. She seemed to be trying to sense something in the air as she drove.

Finally, they turned down the long, overgrown lane that led to the house of Takes the Hawk. The trees along the way seemed to reach out for them, as if to delay their progress. Even Doc, one of the steadiest and calmest horses Mike had ever known, was nervous. He tossed his head and strained to look from side to side, white showing around his eyes. The wind sighed through the leaves and branches moaned as they rubbed together. Things skittered through the underbrush, making unimaginable sounds, and through it all, Anna drove like an arrow toward a target.

They crossed the creek, and pulled up in front of the house. The windows were dark, and no smoke curled out of the chimney. The door opened, and Black Bird Shows stepped out, peering at the new arrivals, trying to determine who they were. When he recognized Anna, he came forward to meet her. Suddenly, he noticed that Mike was with her. His black eyes turned to regard the boy who had helped him escape from the school. Even though both of them were a little older, their shared experience still created a tie unsullied by the length of time since their last contact.

Mike was happy to see that his friend looked healthy and the haunted expression had completely left his face. He had grown taller, and the only sign of his escape was a small scar on his cheek.

"*Kahée*, my friend," Black Bird Shows said. "It's good to see you again,"

"Same here," Mike replied.

Then to Anna, Black Bird Shows indicated the door.

"Come in. He's expecting you."

Anna and Mike stepped into the house. While the furnishings were sparse, the interior was clean and neatly kept. The kitchen woodstove was polished, its few chrome ornamentations glowing in the low light from a single kerosene lantern that sat next to it. A plain wood table with two chairs occupied one side of the single room, and there was a bed against the wall. The old medicine man reclined on the bed, watching the visitors enter. His long white braids were neatly plaited, held in place with strips of soft leather the same color as his wizened face.

Anna went to kneel next to the bed.

"Takes the Hawk," she said. "What is it that brings us here?"

The old man gazed at Anna for a long time. They had shared much. They had overseen many healings and treatments, and their respect and fondness for one another was obvious.

"It is time for me to go from this place," he said, his English careful and perfectly enunciated. "I wanted you to be here when I cross over."

"Would there be somethin' y'd be wantin' me t' do?" Anna asked, as if this was something he said to her every day.

"No. Just be here with Black Bird," the old man moved his gaze toward his nephew.

Black Bird looked back at him, then he turned his anguished and helpless eyes back to Mike.

"Mike Lorrah," he said, his voice breaking. "I don't know what I will do without this old man. He is all I have. I have so much to learn from him yet."

Hearing him, Takes the Hawk spoke again.

"You have learned what I know," he said. "You'll have this house to live in, and Missus Anna will work with you like she did with me. You don't have to be alone."

With a sly smile, he added, "You can marry and have someone to cook for you. Probably you should. Your cooking is not good."

This brought the hint of a smile to Black Bird's face. He rolled his eyes for Mike's benefit and shook his head.

Takes the Hawk struggled to sit up. Everyone moved toward him as if to catch him. His piercing black eyes took in the scene.

"I am not dead yet," he said.

All three stepped back.

"It is time to go outside into the grove."

Pushing back the blankets, he carefully placed his feet on the floor. He still wore the old-style buckskin pants, along with a calico shirt. Black Bird Shows hurried to put the old man's moccasins on for him, then he and Anna each took one of Takes the Hawk's arms and helped him to stand.

Straightening, Takes the Hawk slid his feet along the floor as they accompanied him outside. Mike trailed along behind them, not sure what he should do.

It seemed to take forever, but eventually, they brought him to a spot in the exact center of the almost perfect circle of trees that grew by the creek. When they stopped, the crickets ceased chirping, and a complete silence descended upon the area. Even the creek rolled over the rocks without a sound.

Takes the Hawk motioned with his hand to indicate that Black Bird Shows and Anna should step away from him. They walked the twenty or so feet to stand where Mike had stopped. Then they turned to watch the old man.

He opened his arms and started to shift from foot to foot, swaying as he raised his voice to sing. It was a haunting, eerie song, rising and falling like the grasses on the prairie. His voice was surprisingly strong for someone so old and frail, and he sang on and on. As they watched him, a change began in the atmosphere. First, it seemed there might be a haze in the air, but the disturbance looked more like the heat waves that shimmered over parched dirt in late August. Initially, these changes were barely detectable, so subtle they might have been missed.

The leaves in the huge trees began to stir, first a single leaf here and there, then all of them, dancing, dancing on the ends of their stems. Except for the ancient man's singing, silence ruled the day. Mike stood stock-still, watching. He had never experienced anything like it before. A small puff of air touched his cheek. A few stray white hairs stirred on Takes the Hawk's head. Black Bird Shows tensed up, all his muscles tightening. Silently as a cloud passing overhead, a huge red-tail hawk appeared over where the old man stood. It spiraled down from a very high elevation, then hung motionless directly above the old man. Still he sang.

The little movements of air turned into a steady breeze from the east. It was pleasant and soothing, and Mike liked the feel of it. More of the leaves on the trees rippled without a sound. The wind increased. Abruptly, Mike felt the wind change directions. Now it came from the south. Then from the north. The hawk did not move.

As the wind increased, more of the old man's hair escaped his braids, fluttering against his face. His eyes were closed now, and he continued to sing. Mike wondered how he could keep it up when he was so frail.

Little by little, the wind shifted to begin coming from two different directions, swirling through the grove. It twirled dry leaves and bits of debris, dancing them into the air and dropping them back in place. The wind picked up speed, surrounding the old man, but not disturbing the hovering hawk. Faster and faster it spun, and the sound of twigs snapping off the tree now broke the silence. The old trees in the grove groaned and creaked with the pressure. Mike worried for the safety of Takes the Hawk, Anna, and Black Bird Shows. He was too fascinated by what he was experiencing to fear for himself.

The old man stood in the midst of the whirlwind, his stance solid and resolute. More loose grass, leaves and twigs spun in the wind, forming a dust devil that threatened to obscure the figure in its midst. The hawk flapped its wings once and rose on the air currents. At the same time, Takes the Hawk began to rise, as well. His moccasins left the ground, and his feet dangled as he hung suspended above the grasses. Mike cried out, but Anna and Black Bird Shows both shushed him. Up, up the man continued to soar, the hawk just above his head. As the three on the ground watched, the man and the bird rose higher and higher until they were just specks in the sky. At last, they could no longer be seen.

Mike gasped, and realized that he had been holding his breath.

"What just happened?" he asked.

"Takes the Hawk has gone to the other side," Anna replied.

"I've never seen anything like that, have you?"

"Oh, yes," she said. "Several times in m' practice of the Old Religion, I've seen people leavin' this world in astonishin' ways."

Suddenly, Mike remembered that Black Bird Shows was standing at his side. He turned to him.

"What will you do now?"

"My uncle has prepared me well. I am ready to be on my own, and to learn more from other medicine people. I know how to get food, how to stay warm, and how to stay out of sight. People will not know my uncle is gone, so they will just think it is him living here. I should be safe enough."

There was a note of sadness in his voice.

Anna spoke.

"I'll be checkin' on y' now and again," she said. "Will y' be lonely here?"

Black Bird Shows thought for a moment.

"I'd like to see you once in a while, Healer Woman," he said. "But I'd like to see you, too, Mike Lorrah."

Mike promised him that would happen.

From then on, Mike and Black Bird Shows spent as much time as they could in each others' company. Mike made sure he completed all his work for Morgan, and usually found that he could get away to ride up Lodge Grass Creek on Sundays after feeding the horses and cleaning the barn. The two boys rode their horses, hunted, talked, and explored the range in the foothills of the Big Horn Mountains. When he could, Mike would bring his books to Black Bird's house and share the lessons with him. Mike felt he had been given a brother, and he relished their time together.

As they matured, they found the opportunity to take longer and longer trips. For some reason, Morgan did not question Mike's absence if it was for hunting, as long as he had enough men to do the work at the livery. All Mike had to do was bring back wild game for the ranch kitchen, and Morgan was satisfied.

His grandfather made him the ultimate gift to assure successful hunting. From his school salary, he bought Mike a Model 94 lever action Winchester .30-30 rifle.

"Every man should have a good gun to hunt for food," Frank told him. "It will make sure that your kills are clean and that your prey does not suffer. It will be your responsibility to make sure you are a careful hunter and that you never kill for pleasure or sport."

Mike treasured the rifle, cleaned it thoroughly after every use, and kept it in a safe place. Black Bird Shows understood how much the gun meant to him, and made an elk skin scabbard for it.

Black Bird Shows and Mike ranged further and further, and Black Bird began to reveal some of the secrets of the Big Horn and Pryor Mountains to his friend. He taught him about Crow legends and history, and showed him how to live off the land. Mike worked hard to understand the Crow language that his friend tried to teach him, but it was very complicated. Often his efforts brought peals of laughter from Black Bird, who would explain how a misplaced accent had given a sentence a completely different meaning.

They had many conversations about spiritual things, and Mike was astonished at the many parallels between the Old Religion of his mother and grandmother and the Crow Indian beliefs. On one occasion, Black Bird showed Mike his own medicine bundle, and talked about how his uncle had shown him how to collect his own magical items for it.

They left boyhood behind. Black Bird Shows grew tall and handsome, his ebony hair reaching waist length, even in braids, and his face classic and strong. His shoulders broadened, and his bearing took on a regal cast that conveyed strength and knowledge. Mike, too, began to develop into the man he would be. His thatch of black hair defied order, and his slim body was wiry and quick at exactly six feet. Time spent in the out of doors left him with a permanent tan that only accented his remarkable blue eyes. Those eyes always seemed to be looking off into the distance, as if he saw things others did not. His open face revealed an empathy for all people and living things, but it was a compassion born of an inner strength that ran through his veins. They reveled in each others' company, and with the energy of young men, they often raced across the prairies on foot, just for the joy of feeling how well their bodies worked. Both smiled easily, and the landscape resounded with their laughter when humor overtook them.

They visited the canyons, with their caves high in the limestone cliffs. Black Bird Shows told Mike legends of the ancient peoples who had used these caves as their homes. From the bottom of the canyons, this seemed impossible. However, when the young men rode to the top, many old pathways and trails were apparent. They often used the same caves as overnight camping shelters on their hunts, and discovered that a number of them had ancient petroglyphs and pictographs adorning the walls. At night, in the flickering light of their campfire, these eerie works of art came to life, the animals racing along the rock and the distorted figures of the shield bearing men breathing and moving. On those nights, Mike would close his eyes, only to have his dreams invaded by the primordial peoples, speaking and dancing and singing. These were enchanted places, and visions came to both young men there.

With Black Bird's help, Mike learned some of the secrets of the sweat lodge, vision quests, Crow Indian legends, and how to move among the wild animals without being seen by them. When the day's adventures were done, the boys talked of their hopes and dreams, and exchanged stories of their own hard times. Black Bird spoke for hours about all he had been taught by Takes the Hawk, and said he was continuing to study with other medicine men of the tribe. He knew for certain that he would eventually assume the duties of a Crow holy man, but told Mike that this would come much later in his life.

It was crucial for Mike to make sure his father did not know of this friendship. Morgan was clear about not being social with Crow people, except to trade horses. Mike never told him he was spending time with Black Bird. Sometimes he offered to check the condition of the cattle, or to ride the fences to make sure there were no breaks. He would do those things quickly, assuring that he had time for his return trail to take him past the house of Black Bird Shows. Anna, too, checked on him frequently, and her visits included homemade bread and wax-sealed jars of jams, or several slices of chocolate cake for Black Bird's sweet tooth. The skills he had learned from his clan uncle were impressive, but she added to his store of knowledge with her own formulas of herbal medicines and natural treatments. When she found Mike there, she included him in these lessons, many of which were straight out of the herbal journal her mother in law, Dr. Flora, had kept.

Mike and his sisters were fascinated by the herbal book. It was a beautiful thing, black leather, embossed with a serpentine design, and a buckled strap of leather that held it shut. Everything inside was written in the precise, strong hand of Dr. Flora, with side notes added here and there by Grandmother Anna. On each page was drawn beautiful sketches of native plants, and then written details about their medicinal use, dosage, and care. Glassine paper between some of the pages held pressed samples of the leaves and flowers. Some of the notes described plants and minerals used by the Crow and the Sioux Indian people for medicine and treatments. The book was a work of art and it obviously had taken years of study to gain the knowledge this volume recorded. It was a treasure. The three children all loved the book, and listened closely when their grandmother read the instructions, histories and thoughts from each page. Often they would all set out to gather plants for these uses. Anna dried these harvests by hanging them upside down in an open shed behind the house for a short period of time. Each plant called for its own method of storage to retain the power of its elements.

As time went on, Mike and the girls were allowed to watch as Anna combined these elements into medicines and potions. She explained the use of each one, and showed them where to store them. Many of these items would be combined, ground with an ancient mortar and pestle, sometimes so fine that it was like flour. These powders were then mixed with the pure clear water from a cold, hidden spring nearby. The resulting mixtures were in great demand by people from miles around.

There were many fresh water springs on the ranch, but the exact location of this remarkable spot was only known to Anna and Velia. Anna had taken the three children to the spring several times, but when they tried to return to it on their own, they could never find it. Visiting it with their grandmother was a mystical experience. It was reached by descending an primeval looking passage through a dense chokecherry thicket, down a small slope, where the track turned to rocks arranged in stepping-stone order. This path brought them to an elegant tree of a type that did not usually grow in the region. It grew in a curving pattern near some holly bushes, also not native to Montana. Nestled at base of the tree on its far side, an even bigger surprise awaited. It was a diamond-clear little pond of ice-cold water, and a strong flow ran from it in a sparkling little brook. It appeared to originate between the roots of the tree, as if it were being constantly reborn.

When the children looked into the pool, they were amazed that, clear as it was, they could not see the bottom. When they asked their grandmother about that, her reply was unexpected.

"It has no bottom," Anna told them. "'Tis a sacred spring, and at certain times of the year, we can be communicatin' with another place through it."

"What other place?" Willow had no fear of asking. But Anna was not ready to tell them.

When asked what she meant by 'another place,' she evaded their question.

"That'll be comin' to ye later, today is not the day," she said.

She led them back to the opening in the chokecherry thicket. They stepped through, and continued to walk toward the house. A few steps beyond, the children looked back. The opening in the shrubbery had disappeared as if it was never there.

There also was a wonderful hot spring just down the hill from the house, always warm enough for the sisters and their brother to swim, soak or just stretch out on the big rocks that surrounded it. It had a deep enough pool, lined by smooth stones, to make it very inviting. Mike liked to soak in it after a day of hard work, Moira approached it very deliberately, attired in swimwear, and carrying several thick towels. Willow leaped freely into the water and glided about in it like an otter. Anna and Velia also came to the hot spring, but it was usually to treat a patient with the 'taking of the waters'.

By the time Moira and Willow reached their teens, their bond was growing stronger and stronger. The girls each had their own magic, and they were beautiful. Moira had inherited her mother's raven-wing black hair, and her skin was so white that it appeared translucent. Willow's mass of untamed fiery curls framed her alabaster skin and magnified her electric blue eyes. Both girls had the kind of bodies that men could not tear their eyes from, and nearly every young suitor in the area had made attempts to woo one or both of them.

In the innocence of youth, arcane things were second nature to them. From the time Willow could walk, one of the sisters' favorite diversions was to tiptoe into Mike's room in the middle of the night and get him out of bed. Stealing from the house under the silver light of the full moon, he sat on the ground while his sisters wove their spells, conjuring sights that he would not have believed without witnessing them. They would dance in the grass, Moira with grace and order, her slippers leaving silvery tracks in the dew, Willow in bare feet with wild abandon, leaving no tracks at all. Their steps stirred webs of evening mist, and surrounded the three of them with lunar rainbows. The moon always appeared to become larger with each circle the girls made, some nights seeming to nearly touch the ground. Finally, exhausted, they would return to their rooms and sleep until dawn.

When he woke from these nights, Mike was never sure if what he had witnessed was real or a dream and he could not remember whether his sisters were clothed or not. What he saw at the breakfast table always confirmed the experience. Each of his sisters would slip into her place, a mystical glow to her skin, and a secret smile on her lips. Both girls would gaze across the table at him triumphantly. He wondered why they wanted him there, and finally he caught them alone during the day and asked the question.

"You two always bring me with you when you dance," he said. "I don't understand why. I don't dance with you, I only sit and watch."

Willow answered, eyes twinkling.

"You didn't know?" she asked.

"I didn't know what?"

"It takes three of us to work the magic. Grandmother and Mother say we are too young to do it by ourselves."

A chill tickled Mike's spine. It was not that he had any fear of the unexplained. He knew his grandmother and mother had skills and powers beyond explanation. It simply had never occurred to him that he had any part in it. It had always seemed to him that it was a female art, not participated in by men. His father certainly did not have the magic, and his grandfather appeared to be removed from it.

One night only Willow came to his room to coax him outside.

"Where's Moira?" he asked.

"This is not for magic," Willow replied. "I have to talk to you. Grandmother and Mother spoke with me tonight. They said they want me to learn all they know."

Mike was impressed.

"Willow, that's wonderful!"

"No it is not wonderful," she sighed. "I don't want to do it."

"It is an honor," Mike said.

"It takes too much concentration, too much work. I only want to enjoy life, and not be tied down studying the occult. If it just comes naturally to me, that's one thing. But I have too much life to live. I can't be committed to something like this. I am going to tell them tomorrow to give the legacy to Moira."

Mike could not believe his ears. Time and again, both his grandmother and his mother had proven how powerful their magic was. How could Willow not want it? She saw the question in his eyes.

"Mike," she said. "It's too much responsibility. I have to be free, and I could never do that if I say yes."

It was an irrefutable argument. Willow had always been a wild creature of nature, as inclined to run barefoot into the night to charm a man as to call down the birds from flight to sing for her. Sometimes she was home, and sometimes she vanished for several hours. Family members, even Morgan, had long since given up insisting that she be where they could find her.

So it was Moira who took on the study of her mother's and grandmother's mysteries with dutiful determination. At the same time, she worked hard to maintain some appearance of normalcy, occasionally stepping out with one of the local young men who flocked around the house in the hope of seeing one of the two Lorrah sisters. She attended the local Catholic Church with faultless regularity, as if that would convince her friends and acquaintances that she was leading a perfectly normal life.

Of all the family, her grandfather understood the load she carried. His adoration for this middle child granddaughter made it easy for him to sense the tension in her. In an effort to acknowledge how proud he was of her, Frank Daly created a beautiful gift for Moira. It was an artful little box that he spent many hours crafting. He used the wood from a rowan tree, exactly the same tree as the mountain ash that grew so abundantly in the mountains nearby. This wood provided the framework into which he inlaid mother of pearl he had brought back from his many past railroad journeys to the west coast. He carved concentric spirals and other mystical Celtic designs into the wood of the box and then painstakingly set in delicate bits of the shell. When he finished, it looked as if the shell was an integral part of the wood. Finally, he built into it a secret latch that required a special touch to open it.

When Frank gave Moira this breathtaking gift, she was stunned. It sat lightly in her hands as she gazed deep into her grandfather's eyes. A profound connection passed between them in that look. Frank smiled at her, all his adoration showing through.

"Use this to keep the deepest secrets you have," he said. "That way, you will always know there is a little part of you that you do not have to give to others."

Moira could only nod in understanding, tears standing in her eyes. Her responsibilities seemed just a little lighter, even though she would continue to work with manic energy to learn the practices of the Old Religion.

Sometimes Mike worried about Moira. She was so zealous that it seemed she might explode from the effort. She was angry, too, and told Willow she was shirking her duty. This exchange created a rift between the sisters. Unaffected by Moira's judgment, Willow ignored the criticism, and continued to try to get her to return to their monthly night-revels. But no amount of enticement would bring her dancing under the full moon with her sister. So Willow danced alone, without the rainbows and misty webs. Mike watched, and felt a sense of loss with Moira's withdrawal. He could not be sure if Willow cared about Moira's remarks, and he did not know how to help.

Then, one morning, Willow was gone, the first of many times that she would disappear for days without explanation. Velia was upset, walking about with her back stiff, looking toward the east again and again. Moira sighed and rolled her eyes, but loyally settled in her room and studied the notes she had taken about the herbal. Days passed with Willow nowhere to be seen. Then, one misty morning, she came walking in long strides through the fields, all wild hair and bare feet, her skin sparkling with the dew from the fog, and sapphire eyes laughing. They all were so happy to see her that no reprimand was voiced. No one could ever be angry at Willow for long.

CHAPTER 8

▼

The tiny country school building stood in a field next to the road. It was flanked by two guardian outhouses and a simple, handmade set of swings. During the school week, like many other one room country schools, it housed eleven or more students of various grade levels for their classes. These kids came from the ranches miles around the area, and the lone teacher taught all grades in the same classroom.

On occasional weekend nights like this one, however, the little building had a different persona. Desks were moved from their neat rows and pushed back from the school's wooden floor, and the people from ranches miles around came to dance.

Mike had been to many of these dances over the years, but he had not intended to come to this one. In fact, he had been high in the Big Horn Mountains with Black Bird Shows. They had gone there to hunt, and the night before, they had camped in the shelter of a quaking aspen grove next to a small creek. They had eaten a good camp meal of rabbit and fry bread, then rolled out their blankets on the ground. It had been a long day of tracking and both young men fell into a deep sleep, barely breathing and not moving at all. If there were dreams, neither was aware of them.

In the deepest part of the night, Mike suddenly awoke. He did not know what had disturbed his sleep, and there were no unusual sounds in the forest. The nearly full moon laid a silver cast across the woods and meadow, and the slightest breeze moved through the trees. He could not shake the feeling that he should come off the mountain, but he could not begin to guess why. It was a voiceless invitation, deep in his spirit, that beckoned him. He rose and paced about, waiting for Black Bird Shows to wake up. When he did, Mike told him what had happened.

"You must go, then," Black Bird Shows said.

"I can't figure out why," Mike said.

"You should not ignore the call that came to you," Black Bird said simply. "There is a reason. You just do not know what it is."

Mike was already moving to saddle his horse and pack up his bedroll. It felt like he was being pulled by an invisible cable, and he could not have resisted it, even if he tried.

So here he was, at the Muddy Creek School, and fiddle music was drifting out of its windows. A number of people were walking toward the place, and it looked like it was going to be a well-attended dance. He dismounted from his horse, still in his hunting clothes, and walked toward the door.

Curley Gallagher, a wrangler from the Mill Iron Ranch, spotted Mike when he arrived.

"Mike! Mike Lorrah! Over here!"

Relieved to see a familiar face, Mike walked to where Curley stood against the wall, next to the tightly bunched row of desks. He glanced over to note that his uncles were the musicians for the night. Their tunes were lively and demanding, tugging at him.

Curley was talkative, and had obviously had more than a few shots of whiskey.

"Have a drink, Mike," he said, fishing a flask out of the same shirt pocket he kept his bag of tobacco for rolling his own cigarettes.

Mike took the flask, brushed a few tobacco flakes off it, uncorked it, and took a long drink. The liquid burned a hot path down his throat and settled in his stomach, putting the beginnings of a warm glow on him. Wiping his mouth with the back of his hand, he handed the liquor back to Curley.

"Looks like a good turnout," Mike observed.

Curley took another big swallow.

"Yep," he said. "And take a look over there. The O'Keefe sisters are here."

Mike looked in the direction Curley pointed out. He saw three young women, and was surprised to note that they were talking with Moira and Willow. He had seen two of the O'Keefe girls before. They were from Hardin, and they often traveled the forty plus miles to get to these dances with one of their friends who had a car. He was aware that there was one more sister, but he had never seen all of them.

Gazing across the room, he regarded them with interest. Most of the eligible bachelors in the area were very much aware of these young women, but the two sisters he had already met did not interest him, even though they were beautiful. Now he looked at the one he had not met.

Willow noticed him, and waved him over eagerly. He smiled. She and Moira always understood him, but Willow was the one who could read his mind. She knew he was not comfortable crossing the room to enter the circle of young women, but her invitation gave him the opening he needed.

"Michael!" Willow exclaimed. "You just *have* to meet my friends!"

Mike nodded his head to the O'Keefe girls.

"I've met Nuala and Deidre," he said, smiling at them. "But I haven't had the pleasure of meeting this one."

"You've heard me talk about them," said Willow. "You say you know Nuala, here, and Deidre and this--" she pulled the blond girl forward " -- is Della, She's been too young to come to the dances until this year."

Deidre held out her hand, and he took it absently. His full focus had turned to Della.

"Glad to meet you," he said.

"Goodness!" Willow laughed, the sound like silver bells ringing in the distance. "You can stop staring any time, Michael!"

Mike slid an irritated glance toward his irrepressible sister. She ignored him, nudging his arm.

"I'm going over to talk to those fellows," she said, nudging him. "Why don't you dance with Della?"

Mike could not have done otherwise. It was as if all the other people in the room had faded back or even disappeared, and in his eyes, Della seemed to have a gilded aura completely surrounding her. Her wavy blonde hair shone like burnished gold, and her clear blue eyes looked from under long lashes deep into his. Taking one of her hands, he pulled her into his arms and they began to waltz to the music of Rory and Sean's fiddle and whistle and the notes of the piano player.

For a few moments, Mike was so overcome by his feelings at holding this beautiful girl in his embrace that he could not speak. Finally, words came to him.

"Willow has a way of coming straight to the point," he said apologetically.

Della dazzled him with an easy smile.

"It's what I like about her."

"How old are you, anyway?" Mike asked.

"Sixteen."

The answer should have given him pause, but logical thought was beyond him.

They danced every dance, and during the breaks, Mike stayed close by Della's side. He was bewitched. No other female had ever had this effect on him. When she left his company to go with several of the women to the outhouse behind the school, he moved quickly to where Curley stood.

"Give me another drink, Curley!" he almost pleaded.

He was at a loss as to how to handle what he was feeling. He was being swept away by the attraction, and he did not know what to do.

It had not escaped Curley's notice, either.

"You sure are monopolizing the youngest O'Keefe sister," Curley chided him. "We get a new girl at the dance, and you take up all her time."

"Tough," Mike said with a laugh, his joke carrying some truth with it. Curley chuckled.

"Better take it slow, Mike," he drawled. "She's awful young."

Mike took another swallow from the flask, thanked Curley, and rushed back to the door of the schoolhouse as Della entered. He did not dare leave her unaccompanied for even a few minutes, or the other cowboys would try to capture her for a dance.

The music went on late into the night, and when it ended, the O'Keefe girls stepped into the car that had brought them. Nuala's escort had driven them over the rough dirt roads to this event, and it was time for them to return to Hardin.

Mike walked Della to the car. Asking to see her again was too daunting, so he simply told her he was glad to have met her.

She came to his rescue, displaying dignity and a presence far beyond her years.

Looking directly into his eyes, she said, "I hope to see you again soon, Mike. Thank you for a fine evening."

And the girls were gone, the Nash 420 Sedan leaving a cloud of dust in its wake under the pre-dawn sky. The late night full moon hung over the scene, giving it an ethereal quality, and Mike watched until the car was completely out of sight. He looked around for his sisters, but both had disappeared. He supposed Moira had gone home at a reasonable time, and it would be hard to guess what Willow might have done.

Once again, Curley was at his side.

"Mike! You ol' dog! You sure kept that pretty young thing entertained!"

Curley's words were slurred, and he smelled strongly of whiskey. Mike accepted his offer of another drink from the seemingly bottomless flask, and the burning liquid diminished his longing for the time being. He caught up the reins of his horse, and set out for the home ranch.

In the following days, Della dominated his thoughts. He had never seen a lovelier girl, and he was obsessed with memories of her—the way it felt to dance with her, the depth of her clear blue eyes, the golden blonde head just under his chin, and her peaceful nature. He thought of a million excuses to go to Hardin and try to see her, but something held him back. Because he was not bold socially, initiating contacts like this frightened him. In addition, he had his doubts that her parents would be pleased to have a twenty-two-year-old cowboy pursuing their teen-age daughter.

He turned to Willow and Moira for advice. They were the only females near his own age that he could ask. And they were so wise about him and about women.

Moira counseled him to be cautious.

"Some of your feelings are probably because she is new to you, and you are fascinated by her." she said seriously. "Of course, she *is* pretty, too, so it's easy to understand why you want to see her again. She's a fine person, Michael, and she's my friend. I don't want to see you hurt her, or scare her either."

Willow was less wary.

"Oh, Michael," she exclaimed. "For the sake of the goddesses! Just let your instincts lead you!"

"But what about her parents?" Mike asked.

"Don't worry about that," Willow said. "I never do!"

Mike shook his head. He should have known that Willow's answer would be brash, and perhaps somewhat inappropriate. She always made her own rules, and continued to do so. It was part of her allure, and part of the danger about her.

Mike fled back to the company of Black Bird Shows. They went riding, and Mike told him what had transpired.

"What do you think I should do?" he asked.

Black Bird Shows was silent, looking out over the countryside from the back of his ghostly grey horse. Finally, he spoke, a twinkle in his black eyes.

"Women. They are too difficult," he said with a sigh. "Maybe if you wait, the question will get answered."

Mike snorted with disgust.

"This isn't a subject to joke about," he said. "I don't know what to do, but I *have* to see her again."

Black Bird shrugged.

"I don't know anything about women. If I did I would not be alone. Do what you believe is right."

Frustrated, Mike dug his knees into his horse's sides and the two young men raced across the valley bottom. It was better than trying to talk about this conundrum.

CHAPTER 9

▼

One cold evening in late autumn, Moira and Mike were both at their grandparents' house in town. Moira was staying there to spend time with Anna, working on her knowledge of herbs and potions, and to see her beloved grandfather. Mike was having dinner before going to the livery to spend the night watching over a sick horse.

As they were finishing their slices of their grandmother's apple pie, a knock sounded at the door. A woman stood on the step, scarf wrapped around her head to protect her from the piercing wind that rattled the leafless branches in the trees and tore at her coat. There was something about her that was familiar. Anna invited her in to get warm, and took her coat, seating her at the kitchen table with a cup of tea. Both Mike and Moira could not help staring at her. She was obviously one of the town's "soiled doves," a lady of the evening, dressed in a suggestive, low-cut and gaudy dress, her face painted with more vivid make-up than any respectable woman would wear.

Anna motioned for the two young people and Frank to leave the room, and she sat down at the table with the woman. Moira stepped to the door and listened to the conversation, just out of sight, but shook her head at her brother's inquiring gaze, letting him know that she could not hear what they were saying.

After a short time, there was the sound of the outside door closing, and Anna came into the room where they were.

"Moira and Michael," she said, "That was Rosie, from the hotel down the street. She has a girl who is very ill and needs our help. Michael, I want y' t' come with me t' the hotel, because we are going t' bring her here and I'll be needin' yer strong arm. Go t' the livery and get me buggy and a bunch of blankets. Moira, please make the bed in the spare room."

Brother and sister exchanged a look. This was very unusual. They knew their grandmother had no reservations about helping people from all walks of life. They had seen her do it countless times, and had heard many stories of the healing work she and their great-grandmother, Dr. Flora, had done in Deadwood. This was the first time either one of them could remember her bringing the patient to her own home.

Mike jogged the three blocks to the stable and got the buggy. Gathering blankets from the spot in the barn where he slept, he piled them on the seat and drove the carriage to his grandparents' house. Anna was waiting for him. She came out, carrying her bag of medicines and other materials and climbed in beside him. At her direction, he drove the four blocks to the hotel, and jumped down, hurrying to the other side of the buggy to help Anna down. Without a word, she strode into the hotel, a run-down building near the railroad tracks, where Rosie was pacing back and forth in the dingy lobby, wringing her hands.

Mike followed the two women up the narrow stairs to a room at the end of the hallway. A dim lamp barely illuminated their path, and Mike mused that it was probably better that he could not see his surroundings. He could only imagine how sordid this place would be in the harsh light of day.

Rosie turned a key in the door, and after pulling and pushing on the stubborn latch, finally shoved it open on its complaining hinges.

As they stepped into the room, they were assailed by a terrible smell of dirt and sickness and stale cigar smoke. Rosie turned up the flame in a small lantern. Mike resisted the urge to pinch his nose with his fingers, and he had to force himself to look at the scene of human misery that spread before him. The walls were cracked and peeling, the middle of the floor was covered with a ragged and filthy rug that defied any guess at its original color. There was a battered little chair in the corner and a tiny washstand with basin and pitcher and a filthy towel hanging from the rack on its side. A chamber pot sat next to the bed, and the odor in the room made it clear that it desperately needed to be emptied.

Anna moved swiftly to the side of the bed. As his eyes followed her, Mike realized with a shock that there was a person in it. Grimy blankets obscured the figure of a very thin woman.

"Bring the lamp, Michael," Anna ordered.

When he did, the meager light revealed a graying pillowcase under the head of a girl who looked very young. Her hair spread across the pillow in greasy black strands, and he could see that she was semiconscious, her eyelids fluttering at the invasion of the light.

"Here's what we are goin' t' be doin'," Anna said after a few moments, "Michael, y'll go down and get the clean blankets from m' buggy. Rosie, y'll get fresh water for the pitcher, and we'll clean her up a bit."

Eager for any task that would release him from that room, Mike bounded out the door and down the stairs. He collected the armload of blankets and rushed back into the hotel. When he returned to the room, Anna and Rosie had stripped the covers off the girl and were washing her face and hands. She was clothed in a grubby little cotton sleeping shift and appeared to be no more than skin and bone. Terrible dark circles underlined her sunken eyes, and she moaned softly and continuously. With every stroke of the cloth that washed her, she flinched and tried to move away.

Anna spoke to her in soothing tones.

"Now darlin', we're goin' to make it better. But y' have t' let us help ye."

The patient remained incoherent, struggling weakly against the hands of the two women who tried to clean her. Suddenly, her eyes flew open, and she stared across toward the corner of the room. Then she opened her mouth and screamed, a thin, keening sound like that of an injured animal. Mike spun around, wondering what it was that she saw, but nothing was there. With that, she lapsed back into unconsciousness, and did not move again.

"All right, Rosie," Anna said. "Put the blankets 'round her and let's get her down to the buggy."

Mike stepped up to help, and between the three of them, they wrapped her up and lifted her out of the bed. Rosie proved strong enough to help carry her down the stairs, and they softly laid her in the sheltered back area of the buggy. Anna motioned for Rosie to get her coat and climb into the seat next to her. Mike helped his grandmother into her seat, and when they moved out, he broke into a run through the darkness to the house, getting there just as they arrived.

Moira heard them and opened the door. All four of them struggled to maneuver the girl through it and down the hall to the spare room. Moira pulled the bedclothes back and smoothed the clean sheets. Gently, they laid the girl down. Moira wrinkled her nose at the ragged, grimy little shift on the girl and rushed to bring one of her own that she kept at the house for the nights she spent with her grandparents. Mike turned away as Rosie, Anna and his sister pulled the girl's nightgown off and replaced it with the clean one. Holding the soiled garment between two fingers, Moira spirited it out of the room.

Once the girl was settled, Rosie turned to Anna.

"You are a brave and good woman, Anna Daly," she said. "Please use this to get whatever you need for Sally."

Mike watched in astonishment as Rosie opened a small bag hooked to the belt of her dress and pulled out a wad of money. Anna held up her hand to refuse, but Rosie would not permit this. She set the money on a small dresser nearby, and walked out of the house.

"What's wrong with her, Grandmother?" Moira asked when she returned.

"The poor girl," Anna said. "She's very young, and got into the 'life' because she's an orphan. She's been a business girl for about a year, and several of her 'customers' have been very cruel to her. To live with it, she's been takin' laudanum and finally even that was not enough. Rosie says she took a very big dose sometime last night, and wasn't found 'til a customer came to see her today. He opened the door of her room, got a good look at her and told Rosie. Rosie found she'd emptied an entire bottle of the stuff. She made her vomit, to try to get all the poison out of her, but she couldn't get her awake again. I wanted her here, because I couldn't help her in that dirty room."

"Now, Moira," she continued, "I need yer help t' get her up and walk her about. Michael, t'isn't proper for y' to be here while we do this, so wait in the kitchen. I'll call y' when yer help is needed."

Mike retreated to the kitchen and poured himself a cup of tea to counter the revulsion he felt. Two cups of tea later, he still felt it in the pit of his stomach, as he listened to the murmuring of his sister and his grandmother in the next room. Two cups after that, Anna called him.

"Moira and I are going t' brew a potion," she said. I'll be needin' ye t' sit with her in case she wakes up."

Mike was apprehensive, but he never refused his grandmother's requests. He knew how much help she had given to people in the area, and he learned something new every time he assisted her. He glanced at Moira. Her pinched face revealed how desperate the situation was.

Pulling up a chair, Mike sat near the door where he could watch and where he could call his grandmother if he needed to. He felt helpless, not only because he could not cure the girl, but because he knew so little about women in general. Why would a young woman allow herself to be lured into this kind of life? Was there no solution for people like her? He felt outraged, as he always did when the helpless were treated cruelly.

From the kitchen, he could hear Anna's quiet instructions as she worked with Moira on the elixirs they would try to use to treat this girl's body and spirit. After a time, the two women came back into the room, and attempted to get the girl to drink a little of the sweet-smelling concoction. She could not be roused from unconsciousness, and their endeavors only resulted in the contents of the cup dribbling down her face and soaking into the nightgown and sheets. This time the women ignored Mike's presence, and pulled the girl to her feet. As she wobbled between them, Anna swiftly pulled off her shift.

Mike was stunned. He hadn't meant to stare, but the girl's back was a mass of bruises, and he could see her ribs radiating out from her spine. He had never seen someone so close to his own age so damaged. The fact that she was naked did not even register with him. The heart-wrenching sight of her was almost unbearable, but he knew he had to do something. He jumped to his feet and tore the soiled sheets from the narrow bed. He raced through the house to the linen closet and pulled out another clean set. Then he returned to re-make the bed while Moira and Anna tried to walk the girl back and forth. Their efforts were futile, since they ended up half carrying, half dragging her while her bare toes plowed their lifeless line along the floor. Finally, they laid her back down, without a gown, on the fresh, clean sheets, and pulled the blankets up to her chin. Her frail body was seized by violent spasms, rattling the items on the table beside her, and then she was suddenly very still.

Anna sat down in the chair Mike had been using, and she leaned forward, peering at her patient in search of any movement or change. The girl seemed to have slipped deeper into a stupor, and her breathing was dreadfully shallow. Mike went to the kitchen and brought in another chair, which he offered to Moira, but she refused it. He sat down next to Anna, and Moira tidied up the room, removing a towel she had used to clean up the spilled potion. When she finished, she came back in, and seated herself on the floor at Anna's feet.

Frank came and looked in on them, patting Anna's shoulder. Anna looked up at him, and sighed.

"T'is a bad one, Frankie," she said. "She's been beaten, and she's poisoned herself with laudanum. I'm not sure I have the power t' fix her broken body and her broken soul."

Frank nodded, and with a little soft pat to Moira's head, he stepped from the room to get himself something to eat. Long experience had taught him that when Anna was working to heal someone, he could not expect her to cook for him. But she always had something good in the ice box and he would never go hungry.

On into the night Mike, Moira, and Anna sat with the girl. Mike was saddened even more to realize that he could not remember what Rosie had said her name was. Around midnight, the wind started to blow harder, moaning through the trees and chimneys and crying in an unearthly way. Anna's head jerked up as she listened. Her face was ashen.

Mike looked at her. He had never seen her react like this to the sound of the wind. Moira, too, looked alarmed.

The level of the sound increased, rising to an ear-splitting pitch, then falling to a low, agonized moan. Anna's eyes widened with fear. Moira leapt to her feet as the windows of the room began to rattle. Mike could taste the terror in both the women, and he looked over at the sick girl.

She was sitting bolt upright, eyes staring and mouth open in a silent scream. All of them were paralyzed in their places. Suddenly, one of the double-hung windows banged open, and the wind entered the room, trailing swirling leaves and debris and smoke from outside. The wind spun into the room wailing and groaning as it ripped some of the blankets away from the bed. All these items were snatched up in the whirlwind created before them.

It took a new and menacing shape. The leaves and debris coalesced into a long and wraith-like figure, and the smoke began to form long, sinuous, white ropes of hair. Mike, Moira, and Anna looked on in horror as this dreadful figure exploded to a full eight feet in height. A glowing, ghastly female face materialized within the twisting, floating strands of hair. It stared at each of them from empty eye sockets, and then at the pitiful figure on the bed. All motion slowed, and time ceased to move as the dark spirit threw back its head and opened its mouth.

A blood curdling shriek started somewhere near the bottom of the phantasm and when the noise reached its mouth it was at full intensity. The windows rattled, the beams of the house trembled, and the air was split into thousands of tiny pieces, raining down amidst the smell of death. The cry went on for what seemed like hours, and when it arrived at a crescendo, the mirror on the wall above the wash basin shattered, scattering shards of glass in every direction.

Ignoring any possible danger to herself, Moira sprinted across the floor and flung herself across the body of the girl. Burying her head in the pillow next to hers, she spread her body over the patient and knotted the sheets in her fists, holding on against the turbulence.

Mike bounded from where he had been immobilized by the sound, and stood between the thing and his grandmother. The specter saw him do this and rushed at him. It collided with his body and penetrated it for a moment, filling him with an unimaginable cold, chilling him to the bone. Then it pulled away from him and swirled to the center of the room.

Anna's hand was in front of her mouth, and she was unable to move at all. Then, as suddenly as it had come, the horrible apparition departed, leaving a few fluttering leaves behind. It oozed out of the open window, which slammed shut on its own, leaving Moira, Mike, and Anna gasping. Moira pushed herself up from the bed and looked down at the motionless girl.

"Oh, no," Moira cried. "I think she's dead! Grandmother! What happened?"

Anna had not moved from her chair. She was trembling and huge tears stood in her eyes. Strands of her white hair had fallen loose, and she could not speak.

Frank was at the door of the room, and had seen most of what had happened. His expression was grim. He spoke rapidly to Anna in Irish. Anna shook her head and tears streamed down her face.

Finally, she crossed herself.

"T'was the *Bean Sídhe*," she whispered, using the Irish words for it. Then, in English, she said it again.

"Banshee." It was pronounced almost the same in both languages.

Mike shuddered, still feeling the appalling touch of the thing. With Frank's help, Anna rose from her chair and slowly approached the side of the bed. As Mike and Moira watched, she placed a finger on the girl's throat, feeling for a pulse. There was none.

As if in a trance, Anna turned to look at her grandchildren.

"The *Bean Sidhe* came for Sally tonight. T'was no savin' her. But the spirit's cry was not only for one. Someone else is doomed 'ere long."

Frank looked at Mike.

"Did that thing touch ye, Michael?"

"Yes," Mike whispered. "I can still feel it."

Frank sighed.

"Y' now have a bit o' the banshee in y'. 'Twill be yer lot t' deal with the dead," he said. "It may be a blessin' or a curse, and it may be a while before y' know which."

Mike looked bewildered.

"What do you mean?" he asked.

"Y'll be findin' out," Frank said. "I had an uncle who could talk with the dead after a banshee touched him. It's different for different people."

Moira was inconsolable, sobbing and smoothing Sally's hair. She had never seen anyone die, and after all the healings she had witnessed with her grandmother, she had expected that they would save this girl. Anna turned to her.

"Moira," she said gently. "Sally's at peace. She wasn't meant to get well and return to her awful life. Let her go."

Moira raised a tear stained face to her grandmother.

"What about what you just said? Is the banshee really coming for someone else, too? Was that true?"

Taken aback, Anna hesitated for just a moment.

"Some old legends say if the banshee comes inside yer house, it's a warning that someone else is goin' t' die. I've never seen it proven true. We're all perfectly well, and we have t' go on as if everything is goin' t' be fine. Let's cover this girl's face and leave her t' her rest. We'll get the undertaker in the morning."

She paused, then added.

"T'would be best if ye didn't go out alone after dark for a time…"

Her voice trailed off in unfinished thought.

Moira followed her grandmother's instructions, but her face was troubled. After her grandparents had gone off to bed, she turned to Mike, who had stayed to make sure she was going to recover from the fright they had all received.

"Mike," she said. "Are you all right? That banshee was the most hideous thing I ever saw. And the worst part was to not be able to help Sally. I just feel like we all failed her."

Mike was preoccupied. The chill had finally left him, except for a small place near his heart, but he wondered what it portended.

It would not be long before they all found out.

CHAPTER 10

▼

Life returned to normal. The undertaker came for Sally the next morning, and Anna made him take the body out of the window so her departed spirit could not come in through the door of the house. After that, she washed the sheets and nightclothes several times in lye soap to be sure no traces of death were left on them. Moira was badly shaken, her sleep plagued every night afterwards by terrifying nightmares that jolted her awake and prevented a return to peaceful rest, even in her own room at the ranch. She lost weight, and paced back and forth when Anna was trying to teach her about the supernatural world.

Mike tried to forget all he had seen. He hated the abuse of any creature, human or otherwise, and what he had seen of Sally's bruised and scarred back haunted him. More than that, there was still a small icy place in his gut from the touch of the banshee, and he carried it with him all the time. Sometimes, to forget it was there, he drank. There was always someone around the livery stable, or hanging around the local card room who was willing and able to offer him a drink. The hot fire from whiskey or moonshine was enough to damper the cold place and the dread, if only briefly.

Then one morning at breakfast, Morgan turned his attention to him.

"Mike," he said. "Get the livery stable squared away early today. I need you to go to Hardin for some medicine so you can treat John Ryan's horse."

Mike could not believe his ears. Here was his chance to get away for a while. Without finishing his breakfast, he rose from the table. Saddling his horse, he loped the distance from the ranch to the livery, his anticipation singing in his mind. Rushing through the chores at the stable, he finished swiftly, and raced to the depot to catch the passenger train. The trip from

Lodge Grass to Hardin was short, but to Mike it seemed to move in very slow motion. He could not stay in his seat. He paced the aisle, and noticed one of the cowboys who frequently spent time at the livery.

"Joe!" he said, "I didn't see you there!"

Joe Johnson looked up, grinned at Mike, and said, "Irish Mikey! How are ya?"

"Good," Mike replied. "Where are you going?"

"Twisted my damn ankle pullin' fence wire," Joe said, nodding toward his swollen left foot, which was wrapped in some kind of bandaging. "Stepped in a prairie dog hole. I'm headed to Hardin to see the sawbones. How 'bout you?"

"Picking up some medicine for one of the horses," Mike said. "My Dad likes to have me talk with the vet to make sure we get the best price."

"Have a seat," Joe said, indicating the place across from him. "And have a drink!"

Joe pulled a flask out of his pocket and offered it to Mike.

Mike hesitated, then reached for it. It was not acceptable to refuse a man's offer of a drink in ranch country. Tipping it back, he took a mouthful, and returned the container to Joe. The raw liquor burned all the way down his throat, but there was something comforting about the heat. He relaxed and stretched out his legs.

"This train seems slower every day. Sure would like to get me a car some day," he said.

"Wouldn't we all," Joe agreed. "But the train does the job, and with it runnin' regular, it works pretty good."

The two of them continued the usual cowboy conversation, covering topics from branding to what ranches were hiring to the latest strangers to show up at the livery barn. The bottle passed between them several more times. When the train reached Hardin, Mike was feeling mellow and a somewhat self-satisfied. He said goodbye to Joe and swung off the passenger car to the platform.

Before going to get the medicine, he decided to walk around the town a little, just to see what might have changed since the last time he was there. He tipped his hat to several of the women he passed on the street, and made his way to the center of the bustling little farm community. Cars and horse-drawn wagons mixed in the street, and he did not see anyone he knew as he strode down the walk.

Finally, he turned to go into the drug store, where the soda fountain promised something sweet for his parched throat. The interior of the store was spotless, the tile floor glistening with the midday sunshine that came in through the upper windows. Displays of bottles and boxes were perfectly aligned on the shelves, offering an array of merchandise not available in the smaller stores of Lodge Grass. The young man working behind the counter looked up and asked what he'd like. He ordered a root beer and settled on a stool to drink it. The little bell on the door jingled as it opened to the street, and when he glanced in that direction, he saw that Della and her sisters had entered.

He stood to say hello to them, and they returned his greeting with enthusiasm. Della was as beautiful as his memories had pictured her, and he was a little tongue-tied at the sight of her. Nuala and Deidre chattered easily, asking after Willow and Moira, and he was able to answer their questions. But he could think of nothing to say to Della. Finally, he grasped onto the one thing he could.

"Would you like a root beer?"

All three girls smiled and nodded, and he rummaged in his pocket for some money. The counter man filled three more glasses, and they all moved to one of the little tables nearby. The foaming glasses were delivered there, and the group sipped on them, exclaiming how good the concoction tasted on this warm day. Mike was nearly silent as the girls continued to chat among themselves, and finally, Nuala stood up.

"I'm sorry, but we have to go now, Mike. Our parents are expecting us home right away, and they'll be wondering what became of us. It was nice to see you. Please say hello to your family."

Mike felt like Della was being ripped away from him, but there was no way to change this. As all three girls strolled toward the door, Della turned to him, her placid blue eyes regarding him thoughtfully.

"Why don't you send me a letter sometime?" she asked. "I would write back."

Mike knew Willow and Moira wrote to the O'Keefe girls all the time, so this did not seem like a strange request. He could only nod, but he felt hopeful that this might open a channel of communication for him and Della. He certainly hoped so, since he was internally cursing his own inability to make easy conversation with her in person.

Della and Deidre went out the door, but Nuala stayed behind for a moment.

"Mike," she said quietly, "I think you should know…our parents are pretty strict with Della, since she is the youngest of us. They would not like to see her associating with someone who drinks in the middle of the day."

At Mike's startled look, she continued.

"The smell of whiskey is very strong on your breath. You won't want that to be the case if you should ever come to call at our home."

Horrified, Mike could only react with embarrassment.

"I understand," he said quietly, resolving never to be caught in that situation again.

Nuala turned and joined her sisters outside, leaving Mike standing in the aisle of the store, wondering what he should do next.

Pulling his pocket watch out, he saw that he barely had time to pick up the horse medicine and catch the return train. The veterinarian's office was just down the street and as he walked there, he began to try to compose in his mind the letter he would write to Della when he got home.

The return train stopped in Crow Agency. Along with a number of Crow Indian people who boarded, a tall gaunt white man entered the car Mike was in. His hand was closed in a tight grip around the arm of a very young Indian woman. She looked frightened. He pushed her into a window seat and sat down next to her, pinning her into the tight space. He removed his hat, revealing a thick head of carefully combed red hair.

Mike recognized him. It was Bart Knight, the same man who had come to the ranch looking for Black Bird Shows. Mike did not like the way he was treating the woman, but was hesitant to interfere, since he did not know the circumstances. When the train reached Lodge Grass, Bart Knight and the girl did not get off. Instead, they stayed seated, Bart holding on to her arm with a vice-like grip that assured she could not move. Mike wondered where they were going, but there were no answers for that question.

When he got back to the livery, he treated the sick horse with the medicine he had bought and then joined the cowboys for a round of poker and drinks. This was becoming routine for him, and there was a comfort in the camaraderie the men shared in the amber light of the lanterns. It was far better than the dark of night. If he drank enough, he found he was more easily able to go to sleep. Without the whiskey, sleep was a disturbing place with little rest. This would be a night that he slept at the barn and did not go home to the ranch.

CHAPTER 11

▼

It was in the very early hours that his sleep was interrupted by Moira. The night before had turned into a particularly whiskey sodden one, and he had been sleeping off its effects for only about an hour.

"Michael!" she cried, voice on the edge of panic. "Wake up! You have to come to Grandmother's right now!"

He roused enough to look at his watch. It was four in the morning. Rubbing his eyes, he peered at his sister. She looked terrible. Her hair was not combed, she was dressed in a worn housedress, and her red rimmed eyes revealed her pain and stress.

"Wha...what happened?" he mumbled, trying to focus.

"It's Grandfather," she said. Her voice came out in a whimper of anguish.

"What?" Mike snapped to attention. The small cold spot was growing to occupy his entire chest.

"He didn't come home after work at school yesterday! Come on...we need you to help look!"

Mike was pulling on his clothes as he listened to her.

"What do you mean he didn't come home?"

"Grandmother is beside herself. At first she thought he was just late finishing up at the school building, but when supper time came and went and he still wasn't home, she became very frightened. And he isn't home yet."

Jamming his feet into his boots, Mike reached for Moira's hand, and together they ran back to their grandparents' house. The stars and moon were obscured by ash-colored clouds rolling across the night sky, and thunder rumbled over the mountains in the distance. When they arrived there, Mike found his grandmother striding back and forth in her kitchen.

"Somethin's terrible wrong, Michael," she whispered. "I tried t' sleep, but dark things kept spinnin' 'round me. And there's been a single magpie here in my trees ever since Sally died. I know it's a bad omen. *One for sorrow*, y' know…"

"I'll go to the school, Grandmother. I'll take the lantern from the shed."

"I'm going with you," Moira said.

"No."

Michael's answer was absolute.

"Please stay with Grandmother. She needs you."

"But it's *Grandfather*!"

Moira was adamant. Her beloved grandfather was central in her life. They had always been close, more so because her own father seemed almost unaware of her at times. Frank Daly had always made time for her, and he had been her pillar of strength as she took on the legacy of Old Religion that her mother and grandmother had handed over to her. Her connection to him was so strong that she could not imagine being left out of the search for him.

"Go!" Anna ordered. "I kin take care of m'self. I've prayers t' say t' the goddesses and to God. I'll be fine here."

Mike lit the lantern, and he and Moira were out the door, running as fast as they could toward the high spot where the school sat above the town. It seemed to take them forever to reach the foot of the hill, and another eternity to run to the top of it where the walkway from the school reached the stairs to the sloping path. Their footsteps echoed on the wood and when they crested the last step, they peered about in the darkness. Suddenly, Mike felt the cold knot inside him coil and unwind like an icy rope. It pulled him hard to the left of the walkway, where a low bush spread its branches like multiple leafy arms.

He raised the lantern and saw the form on the ground. Frank Daly lay motionless next to the shrub, one hand outstretched toward his railroad watch which lay beyond his fingers in the dirt. Moira caught up with Mike and fell to her knees next to her grandfather. Mike knelt beside her, setting the lantern down. Moira groaned, the muffled sound rising from deep in her soul. She crossed herself several times, slid from her kneeling position to lay prone on the ground beside the body and she began to chant miserably.

"Grandpa-grandpa-grandpa-grandpa-grandpa-grandpa-grandpa-gran…"

Then her voice broke and she could no longer speak around the sobs that shook her entire body.

Mike felt the tears streaming down his face as well. With strength he did not know he had, he reached down and lifted his grandfather up in his arms.

"Moira," he said. "Let's take him home."

Moira did not respond, remaining crumpled where she had collapsed.

Mike stood still, cradling his grandfather's body.

"Moira! Come with me! You can't stay here alone in the night!"

A sheet of lightning illuminated the backs of the roiling clouds overhead.

"Moira!" Mike cried again. "Get up and come *now*!"

Finally, she looked up, her devastated face wan in the dim illumination of the lantern.

Mike thought he heard her moan again, but realized the sound came from behind him. That horrible resonance began to build, and both of them recognized it from the night Sally died in their grandparents' house.

The wind picked up and the rustling sound of leaves and debris could be heard. Moira staggered to her feet, and turned to face the horrible thing she knew was there.

Behind Mike, the banshee took form. If possible, it was larger and more terrible than the first time they had seen it. With it in back of him, it was out of Mike's field of vision, but he could hear and feel it. He could only stand there and hold his grandfather's lifeless form.

Moira stiffened her back and glared at the empty face as its cry mounted toward the shriek that chilled the bones of anyone who heard it. Her long housedress blew about her slim body, giving her the appearance of levitation. Her hair, blue-black in the night, billowed about her face, undulating on the wind. Drawing herself up to her full height, Moira screamed into the wind.

"Go! Get away from us! You've done enough!"

Still the banshee advanced toward them.

"Enough!" Moira cried, her rage carrying a force behind it that Mike had never witnessed. Could this be his sister who never lost her temper? He had never seen her so angry or so forceful. She threw up her arms in a wide arc, and pointed her left hand at the banshee.

"Now be gone and do not come back!"

The specter seemed to hesitate. Moira advanced on it, screaming incoherently now. The ghastly thing seemed to draw back on itself and then it released a howl backed by a blast of wind that rocked Mike and his precious burden where he stood. With it came the smell of death and decay and the cold chill of all the horrors it had wrought.

Moira was not cowed by this. She raced directly into the face of the thing, and continued to shout angrily. Mike realized that she was not actually incoherent, but that she was speaking the Irish that his grandmother had taught her.

The banshee backed up. First the retreat was almost undetectable, and then it moved away from her furious charge more quickly. At last, it took flight, screaming into the air, ultimately disintegrating back into the original aggregation of leaves and debris and smoke. A few remaining particles swirled around Mike's feet, and he began to walk back to the house.

Moira caught up with him after a while, but she only stared straight ahead as she walked. Neither of them spoke. When they reached the Daly house, Moira mutely opened the door and held it for Mike to carry their grandfather inside. She seemed to want to put Mike between her and Anna, and instead of following Mike, she went directly to the bedroom she usually slept in, closing the door behind her.

Anna stood in the kitchen, as if she knew what dreadful cargo Mike was bringing to her. Gigantic tears rolled down her face and she seemed diminished, smaller somehow. Mike carried Frank's body into their bedroom and gently laid him down on the bed. Anna was right behind him, and she tenderly removed her husband's dusty work shoes. Laying a hand on Mike's shoulder, she reached around him to use two fingers to close Frank's partly open eyes. The expression on the dead man's face was calm, as it had been in life, and if he had seen the banshee, he had accepted its call on his own terms.

"I'll go to the ranch and tell Mother," Mike said. "Moira's here in her room. Tell her if you need something."

"I'll not be needin' anythin'," Anna sighed sorrowfully. "Just a bit o' time t' sit here with me Frankie."

Mike brought a chair to the bedside, and wrapped a light shawl around Anna's shoulders, as she held Frank's hand in her own. As he left the bedroom, he could hear her talking to her husband as if he were still alive.

"Oh, Frankie…I begged y' not t' be in the dark alone."

CHAPTER 12

▼

Mike's ride to the ranch was swift. The clouds had cleared completely from the night sky and the moon provided brilliant light. When he reached the house, his mother was on the front porch, fully dressed and wearing her coat. One of the hired men had hitched up the carriage, and it was waiting by the gate. Neither Morgan nor Willow were home, so Mike tied his horse to the wagon, helped his mother in, and drove her back to the Daly house. He was not surprised to see that she already knew. Her eerie awareness was a fact of life for him. His own stunned mind was too muddled to think beyond transporting her safely.

By the time they arrived, the pre-dawn was beginning to show a few fringes of light along the ridges of the Wolf Mountains. Several horses were tied by his grandparents' gate, and there were lights in every room of the house…except one. The window of the room Moira usually used was dark. Opening the door, Mike followed his mother into the kitchen. Uncles Rauirí and Seán already were there. How they had known was anybody's guess, but it was surely part of the interconnection between his grandparents and their children. Their fiddle and whistle lay on a side table, ready for the music that would surely come. The undertaker stood in the kitchen, talking in low tones with Anna. Her white hair in disarray, and her shoulders slumped with the weight of her immense sorrow, Anna was none the less in command of this scene. She nodded as the undertaker suggested something to her, then shook her head emphatically at the man as he continued talking in hushed tones.

Finally, she raised her voice so her children could hear what she was saying to the man.

"We'll be havin' the wake here at the house fer the next couple of days," she said to him. "And then we'll have a Catholic service. Once Frankie's in the ground, we'll have our own service, m' family and me, and you'll leave us alone at the graveyard t' do it. When we're done, we'll leave, and y' can come back t' do whatever needs doin' at the end."

Abashed, the undertaker said he understood, and he went into the bedroom to take a last look at Frank. Then he was gone. Velia put her arms around her mother, and the two stood in that embrace for a long time. Then both women went into the bedroom with a washbasin and some towels, to get Frank ready for viewing. After a time, the heart-wrenching sounds of keening, the sorrowful wailing lament, drifted in from where they were working.

Mike looked around. Someone had stopped the wall clock, and the mirrors were all covered. He greeted his uncles, shaking their hands, as they thanked him for carrying Frank back to the house.

"Where's Moira?" he asked them.

Rauirí shrugged.

"We haven't seen her since we got here," he said. "She's in her bedroom and she hasn't come out."

Mike went to the door of that room.

"Moira!" he called through the door.

There was no answer.

He turned the knob and went in.

Moira was lying on the bed, still in the same housedress she had been wearing when they found Frank. Her vacant stare was aimed at a part of the ceiling and she did not acknowledge Mike's entrance. He reached down and struck a match to light a small lantern on the little table by the wall.

"Moira," he said softly. "Are you all right?"

She did not answer.

"Everyone is concerned about you. Can I bring you anything? Do you want some company?"

Still no answer.

Mike went back into the kitchen and poured a cup of tea from the pot that was steaming on the stove. He brought it back to Moira, and carried a chair over, sitting down so he could be next to her.

"I brought you some tea," he said. "Mother is here, and I know both she and Grandmother would like to see you."

She only blinked her eyes.

He tried again.

"You were very brave up there on the hill," he said. "I've never seen you like that."

Finally she turned her eyes to him. In a broken voice that sounded like it came from someone far older than her, she spoke in a monotone.

"There is no use in magic that cannot save the person you love as much as I loved Grandfather," she said. "All the studying and practicing, and it was not worth anything."

Mike shook his head.

"That's not true. You drove away the banshee before it could harm me or you or Grandmother."

"It was such an evil force," she declared. "Our good magic is no match. Of course it is gone for now, but it will be back, and then it will take someone else we love. I'm not strong enough for this."

"You looked incredibly strong when you faced that thing," Mike argued. "I don't know what would have happened to me if you had not been there."

"You have a piece of it inside you," Moira said. "No banshee will hurt you as long as that is there."

This shocked Mike.

"How did you know about that?"

"Grandmother said you had been left with a 'bit o the banshee', that you are now fated to find the dead who have been lost or who die where no one can find them."

Mike felt his entire body turn to ice.

"She never told me that," he said.

"I thought you just knew," Moira responded. "Well, there, I've told you now, so you know for sure. I don't care any more. Grandfather is gone and I could not save him."

Tears left wet tracks on her pale cheeks.

Mike rose from his seat and left her there. He went into the kitchen where his uncles were sitting, and leaned against the pantry cupboard. The two older men had a bottle of whiskey and some glasses on the table. They were sipping on their own drinks, and Rauirí poured one for him.

"Here, lad. A drink to ya, and to our da' as well," he said.

Mike threw back the searing liquid in a single swallow.

"Slow down, Mikey boy," Seán said. "It's goin' t' be a long day. Y'll need yer head about ye."

"I've got to go back to the livery," Mike said. "Thank you for the drink."

He left the house, untied his horse from the wagon, and rode him to the barn. Once there, he went inside, dug around behind his cot, and pulled out a full jar of moonshine one of the local ranch hands had given him, and got back on his horse. He rode to a secluded spot near Lodge Grass Creek and set about drinking the entire contents of the jar. Above him, in the big cottonwood tree, a single magpie sat, still and watchful, the white parts of its feathers glowing in the pre-dawn light. Mike was sure it was staring at him. As he drank more and more of the 'shine,' his head spun with the old Irish magpie poem his Grandmother often recited:

> *One for sorrow, Two for mirth,*
> *Three for a wedding, Four for a birth,*
> *Five for rich, Six for poor,*
> *Seven for a secret...I can tell you no more.*

Around and around it went in his thoughts until he could think no more. At some point, just as the sun broke the horizon in a clear dawn, he passed out, face down, on the bank of the creek.

It was close to noon when he came to. Grunting with the effort of moving his stiff limbs, he rolled to his side and peered up at whatever was casting the shadow obscuring the late autumn sun that had begun to warm him where he lay.

A deep voice penetrated the fog he was in.

"This is not a good way to honor your grandfather," it said.

"Jesus, Black Bird, you half scared me."

"I won't let you disgrace yourself by hurting Missus Anna like this. Get up, and let's get you ready to go to her house."

Flooded with shame, Mike reached up to grasp his friend's proffered hand. Black Bird Shows pulled him to his feet, and turned to pick the empty moonshine jar. He sniffed it, wrinkled his nose, and said, "This is poison, my friend. It will kill you and destroy what you love."

Mike nodded.

"I know. But sometimes it is the only thing that helps me go on."

"It's bad. Get control of it," said Black Bird Shows.

Mike took a look at his friend. Black Bird was attired in his best buckskin shirt and moccasins, but he had put on white man's pants to come into Lodge Grass. His waist-length black hair was neatly braided, and he wore a new tall black "reservation hat" adorned with one eagle feather in its beaded hatband. It was obvious he had dressed with great care.

The two young men walked back to the livery stable, leading Mike's horse. Mike shaved, combed his hair and put on a clean shirt and pants. He brushed the dust off his boots, pulled them on, and presented himself to his friend.

"How do I look now?" he asked.

"Good enough."

Together, they walked to the Daly home. Now there were many horses, a couple of cars, and several carriages and wagons parked along the street.

They entered the house, and Black Bird immediately removed his hat. Anna saw him, and came striding across the room. As all the townspeople and neighbors present watched in amazement, she hugged Black Bird Shows warmly, and offered him tea. He accepted, and went to stand and talk with Rauirí and Seán. Morgan had arrived by this time, and he fixed his eyes coldly on Mike.

In a loud voice that everyone could hear, he spoke.

"It's about time you got here. Where the hell were you?"

"At the livery," Mike replied.

"Try again. I stopped there and you were nowhere to be seen."

Anna heard the exchange, and disengaged herself from the people who surrounded her.

"I asked him t' go up t' the cemetery and look at the plot the undertaker set aside for us," she said, cutting off the rest of the insults Morgan was about to launch. "What did you think of it, Michael?"

Her level gaze was more punishing than anything Morgan could have said to him.

"It will be fine," he said, "But I'd like Rauirí and Seán to see it so we could get their opinion."

Morgan's penetrating stare did not waver from Mike's face, but he had had enough confrontations with Anna to know when to back off. He turned to go check on Velia and see how she was doing.

"Thank you, Grandmother," Mike whispered to Anna.

"I can't be savin' y' forever, Michael," she sighed. "Don't make me have t' do that again."

Mike smarted at this. Of all the people he did not want to disappoint, Anna was first on the list. He looked over to the side of the room, and met the level gaze of Black Bird Shows. The look his friend gave him was direct and thoughtful, and Mike dropped his eyes to avoid it.

A subdued Moira came into the room then. She had changed into a severe black dress that revealed how thin she was. Her face was pale, and her eyes red-rimmed, revealing her fragility. She came to stand next to Mike.

He put his arm around her, sensing that she was holding on to her self control by a thread.

"I'm glad to see you out of the room," he said to her in a low voice. "I know this is really difficult for you."

"I am only here to honor Grandfather," she said, a single tear slipping down her face. "I could never fail to be here for that."

"Has anyone heard from Willow?" he asked.

Moira's voice took on a bitter edge.

"Oh yes," she sighed through gritted teeth. "She's here in all her glory. She's in the room with Grandfather."

Mike hugged Moira, something he had never done since they were children. Morgan frowned upon any open displays of affection by Mike. But now, he felt like she was slipping away from him, and everything in him wanted to hold on as tightly as he could. There was a remoteness to her and he did not know what to do. She allowed the hug, but did not return it. Finally, he released her and walked into his grandparents' bedroom.

The room was dark, lit only by a single candle on each side of the bed where Frank Daly was laid out in his best clothes. Standing on the far side of the body was Willow.

Mike took in the sight of his youngest sister. She was as beautiful as ever. Her unruly copper curls tumbled to her shoulders, and unlike the rest of the women in the house, she was not dressed in black. The dress that draped her perfect body was dark kelly green velvet, graced with a delicate white lace collar. Pinned to her breast was an impossible corsage of spring wildflowers, shooting stars, buttercups, and sego lilies. She held Frank's left hand in both of hers as she looked into his face with a small smile.

When she saw Mike, that expression changed, lighting her face. Suddenly, she was in front of him on his side of the bed with both arms held wide to him. He stepped into her embrace, and felt all the tension go out of his body. Willow always had that effect on him. Her ability to heal his internal pain was something he always could rely on, and he was grateful.

At last they let go of one another. Willow spoke first.

"Grandfather is very happy that you were there when he went to the Otherworld," she said.

"He was already gone when I found him," Mike said.

"Oh, Mike…he just wasn't in his body any more. He saw you find him, he saw Moira stop the *Bean Sidhe*, and he saw you carry him home."

"How did you know about all that?" Mike was taken aback. He had not told anyone the details of the encounter.

Willow's reply was simple.

"Grandfather told me," she said.

"Grandfather is dead," Mike said flatly.

"Of course he is. But that does not mean he cannot talk to us. Or at least to me."

Mike was skeptical.

"What else did he tell you?' he asked.

"He told me about the touch of the *Bean Sidhe* that was left on you."

Mike shuddered involuntarily.

"Did he tell you how I can get rid of it?

"No. He said it will be with you all your life. You have to learn to use it for good."

This was terrible news, as far as Mike was concerned.

"I'll never have a normal life, then," he muttered.

Willow smiled, placing a hand on his shoulder.

"In this family, *none* of us gets to have a normal life," she said.

CHAPTER 13

▼

The wake went on all night, with a long procession of people through the house. Mike was astonished at how many people had been touched by Frank Daly or Anna. Standing with Black Bird Shows by the kitchen wall as the dozens came to honor his grandparents, he struggled with the desire to take a drink of whiskey. If Black Bird Shows had not been there, he would have succumbed to the temptation. A bottle of whiskey sat between Seán and Rauirí as they began to play their music, underlaying the sad time with beautiful Irish laments and ballads, all of them Frank's favorites. Every one of the women who came brought dishes and plates of food, and these were set out on the tables and shelves for all to share. Children accompanied their parents, and many of the younger ones were curled up in the laps of adults or even on the floor, already asleep.

Black Bird Shows stood silently, observing these Irish mourning customs for the first time in his life, yet finding a remarkable number of similarities to those of his own tribe. The wake, the food, the special music, and the people staying up with the deceased all night, these were all the same. Most amazing of all, the keening was identical. Crow Indians mourn their dead with wailing cries and songs, and Black Bird Shows had not expected to hear the same sounds of grief. He felt even more closely bound to his friend Mike and to Anna, and was glad that he was there to pay his respects. Rauirí's fiddle had a pleasant enough sound, but it was Seán's penny whistle that had the greatest familiarity to Black Bird. It reminded him of the wooden flute his uncle Takes the Hawk had played. But something was missing. Black Bird suddenly went out the door to where his horse stood tied to the hitching post. When he returned, he carried a small hand drum, made on a hoop of wood with stretched rawhide. Standing near Rauirí and Seán, he took up the rhythm of their music, adding a soft drumming to their tune.

When they finished their song, Rauirí set down his fiddle, leaned back in his chair and reached out a hand in a request to see Black Bird's drum.

"Where did you get the bodhran, sir?" he asked.

"If you mean my drum, I made it," Black Bird replied.

"It looks and sounds like a bodhran, an Irish drum," Rauirí said.

"Never seen one," Black Bird said. "This is just a plain Crow drum."

"Sounds good, whatever it is," Seán said. "Join us in another tune, friend."

If anyone thought it strange to see and hear a Crow Indian playing his drum with two Irish brothers on fiddle and whistle, they did not say so. For Mike, it just seemed right.

The wake continued through the following day. Mike knew he should be tired, but he could not think of sleeping. It was tradition not to leave the deceased person alone, and he took his turn sitting with his grandfather's body late the next night, when few people came and went in the bedroom. It was peaceful in there, and a welcome escape from the numbers of friends and neighbors who came to sympathize and express their regrets to the family. In death as he had in life, his grandfather provided a respite from difficult times. Alone in the room with Frank, Mike could allow his memories to flow.

He remembered Frank making toys for him and his sisters, and he could recall the moral values of the man. Nearly everything he had learned about caring for his family and friends and about being a good man he had learned from his grandfather. Now he was gone. Mike felt lost in the depths of loneliness and sadness. The cold spot next to his heart was quiet, having done its work and now letting him rest. For the moment in this place and time, he did not feel he needed a drink. The funeral would be the next afternoon, and then life would continue on. Finally, he fell asleep in the chair, and only wakened when Willow came to call him in the morning.

Mike got up from the chair, stiff from sleeping in the cramped position, and walked out into the kitchen. His grandmother and mother sat at the table drinking tea. Both looked exhausted, but they were dressed for the day.

Anna looked at Mike.

"I'll be needin' y' to get dressed, Michael," she said, "Y've got a train t' meet."

Without questioning the statement, he nodded.

"I'll be back in a few minutes," he said. "I have some extra clothes at the livery."

Patting her shoulder as he passed by, he kissed his mother's cheek and went out the door. Black Bird Shows was sitting on the grass of the yard, leaned against one of the cottonwood trees. Mike stopped beside him.

"Is this where you slept last night?" he asked.

Black Bird nodded.

"It's a good place," he said, "Out here with the trees and grass. I wanted to see you before I went home."

Mike instantly understood that his friend would not be present for the Catholic services that afternoon. The two exchanged a long look, and then Mike spoke.

"Thank you for being here," he said, and remembering how Black Bird had found him by the creek, "and for everything else you did. I'll visit you very soon."

Black Bird nodded again.

"Come to my place when you can, Mike Lorrah. I'll be glad to see you."

Mike quickly shaved and changed his clothes in the little space that had become his second home at the stable. It was his last clean set of clothes, but luckily, they were his dress clothes. He always kept them in town now, since he never knew when he would be going to a funeral, a wedding or a dance. He never wanted to be unprepared.

He returned to his grandmother's house to check on his mother and Anna. He found both of them with his grandfather's body in the bedroom, where they had taken up keening again. The lament sounded so lonely and bereft that it broke his heart. Rauirí and Seán were up and dressed in their best clothes as well. They accompanied Mike and the carriage to the train depot.

The 10:06 a.m. train from the east was slowing to a stop, belching steam and smoke as it did. The conductors stepped off, and placed the little platforms at the foot of each set of stairs off the train. Passengers began to disembark, and Mike stood, a little unsure of whom to expect. Rauirí and Seán, on the other hand, knew exactly who they were looking for. After several Crow women exited the middle car, two strangers placed their feet on the platform, and watched as their luggage was set beside them.

There was no question who these people were. Anna's brother and sister, Ristéard and Úna, looked exactly like her. The Hughes siblings were older than Anna, with thick, curly white hair and fair skin, and amazing blue eyes that looked around at this new place with calm curiosity. They were dressed for traveling, Ristéard in a suit and Úna in her gray dress with lace collar and a classic hat. Despite the ordinary attire, they had an otherworldly appearance. Both were tall and very slim, distinctly different from Anna in that aspect. Their crystalline blue eyes seemed almost transparent, like the reflection of clear sky in a mountain lake. Rauirí and Seán hurried up to them, greeting them with warm handshakes and hugs, while Mike followed behind. Rauirí turned to him and said, "Michael, here's your Great-uncle Ristéard and your Great-aunt Úna, all the way from Iowa. Uncle and Aunt, this is Velia's oldest child, Michael."

Ristéard studied Mike for a moment, gazing deep into his eyes as if he could see his soul. With a beatific smile, he shook Mike's hand and turned to Úna.

"This is Michael! The one with the magic."

Úna's expression was puzzled.

"No, Ristéard," she said. "The magic is with Moira."

Ristéard shook his head forcefully.

"No. It is here. I can feel it in his hands."

Mike was very uncomfortable. This conversation was awkward and strange, especially with Rauirí and Seán standing right there.

"Let's get you to the house," he said. "Here, let me take your luggage to the carriage."

When they reached the house, the undertaker was there with the hearse. It was a black horse-drawn vehicle, with large curtained windows all around. The coffin already had been taken out of it and into the house. Mike helped Úna step down from the carriage, while Ristéard swung down with the grace of a much younger man. Rauirí and Seán showed them inside, where they were greeted with much affection by Anna and Velia. Anna took them into the bedroom to spend a moment or two with Frank. She had delayed the undertaker's moving Frank to the coffin until their arrival. Once they had seen him, and spoken their own words to him, Frank's body was gently placed in the casket. Rauirí and Seán, the undertaker and his assistant, and two other local men helped move it out through one of the larger windows. It was placed into the hearse for its ride to the little Our Lady of Loretto Catholic Church. The family followed the hearse closely, on this last journey for Frank Daly.

Because they were seated in the front of the church, there was no way for the family to see how many people came from all over the reservation to pay their respects to Frank. When the funeral ended, the family walked out behind the six men who bore the coffin on their shoulders in the old Irish way. As Mike made his way down the aisle toward the door, he nodded to several of the people he recognized. Suddenly, his heart fluttered with excitement and warmth. There, in a row toward the back of the church, stood Della O'Keefe with her sisters and two older people who had to be her parents. He could hardly believe it. Their eyes met and held for a long moment as he passed by.

At the cemetery, the final words were said by the priest, and as Anna had ordered, the undertaker and the priest left the area, taking the rest of the gathered people with them to the town hall where a great reception would be held for all the mourners. Anna, Velia, Morgan, Ristéard, Úna, Ruairí, Seán, Mike, Moira, and Willow remained there. Ristéard took the lead in the ceremony that followed.

He raised his hands to the sky and spoke a long soliloquy in Irish. As he finished the initial part of his address, a lone blue heron appeared in the sky. It swooped down to glide in a graceful arc over where the family stood, and dropped a single red rose from its beak. The flower spiraled down, and landed directly in the center of the coffin as it sat in the hollow of the grave. The huge bird paused in the sky, as if to make sure its gift had landed in its proper place, and then turned and flew directly to the east. The women began to keen again, and Ristéard joined in, singing the story of Frank's life in a wrenching and sorrowful lament. Mike stood, an arm around the waist of each of his sisters. When he stole a glance at Morgan, he could see that his father was struggling to stand still. This ceremony was certainly beyond his understanding, and it was apparent that he barely had the patience it called for. Earlier he had made it clear that he considered this kind of ritual uncivilized and primitive.

Mike found no satisfaction in his discomfort. He had rarely seen his father do anything that he did not want to do, and it was good to know that Velia and Anna had insisted upon his presence. Because of Morgan's own brand of honor, he had agreed to tolerate what he did not understand for the sake of his beloved Velia. Mike was a little impatient himself, because he was eager to get to the reception and see if Della and her family had stayed. But he also was awed by the presence of Ristéard and Úna. Their visit had been remarkable, from the timing of their arrival just before the funeral, to this ceremony, and to the sheer elegance and mystery of their presence. There was an aura of power and dignity around them, and it was riveting to watch them. Ristéard conducted most of the ritual, and when he finished, Úna began to sing. Her voice was angelic and pure, rising and falling and swirling around the mourners to embrace them in sound so comforting that all could feel their spirits rise on the tones and soar above the place they stood. Her song ended, its crystal notes glimmering in the air, and then it was over.

Anna was the first to bend down, take a handful of the dirt, and sprinkle it on the wood of Frank's coffin. Each followed in turn, and Willow was last. She stood at the edge of the grave, scooped up her share of soil in both hands, and tossed it straight up. It was earth as it rose into the air, but flower petals as it showered down, fluttering to spread over Frank. They all began walking back to the carriages and wagons that had brought them to the cemetery.

Morgan led the way, his relief to leave the place written all over his face. He helped Velia and Anna into the carriage, and drove back toward the town hall. Mike had the feeling that if the man could have done so, he would have driven the horses at a run instead of walking them as he was doing.

Mike drove Willow to the reception in Anna's buggy. At the hall, there was no sign of Ristéard, Úna, or Moira. Mike wondered about it briefly, but he was so eager to learn whether Della had stayed that his curiosity was only fleeting. He led Willow inside where they were greeted by numerous friends and acquaintances, and he scanned the room. Della and her family were near the tables of food and drink, visiting with others they knew from Lodge Grass. Mike hurried to where they stood, and Della smiled at him, her radiance lighting the room from wall to wall for him.

"Mike!" she said. "I am glad you are here. We are going to have to leave soon to go back to Hardin, and I was afraid we might miss you. I am so sorry to hear about your grandfather. My parents knew him and they wanted to be sure we all came to the service. I'd like you to meet my mother and father. This is my father, Seamus, and my mother, Evangeline."

She turned to her parents.

"Mother and Father," she said, "This is Mike Lorrah, Frank's grandson and Moira and Willow's brother."

Evangeline O'Keefe smiled pleasantly, nodding at Mike, but Seamus's penetrating eyes measured him where he stood.

"We've been hearing a lot about you, young man," he said. "Our daughter mentions you often. And we've known your parents and grandparents for several years, so we have an idea of your background."

Pink crept into Della's cheeks.

Mike was quick to respond.

"You have three lovely daughters, sir," he said. "I am proud to know all of them. Would you permit me to come and call at the house?"

Seamus paused, an eternal moment that made Mike squirm. It was apparent that he had some reservations, but at a nudge from Della's mother, he finally cleared his throat.

"Yes, fine. But she is very young, and you must always remember that."

Mike put on his most earnest face.

"Yes, sir," he said. "I'll be at my best. I promise I will take my time and not rush anything."

He was rewarded by a radiant smile from Della, a smile which made it clear to him that he would not be able to keep his promise.

CHAPTER 14

▼

The next morning, Mike, Rauirí, Seán, and Willow were saying their goodbyes to Ristéard and Úna, and getting ready to accompany them to the depot to board the train.   Moira came into the living room with a small traveling bag. Her expression was calm and determined.   She wore the same simple black dress she had worn to the funeral, and carried a coat over her arm.

"Are you going somewhere?" Mike asked.

"Yes."

There was a long pause while Mike waited for her to say more.   Finally he broke the silence.

"Well, where?"

"Illinois."

The word hung in the air like a bomb suspended above the earth on the verge of exploding.

"What's in Illinois?"

At this point, Velia and Anna stepped into the room.   The look on their faces was bleak.

Velia answered Mike's question.

"Moira has decided to go to a Carmelite convent there," she said.

"What?"

Mike could not hide his shock.

"Moira, what the hell are you doing? You've never wanted to be a nun! It doesn't have anything to do with who you are!"

"Please try to understand, Michael," she said, using his full name, "It's the only place where I can get some peace.   The community at Our Lady of

Perpetual Succor is cloistered, and it will give me shelter. I'll be able to go part of the way with Uncle Ristéard and Aunt Úna, so I'll be very safe on the trip."

"You won't be able to escape your destiny there," Mike said, ignoring her serene logic. "It will find you."

"Not with enough prayer," Moira declared. "The nuns will help me."

Willow placed her hand on Mike's shoulder.

"We cannot change Moira's mind," she said to everyone in the room. "She has a right to decide about her own life."

Mike stopped speaking. He knew Willow was right, but he wanted to try to keep Moira from leaving.

It was nearly time for the train to arrive, so there would be no more opportunity for discussion. The entire family went to the train station to see the travelers off. For Mike, it was a double loss. His grandfather was dead, and now his sister was leaving with no intention of ever returning. At the station, Morgan gave Moira a brief hug. It was an awkward gesture, made more so by the fact that he had little practice at such displays.

He handed her some money, and said, "If you need anything, just let us know. And if you change your mind, you are always welcome here. This is your home."

Mike was surprised. This was as much emotion as he had ever seen his father display toward Moira.

She looked at Morgan with an unfathomable expression. Her voice was cool and level.

"Thank you, Father. I'm sure I'll be fine."

Velia was next. She wrapped her arms around Moira and held on as if she might be able to keep her from going by sheer physical presence. A huge sob racked her body. Then came Anna. Her expression was one of shock and loss. She took both of Moira's hands and held them for a long time while she gazed into her granddaughter's eyes.

"Blessin's be with ye, child," she sighed. "I hope y' find the peace y' seek."

Then she hugged her.

Willow threw her arms around her sister.

"Take care of yourself, Moira. You deserve whatever happiness this may give you. Remember that we all love you and we are here if you need or want anything."

Mike hugged her, too, feeling more and more empty by the moment. He could not imagine life without both his sisters. Different as they were from one another, the three of them had always been together.

The train chugged into sight and hissed to a stop at the platform. Holding Moira's hand, Mike walked her to where the conductor stood, waiting to help her onto the step of the passenger car. Ristéard and Úna got on first, and giving Mike's hand a final squeeze, Moira climbed the steps. Tears stinging his eyes, Mike turned away, only to nearly run directly into Morgan. His father stared at him.

"Oh, for God's sake, boy, cowboy up," he said, almost shouting in front of the people on the platform. "Don't cry over yer sister like a God damn baby. She's not dead. She's just going away."

Mike straightened his back before this onslaught. He looked directly into Morgan's eyes.

"Are you happy with this?" he asked.

"Better than the hocus pocus her grandmother wanted her to practice, don't you think?"

Morgan's voice was cold. Mike looked past him at his mother and Anna. Anna's eyes glowed with an unearthly anger, but she did not speak.

Mike could not stay quiet.

"Father," he said, with his voice level, "If you think that, then you are saying the same about Mother and Willow. I don't believe you want to stand hard on that thought."

Morgan, who had not realized that Velia could hear him, turned quickly to see the icy expression on her face.

With a sidelong glace at Mike, he muttered, "You drove me to say something in anger, son. You *will* pay for that."

Then he walked away from the three women, Rauirí, Seán, and Mike. Willow shrugged her slender shoulders. She had no fear of her father and his outburst had meant nothing to her. As the steam billowed out from the engine, the wheels of the train began to turn. Mike looked desperately at the windows of the passenger compartment, and he saw Moira looking back. Her face was expressionless, and he had the oddest sense that she had moved on to another plane, somewhere beyond reach to any of the rest of the family.

Ristéard and Úna waved their farewells, and they were gone as the train picked up speed and rounded the bend heading east out of Lodge Grass. Mike watched until he could not even see the steam cloud, then he turned back. He saw his father mounting his horse. Anna, Velia and her two brothers stood there, and Willow had vanished from sight.

CHAPTER 15

▼

When they returned to Anna's house, Rauirí and Seán sat down in the kitchen and began to tune up their instruments for another session. Velia and Anna took Mike to the sitting room, and asked him to sit with them. Anna went to the kitchen for tea, and when she returned with the steaming cups, she took her place in the bentwood rocker that Frank had made for her. The morning light streamed in through a window and created a halo of her white hair. Velia was in a small arm chair to her left.

It was obvious that Morgan would not be coming to the house. And Mike knew Willow would not be back at all on this day.

Anna started the conversation.

"Michael," she said. "It is up t' ye, now."

Recognizing what she was talking about, Mike stalled for time.

"What is up to me?"

"Y' will inherit the knowledge, the powers…before death takes me."

"Oh, Grandmother, you aren't going to die for a long time."

"T'will be sooner than y' think!"

"Grandmother, I just can't do it," he said, making his declaration as strongly as he could without sounding defiant.

"Y' must."

Mike's voice took on a pleading tone.

"It's enough that I have a piece of the banshee," he said. "I just can't take on any more."

Anna refused to be swayed.

"Michael, y' are all that's left to us. Moira has gone t' the convent, Willow has gone t' the wind, and y' are the only steady one."

"Grandmother, I've never refused you anything. But I have to say no to this. I'm not the right one. I have too many weaknesses, and I would fail you if I tried."

Velia could not be silent any longer. Two of the people she loved the most were disagreeing, and she knew the hearts of both of them. She reached out a hand to touch her mother's sleeve.

"Mother," she said softly, "It's too soon. Moira has gone, but she may change her mind and come back. And we don't know that Willow won't come 'round. She's got a good heart, and if she knows it means the survival of the legacy, she might just be persuaded. In the meantime, I have all the knowledge you have given me and I can carry on."

Anna turned her clear blue eyes to her daughter.

"Can y' do it with Morgan so opposed?" she asked.

"I'll just have to make sure that he doesn't know," Velia said. "He is gone much of the time, and I can keep up the practice when he is traveling. We just can't ask this of Michael. He knows he is not ready, and he's right, the forces of the unknown would find his weaknesses and destroy him. He must first learn to control certain parts of his life."

Mike was taken aback. For the first time, he realized that his mother was fully aware of his drinking. Her comments hurt. He had never wanted to disappoint her. Now he was acutely aware that he had been deceiving himself by believing that her extra sensory ability would miss his shortcomings.

Finally, he fled the house. At the livery, he changed into his everyday clothes, saddled Pal, and headed up Lodge Grass Creek at a trot. The horse, happy to stretch his legs, picked up the pace at the edge of town and broke into an easy, gentle gallop. Mike shut off his thoughts, and allowed himself the luxury of feeling the Indian summer breeze in his face. When they came to the gate of the ranch, the horse hesitated slightly, expecting to turn in. Instead, Mike urged him past and on up the valley. A few miles more, and they veered down the wooded lane that led to the house of Black Bird Shows.

The horse's hoofbeats died down, and they traveled the last hundred yards in silence, making no sound even when they transversed the shallow creek crossing. Mike dismounted at the edge of Black Bird's front step, and looked around. He could not see any sign of his friend.

Why had he come here? What had he hoped he would find in the company of Black Bird Shows?

He gazed around, listening for any sound as he did so. Birds sang in the trees, and as he turned this way and that, he saw a single magpie swoop down from its perch high in the big cottonwood. It glided to a spot in the grass nearby, and landed gracefully, never taking its eyes off of Mike.

The smell of wood smoke reached Mike, and he wondered where it was coming from. He tied Pal to the post next to the house, and made his way along the meander of the creek. An almost invisible deer path followed the bends and turns of the stream, and then he saw the source of the smoke. Black Bird Shows was tending a small fire about twenty feet away from a rounded structure of arched willow branches and deer hides. There was a sharp bend in the creek at this point, and the current there had carved a deep hole overlain with mirror smooth water. He straightened up and looked at Mike.

"So. You are here. Good."

It sounded as if he had been waiting for his friend to arrive.

"Ka-Hay. Sho'o Daa' Chi," Mike said, using the Crow greeting his friend had taught him.

"Your sister is gone?" Black Bird asked after returning the greeting.

Mike answered with a question of his own.

"How did you know?"

"I could see that she was already gone in her mind," Black Bird said. "The death of your grandfather was too much for her."

"It is more than that," Mike said. "It was the banshee, the death spirit, that she could not stand."

Black Bird Shows nodded his understanding.

"Yes. She saw it. That is enough to make anyone go away."

"She saw it, but the thing *touched* me," Mike said with a grimace.

This brought Black Bird up short. His black eyes widened with surprise, then narrowed as he contemplated what Mike was saying.

"What did that do to you?" he asked.

"It left me with a connection to the dead," Mike said. "Grandmother tells me it will always be with me."

Black Bird was quiet for a long time. When he spoke, his voice was very calm.

"Join me in a sweat, my friend. It will cleanse your spirit and help you see what you are meant to do. Then we will talk about this some more."

Mike knew that Black Bird often went to his sweat teepee. Most Crow men and some women did this for a variety of reasons and rituals. But this was the first time he had ever invited Mike to participate. Black Bird had always respected his white culture, as he had appreciated the Crow tribal culture. Black Bird would not invite him to a sweat without a reason, so it would not be fitting to refuse. Besides, he was desperate to find his way in the wake of all the confusion and maddening experiences he had just been through.

"I don't know what to do or how to do it," he said.

"I was just getting ready," said Black Bird. "This fire is heating the stones we will use inside."

Mike examined the sweat teepee more closely. It was artfully built, almost a perfect dome, with the opening facing the fire, which was exactly to the east of it. The flap that would cover the opening was laid over to the side, resting on the curve of the lodge. The deer hides were carefully placed on the ribs of willow, completely covering the framework and forming an organic connection with the earth. Black Bird began to move the superheated stones one by one from the fire into a pit inside, just to the north of the doorway. Two handmade strong wooden fork-like branches of wood were used to transport them. He arranged the superheated stones according to some predetermined pattern, until he was completely satisfied. The first four stones seemed to be the most significant. He was praying in the Crow way as he worked.

"Take off your clothes," Black Bird instructed, while pulling his own shirt off over his head.

Mike hesitated, although the statement was not particularly strange, since they had gone skinny dipping many times since they were boys. He followed Black Bird's example, pulling off his shirt, pants, and underwear, folding them neatly and stowing them under another hide laid on the ground. With the onset of late afternoon, the air was getting colder, and goosebumps rose on his skin. He shivered involuntarily.

Black Bird produced a braid of dried sweetgrass, and lit the end of it in the embers of the fire. He began Mike's cleansing by wafting its smoke all around him, fanning it with an eagle feather, bathing him in its essence. Then he did the same to himself.

He motioned for Mike to enter the sweat teepee through the little opening, indicating that he should take his place by turning left inside the door and making his way around the inside perimeter clockwise, in the direction of the sun. As Mike settled himself, he gazed about at the inside of the structure. It seemed to be perfectly circular on the inside, and the packed earth floor was swept clean. The place Black Bird had indicated he should sit was covered with a layer of grasses and sage leaves, and he was surprised at how comfortable he felt. The heat radiating from the stones already made it very warm in the enclosed space, and when Black Bird Shows entered carrying a bucket filled with water and a dipper, Mike felt the temperature rise noticeably. Black Bird set the bucket down, reached over and closed the flap, plunging them into darkness. Some subtle illumination came from the red-hot stones. He continued to speak his prayers and chants as he settled into his place.

Then Black Bird said, "Now we will release the rock people."

With the dipper, he scooped up some water and poured it over the hot stones. The water instantly flashed into searing vapor, filling the sweat teepee with steam. Mike almost panicked, feeling as if he were being cooked in a big dark oven. Sweat burst from all his pores and black spots danced in his vision. He wondered if his brain would explode from the sweltering heat. He was certain that his lungs were being totally scorched by the blazing hot air he had drawn into them with his first gasp.

Black Bird Shows was sweating, too, but he looked much more comfortable than Mike felt. In fact, he was using a small willow switch on himself to encourage the sweating. Eventually, the steam died down a bit, and Mike felt like he could breathe normally again. At that point, Black Bird poured another dipper of water on the stones, and the steam engulfed them as before. He repeated this two more times. Just when Mike thought he was totally exhausted from the steam, Black Bird uttered another prayer in Crow and made his way to the door, where he lifted the flap, allowing cooler air to flow into the sweat teepee. Mike thought he had never drawn a sweeter breath.

In the light from the door, Black Bird looked intently into his face, as if seeking some kind of information. After they had taken several more breaths from the outside, Black Bird Shows dropped the flap down again. He emptied another dipperful of water on the rocks, and the process started over. This time it did not seem so intense. Mike wondered if he was getting used to it, or if the rocks were cooling off, losing their ability to cook the water. Since he could barely make out the thread of light that came in around the door, he decided he must be getting more accustomed to the heat. Black Bird Shows handed him a willow switch. He applied it to his back and shoulders, and was astonished at how it seemed to magnify the sweating. Black Bird continued to pray in Crow. Mike felt himself begin to separate from his own body. He thought of the previous several days, of the banshee and his grandfather's death, of Moira, and of his grandmother's desire that he begin the practice of the Old Religion. A prayer for relief escaped from his lips, surprising him with its spontaneity. Black Bird Shows did not appear to hear him, but sat, rocking, his eyes closed.

They stayed in the sweat teepee until the rocks had cooled too much to heat the water poured on them. Mike felt like the heat from the rocks had been transferred inside his body, until he was broiling from the inside out. At last, Black Bird moved to the doorway, pulled the flap aside completely and stepped outside. He motioned for Mike to follow him. When Mike emerged from the hide covered structure, he saw his friend standing at the edge of the creek above the deep waterhole. When he was sure Mike could see him, he plunged off the bank and into the cold autumn water.

Mike ran to the rim and dove into the water, his body shrinking at the shock of the icy ripples. Wheezing, he surfaced, spitting water and looking around for Black Bird. His friend was floating on his back, smiling and breathing easily.

"Welcome to the sweat, Mike Lorrah," he said. "I hope it brought you the cleansing you were seeking."

When Mike could no longer stand the cold of the water, he climbed out, and grabbed a blanket that Black Bird had laid on the bank. Wrapping it around himself, he was tempted to retreat back into the sweat teepee. As he became more aware of his body, he discovered that he had never felt so clean or so invigorated. He was lighter, less laden with the weight of his grandmother's expectations. Then the euphoria passed. He could still feel the small cold thing next to his heart, and understood that he would never be rid of it. It would be his constant companion for the rest of his life.

Black Bird had gone into the house. He came out with two hot, steaming mugs of traditional tea made of a Crow recipe of rose hips, willow bark and a number of other ingredients Mike could not recognize by taste. The two of them sat, sipping and watching the twilight come over the land. As they enjoyed this companionable moment, Mike told Black Bird of seeing Bart Knight on the train.

"Do you think he has any idea you are still in the area?" Mike asked.

"No. If he did, he would have come looking for me. He will never forget that I got the best of him, and he will want to even things."

"Even now that so much time has passed?"

"He will never forget."

This answer chilled Mike's spirit. He could not imagine such hate, and suddenly felt more protective of Black Bird than he had since helping him get to his uncle.

"Be watchful," he told him. "And if you need my help, you know how to reach me."

"My animal guides will help me," Black Bird declared.

But Mike was not so sure.

They sat in silence for a while longer. Then Mike stood up to leave.

"Oh, I almost forgot," he said. "Grandmother wanted you to have this. It was Grandfather's."

He reached into his saddlebag and brought out a package cushioned in a towel. Unwrapping it, he removed a simple white clay Irish smoking pipe.

"In Irish, it's called a dudeen. Grandmother said you have a number of ceremonies that require tobacco, and she knew Grandfather would want you to have it."

"Tell her I am honored," Black Bird said, taking the pipe reverently in both hands.

As he prepared to leave, Mike spoke, emotion filling his voice.

"Thank you, Black Bird Shows," he said, using the man's full name. "Thank you for the sweat, thank you for standing by me, and thank you for trying to help me. I do feel better, but I have a lot of problems to solve. I will always remember how you have stood by me."

Black Bird shrugged.

"You saved my life," he said. "I am always here. But I can only help you as much as you are willing to be helped. Whiskey will not help you. Remember that."

Mike swore to himself that he would not drink again, but something prevented him from saying so to Black Bird Shows. He did not want to break a vow to this man, his most trusted friend.

After that, the rains finally came, softening the earth, quenching the thirst of the plants and trees, and preparing them for winter. Everything settled under the healing showers, and peace fell over the Lodge Grass Valley. The steady mist obscured the view of the dreamers and they began to return to the present.

The three sitting around the campfire drifted back to reality in a lazy, relaxed manner. The transitions were getting easier for them now. It was dawn, and the day was bright and clear.

Colleen's first concern was Black Bird Shows. Since the old man had not been dreaming with them, she worried that he had not slept. But when she looked at him, his eyes were closed, and there was a gentle smile on his face. He was resting comfortably, sitting up, and wrapped warmly in a wool blanket he had retrieved from his bedroll.

Colleen tapped Andrew's knee, and quietly touched Aisling to make sure she was awake. With her finger to her lips, she motioned for them to get up and follow her over to the spring. They filled cups with the sparkling fresh water and drank deeply, quenching a physical thirst that reflected the craving for information that had gripped them through the past hours.

"Let's go for a short walk," Colleen said. "Black Bird can use some rest, and I could use a stretch of the legs. How are you doing, Aisling?"

"It's a lot to take in," the girl replied. "Great-grandmother Della was not much older than me when she met Great-grandfather Mike. I don't know what to think of all this. Did Mike have that banshee in him all his life? It's like the worst horror movie ever, seeing that thing."

"His part of it was not that monstrous presence we saw when his grandfather died. As I recall, it was more like an intuition," Colleen replied. "He really did find a lot of lost dead people. He said he did not know why, but now I see that he worried people would think he was crazy if he had told all the detail about it. I never understood that part of it before."

"His sisters are a lot like me," Aisling said. "They couldn't see themselves with the legacy, either. I don't know where this dreaming is going, but I still don't see what it has to do with me."

Andrew spoke up.

"Aisling," he said. "If you have the patience to dream the whole story, there may be answers here. I didn't know why I was burdened with <u>my</u> family's history, either. Eventually, it becomes apparent. Took me a number of years. What do you say?"

Aisling smiled. Her admiration of her uncle knew no limit.

"Well, I have to admit this is really interesting. Lots better than any movie."

Colleen breathed a sigh of relief.

"Let's go in and make a little breakfast for us and Black Bird when he wakes up. It's not good to dream on an empty stomach!" she said.

They prepared a pot of hot cereal and they filled cups again with the cool water of the spring. Colleen made some camp coffee for Black Bird Shows, but she and Andrew decided not to drink any themselves. It might interfere with the dreaming. She set the tea kettle on the stove to heat the water that might be needed for the Dreaming Tea, and they carried the food outside. Black Bird was exactly where they had left him, but he seemed to sense their approach.

He opened his eyes and looked at them.

"Did you think you could sneak off and leave an old man sitting here?" he asked with a small grin.

"Yes," Colleen laughed, "but you are far too smart for us. You have all the good stories, so we had to come back."

"We would not want to miss anything!" Andrew joined in the jest. "Especially since the young one is starting to like this. There must be something to it!"

They ate together, and Black Bird Shows demonstrated a remarkable appetite for the hot oatmeal Colleen had cooked. He drank several cups of coffee, and stood up to stretch. Walking about, he had a light step, and movement akin to that of a much younger man. Andrew watched him for a few moments, then joined him in his striding about. They ranged out into the meadow, and back in toward the cabin. Black Bird Shows seemed to be chanting something under his breath, but Andrew just enjoyed his company. When they reached the edge of the open area for the second time, Black Bird stopped and looked into the trees.

Four pairs of brilliant black eyes looked back at him. They belonged to four magpies, who sat, silent observers of the tableau below.

"They are here," Black Bird said, pointing at the birds with an upward motion of his head. "They are watching to be sure you dream the truth. It is time to go back to the women and back to the past."

They turned and when she saw them approaching, Colleen went into the cabin and prepared to make another pot of the tea. Black Bird rearranged his blanket around his shoulders and easily sank into the spot he favored. Andrew took his place, and Aisling remained standing until Colleen came out with their cups. She took hers and moved a little closer to Black Bird than where she had sat previously. Colleen offered Black Bird a cup of spring water, and he took it, sitting it next to him.

When everyone was seated, Black Bird started his otherworldly singing. The sunlight of the splendid day began to shimmer, distorting the trees and grasses and blue of the sky, and they were transported again. Mike came into view.

CHAPTER 16

▼

With his mind clear and refreshed, Mike returned home. His ride back had been dominated by thoughts of Della. He desperately wanted to see her, and immediately posted a letter to her asking if he could call at her home on the weekend. Her reply came by return mail, a sweet note making it very clear that she was as eager to see him as he was to see her. Impatient, Mike did his work at the livery and the ranch, but his mind was preoccupied until the weekend came and he could go to Hardin. On Saturday, he dressed carefully, combed his unruly hair as best he could, and caught a ride with one of the cowboys, Curley Gallagher, who owned a car. When they got to Hardin, Curley pulled up in front of the Mint Bar. With a grin, he turned toward Mike.

"I'm not goin' anywhere but the Mint," he said. "Why don't you take the car to go call on your girlfriend?"

Mike was dumbfounded. He had a good idea of how to drive, but he had never had anyone offer him the use of their car.

"Jeez, Curley, I don't know. I'd hate it if I did something wrong and busted your car," he said.

"Mike, you're gonna be just fine with it. Don't ya' think you'll make more of an impression if you show up in a car than if you have to walk halfway cross town to see her?"

With Curley standing at the side, Mike got into the driver's seat, experimented a bit with the controls, and looked toward his benefactor for comment. Curley waved, and Mike was off to the O'Keefe house, picturing himself as a knight approaching a castle in which his princess resided.

When Della looked out the window and saw him arrive in front of the house, she took one look in the mirror to be sure her hair was exactly right, then she went to the door before one of her sisters could beat her. She invited him in to meet her parents, and once that was accomplished, she suggested they step outside.

Mike said, "My friend Curley let me use his car. Do you want to go for a ride?"

Della smiled with delight.

"Oh, yes. I'd like that very much."

"Do you need to get your parents' approval?"

Della did not pause to think of asking her parents. She would die of embarrassment if they said she could not go.

"Oh, no," she said, trying to appear nonchalant. "My sisters and I go for rides with fellas all the time. My parents won't mind."

He held the door open for her and she stepped into the vehicle. It was not brand new, but it was a passable car, and she was happy Mike had arrived with his own transportation. It was not unusual for young men to come calling at the O'Keefe house on foot, but this was much more sophisticated, as far as she was concerned.

Mike got in and carefully drove out of the neighborhood. He decided that it was not a good idea to drive around the town and he really was not able to concentrate on his minimal driving skills with this beautiful girl sitting next to him, so he went out one of the several country roads. The evening was just coming on, so he chose a place along the Bighorn River, and parked so they could talk. This car was like having your own private living room, and he liked the feel of it.

Once they were parked, he turned to Della. She was breathtakingly attractive, blonde hair perfectly styled, and he found himself lost in her bright blue eyes. He wanted to reach out and touch her face, to feel the softness of her cheek under his fingers, but he was afraid his work-roughened hands would offend her. For a few minutes, neither one of them spoke. At last, Della broke the silence.

"I couldn't wait to have you come and see me," she said. "I have to admit, I have thought of you often since we met at the dance. I hope you don't think it is too forward of me to say so."

"I...I was happy when you invited me," Mike stammered. "I have had you on my mind quite a bit, too."

In his mind, he cursed himself for being so awkward. He wanted to make an impression, and he sounded like a complete fool. What must she think of him?

He need not have worried.

Della smiled.

"My sisters told me you were pretty wild," she said. "They said you did not take life seriously, that you drink too much liquor, and that you never have been dedicated to any girl. But I can see how shy you are. I don't see how you could be wild and shy at the same time."

Mike was relieved. And then he noticed something else.

In her company, he did not feel any sense of the bit of the banshee that inhabited his soul. For these few minutes, he was free of the thing, and he felt light and carefree. Warmth spread through him, and his muscles relaxed, allowing him to be swept into the slow whirlpool that was his infatuation for this lovely girl. If there were ever something called fate, his meeting her had to fit the definition. Now the only thing was to find a way to make her feel the same. It was Della who noticed the time was getting late.

"I really need to get home," she sighed. "I don't want to give my father any reason to say I can't see you again."

Mike was disappointed, but thrilled to hear she wanted to see him again.

"I don't want this evening to stop," he said. "I feel like we are just getting started."

Della was firm. Mike acquiesced and started the car. He delivered her home and walked her to the door. He leaned over her and gave her a short, soft kiss which she returned with a promise of something more to come. Reluctantly, they parted and she stepped in the door, where she stood, watching as he departed.

When he walked into the Mint Bar to pick up Curley, Mike found his friend finishing a poker game with several other men. He saw Mike and pushed his chair back, standing up.

"Hey, Mikey!" he said, his words slightly slurred. "Didja have a good time? Is my car still in one piece?"

Mike smiled easily.

"I had a great time. Thanks for letting me use the car. You didn't lose it in the game, did you?"

The other men laughed.

Mike looked at the table in front of where Curley had been sitting. It was devoid of chips.

"Did you plan to buy into another game, or are you ready to go home?" Mike asked.

Curley shook his head ruefully.

"These boys cleaned me out, Mike. Let's hit the trail!"

They left the bar and Curley climbed into the driver's seat. Mike got in and they headed out of Hardin. It was a nice night with the full moon illuminating the hills and the road. They rolled along in the Little Big Horn valley. Everything seemed idyllic to Mike, who was enraptured by his evening with Della.

They had covered about ten miles when the unthinkable happened. At first it was a small feeling of unease. They drove a little further and then Mike was horrified to feel the cold thing near his heart come to life. It started to fill his spirit with terrible dread, slithering and writhing inside his chest. Then it began to pull at him. Just north of Crow Agency, near a small grove of cottonwoods, Mike could not fight it any more.

"Curley," he said. "I'm sorry. Can you stop and back up to those trees? I have to get out for a minute."

Curley looked at him and what he saw made him respond quickly. Mike's face was pale and drawn, and his body was tensed like a coiled spring. He stopped the car, and began to back up. Before he reached the cluster of trees, Mike flung open the car door and leapt out. He hit the ground running hard and as Curley watched in stunned silence, he disappeared into the brush between the road and the trees.

Mike could only go where the awful thing dragged him, and he found himself standing over the prostrate form of a young Crow Indian man. Even in the pale light of the moon, he could see the man had lain there for a time. He was face down, his long black hair spread around his head like a small shroud. The smell of death was all around him, and Mike felt dizzy and nauseous. After several long minutes, he emerged from the shrubbery. He stumbled to the car, got in, and said, "Curley, we have to stop in Crow Agency. I just found the body of a young Indian fella. Looks like he's been dead a while."

Curley was speechless, staring at Mike as if he had never seen him before.

Recovering after a full minute, he asked, "What made you stop there?"

Mike hesitated, formulating an explanation he hoped would not make him sound insane. Telling Curley about the 'bit of banshee' that inhabited his psyche would not be well received. In fact, Curley might judge him so crazy that he would leave him standing there without a ride on this dark stretch or road, only a few paces away from the body. What could he say that would be acceptable?

He blew out a breath.

"I don't' know," he said. "I just felt like I had to stop here. Couldn't say why. It was just a hunch."

Cowmen understood hunches. They had to exercise them every day in handling livestock. Curley engaged the gears and drove to the tribal police office in Crow Agency. Mike felt the dreadful banshee settle and contract until it was the small frozen knot that he lived with every day. When they got to the Agency, they walked into the tribal police building through the door with the tiny light illuminating it. A very tired looking policeman named Henry Bear Claw looked up when they entered. Henry had an excellent reputation as a lawman and Mike was glad he was the one on duty.

Mike quickly recounted what he had found, along with the location of the man's body. Henry took many notes, and said the authorities would go there at daylight to bring the corpse home. He told Curley and Mike that the man, Robert Whitecrane, had been the subject of a search since he had been reported missing by his family. Whitecrane had been suffering from a bad fever and delirium when he vanished from his home.

Mike and Curley got back into the car, weary from the night, and drove on to Lodge Grass. It was just past midnight when Curley dropped Mike off at the livery barn. Mike was too tired to try to go on to the ranch. He rolled out his bedding on the cot and collapsed into the welcome oblivion of the darkness. He did not want to think about the lonely body of Robert Whitecrane. It had been impossible to tell what the cause of his death had been, but most likely it was exposure and hunger. He was glad to believe that his discovery might have brought some comfort to the man's family, but it did not keep him from feeling sad.

After staring into the darkness for what seemed like an eternity, Mike allowed his thoughts to turn to Della. His agitated spirit calmed immediately as he reviewed every second of his time with her. He could smell her lavender perfume, and feel the velvet touch of her lips on his.

The more he relaxed, the more his memory of the evening took possession of him. He forgot the banshee, forgot poor, dead Robert Whitecrane, and forgot Curley. Every iota of his senses was engulfed by thoughts of Della. He was swept into a vortex of emotion and there was a curious sense of being launched upward. It was as if he had taken the end of a pulley rope just as a very heavy object was dropped at the other end. It catapulted him upward, only to jerk him to a halt at the apex of his flight, just short of where he might be smashed to death.

He opened his eyes wide, completely disoriented at where he found himself. He was not where he had gone to bed. Instead, he was in an unfamiliar room where two people appeared to be sleeping under quilted covers in two single beds. The two were young women, and as he gaped, one turned in her bed and opened her eyes, looking directly at him. It was Della.

"I knew you would come back," she whispered.

"I don't know how this happened," he stammered, "I shouldn't be here in your room."

She sat up, adjusting her snowy white sleeping shift. He did not miss the fact that it was sheer and that he could see some details of her body. Her eyes were huge, trying to see in the dark.

"But I wanted you here," Della said. "I wanted you here so bad I couldn't think of anything else."

"I felt the same way," Mike said, crossing the space between them in two giant steps.

He wrapped his arms around her, marveling at how his embrace seemed to engulf her completely. The heat generated by their touch was so intense, Mike finally pulled away, kissing her so lightly on her lips that it might have been a butterfly wing that grazed her.

"It is wrong for me to be here," he declared. "Even if this is just a dream."

Della's expression was one of immense disappointment. She clung to his hand, holding him there until she could press a piece of paper into it. Using her fingers, she closed his fist around it. As she did so, the other sleeper, her sister Nuala, stirred in the next bed, alarming Mike.

As suddenly as he had materialized in this place, he descended into a dark whirlwind that sucked him away and brought him to a jolting stop back in his own bed. He tried to open his eyes, but it made him dizzy. He slid into a deep sleep and did not wake until the rooster across the road greeted the sunrise. When the sun stabbed its way into the back area of the livery, Mike swam into wakefulness, his first thoughts jumbled. Something was clutched in his palm.

Opening his fingers, he looked at it. It was a small square of lavender scented paper with six simple words written on it in perfect penmanship. Warmth and shock cascaded over him as he read them.

"You are in my dreams--Della."

CHAPTER 17

▼

Mike rushed to dress and complete his work at the livery. When he was satisfied that he had left nothing for his father to criticize, he walked quickly to his grandmother's house. He found her in the garden, plucking some leaves and an odd, blood-red blossom off of what appeared to be a wild rose bush. She placed the leaves and blossom in a flower press to preserve them.

"I need t' be writin' this down, Michael," she said, picking up the journal, "Then we kin talk."

He watched her make notes in her small, precise hand. The journal seemed to have many more pages since he and Moira had last taken instruction from her. She finished with a flourish on the last word she wrote, and closed the book carefully. They moved to sit in the shade of the porch.

"Now, Michael," she said. "What would be on yer mind?"

He poured out the events of the night before, describing briefly his date with Della, then the discovery of the dead man, and finally his transportation back to Della's room.

Anna listened quietly, her eyes widening a bit at the last part of his tale. When he finished speaking, she sat, contemplating what she had heard. Then she began her response, item by item.

"'Tis a great amount t' ponder, Michael," she said. "I've met yer Della and can understand yer attraction t' her. She's very young, but she's a fine person, too. Take yer time wit' her."

She paused, then continued.

"As to yer dead man, this seems t' be the pattern the bit o' banshee is goin' t' take. It's given y' the dark gift of easin' the hearts of those whose dead ones are lost."

Another pause.

"But the last thing," Here she shook her head in wonder. "I've only heard of this from storytellers. Always thought t'was a myth. The old ones say ye can transport to another person if y' both want it enough, under enough emotion on both yer parts. With all y' were feelin' last night, things might just have been right. Y'll just have t' see if it ever happens again."

Mike rose from where he was sitting.

"Thank you, Grandmother," he said. "Here I am, bothering you with my worries, when you are now all alone. Is there anything you need, here by yourself? Can I do anything for you?

"Nay, Michael. Yer mother comes t' see me, and Willow appears now and again. And I know yer there. I'll send fer y' if I need y' before I see y'."

Mike looked at Anna for a long moment. Frank's death had eroded her. She was a little smaller, although no less dynamic. Her sturdy body was healthy and she obviously had a great deal of energy, caring for the house and garden mostly by herself.

Mike carried on for the next few days, working at the livery, and picking up some small wrangling jobs with some of the area ranchers. He went to the home ranch each day to take care of the work Morgan had for him, and he spent time with his mother. She seemed sad to have Moira so far away, and with Willow's visits so fleeting and unpredictable, she was lonely. Her times with Mike were treasured by her, and she told him so often. He tried to time his visits to those occasions when she was alone. Morgan's presence put a damper on the range of subjects they could discuss. Whenever he was home, there was no mention of anything magical. Only work would be discussed.

He stayed at the ranch as often as he could, since having dinner there gave him some additional time with Velia. She was pleased to learn that he was seeing Della, and he had told her as much as he could about this blossoming romance. She shuddered when he shared his story of locating the body, but told him she knew he must have given the dead man's family peace. Staying at the ranch had another purpose for him, too. He had vowed to himself that he would try to cut back on drinking, both to avoid his father's disapproval, but also to keep himself from making any mistakes when it came to Della. In the company of the cowboys and others who hung around the stable, the temptation to drink was always there.

One day, he finished up at the ranch and rode into town. Curley was in for some machine parts, and said he needed to go to Crow Agency to pick up a stock dog for one of the ranchers. Mike asked if he could go along to check with the tribal police on how the family of Robert Whitecrane was doing. Curley dropped him off at the police headquarters and went on to get the dog. Mike started up the steps, and ran into the same policeman they had talked to the night they found the dead man.

"Hello, Henry," he said. "I just wanted to see how Robert Whitecrane's family is."

The officer told him the family was very grateful to him, and that they had given Robert a good funeral and burial. As they stood there talking, a tall, gaunt man in a rumpled black suit approached them.

Henry's demeanor changed, and Mike immediately detected the tribal policeman's intense dislike for this man. Henry introduced him. It was Bart Knight.

Bart's eyes glinted, the cold reflection of glaring light on crushed coal. He stared unblinking at Mike.

"Mike Lorrah," he said. "I done some horse trades with your old man. And I met your mother once when I was hunting a damn runaway injun kid. I always believed he run up Lodge Grass Creek, but when your ma told me no one seen him, I believed her. Still wonder, though. Only redskin ever got the best of me. Figgered he musta died, out on his own. If I ever find out otherwise, we're gonna settle things, him 'n me. Then I'm takin' care of anyone who hid him or lied to me."

Mike kept his expression impassive, but his blood ran cold in the face of such evil.

"I've heard of you, Mr. Knight," he said. "I'll let my dad know I met you."

His tone was level and hard as he acknowledged the man.

Mike watched Bart's eyes. They were reptilian, reminding him of a snake, as he saw Bart instinctively sense his animosity, and take a second measure of him.

"You just do that," he sneered. "You don't know anything 'bout the injun Joe Black, do ya', Mike Lorrah?"

"I don't know anyone named Joe Black. I'll let you know if I ever come across him."

Bart continued to brazenly examine Mike as Henry turned aside for a moment to answer a question from a woman who had come up to him.

"Ya' know, I *have* seen you before," he said. "Seen you on the train from Crow. Ya' saw that squaw I had? I'm lookin' for her. She ran away. These useless Indian cops ain't been any help findin' her. You see her, you can let me know about that, too."

"I haven't seen her," Mike said, struggling to keep himself under control. "Sounds like you have a lot of trouble with runaways."

Bart's expression became even colder.

"I don't like smart asses," he said in a voice too low for Henry to hear. "You'd better not cross me, kid. I can make you *real* sorry."

Henry turned back to the conversation, and Bart redirected his irritation toward him.

"You're not much of a cop, Bear Claw. You oughta be able to find one stupid girl. Call me when you do."

With that, Bart pivoted on the heel of his dusty boots, and strode away.

Henry turned to Mike.

"Actually, I do know where she is, but damned if I'm telling him. Her name is Agnes Little Moon. He beat her up so many times she finally decided to risk coming to us. Figured it would be better than staying with him until he killed her. I got an uncle over in Busby and I sent her there. Never saw anyone as scared as her."

"You did the right thing, Henry," Mike assured him. "Didn't Bart Knight work for the boarding school?"

"Yes. Right up until it closed. Now he goes around collecting debts and generally terrorizing people he can bully. He's a mean bastard, but smart enough to stay just inside the law. There's stories of people he hurt when they did not pay, but they're all too afraid to come to us and file a complaint."

Mike felt his gut twist with anger and pain for the people who had to fear this thug. He wished he had the power to make the man go away, but on his second thought, he did not want that kind of control. His grandmother had always declared that such evildoing would eventually suffer its own brand of justice, and he decided to rely on her assurance. He shook Henry's hand.

"Sure glad I don't have your job, Henry," he said. "Thanks for all you do."

That night, Mike laid awake, trying to duplicate the circumstances that had projected him to Della. Anna had told him they both had to want it desperately. He had no doubt that he wanted it. He felt his life depended upon being with her. It was the way he could obliterate the feel of the unspeakable thing that lurked inside him.

Did Della want to be with him as much?

Was the wanting enough?

He recognized that there had been other factors the night he had been able to move across time and space to her room. The piece of banshee had acted that night, and the emotional upheaval had been different. Locating the dead Crow man had changed him at the time. Did that mean the bit o' banshee was part of the equation? That would be too awful to accept.

After several hours, Mike fell into a restless sleep. His dreams were populated with dark scenes and memories, and he was tired when he awoke. Some of the gloom was dispelled by a glorious morning with cloudless skies and birdsongs. The day invited him to ride out to the foothills to clear his thoughts. He would check the fencelines and make sure the cattle were where they should be.

When he topped a ridge that opened to a panoramic view sweeping across several drainages, he paused to drink in the sight. Standing up in his stirrups to stretch his legs, he twisted a bit and found himself staring into Black Bird's amused face. They grinned at each other, even though Mike wondered about the fact that he had not heard the man's approach.

"Black Bird!" he said, "You and that spooky grey horse get quieter every day. How the heck do you do that?"

Black Bird grunted. Humor danced in his eyes as he replied.

"Horses are pretty quiet when they don't have big iron shoes on."

"That's not the only reason," Mike retorted.

"These grulla horses been on the mountain for a long time," Black Bird said. "He's a wild horse, and he has some ghost in him."

Mike had to agree. His friend's slate colored horse had some primitive markings that set it apart from the horses his father traded and from the mounts of most of the Crows. The animal was a mustang stallion that Black Bird Shows had charmed in the Pryor Mountains. It came from a herd of wild horses populated by descendants of Spanish mounts brought to America centuries earlier. His handsome Arab-like head was darker than his body and his grey ears were edged in black. He had a black stripe down his back and his mane and tail were black, frosted with strands of silvery grey. The markings on his legs constituted the most ancient feature. While they were charcoal grey around the feet and up to the knee, the color tapered off into ghostly dark stripes on the upper legs and withers. All this was topped off by grey-blue eyes that reflected deep intelligence and calm. Black Bird liked riding on a blanket held on with a surcingle strap, and he never used a bridle or halter to guide the horse or make it stay where he wanted. Rider and animal seemed to have a telepathic connection that Mike had tried to emulate but never succeeded in duplicating.

Mike changed the subject.

"I'm glad you're here. I wanted to tell you I ran into Bart Knight in Crow Agency yesterday."

Black Bird gave him his undivided attention.

Mike described his encounter with Knight, including the man's parting threat.

"I don't like it, Black Bird. Knight is mean and filled with a hunger for revenge. If he ever gets wind of the fact that you are right here up Lodge Grass Creek, he'll come looking for you. Is there anything you should do to stay safe?"

Black Bird gazed off into the distance, considering what he had been told.

"No. He probably won't find me. And if he does, there are ways of defending myself from him."

"I'll help you," Mike volunteered.

"I do not think that will be needed, my friend."

As if to demonstrate, Black Bird nudged the side of his horse with his knees and moved off. Almost instantly, the air vibrated and he vanished without a sound.

CHAPTER 18

▼

Mike composed and sent a letter every day to Della. Every next day brought a reply from her. To him, it was as if they were able to carry on a conversation, and it was the only way he could feel connected at the times he could not be with her. Thoughts of her occupied him, whether he was working, riding, reading, walking. Haunted by the one night he had been able to project himself to her, he continued to try to replicate it as he drifted off to sleep. After a time, frustration with these attempts led him to the one place he did not want to go. He turned to spending time with the hangers-on at the livery, and he began to have several drinks before riding back to the ranch or crawling into his cot at the stable. He hated himself for this, but he could not bear the longing that clenched at his heart.

Willow came home from one of her many excursions to unknown parts. Detecting her brother's angst instantly, she broached the subject.

"Would you like me to invite Della and her sisters to come to visit? Mother would be happy to have me associate with people as nice as they are, and they can all stay at the ranch house," she proposed.

Mike was beside himself with excitement at the idea. To have Della at the ranch and overnight, at that! It was a dream come true.

"Willow! You're a life saver!"

The invitation was extended and accepted. It happened that there was to be a dance at the Lodge Grass town hall that weekend, so there would be something special to do. The anticipation was joyful, and Mike thanked Willow and his mother several times for making this possible.

Velia was relieved to see her son so happy. She had observed the tension in him after his grandfather's death, and she was concerned. Anna had alluded to the banshee curse, but had not given her all the details. Velia did not know if it was a one-time thing, or if there was more to the incident than she understood. What she did know was that the events surrounding it had caused Moira such unbearable pain that her middle daughter was lost to the family, and she did not want the same thing to happen with Mike.

Mike stopped to see his grandmother two days before the visit, and told her how excited he was.

"Grandmother," he said. "Della is coming to the ranch with her sisters to visit Willow. Actually, she's coming to visit me. I want this to be a very special time for her. What should I do?"

Anna smiled. It was so good to see her grandson's elation. She went to her herbal cabinet and came back with a small packet wrapped in paper.

"This is a special herb mixture, Michael," she said. "T'will open her heart t' yours."

"I hope her heart is already open to me," he said. "But I will take it with me, just in case."

Hugging Anna, he danced her around her kitchen, causing her to laugh aloud for the first time since Frank's passing. Breathing fast, she put a hand on his cheek to stop him, and gazed into his eyes.

"Michael, be careful. Dark forces are waitin' t' make things hard fer ye. Keep control at all times."

At this statement, Mike felt the cold thing in his chest twitch. Would it always cloud his happy times? No. He would not stand for it. This was to be a wonderful occasion, and he would not allow it to be otherwise. He rushed back to the stable to finish his work, whistling as he fed and watered horses, cleaned stalls, and stacked the new hay that had been delivered.

The week dragged by, but finally it was Saturday.

Willow sashayed into the livery where Mike was tallying the payments and checking the bills for feed. Several other cowboys were in for the weekend, and when they saw her walk in, they were struck dumb. She wore a lavender, frothy concoction of a dress that seemed to float about her while revealing every curve. The scent of lilies of the valley drifted in with her and sent out ribbons of allure that touched every man there. Flowers perched in her hair without any visible means of attachment, and her cobalt eyes finished off any resistance that they might have tried to put up.

"Hello, boys," she sang, in tones like the finest wind chime.

Curley Gallagher put a hand out to try to lean nonchalantly against the wall, and knocked over a pitchfork next to him. Jimmy Swensen swallowed wrong and broke into a coughing fit. Buck Sullivan did his best to look casual, but a brilliant red flush crept up from his collar to his ears. Mike smiled. These men were strong in the face of almost any challenge, but they turned into adolescent boys when confronted with Willow.

"What's wrong with you guys?" he asked, laughing. "This is just my sister. You all have known her since she was a kid."

There were sheepish looks to go around, and almost in unison, the three of them said, "Hullo, Willow. Good to see you."

"Are you ready to go to meet the train, Mike?" Willow asked.

"Sure," he said, peering into the little shaving mirror nailed to the post beside the cot he used. He put his hand up to try to arrange an errant lock of his hair. It didn't work.

Willow motioned for him to sit down, and she ran a comb through the curly black thatch. A couple of passes, and it was perfect. The men watched this open-mouthed, as if hypnotized, and when she straightened to admire her work, they released a collective breath.

"Let's go," Mike said to her, "before one of these yokels has a heart attack."

They strolled the half block to the station just as the Hardin train rounded the bend. The platform was occupied by the usual cast of locals. The station master was there, along with parents waiting for children, several Crow Indian families with tickets to ride to Wyola, and a number of stock buyers ready to go to Sheridan as part of their circuit. Some of the locals were just there to watch who got on and who got off. The arrival of the passenger train was always an event in this little community.

The train huffed to a stop, brakes screeching wheels against the tracks, and people began to disembark. As they did, the station crew unloaded bags of mail, and hefted cans of fresh milk from the local farms onto the cars. People milled on the platform, enjoying the unusually warm weather that had hung on until this first week of October.

The O'Keefe girls were the last to get off the train. Mike had begun to worry that they had not come, but when Nuala led the way, followed by Deidre and Della, he relaxed. The girls had traveled in casual clothes, wearing blouses and trousers that were fast becoming popular with young women in these liberated times of the late 1920s. The style was daring in the eyes of the older generation, showing off the curves and revealing that women actually had legs. Parents found this attire discomfiting, but they understood that there was little they could do to change the minds of these girls. It was, after all, a new age, and an exciting time in the country, with new kinds of music, modern inventions, and more and more people driving cars.

Willow rushed forward, opening her arms as if to embrace all three of the O'Keefe sisters at once, but then sweeping the gesture wider, taking in the entire day.

"Nuala! Deidre! Della! You really are here! This is going to be *so* much fun!"

Then tilting her head to Mike, "Gather up their bags, Mike! And follow me!"

Unable to do more than say hello, Mike followed her lead and easily swept up the three valises. He started to walk toward the stable, where he intended to hitch up a carriage to take them to the ranch, but Willow called him again.

"No, Mike! Over here!"

He looked where she was pointing and saw that she was standing next to a shiny Nash 266 Roadster with its top down.

Whistling with surprise, he asked, "Where did you get that?"

Willow tossed her head.

"Won it fair and square…well, maybe just square. Played poker with some fellas over in Parkman last night, and one of them wasn't a very good gambler. He had trouble keeping his eyes on his cards," she said, a trace of a smile curving her lips.

"You mean you own it? It's really yours?"

"Yep. Gave me the papers and everything."

Mike winced, thinking of some poor cowboy who had probably spent all his earnings to buy the vehicle, only to lose it to Willow's extraordinary card skills and his own distraction. The wretched man had probably awakened this morning without any memory of why he no longer had his fine new car. Of course, his fellow gamblers would probably be more than happy to re-live every moment of his humiliation for him.

The O'Keefe girls were already in the car, exclaiming over its features, and enjoying themselves completely. Deidre and Nuala had squeezed into the front, and Della was sitting back in the rumble seat. Willow slid in behind the wheel.

"Mike, once you load those bags, why don't you sit back there with Della?" she said, waving her hand in the general direction. He climbed in, and they were off.

Willow drove like she lived – without fear and as fast as the car would go. The Nash fishtailed around corners and clung desperately to the gravel road all the way up Lodge Grass Creek to the ranch. Her passengers might have been nervous, but no one said anything. The girls in the front were accustomed to riding in cars, and Mike was so overwhelmed to be this close to Della that he was oblivious to anything happening around him. They covered the ten miles quickly, and as they skidded to a stop in front of the ranch house, Velia came out onto the porch. She smiled a welcome that turned to dismay as the dust cloud Willow had created caught up to the car, almost obscuring her view of the guests.

Willow stepped out, completely unaffected by the commotion, with a bright smile for her mother.

"Look who's here, Mother! Nuala, Deidre, and Della. And, of course, Mike!"

Velia regained her composure.

"I'm so glad you girls could come for a visit," she said graciously. "Welcome to the ranch."

Mike helped Della out of the cozy seat at the back of the car.

Willow pulled Nuala, Deidre, and Della along with her as she showed them the lawn with its large cottonwood trees and comfortable wooden outdoor furniture. Then she ushered them inside the house to the rooms they would use. Mike tagged along until they went into the house. Excusing himself, he went to the barn to take care of the afternoon chores.

Willow assigned the older sisters to the room that had been Moira's, and brought Della to her own bedroom. Once they placed their luggage, she took them outside and walked them around the garden, down to the creek, and then on to a hot spring at the bottom of a slope a few hundred yards from the house. It rose up with substantial flow from beneath a big granite boulder, filled a large stone-lined pool with clear, warm water, and then overflowed toward the creek. A portion of it was shallow, but there was also an area where the water was a good six feet deep. It had always been used as a soaking and swimming pool by the Lorrah family, and Frank Daly had even built a bath house with a huge cast-iron tub inside right next to it. In an ingenious arrangement, Frank had piped in a little of the water inside so people could sit in the tub and soak. Anna and Velia often used it to provide therapy to individuals who came to them with sprains or sore muscles. The pool often provided relief to Mike after riding broncs for his father. It was hidden from sight by a wall of chokecherry, buffalo berry, and juniper bushes.

As the girls watched in amazement, Willow stripped off all her clothing and dove into the pool, barely disturbing the surface. She glided through the water like an otter, effortless and graceful. Nuala, who was the strongest and boldest of the O'Keefe sisters, followed suit, leaving on her undergarments. Deidre and Della hesitated on the rim of the pond.

"Come on in!" Willow sang out. "This water is so nice, and no one will see you. Look how the bushes block everyone's sight of this place. Father is on a buying trip, and Mike has a lot of work to do!"

Cautiously, looking around them as they did so, the other two girls disrobed to their underwear. Della was the first to put a foot and then her entire body into the water. It felt incredible. The water was somewhat warmer than body temperature, enough so that the cooler temperature of the air did not cause the swimmers to feel a chill. They lazily floated on their backs, sat on some of the rocks around the edge, and relished the daring and sensual experience. The O'Keefe girls kept their underclothes on, self conscious about revealing their bodies. Willow ignored their efforts to avert their eyes from her nakedness, and pulled herself out of the pond to perch on a flat stone, water beading on her skin like so many diamonds sparkling in the light. It was so natural with her that eventually the others became comfortable with her unabashed exhibitionism. Della could not contain her awe at the wonders of the hot spring.

"Willow! This is absolutely marvelous!" she said. "I've never seen anything like this. You are so lucky to have it right by your house!"

Willow's mouth formed a satisfied smile. The ranch's hot spring had always been a part of her life, and she knew it had been a privilege for her and Moira and Mike to enjoy these waters year round since they were children. Playfully, she splashed water at the others, causing a trill of feminine laughter that caught Mike's attention as he walked back up the road from the barns. Curious, he nearly walked over toward the hot spring, and then stopped himself, remembering Willow's predilection for swimming in the nude. If the others were in the same state, he did not want to disturb them. It was a huge temptation, especially when he contemplated the vision of Della participating in a naked swim, but he did not want to embarrass the O'Keefe sisters or give them reason to go home before the visit began. His imagination would have to be enough for now.

CHAPTER 19

▼

Willow and the O'Keefe sisters returned to the house in a swirl of talk and laughter. They changed their clothes and did their hair before dinner, taking pleasure in these feminine rituals. They compared clothing, talked about the dance in town, and then came into the kitchen to help Velia with preparing and serving dinner. Mike had bathed and dressed in his best clothes to escort them all to town that evening. He had struggled mightily with his curly hair, and had some semblance of control on it when he came into the dining room.

Della looked up from setting the table, excitement lighting her eyes. It was hard to imagine that such a handsome man was interested in her. Yes, she had her share of admirers, but Mike was the kind of man a girl conjures up in her fondest dreams. And to be staying in his home where she could see him at will over this weekend was more than she could have ever hoped for.

She wanted to have a private moment to talk with him about the night visit he had made to her after their date in Hardin. It seemed impossible that such a thing could have happened, but she had written him the note, and she could not find it after he left. Then when he wrote and told her that he had awakened the following morning with it clutched in his hand, she struggled to find any logical explanation for it. Such things happened in fairy tales, not in the experiences of real people.

"Hello, Della," he said when he saw her.

The greeting was all he could manage, his breath nearly cut off by his wonder at the sight of her. She wore a sweet floral dress that she had made herself. It graced her every curve, and flowed elegantly as she stepped around the table, placing napkins and silverware. The waves of her blonde hair were caught up with barrettes on the sides, making her look like the young schoolgirl she was. She smiled at him, melting his heart instantly.

"Hello, Mike," she said. "Willow took us to the hot springs pond. We had such fun! I've never seen anything like it. Did your family build it? Do you ever swim in it?"

Her questions made it easier for him to speak.

"Yes. I've swum in it ever since I was a kid," he said. "It's very old. In fact, it was here long before the ranch was. No one knows who built it originally. When my father and grandfather decided where to place this house, they chose this location because of the pond."

"It is so warm, and so clear," Della observed. "And Willow…she's like a mermaid!"

Mike laughed at her open admiration of his sister.

"Willow's a creature of nature. She is good with anything outdoors, swimming, riding, camping, tracking animals…sometimes I wonder if she can fly, too!"

"Well, I think she's wonderful," Della said. "I wish I could be more like her. She told us she swims in the pool at night, too. Is that true?"

"Yes. I've known her to do that," Mike said.

At that point, Willow sauntered into the room.

"Hey, you two. Are you talking about me?"

Mike threw an arm around her shoulder, wishing it was around Della's instead.

"Of course we are. You're always the heart of the conversation," he said.

"Well, I'd better be!" Willow declared. "I would expect nothing less!"

At the sound of their laughter, Nuala and Deidre came in bearing the first of the dishes of food. Velia entered behind them with more, and Willow and Della hurried to assist them. As soon as everything was in place, they all took their seats, Velia at the head of the table.

She looked at the five young people, and bowed her head. Mealtime grace was traditional in the Lorrah household, but always in silence. Velia had told her children that this enabled everyone to pray to whatever deity they believed in, and that no one would be embarrassed by differences. The O'Keefe girls looked at each other, then followed suit. When they finished, Velia spoke.

"Morgan had to be in Sheridan for some business tonight. He asked me to convey his regrets that he could not be here for dinner, and said he will see you all for breakfast tomorrow."

Mike was relieved. It would be uncomfortable to be under his father's scrutiny as he deepened his acquaintance with Della. He tired of Morgan's continued criticism of his every move, and he was enjoying the freedom from his watchful eye.

When the meal was finished, the girls cleared the table, put on aprons and helped Velia with the dishes. These tasks complete, they went to their quarters to put the finishing touches on their appearances, and then came outside to where Mike waited by Willow's new car. In a burst of typical generosity, Willow asked Mike to drive, and the girls took their places. Nuala and Deidre got into the rumble seat, and Willow nudged Della to sit in front next to Mike. Once she was in, Willow squeezed in next to her, pushing closer to him. The trip into Lodge Grass was merry, with lively comments and much laughter trailing in the air behind them. Mike drove more carefully than Willow, but the trip did not seem to take any longer. He liked the feeling of Della sitting so close, her arm touching his, and would have been happy driving forever. In no time, they arrived at the town hall, where many other cars, horses, and carriages were clustered in the open area. Strains of a waltz played by a local band drifted out the windows and the door, inviting people of all ages inside.

Mike and the four young women crossed the big porch that spanned the front of the building, where a number of cowboys and couples stood. It was a wonderful place to catch a breath of fresh air, or, in the case of the cowboys, to take a drink or two. A number of people hailed them with greetings and smiles. Mike loved being seen with Della, and felt it did no harm to have three other beautiful women with him. Nuala's usual escort had arrived from Hardin with one of his friends, and they made their way over to where she and Deidre stood. Soon they left the others for the dance floor. Mike glanced at Willow, who motioned that he and Della should do the same, and as they stepped away from her, Mike could see at least four of the local young men rushing to try to be first to ask Willow for a dance. There was some pushing and shoving, and the fastest one claimed her hand.

Willow's laugh chimed across the crowd, and the evening was under way.

Mike was possessive about Della's dances. He permitted a few of the older gentlemen to take her for a spin around the floor, but he was quick to cut off access by any of the younger swains. When the band took a break, he walked her outside onto the porch. Curley strolled up to them.

"Howdy, Mike and Della," he said. "I hope you two are enjoyin' the evenin'."

"We sure are," Mike replied. "How about you?"

"It's a good one, to be sure," Curley replied. "Wondered if you two'd like a little drink. I have some fine whiskey over there."

He tilted his head in the direction of the railing where he had been standing. A tall, elegant bottle of what appeared to be very expensive liquor sat, the glass sending off a golden glow in the light of the lanterns that hung from the pillars of the porch.

"No thanks, Curley," Mike said earnestly. "I want Della to think the best of me. And you and I know that I don't always know when to stop once I start. Think I'll just have some of the punch the ladies have ready inside."

Curley put a hand on his shoulder.

"I don't usually let a man refuse a drink from me," he said. "But in this case, I'll make an exception."

Della patted Mike's arm.

"Mike, don't decline your friend's offer because of me," she said, "I know you'll be a gentleman. You always are."

With this encouragement, Mike and Della followed Curley to where his bottle was, and Mike took several good long pulls from it. It was fine whiskey, indeed, and he thought as such, it was probably safer than the run of the mill stuff the cowboys drank at the livery stable. They talked and several more drinks passed between them. Della demurred when they offered her a drink, saying she would be happy with the ladies' punch.

It was time for the band's break to end, and everyone began to head back inside. Mike was feeling warm and happy inside and out. He cherished this evening with his lovely date on his arm and the glow spreading through his body. Arm around her waist, he guided Della across the porch toward the door.

Just as they were about to enter the hall, Mike stopped short, pulling Della even closer to him. Just ahead of them, Bart Knight was climbing the two steps from the parking area, and it was apparent that he was coming to the dance. Every muscle in Mike's body tensed, and he looked for an avenue to avoid being anywhere near the man.

Bart was peering around the main room, as if looking for someone. Mike kept himself and Della at a distance but watched his actions closely. He was dressed in the same black suit, although it appeared to have been pressed for the occasion. While the custom was for men to remove their hats when they were in the presence of ladies or whenever they came inside a building, Bart did not do so. His expression was one of immense disdain for everyone there, and it was apparent that his visit was not for social purposes. Just before the band started playing again, he stepped up on the platform in front of them, and made his announcement.

"I'm lookin' for the squaw Agnes Little Moon. She's a runaway, and she belongs to me. I have reason to believe someone here might be hidin' her, and I want her back. I don't like being lied to, so if you know anything about where she is, you'd better come clean. If I find out any of you have anything to do with her disappearance, you're goin' to pay."

His black eyes gleamed beneath his red brows as he stared at everyone there. Several of the women had their hands over their mouths in alarm, and some of the men were muttering among themselves. The atmosphere in the room was charged, and tension ran high. Big fights had started at dances for less than this. But Bart did not wait for anyone to confront him. He spun on his heel and stomped down the little set of steps from the platform. As he walked to the door, he saw Mike, and made a beeline toward him. Mike looked behind him, and saw Willow move quickly to grasp Della's hand and pull her away, into the crowd.

Bart stopped in front of Mike.

"Mike Lorrah," he hissed. "*You're* an Indian lover. Bet you know something. Seen you talkin' to that good for nothin' Crow cop, Bear Claw. You'd better not have anything to do with Agnes's escape."

"Look, Bart," Mike said. "This is not the time or the place for this kind of talk. These people are just out to have a good time tonight. Why don't you take it up with the sheriff?"

A sneer lifted the corner of Bart's mouth.

"Him and everyone else in this stupid town protects the redskins," he growled through gritted teeth. "They ain't worth it, and you all better figure that out. They're subhuman, and they'll rob you blind if you're too good to 'em."

Mike felt blistering anger building inside him. Several of the local men stepped to back him up, and he was trying hard to maintain a reasonable demeanor. Problem was, this man was oblivious to civilized discourse. And just when Mike wanted a cool head, the alcohol he had consumed on the porch kicked in. The only cool he had was the sudden awakening of the cold thing next to his heart. It did not move, but just made its presence known with an abrupt attack of ice inside him.

This only made Mike angrier. It had all but disappeared in Della's company, and now Bart Knight had stirred it up. He knew he did not want to get into a physical exchange with him, but he could not let these insults slide, either.

Suddenly, in a voice he hardly recognized as his own, Mike spoke.

"Funny you should hate Indians so much, Bart – since you are one."

Bart froze, a hot red flush rising in his pasty cheeks.

"What the hell do you mean by that?" he asked in a low, menacing tone.

"I mean," Mike said, formulating every word slowly and carefully to be sure the alcohol did not hinder his pronunciation, "that I know you are a Sioux named Bartholomew Kills in the Night. I know you were born in the

Black Hills and that as soon as you were old enough you ran away, trying to escape the Indian part of you. Don't you know you can't run away from yourself?"

Without any warning, Bart's fist shot out and caught Mike squarely in the jaw. Mike went down hard, sprawling on the floor, and Bart was about to stomp on him when two big ranchers grabbed him by each arm, dragging him toward the door. Bart pulled away from them, and drew himself up, struggling to regain his composure. When he reached the exit, he stopped, turned, and spoke to the onlookers, voice ice-cold.

"Mike Lorrah is a liar. What he just said is not true, and it was the ultimate insult. If you believe him, you are just as bad as he is, and you will all pay for such slander."

With that statement, he left. The two ranchers picked Mike up and started to brush him off, as a rumble of excited talk broke out in the crowd. Self-consciously, Mike looked around, wondering what everyone thought about this exchange. He looked toward the door and was mortified to see his father enter the hall, fresh off the evening train.

Morgan walked up to him, and looked at his dusty clothes and the bright red mark showing on his jaw. He took in the scene, and glared at Mike.

"Jesus, boy," he said loudly. "You come to the dance with the nice girl your mother's been telling me about, and you can't even spend part of the evening without drinking and getting into a fight. What the hell's wrong with you?'

Al Anderson, the owner of the general store, stepped up.

"Now, Morgan," he said soothingly, "It wasn't like that. Mike stood up to Bart Knight when he came in here swaggerin' around and threatening people."

Morgan shook his head.

"You're wrong, Al," he said. "Mike drinks too much, and he doesn't know when to shut his mouth. Damn fool."

Mike could only look miserably at his father, completely humiliated by his comments. He waited to see what more Morgan might have to say.

Willow rescued him. She came up to them, Della in tow, and introduced her to Morgan. Then she tugged her father's sleeve, giving him a winning smile.

"Give me one dance, Dad. You know how I love to dance with my handsome father!"

Like any other man, Morgan was helpless in the face of Willow's charms. He allowed her to lead him away to the dance floor.

Della took Mike's hand. She led him to the side of the room, near one of the lanterns to examine his jaw.

Placing a cool hand on his face, she said, "It doesn't look like it will bruise very much. Does it hurt?"

Mike felt the heat of his anger and disgrace cool immediately. Della had such a healing effect on him. If only she could be with him at all times. He swept her into his arms and they began to dance. She assured him she had seen and heard everything and that she thought he was very brave to take a strong stand against such a bully. When the dance ended, several of the local men assured him of the same thing.

"Your dad's awful hard on ya', Mike," Curley told him. "Don't you worry. I saw it all, and you were absolutely right to stand up to Bart. Is it true, what you said to him?"

"Yes," Mike said. "I know it for a fact. But I also know I probably made a real enemy tonight. Bart's not going to forget I said all that in front of so many people."

"He's a coward and a weasel," Curley said. "That was a real sucker punch he caught you with. Just watch your back, and always be ready for him. He's never going to face you in a fair fight."

These words sent a chill up Mike's spine. He was concerned for himself, to be sure, but far more concerned about Black Bird Shows. Dismissing the thoughts for the moment, he concentrated on enjoying the rest of the evening with Della.

When the dance ended, she looked up into his face.

"Oh, Mike," she said, "this was a wonderful evening. I loved the music, the dancing, and the people here in Lodge Grass are so nice. You must not worry about that awful Bart Knight. You showed him you are not a person to be intimidated, and I admire you for that."

"I hope I didn't embarrass you," Mike said.

"Never. You made me feel safe and protected. And I love it that you did not back down."

"Wish my father felt that way," Mike said sadly.

"He just did not see the entire thing," Della said. "I'm sure he'll hear more from the people who were here when it happened, and then he'll be very proud of you."

"I don't think that day will ever come," Mike whispered, arm around her as he walked her to the car.

Willow sailed up to them on the scent of her lilac perfume.

"I got Dad settled down," she said. "He'll be fine. Now, Mike. Can you take Nuala, Deidre and Della out to the ranch? I found a couple of fellas here who never dove off the sand cliff into the river at night. I'm going to show them how, and then I'll come home on one of the horses from the livery."

She vanished before any of them could respond.

CHAPTER 20

▼

Velia and Morgan were asleep when Mike delivered the O'Keefe sisters to the house. They entered quietly, and made their way to their rooms. Della paused to give Mike a light kiss on the lips, but she did not linger. Mike was too wired up to sleep, so he gathered up a towel and a lantern and made his way down to the hot spring pool. He stripped off all his clothing and slid into the water. As he floated on his back in the warmth, he gazed upward into the star-strewn blackness of the sky. He began to relax, muscles letting go of tension and aches leaving his body. He closed his eyes for a moment, and then opened them to find a gigantic white owl gliding in over its perfectly mirrored reflection to perch on one of the rocks at the edge of the pond. Mike righted himself, treading water and staring at this magnificent bird. It looked back at him, its eyes glowing gold in the darkness.

Was it an omen of some kind?

He had heard his grandmother and mother talk about such precursors many times, but could not imagine what the owl might be trying to tell him. Then he remembered something Black Bird Shows had told him about spirit animals. Could this be his? If so, he was satisfied that he could trust this creature with his life. They looked at each other a while longer, and when Mike raised one hand in a traditional Crow greeting, the bird spread its wings and lifted off from the rock with no effort. It seemed to hover over him for a moment, its perfect reflection glimmering in the water like an otherworldly creature beneath the surface. When it seemed like it might drop from the air, it swept its wings in one huge, silent beat and soared away without a sound.

Mike laid back in the water again, floating in peace. He did not even remember getting out, wrapping the towel around himself and making his way back to the house and bed. In deepest relaxation, he slept through the night. When he arose in the morning and looked in the mirror, he was pleased to note that Bart's punch had not left a bruise. The other remarkable thing was that he felt wonderful, a blessing in the wake of all he had had to drink the night before. Perhaps the hot spring did have curative powers.

He was up long before the girls, and he made sure the chores were taken care of at the barn. Morgan's horse was still there, so Mike knew he would be facing his father over the breakfast table. He sighed.

Back at the house, everyone was up. The girls looked refreshed. Morgan and Velia were sitting at the kitchen table with their cups of coffee and tea, and Willow was telling everyone about the dance. When asked about her adventure with diving at the sand cliff, she admitted that she had enticed four of the local young men to go to there in the darkness.

"Did you make the dive yourself?" Mike asked.

"Yep. I've done it so many times I can do it with my eyes shut," she chuckled, adding, "Nothing's more fun than beating luck at its own game."

"What about the fellas?" Mike asked

"You'd have to ask them."

They all knew no details would be forthcoming in front of her parents. She did not like to frighten them too much.

"Willow, you live too dangerously," Nuala laughed. "Of course, the rest of us get to experience your escapades vicariously through your stories. And we all wish we were as brave – or is it as reckless? – as you."

At this point, Morgan looked across the table at Mike.

"You look a lot better than you did last night, boy," he said.

A thousand meanings hovered just beneath the surface of the comment.

"Thank you, sir," Mike replied, hoping the deference he showed his father would keep the conversation from dwelling on the subject.

Velia sensed his discomfort, and rose from her seat.

"Let's get breakfast on the table for all of you," she said. "Then we can put together a picnic lunch, and you all can go down to that grove Willow knows about this afternoon. I know it seems a little cool, but she says it is always so nice there. It might be your last chance to take advantage of this glorious Indian Summer weather."

Nuala looked at Deidre, then back at Velia.

"That is kind of you, Mrs. Lorrah," she said. "but we agreed to go for a ride with our dates from last night. They stayed in Lodge Grass with friends and plan to come for us at ten o'clock."

"What about you, Della?" Velia asked. "Would you like to go with Mike and Willow for a picnic in the grove?"

Della smiled at Velia, and then at Mike. He felt his heart flip over.

"That sounds lovely," she said. "Please let me help you get things ready, Mrs. Lorrah."

"I'll help, too," Willow said quickly. "I can make the lemonade."

She stepped over to where Mike was sitting, tapped him on the shoulder and said, "Go on outside and enjoy the nice day until we're ready."

As Mike stood up, Willow's quick fingers reached into his shirt pocket and deftly fished out the small packet Anna had given him. Mike glanced around, but no one else was looking.

As the noon hour approached, Mike, Willow, and Della packed the lunch baskets, jars of lemonade, and blankets for sitting on the ground in Willow's car. Then they set out for a remote corner of the ranch, with Willow driving. She maneuvered the car over ruts, rocks and what appeared to be impossible obstacles, penetrating deeper and deeper into a hidden canyon cut through ancient rock by long ago streams. Della gave herself over to Willow's skill as she gazed in wonder at the fantastic stone formations. What an amazing place. It seemed so mysterious and hidden, as if straight from a fairy tale. As the canyon narrowed, the creek came closer to the track, sparkling as it rushed over boulders in its bed. Completely out of keeping for the season, the plant life became more verdant and lush, and the songs of many birds circled in the atmosphere above their heads.

At last they bounced to a stop and got out of the car. Mike gathered up the picnic supplies, and Willow and Della got the blankets to spread on the ground. They walked another fifty yards down a path that opened up into the most delightful place Della had ever seen. Massive cottonwoods grew in an almost perfect circle around a luxuriant swath of grass and wildflowers. An outer circle of mountain ash formed a tapestry of color. These were interspersed with quaking aspen trees which added their tiny applause of leaves as the three entered the space. Just outside the arc of trees was a magnificent narrow strand of a waterfall that shone like a pastel satin ribbon as it plunged some thirty feet from the cliff above, through a slot in the stone to the streambed below.

Willow kicked off her shoes and walked barefoot on the grass. Despite weather that felt chilly when they set out, this place was warm and dappled with sunlight. They arranged the food and poured themselves glasses of lemonade. Della sipped hers, finding the flavor different from any she had tasted before. The fried chicken and coleslaw vanished quickly, with all three of them exclaiming that they did not know they were so hungry. Laughter rang out as Willow finished telling them the details of the cliff diving adventure from the night before. She noted that she was not sure if she would ever hear a civil word from any of the four young men she had dared to participate. Her account of them following her determinedly to the top of the cliff, perhaps assuming that she would not actually dive off, and then three of the four backing out struck Mike and Della so funny that they laughed holding their sides.

"What happened to the fourth one?" Mike asked with a grin.

Willow shrugged.

"Who knows? I didn't stay to find out! I figured he had three friends to help him out when he got to the bottom, one way or the other."

Mike and Della chuckled to imagine the four young men thrashing around in the brush without any light. Mike knew from experience that Willow would not deliberately injure any of them, and that they might not even remember what happened the night before.

The grove was a magical place, separate from the rest of the world, and hidden from the eyes of any but those who knew it was there. Della felt she could stay there forever.

When they finished eating, Willow stood, twirled in place in a way that made Mike wonder if she was going to perform her "moon dance" here in broad daylight. As she spun, there was a quiver in the air, and it seemed the molecules of one of the big trees parted. They stared as a magnificent red fox vixen appeared there. It was bigger than an ordinary fox, and its coat was exactly the same color as Willow's rich cinnamon locks. After standing stock-still, looking at Willow for a long moment, it rose up on its hind legs to dance with her. Mike had seen her with this vixen a number of times before. As always, he remembered the fox kit that had danced with her as a toddler. Each time he saw this ritual, he wondered if it was the same animal. The dance went on, in time to the music of the birds and trees. Each step seemed to intensify the light in the grove, and when it reached its pinnacle, both Willow and the fox shimmered and then vanished.

Della gasped. Mike held his breath, waiting to see her reaction.

Wide blue eyes on his face, she asked, "Where did she go?"

Mike measured his words. What would she be able to accept?

"I'm not sure. She does this once in a rare while, and I don't know where she goes."

Della was silent. Mike waited. Finally she spoke.

"I've never seen anyone do that before. Have you?"

"A few times. Many of the Crow medicine men are able to do it."

"It looks like some kind of magic," Della said. "It isn't a parlor trick, is it?'

"No. It is real."

Mike struggled with himself for a moment, and then decided to take the plunge. He took her hand and looked directly into her puzzled eyes.

"Look, Della," he said, "you and I had a touch of this experience after our date in Hardin. I was able to come to you, even though I was in Lodge Grass.

I don't know how it happened, and I have never been able to do it again. My family has some mysterious abilities and most of them seem to be stronger in the women than in the men."

"Can your grandmother or your mother do things like this?"

"I know my grandmother has a lot of powerful skills. My mother keeps her abilities more to herself. I think that is probably because my father does not approve. My grandfather had some magic, but he did not show it to the family. I only know he did because my grandmother told me about it. He just liked being part of her life, and he was a real helpmate to her."

Mike stopped, dismayed that he had said so much, and terrified that he might be frightening Della. Desperately, he scanned her face, expecting to see fear, disbelief or revulsion. Instead, he saw a reverent and fascinated expression, magnified by the soft glow in her eyes.

"Mike," she breathed. "I knew there was something very special about you from the first moment I saw you. When you came in the door at the dance that night, my heart reached out for you. I tried to resist it, but there was no way I could."

Relief flooded over Mike.

"There is more than one side to this mystery world," he said. "I must tell you the dark side, too."

With that, he told her in detail of the night his grandfather had died, and every aspect of the dark force that resided inside him.

At the end of his tale, he said, "I will live with this thing for the rest of my life. It forces me to find people who have died and cannot be found. It haunts my dreams. And sometimes it is so unbearable that I drink to forget it is there. And when I drink, I don't stop when I should. The only time I feel safe from it is when you are with me."

This touched Della's heart and she rose to her knees, putting her arms around him. He buried his head in her shoulder, and gave a long sigh of release. The light in the grove made a gradual shift from the bright sunshine of midday to a warm golden glow. At the same time, the sounds of birds and leaves merged into a barely perceptible electric hum that vibrated in their skin. Mike lifted his head and barely brushed Della's lips with his own. It was a sensual kiss that blended their spirits and made them both lighter than air. Della pulled back for a moment.

"What about Willow? What if she comes back?"

Mike shook his head.

"She won't. When she goes off with the vixen, it is always for a very long time."

He was not sure that would be the case, but he knew Willow would not interfere with the magic of this day for him.

The light softened even more, and the humming intensified. It was not that it grew louder, but that it grew stronger. Every pore of their bodies tuned in to it, and the beating of their hearts synchronized exactly. Della wondered if she should be afraid, but she felt more serene than she ever had. Even though the day had seemed cool earlier, she now felt comfortable and content. Her body was warming inevitably to the feel of contact with Mike's, and she wanted to be closer and closer to him.

Mike was experiencing his own reactions. For the first time since he was very young, he felt completely safe and sheltered. In Della's arms he found tranquility and warmth that had long been missing from his existence. There was no awareness of the icy thing next to his heart, and he was sure that Della was the reason. He tightened his embrace, and kissed her more deeply. She responded with an ardor that she did not realize she was capable of, creating heat that built in both of them. Their kisses grew hot and more demanding, and the grove seemed to move in and conceal them. The waterfall fragmented the light, casting rainbow reflections into the gilded light within the trees. Their hands explored each other's bodies, and wherever they touched, golden paths were traced on their skin. The heat increased to blast furnace level, melding the two of them into one, neutralizing their physical presence into silvery mist. Their weightlessness levitated them above the earth into the canopy of the trees, and they made love in another dimension.

Slowly settling to the ground afterward, they reluctantly loosened their arms and legs from one another. Both were dazed to discover that they were undressed. Even though they knew they should be embarrassed, that was not the case. They looked at each other for a long time, drinking in pleasure at seeing each other's bodies fully for the first time.

Finally, they gathered up their clothing and began to dress. As ordinary light began to replace the mystical illumination among the trees, reality seeped into Mike's consciousness. He was alarmed. He looked deeply into her eyes, seeking answers she could not voice.

"Della," he said softly. "Are you all right? Did I hurt you in any way? It would break my heart if I did anything I should not have done."

He was terrified that he had taken advantage of how young she was.

"I should not have allowed Willow to leave us alone here. This grove is the place Crow people often come to experience the same thing we just did. Willow learned of it from several Crow holy women, and she comes here frequently. It never occurred to me that this would happen, and if you are troubled about it, I am so very sorry."

Della did not answer. She continued to look into his face with an unwavering gaze, and her expression was impossible to read.

Mike began to feel frightened. Now that he had found her, he could not lose her. He felt as if his life depended upon keeping her close to him. It was the only time he found any peace from the turmoil inside.

Still she did not speak. Looking away, she bent to pick up her sweater, which was the only piece of clothing she had not put back on. Slowly she shook the grass out of it, and then focused on picking imaginary leaves off it. At last, she put it on.

Eyes stinging, Mike was afraid he might cry if she did not say something. "Della?"

Deliberately, she raised her eyes to his.

"Mike, you could never do anything to hurt me. I was saving myself for the man I would marry."

This comment devastated Mike.

"Oh, God, Della. I am so sorry. I don't know why I wasn't strong enough to resist the temptation to do this. It can't be undone, I know, but I will do anything you want to make up for it."

"Mike," she said patiently, as if explaining to a child, "You aren't hearing what I am saying. I saved myself for the man I would marry. I love you. I want to marry you."

"But your parents will never approve," he said. "You are so young. We should have waited for this moment until after we were married."

"Mike! Do you mean that you *would* marry me?"

He could not understand how she could have any doubt.

"I cannot imagine life without you, Della. Of course I will marry you. The bigger question is whether you would want to be part of a family with so many mysteries. It is not an easy life, and you should think about it very carefully."

"Well," Della said. "It would all be worth it, just for a life with you. And we have time. No one needs to know what happened here in the grove. We can just keep seeing each other until I am old enough for us to marry."

A huge bubble of joy began to build in Mike's heart. He took Della's hand and dropped to his knees.

"Miss Della O'Keefe," he said, looking up at her flushed face. "Will you do me the honor of becoming my wife...when you are old enough?"

A blissful smile spread across her face.

"Mr. Michael Lorrah, of course I will be your wife. I don't believe either of us has any choice about it."

And with that, she allowed a quiet laugh to tumble from her lips, carrying with it a measure of ecstasy that wrapped itself around them both. She bent her face to kiss him on the lips, sealing their secret and their oath.

A few moments later, the sound of footsteps splashing through the stream heralded Willow's reappearance. Leaves perched in her hair, several birds flew about her, and she carried a basket woven of fresh cattail leaves. When she reached them, she tipped the basket and dozens of completely out of season wild strawberries rolled out onto the blanket. Her knowing eyes looked them over, and she laughed a full, throaty laugh filled with delight.

Dropping cross-legged to sit beside her bounty, she offered the berries to Mike and Della.

Nothing had ever tasted so sweet.

The dreamers emerged from the grove by the stream into awareness of the campfire and the forest by Clear Spring.

Colleen awoke first, with a start, and looked at Black Bird Shows.

"I need time to think about this," she said. "I don't exactly feel comfortable seeing that part of my parents' lives."

Black Bird smiled at her.

"You have just used the right words, Mike's daughter. It is part of life. These are not things to hide from those closest to us. They are things to be celebrated."

"I know, but it's my parents!" she exclaimed.

Andrew and Aisling had awakened by now and both heard what Black Bird and Colleen had said to one another.

Andrew kept his silence, but Aisling stated her observation.

"That was the most beautiful thing I have ever seen," she said. "And to think, Great Grandmother was only a few years older than me!"

This did little to calm Colleen's concerns.

"This just feels like it is getting too close for comfort," she sighed, turning to check Andrew's reaction.

He had gotten up, stretching to loosen his muscles. He leaned down, offered Colleen a hand to stand up, and planted a small kiss on top of her head.

In a low voice only she could hear, he said, "You did not seem to mind when it was you and me."

Then to Aisling, he said, "Come on, little one, let's move around a bit."

"What about you, Black Bird?" Colleen asked the old man, "Can we get anything for you?"

"I will get some water from the spring, and maybe rest some while you walk. My bones are craving a softer place. I think I will lie down on your bed in the cabin."

"Of course," Colleen assured him. "Our home is your home whenever you want. You know that."

Colleen walked a little behind Aisling and Andrew for some time as they followed one of the paths along the rim of the canyon. The awe-inspiring scale of the area always made her feel protected and separated from the confusion of the rest of the world. She was not sure what time it was, or for that matter, what day it was. Gratitude for the rich dreams filled her mind, and she was happy for the answers they brought. However, she felt like she was spying on her parents and other ancestors, now long dead, and this set off a dissonance in her heart. The events of the family's past were mysteries she had longed to penetrate, but this felt very strange to her. She caught up with her two companions.

"Andrew," she said, "Does this feel right to you? Should we know this much?"

"Black Bird would not take us down this path if it was not important," he said. "Aisling, what do you think?"

The girl was took a moment to answer..

"I wasn't sure at first," she said. "Now, I feel like it is leading us somewhere. I already learned something really important, and I really want to know even more."

"What did you learn?"

Colleen was afraid her answer would be about sex, and she was not sure it was the kind of knowledge her parents had sent her to seek on the mountain. The last thing she wanted to do was violate the trust Hugh and Naima had placed in her and Andrew. This girl was precious; maybe even the shining hope of the family legacy, and the wrong knowledge could put a stop to all of it.

Aisling smiled at her great aunt.

"I learned that there is magic in everyone. So far, we know that Great-great-great Grandmother Anna could heal, Great-great Grandmother Velia learned everything from her, and Great-grandfather Mike could solve the mystery of where lost dead people were. Great-great Aunts Willow and Moira had magic, too... Willow was all about nature, and Moira was the strong one. I have to know what happened to Moira, and whether she ever opened her spirit to what was inside of her. Can we please dream some more?"

Colleen gave Aisling a quick hug.

"I don't think we have any option," she said.

Holding hands, the three of them returned through the woods to the campfire. Black Bird emerged from the cabin. He was carrying the tea kettle.

CHAPTER 21

▼

The dream was nearly instantaneous this time. They barely had time to set their cups down before they were moving quickly through an inky sky roiling with pewter clouds. They were winged things now, no longer trees, and the Lodge Grass valley lay under two feet of swirling snow. Even in the air, the visibility was limited, and they fought to keep their direction. Finally, they could see the dim lights of Hardin, and they circled down to land on the porch of the O'Keefe household. Della and Mike were in the parlor with Seamus and Evangeline. No one looked happy.

"We want Della to finish her education," Seamus said. "I can't believe you two are so foolish."

"I did not intend to get pregnant," said Della.

"It is not your fault. Mike, you are much older than her. You should have known better. She's just a child."

Della was furious.

"I am not a child, Father. I made the decision myself, and Mike is not to blame."

Seamus did not acknowledge her statement.

"Were y' drinkin', again, Mike? It is bad for you to take advantage of an innocent young woman."

Mike tried to formulate his answer, recalling the day in the grove, and how neither one of them could have done anything differently. There had been no way to know that one mysterious afternoon would result in Della becoming pregnant. When Della had written to tell him that she was sure she was expecting, she had assured him over and over again that it he had done nothing wrong. They agreed that her parents had to be told. Mike knew she was fearful and he wanted to stand by her with her family, but he had no idea what they should do beyond that.

"It wasn't like that, sir. I love your daughter and I want to marry her."

"Her mother and I cannot give you permission for that. She'll stay with us and finish school this year. She should be able to do that without anyone knowing. Then she'll go to relatives and have this baby. I have a sister in the East who will adopt it, and she can come back as if nothing has happened. We can't have her shamed in front of our community."

Seamus's stern declaration left no room for anyone to argue.

"I think you'd better leave now, Mike," Evangeline said.

Della rose to see him to the door.

"No, Della," her mother said. "Let him find his own way out. We don't need the likes of him spending any more time with you."

Della ignored the order. Tears streaming down her face, she took Mike's arm and walked him through the house to the door.

"I'll come with you tonight," she said simply. "They can't keep me from marrying you."

Mike reached in his pocket for a handkerchief. He wiped her tears, then took her face in both his hands.

"You know, my love, they are right about you getting your education. Please stay in school and I'll come for you when classes end for the summer."

He squeezed his eyes shut to hold back his own tears, then looked at her earnestly again.

She shook her head violently.

"No! I don't want to be apart from you for that long. Please don't make me do this!"

She began to cry again.

"It will be fine. I'll write to you every day, and we'll be together when summer comes," Mike assured her. "I want you and I want this baby. It was conceived in powerful magic and it will be a powerful child. We must be together."

With a final soft kiss on Della's lips, he opened the door. The storm hit him full in the face, pelting his cheeks with bits of ice and snow. For once he was glad he had come on the train. Trying to drive any car in this weather would be hazardous, and he did not want anything to threaten his safety or hers. Shoving his hands deep into his jacket pockets he slogged miserably through the drifts to the depot to catch the last train to Lodge Grass that night. His spirit was turbulent, one regret chasing another through his mind. How could things have gone so wrong? A love that should have been the best thing in his life now had him at odds with Della's family. And to have put her in such an awkward position made him furious with himself.

Up until a month or so ago, he had believed that he could handle any adversity. There had been excellent prospects that the part-time job he had picked up working on an oil rig in the area would expand into something permanent. It would have meant a good wage that would support a bride and a family. The Depression put an end to that, and now even the wrangling jobs on local ranches were either gone or paid only in room and board for the cowboy.

He kicked at a lump of snow in the street, venting his frustration.

It made a clinking sound as a piece of the lump broke loose and rolled along the stones of the street. He bent down and peered at it. It was a half-empty bottle of cheap whiskey that must have been lost by some cowboy or sheepherder in town for the winter. Mike picked it up, and wiped the mud and snow off it, then tucked it into the big inside pocket of his winter coat. He could use a little antifreeze while he waited for the train to come.

When he got to the depot, it was deserted except for the station agent, who was a stranger to him. Mike told him he was there to catch the late train, and the man told him it was on time despite the weather. Mike took a seat on the wrought iron and wooden bench that sat against the wall. The agent went back to his work.

Uncorking the bottle, Mike took a long draught from it and nearly choked. It was some of the worst tasting liquor he had ever encountered, including the local moonshine. However, the heat it spread through his body as it sluiced its fiery way to his stomach brought comfort and drove the chill away. If one drink felt that good, another should feel even better. He drank again, a bigger swallow this time.

The remaining whiskey was nearly gone by the time the train arrived, but Mike tucked the bottle back into his pocket before he boarded the passenger car. When he tripped on the steps, he was sure the ice and snow had created the problem, and he pointedly did not look into the disgusted face of the conductor. Holding on to each aisle seat, he made his way to an empty place and sat down hard as the train started to move. The next thing he knew, the conductor was waking him up to get off in Lodge Grass.

In the late hour, the train station was as abandoned as the Hardin depot had been. Mike's feet skidded on the wooden walkway as he made his way to the livery barn. He dimly remembered that the discussion with Della's parents had gone badly, but the evening was pretty much lost in the mist of alcohol that fogged his mind. He stumbled into the back room and fell onto his cot fully dressed, pulling a blanket partly over himself. The cold had little effect on him through the layers of his coat.

Morning arrived too soon, and he came to consciousness slowly and painfully. The sounds of the night man moving about to feed the horses seemed far too loud. As a matter of fact, even the sounds of the animals chewing their morning ration of oats sounded like the smashing of a rock crusher. Mike moaned.

Jim, the night man, looked down from the hayloft ladder at the miserable young man.

"Hey, Mike!" he called, grinning as he saw his audience flinch at the sound, "Your old man's lookin' for ya'!"

Could things get any worse?

"Where is he?" Mike asked.

"Over at the café. He came by here last night, and didn't seem happy that you were gone."

Mike stood up shakily. He moved over to stand closer to the little potbelly stove, grateful for its warmth. After pouring himself a cup of coffee from the old enamelware camp coffeepot, he peered at himself in the tiny shaving mirror and was embarrassed at what he saw. The day-old growth of beard, the bloodshot eyes, and the hang-dog expression made him think of the depression bums he often saw begging for a handout near the bars in Hardin. He could not do much about the bloodshot eyes, but he hurried to take care of shaving, brushing his teeth, and combing his hair. A clean shirt made him feel like he was presentable enough to go talk to Morgan.

When he stepped out of the livery, the light of day nearly knocked him back. The storm had left a layer of fresh white snow over everything in the town, and the sun was bouncing off it with such intensity it felt like hundreds of shining needles piercing his eyes. He was tempted to go back to bed. But he knew he had to face his father sooner or later. Now was as good a time as any.

Morgan was sitting in the café with two other men, eating breakfast and drinking coffee. He looked up when Mike entered, and motioned for him to come to the empty seat next to him.

Mike braced himself for whatever criticism might be leveled at him, but none was forthcoming. Instead, Morgan introduced him to the men he was with, keeping the insult subtle.

"This is Bronc Williams and Tony Jamison," he said. "They came in yesterday to talk about running sheep up in the Dryhead. They think they'd like to hire you to work for them up there, tending camp and moving the herders. I told them you're a little soft when it comes to handling horses and cows, but sheep might be the perfect thing for you."

Bronc Williams pointedly ignored Morgan's jab and looked Mike directly in the eye.

"Mike," he said, "We've heard good things about you from several of the ranchers in the area, and we know you have a good relationship with the Crows, too. As you probably know, the tribe can make it easier or harder for a man working that country. It means a lot to them to be able to trust whoever's up there. In fact, that's what happened with the last ranch manager. He crossed the Indians, and they ran him off. Let his horses loose, scared the sheep away, and generally made his existence miserable. From what we hear, that won't be a problem with you."

Mike was familiar with the Dryhead Ranch. It was in country that he had explored with Black Bird Shows on several hunting trips, and he had been there to look for stray cattle a few times. It was deep in the Pryor Mountains, and the road was nearly impassible once winter came on. You could make your way into the area on horseback through the Big Horn Mountains, and it was likely that hauling hay and other supplies would have to be done with a big horse-drawn sled.

"I don't know anything about sheep," Mike said.

"Got anything against 'em?" the man named Bronc asked.

"No," Mike said. "When would this job start?"

"Not 'til spring. The herders are all in for the winter, except one who stayed at the place, and we'd be trailing the sheep up there when the grass gets good."

"I'll go look at it. You're sure you don't mind if I take a few days to think about it?" Mike asked, noting his father's annoyed expression.

"Look, boy, these men are offering you a perfectly good job, and they don't need to be kept waiting," Morgan growled.

Tony Jamison spoke up.

"Morgan," he said, "It's a big decision. He can have some time. Mike, we're going to be here in Lodge Grass for a couple of weeks, getting some leases in order. I'd suggest you get up to the Dryhead and see what you think. As I said, one of the herders, Dónal O'Reilly, stayed up there for the winter, as caretaker and watchman. You go up, and when you come back down, we'll talk again."

"I'll be glad to go and have a look. Probably take me longer each way with this weather. I'll have an answer for you no later than two weeks from now," Mike confirmed.

"Fair enough," Tony agreed.

"Thank you, sir," Mike said, standing and shaking each man's hand.

As he started to walk out of the restaurant, Morgan followed him to the door.

"Mike," he said in a cool, quiet voice, "You'll take this job if you have any sense. With the bad news at the banks these days, there aren't a lot of good jobs around. And with all the drinking you're doing, you'd do well to be up there away from temptation. You're a real embarrassment to the family, and your mother's pretty unhappy with what she hears about it."

Mike stared at the toes of his boots. Morgan was an enigma to him. This morning, when he had fully expected him to attack with recriminations, his father seemed to be trying to find a way to set him on the straight and narrow. Or was this a way to get him out of town and out of the way?

Looking into the older man's eyes, Mike asked, "How much do you know about this sheep operation?"

Morgan's gaze was level and impossible to read.

"Actually, I bought into it. The cattle business is suffering right now with the tough winters and the drought. I sold off some of my cows, and figured sheep couldn't do any worse. Ain't a lot of prestige in 'em, but they're a better bet than cows right now. I know you'll be honest and that I can trust you, at least as far as work is concerned. And I want you out of town. Seamus O'Keefe called me this morning, and he's plenty mad at you and Della. It won't hurt for you to be away from that."

The breath caught in Mike's throat. Of course his parents would find out sooner or later, but he had hoped for later. The very thought of being away from Della was wrenching, yet he needed steady work in these hard times. Marrying Della when school was out in the spring was his number one goal, and he would have to have a job if that was going to happen. He would not be required to go to the Dryhead until then, so he could stay in Lodge Grass through the winter. The prospect of working for his father was not ideal, but in view of the circumstances, it might be best for all involved. The other side of that thought was that he realized his father thought he was trying to help Mike with his problems.

Mike nodded.

"You're right," he said. "Thank you. Does Mother know?"

"Yep," Morgan said matter-of-factly, I told her you'd do this, so I'm glad you see the light. She's very upset about this thing with the O'Keefe girl."

Mike turned and trudged out of the café into the windblown snow. Melancholy sat heavily upon his heart, and he wanted more than ever to talk with Della. He went back into the livery stable and sat down heavily on his cot. Then he gathered his things into a bundle and took them to his grandmother's house.

He knocked, opened the door and walked into the kitchen area. Anna was just pouring herself a cup of tea. He sat the bundle down and gave her a quick hug, trying not to get too much snow on her. She filled another cup for him, and they sat down together without saying anything. Silence filled the room for a minute or two, then Mike told her everything about the confrontation with Della's parents, and Morgan's plans for him to go to the Dryhead Ranch.

Anna looked at him for a few moments, considering what he had told her.

"What will ye be doin' next?" she asked.

"I figured I should go up to the ranch and see what is there. I'm going to have to spend the winter educating myself about the sheep business. I want to talk to some of the other ranchers and find out what I need to know. The herd is down in lower pastures for the winter, so I can see them on my way up or down from the mountain."

Anna's face took on a peaceful demeanor.

"The raisin' of sheep'll be comin' easy to y'," she said. "The Irish have had sheep for centuries. It's in yer blood."

"I don't think it works like that, Grandmother," Mike said gently. "I know I have an awful lot to learn. They are so different from cattle."

"Y'll be surprised, Michael. Y'll do fine."

"I'll just have to feel my way along," he said. "There's another thing I wanted to talk to you about. It's about Della and me."

Anna smiled.

"And the wee baby," she said.

"You already know?"

"I knew the day he was conceived," she said. "Four magpies were in me trees...*Four for a birth...*"

"What shall I do?" Mike asked. "My dad wants to send me up the Dryhead Ranch in the spring, but that will put me awfully far away from Della until school is out. I don't think I'll be able to stand it."

"Michael," Anna said patiently, "All things in good time. When the two of ye are ready, I'll help with the ancient words. Let things settle a bit, see how events move along."

Her statements eased Mike's concerns, although nothing had changed for him and Della. He knew his grandmother would not tell him more at this time, but he also believed that she was indicating that he and Della would be together to welcome their baby into the world. He finished his tea and stood to embrace Anna.

"Thank you, Grandmother," he said. "I hope you are right. If you don't mind, I'm going to leave this bedroll with you until I go up to the Dryhead. I'll pick it up when I get supplies. Right now, I want to go out to the ranch and see Mother."

The snow was still skittering along the icy street when he returned to the livery barn to saddle his horse. Pal was ready and willing, as usual, and Mike talked softly to him.

"Sorry to take you out in this awful weather, old boy," he murmured. "Lucky you've got a good coat of winter hair. I'll put you in a nice warm stall when we get there."

CHAPTER 22

▼

When Mike arrived at the ranch, he kept his promise to Pal, and tucked him away in a stall with fresh straw, a portion of oats in the feeder, and a bucket of warm water from the spring. Then he walked up the hill in the snowy track, wondering what state of mind he would find his mother in when he reached the house. He was relieved to see that Morgan had not come home yet, and hoped this would give him the opportunity to have a good conversation with Velia.

"Hello, Mother," he called as he went in the door and bent to remove his wet boots.

"Hello, Mike," she replied quietly.

He made his way up the short flight of steps and entered the warmth of the kitchen with its wonderful smells of cinnamon and fresh bread.

His mother was sitting at the table, peeling apples from the root cellar. She looked at him with a direct gaze that made him uncomfortable.

"Father tells me you know what has happened," he said.

"I do."

"I'm sorry if I have embarrassed you, Mother. I would never hurt you intentionally," he said.

"I know that, Mike," she replied. "And I believe this will all turn out all right. It was a shock, but things seem to happen for a reason. A man with as much magic as you have is not meant to have an ordinary life. There is something in the fates that makes it important for you to have your son now."

"Father was calmer than I expected," Mike said.

"He has hope that this may cause you to turn your life around. The alcohol is eating away at your future."

"I know," he admitted. "The Dryhead Ranch will certainly take me a long way from temptation."

"Temptation is always there. You can not just go away from it. It will follow you, and you have to learn to fight it."

He was silent at this comment. Deep inside, it rang true, but it was not something he wanted to admit just yet.

Velia gave her son lunch, and they ate in companionable silence. Willow was not at home, and Morgan did not return. Mike went back down to the barn and made sure the other horses had hay and oats for the day. Then he began to pull together the supplies he would need to make the long trip to the Dryhead. It would take him at least three days of steady riding to get there, and he made sure he had enough food and gear to allow for overnight camps and meals. There would be supplies at the place itself, and ranchers along the way would offer hospitality, too. He would start out the following morning, after talking with Morgan about what else he should take. That night, he wrote a letter to Della, detailing the offer he had received to go to the Dryhead, and declaring his love for her.

> *My darling Della,*
>
> *I hope you are doing okay after our discussion with your parents. It tears me apart to find myself separated from you at this difficult time. I dream of you, I think of you, I feel you in the very core of me. I know in my heart that eventually, your mother and father will understand we are meant to be together, along with our baby. I have been offered a job working with sheep up at the Dryhead Ranch...that's in the Pryor Mountains...and tomorrow I will leave to go see the place. It will be a while before I can write to you again, so please read this same letter over and over, and pretend it is a new one sent to you every day until I am back to a place with a post office.*
>
> *Your father has talked with my father, so both he and my mother know about us. My grandmother assures me that things will turn out all right, but both my parents worry about my drinking, and tell me I should have been more responsible in my actions. I know I can be a better man and by the time school is out maybe we can make a home at that distant ranch, away from everyone who might judge us and those who might try to get me to drink with them.*

You are my love and my life, and all I think of night and day.
Please keep me in your heart until I come back, for you are
surely in mine.

With all my love,

Your Irish Mike

He put it into an envelope, sealed it and placed a stamp on it. Then he crawled into his bed, and lay awake, remembering earlier times when he had slept in this room. He missed his sisters, and all the enchantments they had shared with him. Adulthood was bearing down on him ferociously, and he was not sure he was ready.

At last he slept, dreams eddying about him but leaving no memories.

When he woke the following morning, physical and emotional exhaustion had settled over his entire being. He peered outside, and his spirit lifted to see the sun beginning to rise in a clear sky, casting pre-dawn light that turned the snow covered fields into sparkling pink carpets. The smells of coffee and bacon drew him to the kitchen, and Morgan was waiting for him at the table.

"It's probably best you are going up to look at the Dryhead now," he said. "It could be a tough trip in worse weather. But it's a good idea to go and see it. When you get back, we can decide when you go up there for good, and what supplies you'll need. Don't take any liquor along. You'll want a clear head to make sure you don't get into any trouble on the way."

Resentment boiled up in Mike. He hated the fact that his father did not trust him to behave responsibly. But he did not respond to the comment. There was no use in getting into an argument with Morgan before he left. Nothing would be gained by such an exchange.

After eating breakfast, Mike pulled on his wool pants, heavy coat, and gloves and wrapped a scarf around his head before putting on his hat. He went to the barn, caught Pal and rigged a Decker saddle on one of the pack horses. He put a few provisions from the ranch into the pannier, then tied a cloth bag with biscuits, bacon, dried beans and venison jerky to his own saddle. Finally, he secured his scabbard with his trusty Winchester, and stepped up onto Pal's back. The pack horse's lead rope was dallied around the saddle horn, and he checked to make sure it was solid. This done, he set off for Lodge Grass, where he bought enough additional supplies at the general store for the trip, loaded them and his bedroll on the pack horse, and mailed his letter. With a sense of finality, he rode out, heading up country toward the mountains. The horses danced a bit with the cold at the beginning, but gradually, they settled into a consistent pace that covered the ground quickly enough.

As they began to gain elevation, the snow became deeper in spots, and Mike was glad to see that the old wagon trail he followed had blown clear where it ran along the ridges. It was easier on the horses not to have to plod through drifts as they ascended the foothills. He stopped in the middle of the day to take a break, near a little creek that had not yet frozen over. Pal and the pack horse drank from the water, and then pawed up a little grass from beneath the snow. Mike dug into his saddlebag for some biscuits and venison jerky to satisfy his own hunger and stood on a high point to gaze back over the route he had just covered. It was hard not to marvel at the panorama that sprawled out in front of him. From where he was, he could see back across the Lodge Grass Creek and Little Big Horn River valleys. White strands of smoke spiraled up out of a few houses and cabins far below, and the early winter sun cast long shadows out across the hills.

It was beautiful, but at the same time, Mike thought he had never felt so alone. He was unsure of what was ahead for him, and he was the only one who could decide on the future of his life. As he stepped off the rock to return to his horses, the same huge white owl he had seen before floated silently out of the trees, and came to rest on a rock outcropping, eye to eye with him.

"So you are back again," Mike said. "I wish I knew what your visits meant. At least I feel a little less alone with you here."

The owl only stared at him with gilded eyes, blinking occasionally, but uttering no sound. Finally it lifted off, and flew into the shelter of a big pine tree.

Mike mounted up again, and Pal stepped into his steady gait, the pack horse following in good order. The trail was becoming steeper, and with the snow underfoot, Mike wanted to take great care in letting Pal choose his way. Suddenly, the owl appeared again, this time soaring in front of them, just up the trail. It landed, and looked at him and the horses, as if to assure them they were following the right route. Mike watched, fascinated. The big bird repeated this action over and over again, keeping him company, and reassuring him about the direction he was taking.

The next time Mike stopped to stretch and let the horses rest, he noticed that the temperature had dropped and he wondered if his weather gear was going to be enough to keep him comfortable. He jogged his feet a bit to warm them, although he was glad to note that the double pair of wool socks he had pulled on seemed to be doing their job. The snow was about a foot deep at this elevation, and the trail was moving up the ridge at a more accelerated rate. He had covered much ground already, and was satisfied that his plan to get to the first line camp cabin for the night was a good one. By his calculation, it was only about two hours away, and that would put him there long before sunset. This realization injected extra energy in his actions as he got back on

Pal's back and rode the rest of the way to the Clear Spring line camp. When he crested the last hill, he could see the little building ahead.

His grandfather and father had built this cabin, along with several others, placing them strategically throughout the grazing range. It was a sturdy, if rudimentary, shelter that served as a camp for cowboys working in the mountains. Mike suspected it had served as an occasional hideout during some of Morgan's questionable horse operations, as well. There was no doubt that the walls still held the secrets and sweat of many such expeditions. It was the mid-way point between the home ranch and the high summer pastures, and a great stopping point on the route through the mountain. Mike loved the diminutive shack, with its wood-burning camp stove, wood floors, and sweet-water spring near the back door. It was his job to make sure it was fully stocked with necessities to welcome the men who might have cause to use it.

There was a lean-to shed at the side of it where he stacked firewood every summer, making sure visitors would be able to stoke the wood stove without having to go out and search for fuel. There also was enough hay and straw to make the horses comfortable. A sealed barrel kept a supply of oats safe from rodents who might wish to lay claim to a share for themselves. He removed the saddles and packs and gave each horse a healthy scoop of the grain, a sheaf of hay, and a bucket of the pure water from Clear Spring. As he did so, he stroked them and thanked them for their hard work that day. Here, as at the home ranch hot spring, his grandfather had diverted a small portion of the water through a pipe for easier access. Mike filled another bucket for making coffee and washing his face the following morning. When he pulled the latch string to enter the cabin after these chores, he found himself face to face with Black Bird Shows, who was sitting in one of the two rough-hewn chairs at the little table.

"Where did you come from?" Mike asked with a laugh. "I didn't see any tracks out there in the snow."

Black Bird chose not to answer the question.

"Thought you might like some company on your ride," he said. "No man should go alone to a new life."

"How did you know?"

"An owl told me."

"I was about to make up a little supper," Mike said. "I've got some of Mother's good biscuits and some beans and bacon. You hungry?"

"I have some elk steak, too," Black Bird replied. "I don't think we are going to starve!"

What had looked to be a lonely night on the mountain turned in to an evening of talk and camaraderie. Black Bird Shows told Mike about his travels, including several forays into Yellowstone National Park. It was part of the ancestral hunting area for the Crow and he had explored it in some depth.

He described it as a place of unique boiling and steaming waters, canyons and a wealth of wildlife. It was apparent that Black Bird had been in many remote parts of the park that were not on the usual sight-seeing routes. Although Mike had read a great deal about the park in newspapers and magazines, it was more compelling for him to hear his friend's first-hand account. He promised himself that he would go there with Black Bird sometime soon.

More importantly, Mike wanted to ask Black Bird about the Dryhead country and the Pryor Mountains.

"I've been up there a few times, including those hunting trips with you," he said, "but now that I'm going to live there, I need to know more."

Black Bird nodded his head, dark eyes looking off into some distant world outside the cocoon of the cabin.

"The Pryor Mountains, we call them *Baáhpuuo Isawaxaawíua* in Crow, which means Hitting the Rock Mountains. They are living things, a part of our lifeblood. Along with the Big Horn Mountains, they are where the Little People, the *Awakkulé,* live. You know about the *Awakkulé?*"

Mike was thoughtful.

"I've heard a lot of the older Crow people talk about them," he said. "I always thought those stories were fables, stories told to illustrate a point. You talk about the Little People as if they are real."

"They *are* real. The main reason I came to ride with you was to make sure you knew about them and knew to respect them."

Blackbird's statement was emphatic and left no room for argument.

"Have you ever seen them?"

"Very few people ever see them. Seeing them matters little. They are the guardians of the Pryors and the Big Horns, the holders of the land. They are very powerful, and they watch over people. If you do good things, they make sure you are helped. If you do bad things, it is hard to tell how they will punish you, but they will find a way to make you wish you had not been on the wrong side. And evil...they have no tolerance for it."

Black Bird told him that the Crow People leave offerings to the *Awakkulé* at certain locations in and around the Pryor and Big Horn Mountains, and he related one of the ancestor stories about them.

"The old ones say the Awakkulé have lived in these mountains for a very long time. They are a tribe of very small people, and they live in caves and other shelters up here. They are not dwarfs, but perfectly proportioned small people. They live according to the old ways long before the reservation and white men. It is a way of life connected to the earth, eating what the prairies and forests give them and disturbing nothing. Their days are tied to the changing seasons and the phases of the moon and sun.

"Almost no one, Crow people or others, have ever seen them. They only show themselves to a few very powerful medicine people they believe they can trust. It is their manner to keep out of sight, because they know how many mistakes we people make, and how we don't always treat each other right. If you pay attention, you may see signs that they are there and when the times are right, you might catch sight of their movements and shadows. They seek caves and cracks in the ground to make sure they stay invisible. There is a place called Arrow Rock in the Pryor Gap where they have been seen most often by the holy people. We believe it is one of the main places where they make their homes.

"The Crow people respect the Little People, and we leave them gifts when we pass through that place. We acknowledge them by placing a rock on the cairn that has grown there. It is a very large heap of rocks now, so you would know that many, many people have honored them.

"The Crow have countless stories of how they have touched our people. The oldest one is about a mother and father whose baby got lost when they were moving camp ahead of an enemy war party. They were moving too fast, and the child got left. They tried to go back, but they were not able to get past the enemies. They looked everywhere they could, but they did not find him.

"Many years they grieved. The mother cried and pulled out her hair. The father cut off one of his fingers, and several pieces of his flesh. Their hearts were on the ground.

"Then one day, many years later, a man came into their camp. They did not know him at first, but it was their son. He had grown, and he looked very well. They were so happy, but they were puzzled, too. They asked him how this could be. He was so young when he was lost that they had been sure he was dead.

"He told them that a tribe of very small people had saved him. They took him to their cave where they kept him warm and fed him. He was never afraid. But the Little People knew his mother and father were very sad. And they knew there were no other children for them. When the Crow people passed this way again, the Little People got him ready, dressing him in fine clothes and telling him his parents were coming. When the time was right, they brought him to the camp and sent him to where his mother and father had their lodge.

"He stayed with his mother and father for the rest of their lives, and while he was like his clan in most ways, he was considered to be big medicine because of what had happened to him. My uncle, Takes the Hawk, said his own father's grandfather saw some of the Awakkulé in the mountains."

Black Bird sat back, filling and lighting his white clay pipe, the *dudeen* that had belonged to Frank Daly. Blue circles of smoke drifted up and traced shadow patterns from the lantern on the cabin's walls and ceiling. To Mike, it felt like they were on another plane, in a different time and place. He

171

was comforted by Black Bird's presence, his stories, and his friendship. The journey he had to make seemed far less lonely now.

They slept well that night, and without alcohol to affect his well-being, Mike awoke clear and rested when the sun probed the interior of the cabin through the diminutive windows. He made a small fire in the stove to brew coffee, and they ate some of the bacon and biscuits and the leftover beans from dinner. They allowed the fire to go out, and stepped outside to prepare to leave. Mike found Black Bird's ghostly grulla horse in the lean-to with Pal and the pack horse, and shook his head. He wondered how his friend did the things he did, but decided it was enough that he showed up when needed. It was the best of luck to have a person like Black Bird as his friend and companion, and it should not be questioned.

They mounted up and set out for the next line camp, traveling as quickly as conditions allowed. The weather continued to favor them with sunshine and little wind, and they made their way with no trouble at all. The big snows had not yet come to this part of the mountains, and the minimal white layer that had fallen was beginning to melt off as the day warmed. Indian summer still had some mild days to offer them.

At one point, they arrived at a rock cairn that appeared to be very old. It was about six feet high, and seemed to have been built one rock at a time in a very careful stacking. Each rock fit perfectly in its place, and there was almost no space between any of the rocks.

Black Bird Shows dismounted and pulled down his parflesche from his horse's back. He untied the leather strings that held this rawhide bag closed, and retrieved an exquisitely beaded turtle fetish. As Mike watched, Black Bird placed it carefully in a niche that had been constructed in the cairn.

"What are you doing?" Mike asked. "That's such a beautiful piece of beadwork."

"It is a gift for the *Awakkulé*," Black Bird replied. "It is important to always leave something for them when you cross their lands."

"Is this part of their lands?"

"Yes. I wanted to be sure they knew you recognized that, and that you mean them no harm."

Mike trusted what Black Bird told him, and he understood the point his friend was making.

"Just a minute," he said, "I think I have something for them, too."

He patted his pockets, and retrieved a shiny silver dollar.

"Will this be the right thing for my first time?" he asked.

Black Bird looked at Mike to see if he was serious. Then a warm smile spread across his face.

"It is exactly right," he said. "You want to hand it down to me?"

"Nope," Mike replied, sliding off his horse. "I'd like to place it here myself, if you think that is all right."

Black Bird stepped back from the cairn, making space for Mike to put his gift next to the exquisite beaded turtle. They stood silently for a moment, thinking about the Little People, then went back to their horses and mounted up again.

They reached the second camp, the one at Sun Point, late in the afternoon. It was unoccupied, and they made themselves comfortable in the accommodation. Since the evening was still temperate, they sat inside, but kept the door of the cabin open. As they were eating the sandwiches they had made from some of the leftover elk meat, Black Bird tapped Mike's shoulder and pointed out the door to the clear space by the front step. A beautiful red fox sat on a flagstone looking in at them. Its russet coat sparkled with drops of melting snow, and its luxuriant tail formed a circle around its feet. It had unusual eyes, blue in color, and it watched them for a long time before turning and loping off across the snow of the meadow.

They spent the evening talking about their previous adventures together, and planning for future hunting trips. Mike was at ease with Black Bird, and they finally decided they should get some sleep so they would be ready for the following day's ride.

Black Bird stretched out and immediately fell into a deep sleep with a practiced skill that Mike envied. Mike remained awake longer, but with the happy tiredness he felt in his friend's company, he finally drifted off.

Mike slept soundly for most of the night. At some point, he drifted into a dream state and he found himself peering through a wall of snow crystals, trying to discern what shadowy being was hidden just beyond his sight. Finally the sparkling barrier lifted, and he could see that it was the fox they had glimpsed earlier. As he watched, it transformed in a shower of frozen particles to take an entirely different shape.

It was Willow. She was dressed in a short, luminous dress that seemed to be constructed of frost, and her bare feet appeared to stand on the snow without sinking in. She stayed outside, and beckoned Black Bird Shows and Mike to come out to where she stood. When they did, she took both of Black Bird Shows hands first, in a warm greeting. Then she embraced Mike and kissed him on the cheek.

Mike stepped back, a hand on each of her shoulders. Looking deep into her eyes, he asked, "Willow...what the heck are you doing here?"

"I couldn't let you go all the way to the Dryhead without seeing you, could I?" she replied. "I had to be sure you were all right."

Mike started to relate to her all that had happened with Della and with Morgan. Willow stopped him.

"I know all that. What happened in the grove the day we picnicked there was by design. Because Moira has abandoned the magic, and you and I are not willing to carry the burden of it forward, the next generation must begin," she said.

Mike stared at her.

"Don't I have any say in this? Why do I have to be the one to provide children for this inheritance? It's a damn curse, not a legacy!"

Then, shocked at his own words, he added, "I *do* want this baby. It is just that the timing is completely wrong."

Willow gave a little shrug of her shoulders.

"Now, Mike, you know Moira will not be having children. She is Sister Mary Cecelia now. And if I ever do have children, it will most likely be a long time from now, and I probably will not be the best mother to bring them to the legacy. Who knows how they'll turn out with me as a mother? You are our best hope for the magic to survive."

In the dream, Black Bird had listened to this exchange impassively. He always had been bemused by Willow. She was like some exotic creature that he could not understand or communicate with, but she fascinated him. She was nothing like the tribal women he was accustomed to, and Mike knew he felt like the earth was not completely solid under his feet when in her presence. But she was Mike's sister, and that had always been enough.

"How do I know these children will be magic?" Mike asked her.

"Mike," she said gently, "You know as well as I do that there is magic in *everybody*. Isn't that so, Black Bird Shows?"

Speechless at the question, Black Bird could only nod, his expression serious.

Willow smiled brilliantly.

"It will all be just fine, Mike. There's no question of it," she declared. "And I'll turn up every so often!"

And with a laugh like the tinkling of a wind chime, she disappeared in a little gleaming whirlwind of snowflakes.

Mike woke up. He found himself standing outside on the stoop, Black Bird Shows at his side. His dream did not fade with his awakening, and when he looked at Black Bird, his friend put one hand on his shoulder. The two of them were silent for a long time.

Black Bird finally spoke.

"That was enough to give you pause, wasn't it?" he asked.

"Did that really happen? Was that *real?*" Mike was very confused.

Black Bird did not answer, going back into the cabin. Mike followed, to bank the fire, clean up the camp dishes, and roll up the bedrolls.

The light of day was coming soon and they would spend this day finishing the journey.

CHAPTER 23

▼

Dawn found them on the trail as the sun cleared the horizon on another cloudless sky. The shots of pink and orange light painted the remaining snow with unworldly colors. Mike and Black Bird talked little, and neither mentioned Willow's appearance of the night before. They both reveled in the spectacle of the mountains and the wildlife that began to move about at this early hour.

Several herds of elk presented themselves, and Mike noted that they did not seem aware of his and Black Bird's passage. Even the huge bulls with their gigantic antlers did not acknowledge them. Later in the day, a pack of wolves, five strong, crossed their path and paused, sniffing the air. The alpha male and female were black, and their sulphur yellow eyes glowed so deep, Mike thought a man might become lost if he looked into them too long. After a few moments, the group began its gliding lope across the snowy meadow, seeming not to touch the ground with their feet. Again, it was as if Mike and Black Bird were invisible.

With a stop for a midday meal, they made good progress, covering most of the remaining distance to the Dryhead before twilight. As they started up the last few miles of the road leading into the ranch, Mike turned to Black Bird.

"I'd probably better ride in first," he said, "Just in case this man Dónal O'Neill has something against Indians."

"I'll ride in with you," Black Bird Shows said. "He won't know I'm there."

Mike glanced at him and saw this assertion was accurate. Black Bird and his horse were hard to see in the gloaming of the day. The setting sun laid a blue grey hue across the country and his friend blended into it. It was spooky, but he trusted Black Bird, and they rode on. The grulla horse made almost no sound in the snow, and since Black Bird rode with little rigging, the quiet was complete. Mike shivered.

In front of the ranch buildings and corrals, Mike stepped down from his horse. There was no light at the main house, but the windows of the bunkhouse glowed warmly and smoke curled from the chimney. Mike knocked at the door and called out for Dónal. The light in the windows told him the man was inside.

He called out again, and there was a sound of a heavy board being removed from where it barricaded the door. The entrance was opened by a tall, black haired man with broad shoulders. He was carrying a rifle, and there was a suspicious expression on his face.

"Hello," Mike said. "I'm Mike Lorrah, and you must be Dónal O'Neill. Bronc wanted me to come up and look the place over to see if I wanted to work here next spring. He told me you'd decided to stay on for the winter, so I'm hoping you can show me around the place tomorrow. Is that agreeable to you?"

The man relaxed visibly, shrugging in apology.

"Of course 'tis," Dónal said. "Sorry 'bout the gun. Y' never know who could be comin' to yer door."

"I have a friend with me," Mike said. "He's a Crow Indian, and I hope you won't have a problem with that."

"'Tis not Indians I'd be leery about," Dónal said. "Tell him to come in."

"We'll put the horses in the corral and give them some oats and hay," Mike said, "then we'll both be in."

Dónal rumbled in agreement, and closed the door against the cold. Mike walked toward the barns, Pal following him, and the pack horse being led by its halter rope, which was still looped around Pal's saddle horn. Black Bird was already in the barn, feeding and rubbing down his horse. They worked together to take care of the other two horses, then made their way to the bunkhouse. When they entered, Dónal was cooking up some bacon and beans on the small wood stove that served as heat source and cooking surface. He reached into a wooden box and pulled out a round loaf of bread. Looking at the cross cut into the top of it, Mike recognized it as soda bread like that his mother and grandmother made regularly. Dónal looked up at the sound of their footsteps, and when he saw Black Bird Shows, his eyes widened. He stared until Black Bird Shows broke the silence.

"Did I grow a second nose?" he asked, the hint of a smile twitching at the edge of his mouth.

Dónal reddened.

"Sorry," he said. "You'd be the first Indian I been this close to."

"What do you think?"

"You have some size on ya'" Dónal said. "I expected y' t' be a shorter man."

"Why?"

"There was a slew of footprints in the snow over by the rimrock next to the corral. I thought they must be Indian tracks. They looked like moccasin tracks. But they were wee ones."

Blackbird's eyebrows shot up.

"How *wee?*" he said, emphasizing the word.

Dónal held up his hand, showing a span between thumb and first finger. "Like this."

Black Bird was thoughtful.

"I'm not so sure those were Crow Indian tracks," he said. "There are more who live in this area than Crow and white."

"Like who?" Mike asked.

"This area is said to be one of the places most important to the *Awakkulé*," Black Bird said slowly. "It's rare to see their tracks, but it does happen. They have to have a reason to be someplace. And the smallest thing can make them go away and not come back. I wonder what they are doing here."

"You seem to be pretty sure that the tracks are theirs," Mike said. "Why?"

Dónal had stopped participating in the conversation, but he had been following it closely, his eyes moving from man to man as it progressed. Finally his curiosity came to the fore.

"Are ye speakin' of another tribe of people up here in these mountains?" he asked.

Black Bird stopped and explained to him, telling him the same story he had told Mike on the trip up the mountain. Dónal was riveted as he listened to the tale.

"Sounds exactly like the little people in Ireland!" he said when Black Bird finished. "They've left many of the places there, too, with the Rebellion and all."

Mike looked at Dónal more carefully now. He knew from the man's accent that he was Irish, but there seemed to be something more. His statement rang of personal knowledge about the troubles in the country.

"What brought you to America?" Mike asked him. "And how long ago did you come here?"

"I've only been here about two years. T'was time fer me t' leave the *auld sod*," Dónal replied. "T'was nothin' left there fer me. When I landed in New York, there wasn't any work that suited me, so I came west. I spent years in the countryside o' County Kerry, helpin' me da' and me brothers with the sheep, so it seemed the best way fer me t' make a livin' in this country, too."

The three men ate their meal, turning in for the night afterwards. The next day, Black Bird took his leave, assured that Mike could come off the mountain through the territory of the *Awakkulé* and back to Lodge Grass on his own. Black Bird mounted his grulla and rode off in the early hours as the sun transformed the fog into an opalescent drapery, obscuring his departure. Dónal toured Mike around the ranch buildings and explained how the sheep operation had been run prior to its purchase by Williams and Jamison. Mike liked Dónal immediately, and he was fascinated by the prospect of working with sheep. Despite his family history in the cattle business, he had little interest in cows. Some part of his ancestral memory was reaching out to the tough wooly critters that eked out survival on any terrain in nearly every kind of weather.

The only sheep still under Dónal's care at the Dryhead were the bucks that were used to breed the ewes currently pastured at lower elevations for the winter. Dónal fed them hay inside the corral, and made sure they could get into the shelter of the sheds in the event of a blizzard. He told Mike the ewes and lambs would be brought back to the mountain pastures in the spring to spend the hot months of the summer in the cooler reaches.

Mike asked if Dónal was planning to continue working for the operation, now that it had new owners. Dónal affirmed that he was, and Mike was relieved to hear that there would be a good teacher on hand to show him the intricacies of working sheep.

Mike's mind was flooded with thoughts of Della. The Dryhead ranch house would be a good place to begin his life with her. The big rambling log structure was surrounded by skeletal cottonwoods, asleep for the winter. They promised a sheltered and a shaded yard around the house in the spring, and a small creek ran past them. Such trees would not grow without good groundwater. Dónal told him there was a well with excellent water. Coming here with their child would provide time to build their marriage and to start their life together outside the scrutiny of family and community. Mike found it easy to imagine being here after the winter ended, but he was not sure how Della would cope with the distance and isolation. She was young and close to her family, especially her sisters. How would it be for her to live so far from the conveniences of town? For her, this could be a lonely place. But Mike chose not to consider the negatives for long. He only knew he wanted to be with her.

He stayed on another full day, helping Dónal with the bucks and talking more about sheep. He made his own departure back to the home ranch the next day. Dónal stood in the doorway of the bunkhouse, watching him leave for several minutes, and finally turned to go back inside. Even though he had covered some distance from the place, Mike could hear the big wooden bar thud into place, securing the building against any and all comers.

The weather held for Mike's journey back to the Lorrah ranch, a quick two day trip off the mountain. He put the horses in the barn, with the usual generous reward of hay and grain, then made his way up the frozen road to the house. His mother paused from baking pies and gave him one of her brilliant smiles. He went down the hall to the office where Morgan was writing long rows of figures in a ledger. He watched him for a moment, then sat down in the generous leather chair that faced the desk.

"Well," Mike said, "if you still are willing to have me go to the Dryhead to work in the spring, I'll be happy to go."

Morgan looked up from his work, and for a moment, Mike wondered if he even remembered their conversation about the sheep operation. Then the hesitation passed, and Morgan replied.

"That's good, boy. You can help run those wooly things this winter, and help lamb 'em out in the spring. Once the pairs are ready to travel, you'll trail 'em up to the Dryhead. I'll look for you to keep up your work at the livery, too."

Mike had expected this, and he nodded in agreement.

Morgan made it obvious that the conversation was over, so Mike rose and went back to the kitchen, where Velia had warmed up some stew for him. He ate heartily, glad for food that was not cooked over a campfire, and went to his room to sleep. Della was the focus of all his thoughts. He wondered how she was, what she was feeling, and whether she was truly willing to become the wife of a sheep man. All his questions and thoughts and dreams eddied around him, forming a whirlpool that sucked him into the vortex of darkness. He was too tired to resist the flow of emotion as it picked him up and cast him through space and time. Suddenly, he felt himself jolt to a stop, and he opened his eyes to see that he was in Della's room. Elation was replaced by concern when he saw that she was alone there, sobbing as if her heart was broken.

"Della!" he whispered, "Are you all right?"

The sobbing stopped as she jerked upright in bed and stared at the shadowy corner where he stood. When she recognized that it was him, she began to cry again, hysterically, sheets pulled up to her face to muffle the sound.

In two quick steps, he was with her on the bed, arms wrapped around her.

"Why are you crying? What is wrong?"

"I...I was just feeling so alone," she sniffed, when she could finally speak. "I don't want to wait until spring for us to be together. I want to be with you *now*!"

More tears poured from her eyes.

Mike rocked her softly, kissing her wet cheeks and smoothing her hair.

"I'll come and talk with your father again," he said. "I have a job now, and I want him to know I plan to take care of you."

"Oh, Mike," she sobbed, "He is still so angry. I don't know if he will listen to you."

"Look, Della, he loves you. He doesn't want you to be sad, and he will listen to reason. I'll convince him, I promise you."

Suddenly, there was the sound of footsteps outside the bedroom door. It would either be Nuala or Deidre, and the sound was enough to break the spell. The swirling whirlwind of darkness flung Mike from Della's arms and into the nothingness that seemed to accompany this kind of astral travel. He crashed to the floor of his own room at the ranch, and laid there a moment, wondering if he had been hurt in his landing. Slowly, he picked himself up and crawled back into the warmth of his own bed. Sleep eluded him after that, and he lay there, scripting what he would say to Seamus O'Keefe to convince him that Della should come with him immediately.

CHAPTER 24

▼

The meeting with Seamus O'Keefe was easier than Mike had expected. He chose not to take the train, but used Willow's car instead, since she was off on another of her adventures, one that did not require a vehicle.

Evangeline met him at the door. She told him that while she and Seamus were both very unhappy with the events leading to this discussion, they had discovered that Della was determined to be with him. It had become obvious that she would settle for nothing less than becoming Mike's wife so they could raise their child together. Most of the time, she had stayed in her room, refusing to speak with anyone who tried to persuade her to take another path. All advice to stay with a relative to have the baby, or to allow it to be adopted was met with a storm of objections and tears, and she had finally worn her parents down. Evangeline escorted Mike to the parlor, where Seamus was waiting to talk with him. When Mike entered the room, he found Seamus almost relieved to see him. Evangeline stayed to listen to their conversation.

"Well, son," Seamus said, "Our daughter is determined to marry you and settle in ranch country. I am not happy that the two of you decided to bring this event about in this way. And I wish Della was older. But she will not rest until the two of you are together. I can't say I'll give my blessing, but I will give my permission."

"Thank you, sir," Mike replied. "I will take good care of her. I have a job, even in spite of these hard times, and she will never want for food or shelter. We won't embarrass you with a public ceremony. We'll get married very privately in another place, and you won't have to worry about a thing."

"That would be for the best," Seamus said. "When will all this happen?"

"If Della's willing, I'd like to come for her next week. I have a few things to arrange."

Evangeline rose.

"I'll call her," she said.

When Della came into the room, she was rigid with concern. She warily looked at her father's solemn face, and at her mother who stood impassively. Finally, she turned her eyes to Mike, seeking some kind of answer in his expression. All seemed to be waiting for someone to speak. After an eternity, Seamus cleared his throat.

"Della," he said, "I don't like this. You are too young. And Mike has not shown himself to be a very responsible man. But he says he's turned over a new leaf. He wants to make a home for you and the baby, and he has a job. I've told him I want you to finish your education, and I don't want the rest of the family shamed by this. You are to be married privately and with as little fuss as possible. Is that understood?"

For a moment, Della's face was blank. She had not known what to expect when she entered the room, and now she was trying to be sure of what she had heard. As she realized that her parents were giving her permission to marry Mike, she became fearful. Was this really what she wanted? Up until a few weeks ago, she had been a girl, caught up in school, social activities and the heady world of being the object of adulation from many male admirers. Now she was on the brink of leaving her family to become a wife and mother. She gazed at Mike whose stressed demeanor revealed how difficult this encounter had been with her father.

Love flooded all her senses. Mike was without a doubt the man of her dreams and the mystery of their connection was beyond understanding. Any doubt she might entertain was secondary to the forces at work inside and outside her feelings of comfort. With a sense that she was poised on a cliff, Della stepped out into the void. Looking directly into Mike's eyes, she spoke.

'I must be with Mike," she said simply, a single tear glided down her cheek. "You are my family, and I don't want you to be angry, but he my future. I will always be your daughter, but now I will be his wife and the mother of this child and any other children born in the future."

Seamus and Evangeline did not respond.

Mike said, "I told your parents I would come back for you in one week, and that we would make our home at the ranch until spring when we go to the Dryhead country."

Della was crying openly now, and the sight of this broke Mike's heart. He crossed the room to put his arms around her.

"Everything will be all right, Della," he whispered. "Once everyone is used to the idea, all this pain will be forgotten. You'll see."

They stood in their embrace until Della's sobbing stopped. Sniffling a little, she walked him to the door, and with a tender kiss, he left her. He scraped the snow off the windshield of Willow's car, and started the engine. He knew it was going to be a long drive home, since he had fought wind-blown snow and sub-zero temperatures all the way to Hardin. And he still had to tell his parents that he would be bringing his new wife to the home ranch for the winter. The emotion of all this made him wrestle with the urge to have a drink. It would be so easy to stop at one of the bars and buy a bottle to accompany him on his trip to Lodge Grass, but on this night, he was determined to win the battle. He might have done so, too, but he felt the awful sycophant inside him begin to awaken.

"Oh, no," he moaned aloud. "Not tonight. Stop! I cannot face this on top of everything else! Let me be!"

But his objections were in vain. He could feel the icy, slithering thing writhing inside his chest, and it was not to be denied. Mike drove straight to the Mint Bar, left the car running at the curb, and walked stiffly inside. He laid his money on the bar, bought a fifth of whiskey, and barely acknowledging the few men in the establishment, strode purposefully back outside. Scuffling through accumulating snow, he climbed into the car. In the privacy of its interior, he uncapped the bottle, and threw a huge drink down his throat. As the savage liquid began to numb his anxiety, he drove off into the darkness.

Peering between the torrents of snow flakes, he drove carefully at first. He could see no other vehicles along the way, and he was glad he was as familiar with the route as he was. It would have been easy to slide off the road, and in the black of the night, he was certain that no one would ever notice him. The cold was penetrating his coat and gloves, so he had more drinks from the bottle, and as he did, he felt his body begin to relax. He did not care so much that the storm was growing worse, and visibility had declined to just a few feet in front of the car. The liquor seemed to be achieving the purpose for which he had purchased it. For a time, he could not feel the presence of his cold internal nemesis.

Then he reached a stretch of road that ran along the Little Big Horn River, three or four miles north of Lodge Grass. All of a sudden, the frigid knot came to life. An icy serpent, it expanded inside him, cutting off his breathing and compelling him to stop his vehicle. Braking caused the car to fishtail a bit, then skid to a stop. Mike flung open the door and felt himself jerked out by the horrifying coiling snake-like thing. In that moment, he found himself overcome with a tidal wave of nausea. He bent over, hands on knees, trying to catch his breath, and then he vomited. Dizziness rendered him helpless for a few moments, and he wondered if the alcohol had overcome his senses, or if he might have eaten some bad food. He could not remember.

As abruptly as it had come, the sickness left him. The cold air revived him, and he felt his mind come to perfect clarity. As the reptilian presence unwound, Mike felt his attention riveted to some faint marks at the edge of the road. The thick snowfall opened up into a black tunnel in front of him, inviting him to enter its maw and follow where it led. Leaving the car where he had stopped, he crossed the road and trudged through the ditch toward the bank of the river. Although the snow had all but obscured the tracks, he could clearly see that something had traveled in a swooping snowplowing pattern. He followed it to the river where there was a jumble of impressions in the snow. Peering over the edge, he could see just below the cutbank. Already freezing around the rim of the frigid black water was a vehicle-sized hole in the ice. Mike started to try to edge down to the water, but when a bit of the bank gave way and plunged to the icy surface, he leapt back.

It was too late to try to save whoever was in the water, he was sure of that. He also knew that by morning, no one would be able to see any sign of the accident. Crying out in agony to the sky, he stumbled back to the road. The only thing to do was to drive on to Lodge Grass and tell the sheriff. Tears were freezing on his face as he got into the car and finished his trip. He was completely sober. Going directly to the home of the current town sheriff, Bud Lamborn, he pounded on the door. It was late, but he had to tell his story now, while it was still clear in his mind.

Bud came to the door, carrying his shotgun.

"Jesus, Mike, what the hell are you doing, waking me up in the middle of the night?" he asked. "You been drinkin' again?"

"I did have a few drinks in Hardin, Bud, but this isn't about that."

"What then?"

"On the way back, I saw where someone went off the road and into the river about three or four miles back. I figured if I didn't tell you about it now, the place might be impossible to find tomorrow, with all this snow."

Bud looked closely at Mike.

"You sure?"

"Yes."

Mike was thoughtful about how to put this information into words without it sounding too strange.

"It was just a fluke that I happened to notice it. I was driving slow because of the storm, and something just didn't look right. When I saw the place the vehicle went in, I was sure no one could have survived it."

"Let me get dressed, and we'll go have a look," Bud said. "What the hell were you doin' out on the roads in this weather?"

"I had some business in Hardin," Mike said, remembering the earlier part of the evening, "Just didn't get out of there until awful late."

Bud brought him inside to wait for him. When he came back, he carried a couple of flashlights. They climbed into Bud's truck, a 1928 Ford Model AA with closed cab and a cargo bed. Bud had thrown in blankets, rope, a couple of grappling hooks, and a set of industrial-sized pulleys on top of his big tool box. There were several large sandbags and some firewood in the back for weight, as well. He sent his teen-age son to alert several other local men and tell them to join him and Mike at the spot.

In the time it had taken Mike to reach town and relay the information to Bud, road conditions had grown even more treacherous. The surface was like glass, and sheets of blowing snow obscured the road itself. They crept along and stopped several times so Mike could get out and clear the ice and snow from Bud's windshield.

As they inched the final distance, Mike suddenly cried out.

"Stop! Right here, Bud, this is the place!"

Bud braked cautiously and brought the truck to a level spot at the side of the road. They got out and waded through snow that had now reached two feet in depth, falling several times before reaching the bank of the river. Bud shone one of his flashlights down in the direction Mike pointed out, and saw that there was still an open spot in the ice, but it looked smaller than a car.

Bud was dumbfounded.

"Holy Mother of God, Mike," he said. "If you hadn't seen this, no one would ever know it was here. It's hard to believe that there could be a whole vehicle in there."

"The hole was bigger when I saw it, Bud," Mike assured him. "I never would have spotted it if it wasn't for the swath it plowed through the snow from the road."

"Well, it's going to be a long night," Bud sighed. "Why don't you and I build a bonfire here so the others'll have a place to get warm?"

They trudged up and down from truck to bank, carrying paper, kindling and logs. Bud brought a small can of kerosene he kept for lanterns and poured a little on the wood to get a good start to the fire.

"That'll make sure we get it going in spite of the snow," he said. "And it'll help the others see where we are."

Soon, they had a sizable blaze going, and Mike filled the time dragging in more dead wood from the surrounding area to add to the pile. Before long, several others began to arrive, and finally there were some fifteen local men there. Ole Swenson brought his old tow truck with its winch, and they all stood on the bank, shining flashlights onto the surface of the frozen river, trying to determine the best course of action.

It was Bud's idea to cast one of the iron grappling hooks down and see if they could snare some part of the vehicle with it. All the men agreed that would be a good place to start. The hooks were heavy and strong, and two ropes were attached to each one. Bud swung hard, with all the power he could put behind it and his aim proved true. The heavy metal broke off a piece of thin, freshly formed ice, and sank into the black water. Three of the younger, stronger men grasped the ropes and pulled hard. The hook hesitated a moment, then rose free from the river, dripping icy drops.

The second toss went deeper, and there was an audible, watery clunk as it made contact with something metallic. This time, when the men heaved on the ropes, the claws would not come up.

"Keep the rope tight!" Ole cried. "Let's hook that to my tow cable up there on the road." While the men held the rope tight, Ole struggled through the snow and released the brake on his tow cable. He pulled it with him to where the men were gathered, and they secured the ropes to his tow hook. He started the motor of the cable reel, and the machinery lurched into gear. To his dismay, his tow truck began to slide on the icy surface of the road, and he grew afraid that it might be pulled down into the deep snow on the bank.

"Stop!" he cried. "We're slidin'!"

Bud came up from the bank, along with another big man, and each of them pulled a sandbag off Bud's truck. They wedged these behind the wheels of Ole's truck, and the sliding stopped. Now the object in the river began to come along in the direction of the tow-line. The roof of it broke the surface of the water, and they all could see that it was, indeed, a car. Heavy with the water inside, it resisted the pull mightily, but eventually, it was dragged to a shallower area near the bank. Black water ran from every seam, lightening the load and making it easier to move. A dozen flashlights were aimed at it, and when the windows were out of the water, it was apparent that there was a person in the driver's seat. It also appeared the accident had jarred the passenger door open.

Mike and another man did not hesitate. They waded into the icy water and worked to open the driver's side door, oblivious to how wet and cold they were getting. Ole threw down a crowbar, and Mike caught it, feeling it freeze instantly to the sheepskin mittens he wore. Using it for leverage, they finally pried the door open and lifted the body out, laying it down on the bank. Bud was waiting for them, and he pushed both men to the fire, where he made them strip and wrap themselves in the blankets he had brought.

Meanwhile, the other men were looking at the body they had retrieved.

"It's Marie Olson," one of the men shouted. "What the hell was she doing out on a night like this?"

Mike was saddened when he heard this. Mrs. Olson was a kindly woman, about sixty years old, who was well-liked in Lodge Grass. She had a little laundry and mending business, and everyone in town knew her. Her husband worked at the post office, and they had several grown children, all of whom had settled in the area. He remembered his grandmother telling him that his special ability was there to make sure people did not wonder what had happened to their loved ones who died. It did not make him feel any better. What would these men think if they knew he had some special extra-sensory ability that drew him to lost dead people? His shiver had nothing to do with how cold it was.

The men decided to leave the car until daylight, and to take Mrs. Olson's body to Lodge Grass. Bud said he would notify John Olson, and he thanked Mike for all he had done in front of all the other men. Mike climbed back into Bud's truck, wrapped in the blanket, and asked to be taken to his grandmother's house. She was the only one who would understand what he had been through.

Dawn was breaking when he quietly opened her door, but he need not have worried about waking her. She was sitting in the kitchen, hot tea and porridge ready, and she looked at him with a steady gaze.

"Well, Michael," she said. "It appears y've had quite a night. The bit o' banshee has led y' on another discovery, is it?"

Mike looked at her for a moment, then sank into a chair at the table, put his head down and sobbed. She went to her bedroom, came out with a down comforter, and wrapped it around his shoulders.

"Y' need not worry, Michael," she said. "That thing will sleep for a while, now. Here, drink some tea, eat some porridge, and I'll let yer parents know y'll be stayin' in bed today."

As obediently as a child, he did as she ordered, then walked into the room he usually used, and collapsed into a dreamless sleep.

CHAPTER 25

▼

It was afternoon when he finally opened his eyes.

Anna was standing at the door of the room with a tray. It held a cup of steaming hot tea, some biscuits, and a generous dish of jam.

"T'is time for y' to be risin', Michael," she said. "I'm goin' t' be needin' y' to go with me."

He squinted at her, rubbed his eyes, and sat up wearily.

"I should be getting to the ranch, Grandmother," he replied.

"Nay, Michael," she said. "There's somethin' more important y' ll be helpin' me with."

Anna set down the tray removed herself from the room. She returned immediately carrying his clothes, dried and warm. She laid them on the foot of the bed,

"Now, be gettin' dressed," she urged. "We need t' move fast."

Mike pulled on his clothes, reaching for a biscuit between each action, and gulped the hot tea as he carried the tray back to the kitchen. When he entered the room, he stopped short.

Sitting at his grandmother's table, her haunted dark eyes staring at him from her pinched and fearful face, was Agnes Little Moon. She was thinner than she had been when he saw her with Bart Knight on the train, but this did nothing to detract from her beauty. Her skin was a flawless brown, and her black hair shone in the morning light, even though she had pulled it back into a severe knot at the nape of her neck. Exhaustion was etched on the classic lines of her face, and she was wearing a coat that Moira had left at Anna's house.

"Where did you come from?" Mike asked gently.

Agnes did not answer. She just kept staring at him as if he might be dangerous.

Anna stepped over to her, and placed a hand on her shoulder.

"Agnes left the people who were givin' her shelter in Busby. Bart Knight beat up an old Crow man so badly he told him where she was, and he came lookin' fer her. She was at the church, but Bart said William Bear Claw was lyin' when he insisted Agnes was not at the house. So he beat up William, ransacked the place, and left t' try to find her. When Agnes came back and saw what had happened, she decided not t' put her protectors in any more danger. She left. One of the mail drivers gave her a ride and he knew Mrs. Olson was in Busby t' visit friends. He asked her t' give Agnes a lift t' Lodge Grass. They were almost here when their car slid off the road into the river. Agnes was thrown out, and she tried t' help Mrs. Olson. When she realized t'was no use, she walked on in the dark. Somehow, she knew this house was safe, so she came here."

"What can we do for her, Grandmother? Are you going to hide her here?"

"Nay. We'll be takin' her t' Black Bird Shows. It's goin' to be hard travelin' with the snow, but it's the best time. Less people likely t' see us make the trip."

"I left Willow's car at the Sheriff's, and it would be useless, anyway," Mike said. "Let me get one of the sleighs from the livery."

Anna agreed, and Mike threw on his jacket and heavy sheepskin mittens. He dug around in one of the closets and came out with a wool hat that had belonged to his grandfather. Opening the door, he plunged into the blinding whiteness outside. The storm had now intensified to a howling blizzard, and snow froze on his face as he ran to the livery. He hitched up a sturdy brown horse to a sleigh that had been stored there, and he fastened a horse blanket over the harness to try to protect the animal. The sleigh handled well as he drove it down the street to Anna's house. When he got there, she brought out an armload of blankets, then went back in and returned with Agnes. Seating her in the back, she climbed in beside her, and wrapped the blankets around both of them, tugging one of them up over their heads.

Mike pulled his wool scarf over his face, jammed the hat down hard on his head, and thrust his hands back into his mittens. Flicking the reins, he leaned into the wind, peering to try to see the road. The horse stepped out in an easy trot, trusting the man to guide it as it made its way. Going was slow, and the snow caked on their coats, the blankets and the front of the sleigh. Periodically, Mike bared one of his hands and wiped ice from his eyelashes. This trip was taking forever, and he was very concerned about Anna. He did not want her to become chilled.

He need not have worried. She had put her arms around Agnes, and the blankets were keeping them warm enough. Conditions were terrible for travel, but the advantage was that no one would be following them. Since they were headed up Lodge Grass Creek, anyone seeing them would assume that Mike was taking his grandmother to the home ranch, so their travel would not arouse suspicion.

They drove for a long time. At last they arrived at the turn down the lane that led to Black Bird Show's cabin. There were no tracks leading in or out, and when they reached the creek crossing, it was frozen and covered with snow. They crossed, and Mike reined the horse to a stop as close to the door as he could come. Chunks of snow broke off Mike's coat as he climbed down, and he hurried to help Anna and Agnes from their seat. The blankets had protected them, and he was happy to see that both of them were still dry.

"Bring the blankets in with y', Michael," his grandmother directed. "Let's dry them as best we can."

He put one of the blankets over the back of the horse, and collected the rest. When he turned, he saw that Black Bird Shows had his door open and all three of his refugee visitors entered quickly. The interior of his cabin was warm from the fire in the wood stove. Agnes stood still in the middle of the room, and Anna looked seriously at Black Bird Shows.

"Well, young man," she said. "This is Agnes Little Moon. She's made a hard journey, and she's in grave danger from Bart Knight. He'd be the man who hunted y' when y' left the boardin' school. He means t' do her more harm when he finds her."

Black Bird spoke softly to Agnes in Crow. She stared at him in silence, and after a few moments, huge tears escaped her eyes.

"I told her she'll be safe here. She can stay as long as she wants," Black Bird said to Anna.

"I heard that," Anna said.

"Why is she crying, then?" Mike asked.

"She's relieved t' feel safe for the first time in months," Anna said. "And she feels lucky t' be alive after the accident last night. Y'd be cryin' too, if t'was yerself."

Mike nodded.

"Come, Michael," she said, "Time t' be gettin' back before anyone looks for us."

Agnes saw that they were about to leave, and she caught hold of Anna's sleeve. She unbuttoned Moira's coat and removed it, handing it over to the older woman. Her stance was erect and graceful, and without the heavy coat, her thin body looked as regal as any queen.

Anna spoke to her in Crow, but Agnes shook her head in response.

"What's happening?" Mike asked.

"She's givin' back the coat," Anna said. "She wants t' wear a blanket like a true Crow woman."

Black Bird had already stepped to the side of the room and returned, holding a colorful wool blanket from the bed that had been Takes the Hawk's. He unfolded it and handed it to Agnes. Still not speaking, she took it from him, wrapped it around her shoulders and stood proudly.

She broke her silence.

The words she spoke were in Crow, and both Black Bird Shows and Anna nodded at what she was saying. Mike looked from one to the other to make sure he had understood.

Black Bird smiled at him.

"She says she does not want to be called Agnes any more. From here on, she wishes to be known as Little Moon," he said.

Mike smiled ruefully at his friend.

"You're going to have to teach me a lot more Crow one of these days, Black Bird," he said. "I hate being on the fringe of these conversations."

"It will come to you easily," Black Bird replied. "You already understand more of it than you think."

Mike stood silently for a moment, drawing on all Black Bird had taught him, then spoke to Little Moon in the simplest Crow.

"Please be happy," he said, watching his grandmother and his friend to see if they indicated he was making any mistakes. "We will always be your friends."

Little Moon looked at him, then at Anna, and then she smiled a little, tentative smile. It lit up the room.

Black Bird's face was a study in peace and courage.

Mike looked at him.

"If Bart Knight figures this out, you are going to be in real danger, Black Bird. Please be careful. Now he has two reasons to come after you!"

"Even if he did know, he wouldn't come in this storm," Black Bird replied. "Like Missus Anna says, you should take advantage of its cover and make your way back home."

Anna took both of Little Moon's hands in hers, and spoke to her again in Crow. Then she fixed a grave look on Black Bird.

"This girl is here t' heal," she said in English for Mike's benefit. "Use your best medicine t' make her well again. And don't be scarin' her with any sudden movements! She deserves some peace."

Black Bird bowed a little toward Anna, displaying the deference he had always given her since his own rescue.

"Missus Anna, you are a hero. Many lives are so much better because of you. Please live a long time so that I may learn more from you," he said.

Anna buttoned her brown coat and wrapped her scarf around her head and neck. Bundled up in this manner, she looked like a small mother bear. Mike followed her example, then gathered up the blankets, which had become warm and mostly dry. Black Bird opened the door quickly, and the storm lashed at the opening, threatening to bring its fury inside the simple house. Mike and Anna stepped out and he closed the door quickly after them.

Ushering Anna to the sleigh, Mike helped her in, tucking the blankets all around her. He pulled the blanket off the horse, shook off as much of the snow as he could and tossed it onto the floor of the driver's seat. Swinging up into place, he twitched the reins. The horse displayed the uncanny sense of direction most horses demonstrate when headed back to their barns. The animal broke into a steady trot and aimed itself down the road without a single misstep. When they reached the gate of the Lorrah ranch, the snowfall and wind stopped. The storm was over, and the few remaining clouds scudded away, revealing a star-filled sky with a quarter moon on the wane.

Glancing back at his grandmother, he saw that she had dozed off in the warmth of the blankets. He would take her to the home ranch for the night and not fight the snowy road any further than he had to. Serenity settled over Mike for the first time in many weeks. The cold thing next to his heart was asleep.

The following morning, Mike came into the kitchen to find his mother and grandmother waiting for him. It was a relief to see that his grandmother was none the worse for the wear of the previous day's adventure. He poured himself a cup of hot tea from the pot on the sideboard and sat down with them. Without any formalities, he plunged into his subject.

"I'm going to marry Della," he said. "I'll be bringing her here to the ranch until spring, and then we'll be going to the Dryhead."

Both women looked at him silently.

Velia was the first to speak.

"The little house down on Goodluck Creek is empty right now. The two of you could stay there until you go to the mountain," she said. "I'll talk with your father."

Mike looked at her gratefully.

"Thank you, Mother. That should work out fine."

"Where will you be married?" Velia asked.

Anna spoke up.

"They'll be married in the Old Religion at the time of the full moon," she said. "We'll take them down t' the ledge by the hot spring. It is important that they be joined next t' water. 'Tis the way things should begin for the special babe who's comin'."

Mike was surprised. He had not thought about how the marriage could be performed privately. At one point, he had considered common law as the answer to this dilemma.

"I've been thinking about all this," Mike said. "I'd like Black Bird to have a part of the ceremony, too. Is that possible?"

Anna nodded. "We will be sure that's how 'tis done."

Velia was quiet. "Of course, you will have my best wishes and I will be a part of this. However, your father will not attend. In fact, it is best that he will be away from home when the ceremony takes place."

Mike set his cup down.

"Thank you both," he said. "If it was not for your understanding, I am not sure how I would be able to make it through this. It surely is not happening in the way I would have wished."

"Sometimes we are not given choices," Anna said gently. "There's a bigger pattern here than any of us might see."

CHAPTER 26

▼

Mike returned to town with his grandmother. After delivering her to her house, he put the sleigh back in its place at the livery. Then he went across to the cafe to use the telephone there. Having telephone service come to rural Montana towns in recent years made things much easier. Of course, a caller had to choose words carefully, since it was easy for local operators to hear any conversation and share it with the entire community. Luckily, the true meaning of his message had already been established in his previous conversation with Della and her parents. When Della answered, he told her that he would be coming for her in two days. Her voice was calm, but the underlying excitement was there and it warmed his heart. Time spent away from her undermined his confidence that she could really want to be his wife. Only direct contact reassured him.

Racing to complete the tasks that lay ahead, Mike finished his work at the stable for the day, saddled Pal and rode back to the ranch through the brilliant white landscape. His mother intervened to get permission from Morgan for Mike and Della to use the little house on Goodluck Creek. Mike rode over to that house to check its condition and found it livable, but without furniture. They would have to stay at the guest house near the main ranch for a time while they got the little place ready. Then they could take any furnishings they managed to acquire to the Dryhead Ranch when spring came.

The next two days flew past, blown on the winds of a chinook. The warm breeze melted most of the snow, turning the roads into muddy quagmires in places. Mike decided the best way to go for Della would be with a horse-drawn carriage. While he would have liked to drive there in Willow's car, he was not certain it would negotiate the difficult parts of the road. This way, they would have no trouble bringing Della's things back.

When the day came, Mike was up and on the way before dawn. Excitement vibrated under his skin and he was buoyant with love for Della. The temperature was still warm and he looked forward to bringing her home to the ranch country he loved so much. Layered over his joy was the belief that marrying her would make a better man of him. He knew without a doubt that this was the most important time in his life.

Della met him at the door, throwing herself into his arms and kissing him. She led him into the house, and her sisters each gave him a warm hug, congratulating him and ordering him to take care of their little sister. Evangeline heard the chatter and laughter in her kitchen and came from the next room. Seamus was in the parlor, she told him, and wanted a word.

Mike was nervous, even though all had been settled. He entered the parlor, and remained standing while he said hello to his future father-in-law.

"Mr. O'Keefe," he said. "How are you?"

Seamus looked at him for a long time.

"How do you think I am? You are taking my youngest child from me."

"I would never take her away, sir," Mike replied. "She will always be a part of your family, and I'll see that she can visit often."

"You make sure you take care of her. If you hurt her in any way, beyond what you already have, it's me you'll answer to. Do you understand?"

"Yes, sir. I love her. It will be my honor to be married to her, and it will be my life-long effort to give her a good life. I can't expect you to believe me, but I will do everything I can to show you."

"I'll be watching."

"Thank you, sir," Mike said. "We are going to try to take advantage of this good weather and get on back to the ranch. Please plan to come and see us once we are married. When you see where we are living and know my parents better, I am sure you'll be satisfied."

Seamus gave a jerky nod and returned to his newspaper, not looking at Mike again. Mike stood for a moment, then said goodbye. He walked out of the room, leaving the man to his reading.

Della's sisters had loaded a number of bags and blankets. There were two small traveling trunks that Mike hefted and carried out, until everything Della was bringing with her was in its place in the carriage. Della wrapped a scarf around her neck, placed the hood of her coat over her head, and pulled on her gloves. She had a muff to keep her hands warm, as well. Mike put several blankets on the seat to help shelter her from the cold. Then he helped her up and they were off.

Once the initial exhilaration of their departure passed, Della turned her head away, and he knew she was crying. It was a huge step, leaving all that was familiar for a life that was unlike anything she had known growing up. She was sure she wanted to be with Mike, but leaving her sisters, her parents, and her warm, cozy home in Hardin was the hardest thing she had ever done.

He tugged on the reins, stopping the horse.

"Della, please don't be sad," he said, putting his arms around her. "I'll make sure you see your family as often as possible. I know you are going to miss them. But we'll be at the ranch all winter, and it's easy to get to the train so you can go back and forth and visit."

Della sniffled, drying her eyes with the sleeve of her coat.

"Don't worry, Mike," she said. "I'm just a little emotional, but I'll be fine. I want this more than anything."

The trip went quickly, with the sun shining brightly and the warm breeze continuing to melt the snow into the thirsty ground. They were at the gate of the ranch house by mid-afternoon. Velia opened the door for them, and ushered Della into the kitchen. Mike said he'd be taking her things to the guest house and putting the horse away before coming in. There was no sign that his father was around, and he trusted his mother to make Della feel at home.

Before long, he was back at the house where a pleasant household sight met him. Velia was finishing up with food for supper, and Della was setting the table. It was as if she had lived here all her life. Mike hugged Della, smiling over her shoulder at his mother, and mouthing "Thank you," to her.

This peaceful scene was disrupted when Morgan came into the house. He had returned from wherever he had been on business, and it was apparent he was not happy with the result of his travels.

"Take care of my horse, boy," he growled.

Catching his coat off its peg by the door, Mike headed out.

"Della's here," he said to his father. "I put our things in the guest house until we get some furniture into the Goodluck place."

Morgan did not reply, but looked toward Della.

"Hello, Della," he said, his tone completely different than the one he used with Mike, "Welcome to the Lorrah place. You tell that son of mine to take good care of you."

Before Della could respond, his eyes settled on Velia.

"Hello, Velia," he breathed.

She came to his embrace, and he gave her a warm kiss. Handing him a cup of coffee, she took his coat and hung it up. Leaning against the wall, he told her the day had been a long one, and he was glad to be home.

Dinner was placed on the table, and even though Mike was not back from the barn, Morgan, Velia and Della took their seats.

"Shouldn't we wait for Mike?" Della asked.

"He'll be along," Morgan answered carelessly.

Della could see this was the usual manner of things. It rankled her, but she was not yet a part of this family, and she hesitated to say anything about this. At that moment, Mike came in, quickly removed his coat and washed his hands. Taking his seat at the table, he looked at all of them.

"Nice to have a few more of us at the table again," he said. "It has seemed strange to have Moira and Willow gone."

Velia agreed, and Morgan said nothing.

When they finished, Della hurried to clear the table and put the remaining food away. She washed the dishes and encouraged Velia to spend time with Morgan. Mike remained in the kitchen to keep her company.

"It is so wonderful to see how you are making a place for yourself here," he said. "How do you feel about it?"

"Your family makes me feel like I belong here," she replied. "especially your mother. I'm still a little scared of your father, but I'm sure it's because I don't know him very well."

"He's not easy to get to know," Mike said. "Just give it some time."

Della was surprised to see that the guest house was almost like a fully equipped extra house. There was a comfortable looking bed and a sitting area with two rocking chairs and a sofa. A wood burning stove heated the interior. The odd thing was that it did not seem to have a kitchen. Since many farm and ranch homes did not have a bathroom, it was only the lack of a kitchen that stood out.

"This was my grandparents' home when they lived out here at the ranch. It used to have a kitchen, but we took it out when they went to live in their house in town. Since it's a guest house, people who stay here always eat at my parents' place," Mike explained. "My mother thought it was important that guests would not think they were expected to cook, so we replaced the cook stove with this heating stove, and the old kitchen cupboards with these closets."

"Would you rather live here, closer to your parents?" Della asked.

"We are going to have to build our marriage, and it will be easier to do with a little distance between us, especially when it comes to my dad," Mike replied. "In the spring, we will have plenty of distance between us at the Dryhead, but for now, I want you to have your own house so we can have our own life."

Della understood Mike's thought, but she wanted some companionship whenever Mike would have to be gone, and she liked Velia. She already missed her own mother and she wanted to know Mike's mother better.

"Will your mother mind if I visit her frequently?" she asked.

"I'm sure she'll be fine with it, but not if you interfere with the time she and my dad have together. That is sacred to my dad, and he doesn't like to share her time. Pretty much how I feel about us," Mike said.

Uttering these words, Mike was surprised at how well he now understood his father's possessiveness with regard to Velia. He took Della in his arms, and kissed her softly. The initial chaste kiss turned warm then very hot as their desire erased the initial awkwardness of the first night they would spend together. The warm, hand-made quilts and featherbed invited them, and they melted into one another before dropping into a deep sleep.

The next day saw the arrival of several townspeople who came with wagons and trucks, each bringing one piece of furniture. In the mysterious way of small towns, word had spread that Mike had brought home a bride, and that they needed to furnish their home. Many of the people who had known Mike since childhood had found at least one piece of furniture or linens or dishes to contribute, and before Della and Mike knew it, they had enough items to make their little house a home. Within two days, they were ready to move from the guest house. When the time came, Anna presented them with several pieces of Irish linen, a packet of her own specially blended tea, and a small package of herbs to bring the scent of nature into the house. She also wove a St. Bridget's cross of reeds, which Mike placed over the doorway, as she sprinkled some herbs and dried flowers around the front doorstep.

After the St. Bridget's cross was hung, Anna stepped back to look at it, and smiled.

"The best of both worlds, Michael," she said. "It does no harm t' be protected by both the Church and the Old Religion. T'was the way of me ma and 'tis my way as well."

She went on.

"T'will be the time of the full moon in three days. I have much to do to prepare things, and I wanted to give you this, Della. It has come down through our family and y'll be after wearin' it on your wedding day."

Della watched as she set a package on the table in front of her. She had given little thought to what she would wear when she and Mike were married. The item in front of her was wrapped in layers of fine tissue and tied with what appeared to be a golden thread. The bundle was light as air, and when Della opened it she gasped at the sight of what it contained.

It was a creamy, glistening white and the texture of a mass of spider web or silk filaments. It almost appeared alive. Della reached a tentative finger out to touch it, but hesitated, afraid. She waited for Anna to direct her.

Anna did not speak. Instead, she delicately took the fragile thing between the thumb and forefinger of both hands and lifted it up. The airy stuff draped in splendid folds that drifted in the air. It was a shift-style dress, gauzy and mysterious, with strange designs woven across the bodice. Prism-like, colors and light played across it, highlighting first one part, then another. It was strangely opaque, despite the initial impression of transparency. Della and Mike both stared.

"Anna!" Della whispered. "This is so beautiful! Please tell me about it!"

"This is a ceremonial dress," Anna said simply.

"Where did it come from?"

"It was spun and woven of the finest wool from the sheep who live in the highest Irish mountains. The design has been handed down through the family for many generations," Anna was contemplative, almost as if speaking from another time and place. "Me mother taught me about it, and I taught Velia. But 'tis seldom fashioned in present days. There wouldna' have been a purpose to it. Now, the secret of this dress rests with our family."

She held it up to Della's shoulders, checking to see how it looked.

Della tried to imagine wearing it, and finally she asked, "Should I try it on to see if it will fit?"

"Y' need not worry about that," Anna replied. "It will fit. It's not t' be worn 'til the ceremony."

Mike had stayed out of this conversation, but now he spoke.

"Grandmother, this is the most beautiful thing I have ever seen. It is so kind of you to offer it to Della for our marriage."

"I would not have done otherwise," Anna said simply. "T'is a magic garment for the mother of a magic baby."

Della began to weep.

"What is wrong?" Anna asked.

"I'm afraid. I don't know anything about magic. I don't know what will be expected of me if this baby really is magic. What if I do something wrong?"

Anna embraced her.

"Y' need not be worried," she soothed, carefully settling the dress back into its wrapping, "All this babe will need at first is what all babies need... food and love. Later, the only thing expected of you besides bein' a good mother is that ye believe in the child. Never tell him anythin' is impossible. The children of this marriage will be treasured. They are the *hope* of a long line of magic and mystery. Yer work will be t' keep their path open."

Della's nervousness did not fade. When Anna stepped back, Mike put his hand on her shoulder and looked into her eyes.

"We would not have been brought together if you weren't the right person," he said. "I believe you will be the perfect mother."

Anna turned and picked up her coat and walked toward the door.

"I'll be goin' home now, and I'd advise ye t' rest as much as ye can. This is an important event in yer lives, and ye'll be wantin' t' be at yer best. Over the next two days, drink the weddin' tea I brought for ye. It's from an old family recipe," she said, an enigmatic smile on her face.

As the door closed behind her, Della collapsed into a chair, her eyes wide in the look of a young child being told about fairies. She frowned slightly, trying to take in everything she had been told.

"Oh, Mike," she said, "do you really think I'm up to this?"

He gently lifted her to her feet, enfolded her in an embrace that made her feel safe, and then he kissed her.

"You have to be," he said. "I felt it from the first time I ever saw you. And you make me feel peaceful, something no one has ever been able to do before."

Kissing her again, he lifted her in his arms and took her to the bed. Settling her tenderly, he placed one of her sisters' quilts over her, and stroked her hair.

"Rest for a while," he said. "You've had a lot to absorb today. Grandmother will make sure everything is fine."

When Della drifted off to sleep, Mike walked outside into the afternoon. The snow was now completely stripped from the trees, and the day was cold and crisp. A stiff wind threatened to escort a cold front through the valley before nightfall, and the air was brilliant and clear. He gazed south toward Black Bird Shows' home and further toward the Big Horn Mountains.

Contemplating the odd turns his life had taken in the past half-year, Mike wondered what was next. The marriage ceremony would come in two days and he and Della would be bound together by ritual. But that was just a formality, unorthodox as it might be. In this short time, they were already so intertwined that he could not remember life as it had been when they were not together.

The two days passed quickly, and Della and Mike awoke on the morning of the ceremony. Della was up first to make breakfast, and when Mike came into the kitchen, he found her staring out of the small window in the direction of the rising sun. She was completely silent.

Coming up behind her, he enfolded her in his arms for warmth. Then he looked out the window. A blanket of silvery fog obscured even the big apple tree that grew in the yard just a few feet from the house. Della leaned back into his arms.

"Why would this happen on our special day, Mike?" she whispered. "It feels very strange."

Mike stood quietly, not letting go of her. All his senses explored this eerie phenomenon, and he was intensely relieved that he could not feel the bit o' banshee inside his chest. As they continued to look out into the vapor, a flash of white and black exploded into view and then disappeared again into the fog.

"What was that?" Della cried.

"I'm not sure," Mike replied, sliding his arms away and taking her hand. "Let's look out of the door to see if it is what I think it is."

They opened the front door and stepped out into the mist. It swirled around them as Mike pulled her along toward the apple tree. As it began to become visible in front of them Mike laughed aloud.

"What's so funny?" Della asked.

"Look!"

High in the tree, perched in perfect symmetry, were three of the biggest magpies Della had ever seen. Their obsidian eyes looked calmly at the young couple who gazed back up at them.

Mike danced Della around in a circle.

"Don't you see?" he cried. "It's a good sign!"

"Why?"

"From the old Irish poem...you know the one!"

She shook her head.

He recited it for her, almost singing it:

> *One for sorrow*
> *Two for mirth*
> *Three for a wedding*
> *Four for a birth*
> *Five for rich*
> *Six for poor*
> *Seven for a secret*
> *I can tell you no more!*

"Don't you see... *Three for a wedding!* We couldn't hope for a better omen than this!" Mike was euphoric.

Wonder echoed in Della's voice.

"I've heard that poem all my life," she said. "My mother and my aunts all used to say it to me and my sisters. I really never thought it would mean anything to me..."

Her voice trailed off and she continued to look at the gleaming magpies. A radiance seemed to glow from inside the birds, making the white of their breasts and wingtips so brilliant that they looked like fresh snow. The dominant black of their feathers shone with the iridescent blue-green and purple magpies are known for, and the eyes...the eyes were rich with intelligence and meaning. Della had never been this close to a magpie, and surely never this close to three of them. She was exhilarated.

After a time, the biggest of the birds opened its wings and slowly glided off its branch. Without any apparent effort it wheeled above Mike and Della and began a lazy spiral upward, followed exactly by its two companions. As they ascended, each of the birds vanished into the shining fog, leaving the young couple on the ground amazed and hushed. Eventually the cold damp of the mist began to penetrate their sensation of well-being and Mike walked Della back into the house. As they sat at the breakfast table, Della realized she was not sure what she should do next.

"Mike," she said, "your grandmother did not tell me what would be expected of me in this ceremony. I'm relying on her and your mother to make sure I don't make any mistakes."

Mike placed his hand over hers.

"If I know Grandmother, she will make sure everything is done in its proper order," he assured her. "All you should do is bring the package with the dress."

The time seemed to pass slowly on that day, and Della busied herself with small tasks. The house still needed to be put into the order she wanted, and her stomach was a bit queasy with morning sickness. She knew from what she had seen with her parents' friends and relatives that she had been lucky. Most of the time she felt very well, and she had suffered little from nausea in this pregnancy. If anything, she had more energy than she had ever had, and she was quietly excited about this baby. She was certain that any child she and Mike created would have a extraordinary place in the world. Even the Lorrah family legacy did not give her cause for concern.

Late in the afternoon, Mike again encouraged her to lie down and rest. As soon as her head touched the pillow, she fell into a deep sleep. Several hours later, she awoke to find Mike sitting beside the bed, watching her with tenderness.

"It's almost time," he said. "Let's gather our things and go up to folks' house."

When they stepped outside into the darkness, Della could see that the fog had not lifted. Mike had harnessed the horse to the carriage, and after placing her things in the back, he helped her into her seat. In a very short time, they arrived, and he lifted her down. Anna was waiting for them at the gate of the yard.

"Y'll be comin' with me," she said, turning them away from the house and walking them toward the hot spring, "The ceremony will be takin' place near water."

Following Anna, they made their way slowly down to the pool. It was shrouded in fog, but seemed to emanate a glow from the surface of the water. Through the mist, several figures were barely discernible. As they approached the group, Mike was astonished to see that Anna's brother and sister, Ristéard and Úna, had returned. Ristéard's white hair glowed in the darkness, and his luminous eyes fell upon Mike and Della. He was dressed in a long grey robe, as was Úna. Their thin figures were even more ethereal in the diminished visibility of the haze. Velia was there, too. Her body was caressed by the silky blue gown she wore, despite the fact that it was cut high at the neck and designed with long sleeves.

The area next to the hot spring pool was warmed by the temperature of the water, and when Della stepped up to the rock ledge, Velia, Anna and Úna took her aside to help her put on the ceremonial dress. When she was ready, they returned to where Mike and Ristéard stood. Placing the young couple in the center, the others formed a four-point group around them. Mike recognized that each of them stood at one of the cardinal directions: his mother to the east, Anna to the west, Úna to the north, and Ristéard to the south. The swirling mist eddied around them.

Ristéard looked around at the gathering and frowned slightly.

"This placement is missing somethin'," he said, "We'd be needin' the right one fer the south."

Úna put a hand on his arm.

"T'will be all right, Ristéard," she said. "She may be comin' yet."

Anna agreed.

"Let's get the placement right," she said, "All things will happen in good time."

She continued: "The East is the direction of Air. Also the direction of Spring. Velia, it is right y' should be there."

Looking at Úna, she said, "North is the direction of Winter and of Earth. Úna represents it well."

A deep breath, and then she said, "West is Autumn. I am in the autumn of me years, so this place is mine."

Suddenly there was a tinkling sound, like chimes of glass. A blue area glittered, half-hidden in the mist, beside Ristéard. Sparkling, thousands of ice crystals flashed, suspended in the night air. The hovering crystals began to change colors in waves, violet, blue, green, yellow, orange and then a brilliant red. The incandescent bits danced about, then showered to the stone ledge, revealing Willow.

She looked up at Ristéard, eyes luminous and smile exuberant.

"You did not think I would miss my big brother's wedding, did you?"

Laughter bubbled up from her, a sound almost exactly like the sweet tones that had preceded her appearance. A low-cut silken seafoam green gown clung to her body, covering but not concealing her every attribute. It was the kind of garment that reminded Mike of paintings of Greek goddesses. Her feet were bare. Tiny drops of mist glittered on her skin. She hugged Mike and Della in turn, and announced to the gathering,

"I'm the one who should be the South, and represent summer!"

"Good," Ristéard said. "I think we are almost ready to begin."

He made a complete turn as if looking for something or someone.

Mike spoke.

"There'll be nobody else, Uncle Ristéard. Moira is in the convent, and my father would never participate in a ceremony like this."

The words had hardly left his lips when he detected motion in the fog. Two additional people were approaching. As all of those present watched, Black Bird Shows and Little Moon emerged from the opaque atmosphere. They were dazzling. Both wore white buckskin, his a shirt and pants, hers a fringed dress that fell to her ankles. Both had moccasins of the same leather. All their clothing was richly beaded, the colors incredible and the workmanship fine beyond description. But most astonishing of all was the change in Little Moon. Her black hair was rich and full, falling in a shining mass to below her waist. Her skin glowed with good health and her eyes shone with pride and strength. Standing next to Black Bird Shows, she was erect and for the first time, Mike realized that she was very tall. The two were beautiful.

Mike walked over to face his friend. He took his hand in a clasp of friendship, and reached out his other hand to lay it on his arm.

"I am so glad to see you, my brother," he said warmly. "Thank you so much for coming."

"I could not be in any other place," Black Bird said.

Little Moon gave everyone a brilliant smile, but said nothing.

Ristéard gazed around at the group.

"Now we can begin," he said. "Please hold each other's hands and face each other."

Black Bird stepped forward. Out of nowhere, he produced a branch of sage, braided with sweetgrass. It ignited spontaneously in his hand, and he began to "smudge" the air to purify the surroundings. He sang an old Crow song, and walked around the entire circle. When he completed his circuit, the sage and grass smoke formed a perfect ring around everyone at ground level. When the last of the smoke touched the layer that marked his starting point, it began to revolve, rising slowly. It reached their knees, then their waists, shoulders and heads. It continued to rise high above them, and as it did so, the fog dissipated, leaving the air absolutely clear.

Black Bird and Little Moon stood slightly to the side of the formation Mike's family had created.

Velia began to speak in a singing tone, reciting a sacrament older than anyone could remember, a ritual handed down through scores of generations of the Hughes family.

"Spirits of the East, Essence of Air, bring to this man and this woman knowledge, intuition, renewal and a lightness of being. For these are the gifts of Spring."

Willow was next.

"Spirits of the South, Essence of Fire, bring them passion, creativity, adventure and a constant fire for their hearth. For these are the gifts of Summer."

"Spirits of the West," Anna sang, "Essence of Water, bring them peace, nurturing, and eternal love. Buoy them up when they are challenged, give them comfort and slake their thirst. For these are the gifts of Autumn.

Úna finished, "Spirits of the North, Essence of Earth, give them stability, strength and support. Make the ground solid beneath their feet, and provide them with a home wherever they may be. For these are the gifts of Winter."

There was silence for a few moments.

Then Ristéard raised his arms high so they formed a "v" above his head. Through the column of clarity left by the smoke ring, they could see the full moon directly above their gathering.

"Air, Fire, Water and Earth, the elementals of Nature...your love must reach beyond even these to give your life together meaning and joy."

He lowered his arms. Producing a cord of gleaming gold, he wove it over and under their hands, binding them together.

"This strand of gold is the binding promise you are here to combine into one," he chanted. "While you may remove it, it will never be gone. Your love must be strong. Greater than yourselves, but nothing without you to give it significance. Do you make this promise?"

Mike and Della looked into each other's eyes, and suddenly they were unaware of anyone else. A long moment passed, then in unison, they both said, "I promise."

"Then you shall be surrounded by the elementals for the rest of your lives," Ristéard declared.

"Air!" he cried.

The still air stirred, and a breeze began to blow softly, tousling Ristéard's white hair, and rioting through Willow's auburn curls. It caressed faces, stirred clothing and touched hair like a thousand tiny fairy fingers. Della's spiderweb fine dress breathed with life and moved sinuously about her body in celebration.

"Fire!"

A flame suspended itself in the air in front of Willow. A motion from her hand sent it in a lazy spiral around Mike and Della, casting a golden hue on their skin and magnifying the glow in their eyes.

"Water!"

The pond beside them began to spout a fine spray like a delicate fountain. A single strand of water played in an intricate pattern, interweaving a design on the pond that remained on its surface, illuminated by the moon.

"Earth!"

Silvery sand sifted into the center of the gathering, coating the ledge with a glistening layer that sang beneath their feet. It ebbed and flowed, sparkling powdered diamond dust.

At that moment, the golden cord slid from their hands into the air, hovering slightly above them. It shimmered there, meandering around itself in a gleaming display, winding tighter and tighter until it formed a delicate ring of gold. Mike reached out and took it from its flight, placing it on the third finger of Della's left hand.

"We are together for as long as we live," he breathed.

Della, eyes large and luminous, nodded.

"I will always be with you, Mike," she said, "Forever."

They kissed one another, a long, lingering kiss that carried all the promises they felt.

"It is done."

Ristéard's declaration left no doubt that the marriage was complete.

Before they departed, Black Bird Shows and Little Moon went to their horses. They returned with gifts for Mike and Della. Little Moon had made an intricate beaded necklace for Della. The beads were of glass, and they sparkled in their hues of blue and green and white. The medallion design was floral, deep blue morning glories in a field of pale blue. Black Bird waited while Della put her gift on, then he held out a buckskin-wrapped package to Mike.

Inside was a wool blanket. It was black with brilliant designs of green, red, and gold.

"This blanket will help protect you," Black Bird said. "It was a gift to me from Takes the Hawk, and it shielded me from those who would hunt me down. I give it to you to protect you from the evils of alcohol that seek to steal your life. Just remember, any time you are away from it, it cannot help you."

Mike took the blanket out and stroked its soft surface.

"Thank you, Black Bird," he said quietly. "I hope you are right about this blanket. I need all the help I can get."

He looked at his friend and saw him smiling more broadly than usual.

"What's on your mind, Black Bird? You look like the cat that swallowed the sparrow."

"I was just thinking, my friend. We have come a long way from those two boys in the barn loft to now...now when we are two married men."

"What? You're married?" Mike laughed aloud. "When did that happen?"

"I did not feel it was right for Little Moon to live with me without being my wife. The spirits told us it would be right for us to be joined. So we were married in the days after I came back from the mountain. My life is very good, and she says she is happy."

"She sure looks happy," Mike said, adding ruefully. "I don't have a gift for you, though."

"You have given us the best gifts. You have given us our lives back. You have given friendship and trust. And Mrs. Anna gave us each other. There are no better gifts."

They turned then and went back to their horses. Little Moon mounted so gracefully it was almost like she floated into the air to her seat on the white horse she rode bareback. Black Bird swung easily up onto his grulla horse. Both raised one hand in a gesture of farewell, and they rode away into the fog that still surrounded the spot where the ritual had taken place. The mist deadened the sound of the horses' footsteps, and a hush settled on the group left behind.

Mike gazed at the older people and Willow.

"I don't know if I can ever come up with the words to thank you all for this," he said. "It has brought joy to a time that could have been very difficult."

Ristéard and Úna smiled. Ristéard spoke.

"T'was our joy t' be alive t' witness this moment," he said. "Every good wish t' ye."

Della was radiant. She was now married to the man she loved, and no one could break that bond. There was some apprehension in the realization that she knew very little about the mysteries of the family, but she would do her best to learn everything she could. For the sake of their baby, she had to find her place in all of this.

Willow glided up to her, stirring the glittering sands at their feet.

"I have another sister!" she exclaimed. "I am so happy! Now, you make sure that brother of mine takes care of you...he'll have me to answer to if he doesn't."

Her statement was punctuated by her silvery laugh echoing through the night.

"We got you married, and now I have to be off," she continued.

Velia heard this and pleaded, "Willow, can't you at least stay the night? Your father would love to see you!"

Looking at her mother, Willow relented.

"Of course, mother. After all, you gave away your only son, and you should not have an empty house on a night like this. Why don't you stay, too, Grandmother?"

Anna shook her head.

"No, I'm tired and I want t' sleep in m' own bed," she said. "Ristéard and Úna'll stay with me so they can take the train in the mornin'. You'll come t' see me soon, Willow?"

"As usual," Willow replied, placing a gentle kiss on Anna's cheek.

There were embraces all around and the group parted. As Mike and Della stepped off the bank of the hot spring, the spray of water stopped and the fog closed in. They made their way to the little house that would now be their home until spring.

Above it all, the full moon kept watch, along with a huge white owl that drifted along directly above the couple.

C H A P T E R 2 7

▼

The trio next to the embers of the fire awoke. Dawn was breaking and the sound of singing birds was punctuated by dew dripping from the trees.

Colleen looked at Black Bird Shows.

"I didn't know you were ever married," she said. "How was it that I never heard about Little Moon?"

Black Bird's eyes took on a far away look, tinged by sadness.

"She was not meant to live long," he said. "But she brought me great happiness while she did. You'll see more of her as you dream, but it was so many years between her life and yours that I did not speak of her to you. It is not the Crow way."

Aisling had already stood up.

Her eyes shone with excitement.

"I never saw anything like that wedding!" she exclaimed. "And is that baby-to-be Grandfather Sean?"

Colleen nodded.

"Yes. I didn't know about the wedding, either," she said. "It is all starting to make more sense to me now. I am learning as much from these dreams as you are."

Andrew sat quietly, contemplating all they had learned.

"Did y' ever wish we'd had a formal ceremony?" he asked Colleen, a small frown on his face.

"No," she replied. "Ours was a ceremony of fire that we lived through. It sealed our marriage completely. I've never had a single doubt."

Colleen gazed at Black Bird Shows.

"Do you need anything, Black Bird? It must be tiring, staying awake while we dream."

"No. I will go to your cabin and sleep some more," he said. "You go into the woods again, and when you come back, you will dream again."

Colleen was worried about the old man. He looked tired and weak.

"Would you like something to eat? she asked.

"No, Mike's daughter. I will be fine after a rest. I am here to make sure this story gets told. You go with the man and the girl. Breathe the mountain air. I will be ready when you come back."

The dreamers returned to find the country had awakened to spring. Lodge Grass Creek was running high and muddy, the pasture grasses were lush and high, and calves and lambs abounded in the fields. As they soared over the little white house, Mike was carrying some supplies to a horse drawn wagon. Della was standing on the front stoop, her face a mask of tension. In the advanced stage of her pregnancy, she was even more beautiful. Her skin was flawless and creamy, and her blonde hair shone rich like burnished bronze. Even though she was weeks away from motherhood, she looked like a young girl.

As Mike looked at her, he was overwhelmed with love and sadness for what was about to come.

"I hate this," he said, "but if we are to have a way to make a living, I have to go to the Dryhead now. I know you love this house, but I want you to go in with Mother and stay with Grandmother until the baby comes. Grandmother has delivered hundreds of babies, and she's the best one to take care of you. As soon as I know the baby is here, I'll come for you. But the sheep have to go to the high pastures now."

Della gazed at him forlornly, resigned to their first separation since the marriage.

"I know this is how it has to be, Mike," she said. "It doesn't make it any easier. I'm glad I have your mother and your grandmother, and Little Moon has been such a friend. I don't know what I would have done if she had not been able to spend time with me over the winter."

Mike smiled at the memory of the two of them in their many visits. Little Moon was reveling in her new life with Black Bird Shows. She reminded him of a bird set free to live as it had been meant to live. She rode her horse to see Della at least once a week, and they would spend hours talking about cooking, sewing, babies, nature, and dozens of other subjects that he and Black Bird were not privy to. With Della, she spoke the English she had learned in the hated boarding school, one of the few times she would do so. After each of these visits, Della was in high spirits for days, which made him happy. Her life on the Lorrah ranch included the companionship of his mother and grandmother, but she needed people her own age. Willow made sporadic appearances, but her existence was on another plane, one so separate that Della felt little connection to it. She enjoyed Willow and the momentary excitement of her brief stopovers, but it was Little Moon who brought her the greatest joy.

When they told Black Bird and Little Moon during a recent visit that Della would be staying in Lodge Grass with Anna until the birth of the baby, Little Moon did not hesitate.

"I'll come to see you there, just like here," she assured Della. "The ride is not that much further."

"Will you be in any danger, coming into town?" Mike asked.

Black Bird shook his head.

"The way she looks now, no one will ever know she's the same person," he said. "And I was a kid when I left the school. If anyone still looks for me, they won't know me."

Mike was concerned.

"Your coming to my grandfather's wake stirred up some questions in town," he said. "I sure would hate to bring any trouble to you."

"I cannot spend my life trying to avoid problems," Black Bird said. "That would not be living. It would be hiding. I am not going to do that."

Looking long and hard at his friend, Mike said, "If you think Bart is still on your trail, you have to tell me. I want to be at your side if he ever shows up."

"He's too much a coward to face me, now that I am a man," Black Bird observed. "He only wants to fight the weak and the helpless."

"I hear he's doing his collections around Crow with a gang of thugs," Mike said. "I don't think he'd come alone."

"We will just have to wait and see what he does. As for me, I'm going to live my life."

Mike knew the subject was closed, and they talked of other things.

Now, as he prepared to depart for the mountain, he reminded Della, "When Little Moon comes to visit, please encourage her to be discreet. The fewer people who see her coming and going from Lodge Grass, the better."

Della nodded, the worried look on her face intensifying.

"You don't really think anything is going to happen, do you?" she asked, voice plaintive.

Mike rushed to reassure her.

"No, of course not. I am just afraid that she is so happy with her new life that she might become a little careless. Where someone like Bart Knight is concerned, you just can't be too careful."

He wrapped his arms around her.

"Please just take care of yourself and our baby. Grandmother will help you to know exactly what to do. And Mother will be there, as well. Dad and Mother will take you to town tomorrow, when Mother goes to church, so you should pack what you are going to need for the next few weeks. I can't wait to see our baby."

Della looked down at her expanded body.

"I feel the same way, Mike," she said. "We are going to be a family, and it can't come too soon for me."

Mike gave her a long kiss, and releasing her reluctantly from his arms, he got into the wagon seat.

"I love you," he called back as he slapped the reins on the draft horses' backs.

Della stood watching as long as he was visible from the front of the house. When she could no longer see him, she went inside and sat alone in their kitchen, tears flowing unabated until she could cry no more. She knew it was usual for men not to be present at the birth of their children, but she wished that was not the case for her and Mike.

The next morning, Morgan and Velia came for her. Morgan carried her bundles to his recently purchased car, and they drove into town. Della watched her little home fade into the distance, and she thought she could not recall ever feeling so lonely.

Once she was settled at Anna's house, she created a routine for herself. Despite the advanced stage of her pregnancy, she tried to help Anna with household tasks. She would keep the older woman company as she worked in her garden tending herbs, flowers and a variety of plants that Della had never seen. There was still a steady parade coming and going from Anna's home for various medicines and treatments, and Della was fascinated by the variety of people represented. There were Crow Indians, Chinese rail workers, Mexican field hands, and the everyday locals who knew Anna Daly and trusted her to help them. Anna turned no one away.

Anna cared for Della like a precious treasure. She made her special soups and teas, and insisted that she eat the freshest vegetables from the garden. Della had struggled to follow her instructions, but with Mike gone, she did not have much of an appetite. Finally, Anna brewed a tea that made her so hungry that she could not get enough to eat.

"Y' kin starve yerself after this baby comes, if y' like," Anna said sternly, "But I'll not be havin' y' starve the babe."

Della obediently devoured her next meal, and never failed to eat enough after that.

Time passed slowly, but good to her word, Little Moon came for her first visit. Anna was stern with her, too.

"Little Moon," she said. " Y'll not be leavin' except under cover of darkness. And the next time y' come, come before light breaks."

Little Moon nodded respectfully to Anna.

"I am not afraid any more, Mrs. Anna," she said. "I'll be fine coming and going in the light."

"Be careful," Anna admonished. "And I want you here when Della's baby comes. I know you can help me, because Black Bird tells me you worked in the agency hospital for a time."

Little Moon's smile was radiant.

"I would not be anywhere else," she said.

CHAPTER 28

▼

Della was helping Anna shell peas for soup when it started. First it was a small twinge, not so different from the baby's usual kicking and moving about inside her. Then came the first clenching pain and when she stood to try to relieve it, her water broke.

Anna was at her side immediately.

"Shush, darlin'," she soothed. "Let's get y' to yer bed."

As quickly as it had come, the pain passed, and Della said, "I think I am all right, now. I'll just go and change my clothes."

Anna went next door to a neighbor who had a telephone. As she walked out of her front door, she saw a huge white owl sitting on the gatepost. Looking into its gleaming gold eyes, she recognized its purpose. It seemed to understand the time had arrived, and launched itself on silent wings, gaining elevation as it flew toward the mountains. Anna stood still for another moment, then continued to the neighbor's where she called Velia. Explaining what was happening, she asked her to notify Little Moon, then come into town.

Since Velia did not drive, she asked Morgan to take her to Black Bird's house, following Anna's directions. Morgan did not like it, but he knew better than to cross Velia when it came to this first grandchild. He remained in the car while she went to the door and talked with the regal young Indian woman who answered.

When Velia got back into the car, he was silent as he drove up the lane to the main road. Once they were on their way into town, he asked Velia a number of questions about the place they had just been, and about the people who lived there. Velia did not like to keep secrets from her husband, so she told him some of what she knew. Her information was spotty, but it seemed to be enough to satisfy Morgan.

Morgan brought her to Anna's house, and then went off to the livery stable. He didn't like to be around when babies were being born. He had managed to steer clear of it when his own children came, and he would avoid it now.

At the livery, he was surprised to see two men from his past horse dealing days. Jack Cole and "Stubs" Schmidt were talking with several of the other regulars who hung around the stable. Neither man had changed much since Morgan had last seen them some twelve years earlier. Jack had seemed old then, but he had aged little. The huge scar running up one cheek still gleamed painfully. "Stubs," so named for the three fingers he had lost in a roping accident, had a few more gray hairs, and if anything, he looked meaner.

Morgan stopped in front of the two.

"Hey. Morgan," Jack Cole said, "How're ya doin'?"

"I thought I told you not to come around the stable," Morgan muttered quietly enough so only they heard.

"Ya' did," Jack said. "We're just passin' through. The horse business ain't been so good lately. Not since we rode with you. So we hired on to help hunt for a couple of renegade Crow."

"Yeah? What renegade Crow?" Morgan's tone indicated how dubious he thought the statement was.

"Ol' Bart Knight, ya' know, the one from Crow Agency," Jack explained, "He had a Crow woman get away from him. Tracked her to Busby, then someone here thought they seen her a few times in town, so we're here lookin' fer her."

"Who's the other one?" he asked.

"Bart had a kid escape from the boardin' school when he was workin' there. Fer some reason, he's obsessed about that kid. I'd guess he'd be in his twenties now. So while we're lookin' fer the squaw, we're keepin' an eye out fer the buck, too."

Morgan wasn't happy to see these reminders of his past in Lodge Grass. He did some quick calculations in his mind, and decided he had the perfect way to get them to leave town.

"I don't know if it'd be any help to you boys," he said slowly, "but I think I might have a good lead for you. There's a pair who might fit your description livin' up Lodge Grass Creek not far from my ranch."

He went on to describe Black Bird Shows and Little Moon. What the hell, he thought. He did not know them, and he didn't like the idea of his family being so friendly with any Crows anyhow.

Jack and Stubs gave him their undivided attention.

215

"Now, I want to know that you won't be coming back to town for anything in the future," Morgan said to them. "Do I have your agreement?"

They both shook his hand. Morgan's handshake was very firm, in the hope that honor among thieves would serve him well this time. He left the men and went across the street to the cafe, in search of more respectable company. They waited until he had gone inside, and they scrambled to get to a phone to tell Bart what they had learned.

Bart told them to meet him on the outskirts of town, and he commandeered the car of an Indian man he had been shaking down for payments. He nearly salivated has he drove, thinking of the revenge he would extract if these people were indeed Joe Black and Agnes Little Moon. It was preposterous that such inferior people could outsmart him, and he had no other aim in life than to eliminate their existence. That would certainly show any other Crow that he was not a man to be trifled with. Fortified with anger, he made the trip from Crow Agency to Lodge Grass and he found the men he thought of as his minions waiting for him as instructed.

"I want you to check things out," he told them. "Don't know if Morgan Lorrah knows what he's talkin' about on this, but if he does, I don't want any mistakes. You go on ahead, keep watch, but don't do anything 'til I catch up with you. First, I got me a little business with a person who told Mike Lorrah lies about me."

The two men looked at him blankly at this comment, then discarded it.

"What do you want us to do, exactly?" Stubs asked.

"Find a spot where you can watch the activity at the Indian's place."

Stubbs nodded.

"I know that country," he said. "There's a hill across from the road out of there where ya' can see anyone who comes or goes."

"Can ya' stay outa sight?"

"Hell yes," Stubs snorted. "Ain't no one goin' to be lookin' fer us, anyhow."

He gave Bart some directions so he could find them, and they saddled their horses. Bart didn't wait to see them off, but headed on foot toward Anna's house.

By the time he got there, Anna was just closing the front door. Bart stopped her, his hand holding the door partially open. His face was white with anger, and his eyes glittered.

"Well, old woman," he said, "Seems you've caused me some trouble."

Anna's gaze was steady.

"Hello, Bartholomew," she said. "I wondered when you'd be showin' up."

"Took me a while to figger out how Mike Lorrah knew about me. Then somebody told me he's yer grandson, and it all started made sense."

"What would y' be plannin' to do about it?" Anna asked.

"I oughta kill ya'," Bart muttered, annoyed that Anna did not seem to be surprised or intimidated by his appearance at her home.

There was a cry from the back bedroom. Della was beginning hard labor.

Anna gave him a cool look.

"There's a baby bein' born here," she said. "It's Morgan Lorrah's grandson, and I'll be after deliverin' that babe. If y' choose t' interfere, it's Morgan y'll be talkin' to."

Bart's thin lips faltered in their sneer. He loved threatening the helpless, but the thought of crossing Morgan Lorrah was not something he favored.

"I got me some Injuns to hunt, so I'll deal with you later. I *will* be back," he hissed, turning his back on her and walking away.

Anna blew a loose tendril of hair away from her face and closed the door carefully. Bart's appearance made her uneasy, and she feared for Black Bird and Little Moon. There was no question that Bart was obsessed with revenge against anyone and everyone he believed had crossed him. Knowing Little Moon was on her way into town, Anna wondered if there was any way to warn her. She walked down the hall to check on Della. Velia was with her, holding the young woman's hand, and occasionally wiping her brow. Anna returned to the kitchen to put a kettle of water on the stove to boil. She would just have to hope that Bart did not have any idea that Black Bird and Little Moon were in the area. The wee one was most definitely on his way, and her first duty was to make sure everything went perfectly with this birth. Della's youth and the fact that this was her first baby meant this would be a long day.

Bart went back to the stable and got into his car. Speeding up Lodge Grass Creek on the gravel road, he stared straight ahead. White hot anger burned in his chest, and visions of revenge circled in his brain. He fingered the pistol he had stuffed in the waistband of his black pants.

An occasional memory of his childhood flitted through his thoughts. He remembered that Anna had tried to pretend to be nice to him back in the Black Hills. But it was all an act. He knew that she hated him, just like everyone else he knew when he was a kid. People said she was a good person, but he knew better. If she was so good, she never would have told anyone about him being Indian. He'd take care of her once he had settled the score with Agnes Little Moon and Joe Black.

They would all pay for their betrayals.

He would make them pay.

And he would be sure they knew it was him making them pay.

When he had covered the distance Stubs and Jack had described, he began to look for them. The area on one side of the road fell off toward Lodge Grass Creek, and on the other side, rose sharply to a bench of land. The high side was covered with brush, chokecherry, buffalo berry, a few errant Russian olives, and other shrubs. He slowed his car, peering up the hill.

Jack Cole emerged from the vegetation cover a few hundred yards further up the road, and waved to him. Motioning toward a hidden track that led off the main road and angled up the incline, Cole directed him to a spot where his car could not be seen. He rolled to a stop, and got out. Cole wedged a rock behind one of the wheels, assuring that the car would not roll back.

"So where's this place ya' thought they might be?" Bart asked.

Cole pointed downhill.

"When we was runnin' horses with Morgan, there was a old Injun livin' in a log place down there. It's across the crick, and pretty well hidden. But if ya' look close, ya' kin see a lane down through them trees."

Bart reached into his car and pulled out a pair of field glasses.

Focusing in the direction Cole pointed, he peered through the glasses. Barely discernable on the downhill side of the main road was an opening in the trees and brush.

"You sure that's the place?" Bart asked.

"Yep. Saw the squaw come rippin' outa there a-horseback 'bout a half-hour ago. She was hell bent for leather."

"What? You didn't stop her?"

"Ya' *said* not to do anything until you caught up with us," Stubs said, voice dripping with sarcasm.

"Jesus Christ! You two are dumb as dirt. Ya' knew I wanted both them Injuns. Which way did she go?"

"Toward town."

"Both of you go there and bring her back. I'll stay here and watch for the buck Injun. Ya' think the two of you can handle one squaw?"

Cole spat a brown stream of chewing tobacco on the ground.

"Take it easy, Bart. Ya' shoulda' been more clear. C'mon Stubs, let's go get 'er."

They mounted their horses and spurred them to a gallop, leaving Bart standing there. It took him a few minutes to focus through the glasses again. Rage nearly blinded him to the detail around him. There was no sign of movement at the opening in the vegetation, and he paced back and forth between taking long looks in that direction.

At the Daly house, Della was deep into hard labor when Little Moon arrived. She brought a medicine packet from Black Bird Shows, and a number of small gifts for the baby. Anna met her at the door and pulled her inside quickly, looking up and down the street to see if anyone saw her enter. Little Moon went directly to Della's side, taking her friend's hand and whispering reassurances.

Velia was at the other side of Della's bed, applying cool damp cloths to her forehead and making her as comfortable as possible. She looked at Little Moon with a smile, glad for the calm that seemed to come over Della when she saw the young Crow woman.

After a few moments, Anna touched Little Moon's arm and motioned for her to come into the kitchen.

Speaking in Crow, Anna said, "Little Moon, it is not safe for you to be here. Bart Knight was here looking for you and Black Bird."

Little Moon's eyes grew dark with apprehension.

"Where did he go?"

"I don't know, but he acted like he knew where you might be."

Now Little Moon was frightened and angry.

"Black Bird is alone. Missus Anna, I am sorry. I must go back."

"That will be dangerous, too. He's sure t' be watchin' for y' along the road," Anna said.

"There are other ways to travel than on the road, old trails that serve me well," Little Moon said. "I am going now. Please tell Della I had to go back for something, but do not tell her about Bart. I do not want her to worry about anything."

Little Moon raced out the door and flung herself onto the back of her white horse, riding at a gallop toward the course of the creek, where brush would conceal her travel. Anna closed the door carefully in her wake, and returned to the bedroom.

Della was between contractions, and she looked up eagerly when Anna reentered the room.

"Where's Little Moon?" she asked.

Anna relayed the message as Little Moon had asked. Della looked disappointed. Tears stood in her eyes.

"I was hoping she would be here when the baby came," she whispered. "I am so happy to have you and Velia, but I wanted Little Moon and Mike, too. I miss Mike so much."

Anna patted her hand.

"I sent a message to him," she soothed Della, thinking of the great white owl. "He'll come as soon as he can."

Mike was feeding the bucks when he saw the owl. It settled to the top rail of the corral fence, folded its wings and stared unblinking at him. There was no doubt in Mike's mind what its visit meant. The baby was being born. He rushed to the barn where Dónal was repairing a wheel on one of the sheep wagons.

"Dónal!" he exclaimed, one word tumbling over the other. "My baby's coming! I have to go back to Lodge Grass!"

Dónal looked at him doubtfully.

"How could you possibly know?" he asked.

"I just know!" Mike said impatiently. "An Irishman like yourself should understand that!"

"'Tis true I've had a hunch or two in m' time," Dónal said. "One of 'em saved m' life. Y' did tell me when you came up here that you'd be goin' back when the wee baby came. I'll be fine with the sheep fer a time. Still don't know how you can be so sure..."

"Much obliged, Dónal!" Mike called over his shoulder as he ran toward the corrals.

He was not sure what to do first. Getting to Della in the fastest way possible was all he could think about. He could almost feel how afraid she must be, and he was sure she was desperate for him to be with her. He started toward Pal, intending to get him ready for the ride down off the mountain. Then he changed his mind and dashed to the house for some clothes. He stuffed them into a saddlebag, then set it aside, remembering that he still had plenty of clothes back at the ranch and at his grandmother's. Back to the corral, where Pal's curious eyes watched him as he grabbed for the saddle, dropped it, fumbled with the rigging, slung it up on the horse, and tugged the cinch tight. He was growing more frantic, and thinking about how far he had to go made him impatient.

As he was cursing his clumsiness, the owl glided off the fence and landed at the base of the sandstone rimrocks that formed one edge of the corral. Mike wanted to ignore it, but it would not be there without a reason. Patting Pal's neck, he left the horse and walked over to the outcropping. In the soft spring soil, he saw a series of small footprints. He remembered Dónal telling him and Black Bird about seeing such prints in the snow, but there had been no sign of them when he had arrived at the Dryhead with the ewes and lambs. Now they were everywhere at the base of the rimrock. Hundreds of them.

Mike looked around in all directions, but saw no movement. Yet he had the strongest feeling he was being watched by dozens of pairs of eyes. The air around him stilled. He could not hear any sounds and he was encircled in light the same color as the eyes of the owl. The ground seemed to move beneath his feet, and he felt like a black hole opened up under him. Wrapped in the amber light, he plunged into the vortex. As with the other times he had been transported to Della's side, he had the sensation of space rushing past him at a dizzying speed, rendering him powerless. There was no way to muster any clarity of thought when this happened. It was all sensation and helplessness. This time it seemed to take much longer to make the transition, but eventually it was over, and he found himself inside the room as Della cried out. It was a long, painful cry, ending on a sobbing note as she bore down in the final stages of delivery. The sound of it tore at Mike's heart.

Once again, he had arrived to a shadowy part of the room, and no one saw him there. He quickly took in the scene. His mother was saying comforting words to Della and the younger woman was trying very hard to be brave. But it was clear that she was frightened. Anna was seated on a low chair, ready to help the baby into the world.

"Now, Della," Anna said calmly. "We'll be needin' y' to make one more good push, and the wee one will be here!"

"I don't know if I can," Della groaned. "I'm so tired. I want Mike!"

"Y' kin do it," Anna declared. "Y've already done all the work!"

Della sucked in a deep breath, squeezed her eyes shut and pushed. Her face was red and ringlets of her blonde hair hung wet around her forehead.

Anna received the baby into a soft wrapping, and handed the tiny being into Velia's arms. The baby mustered a lusty cry almost immediately. Working quickly, Anna tied and cut the umbilical cord and finished what needed to be done to make Della more comfortable. Velia cleaned the baby and placed him into the new mother's arms. As she gazed into the miniature face, Mike stepped out of the darkness along the wall and went straightaway to Della's side.

Velia looked up, startled.

"Mike!" she cried. "How did you know?"

"Grandmother sent me a message," he replied, staring in awe at his son in Della's arms.

Della's smile illuminated the room.

"Oh, Mike," she breathed. "I knew you would be here. I wanted you here so much. Isn't he beautiful?'

Tenderly, he kissed Della.

"Are you all right?" he asked.

"Never better," she whispered. "Oh, a little tired, maybe. But it was worth it. Isn't he a miracle?"

"He's perfect," Mike replied, removing his jacket and taking the seat that Anna offered him.

Della handed the baby to him, and he was amazed by the joy he experienced when the little body was snuggled in his arms. He reached out his free hand and took Della's.

"I love you, Della," he breathed.

Then to the baby, he said "And I love you, too, son."

The baby stared up at the man who held him, and a potent connection passed between them. The moment was electric. A rich and bewildering mix of emotions filled Mike. Joy at seeing this baby was foremost, but everything was made more powerful by the instantaneous love and devotion he felt to both his wife and his child. He was grateful to the family legacy, perhaps for the first time, because it had made his swift journey to their side possible. But even more startling, he felt a ferocious protective emotion rise up inside him. Nothing must ever harm them, and he knew he would lay his life on the line to make sure they were always safe.

Velia continued to tidy the room as her son and his new family sat together. Anna took some items to the kitchen. There were only a few moments of peace before a loud banging on the front door sounded through the house.

Mike and Della heard Anna open the door, but her greeting was followed by a crash. Mike placed the baby in Della's arms and crossed the room to peer down the hallway. He heard his grandmother's commanding voice.

"What do you men want?"

A rough voice shouted, "Where's the squaw?"

"Who do you mean?" Anna's voice was cold.

"The squaw, Agnes Little Moon."

"She's not here," Anna replied.

"Don't lie to us, old woman, we know she came here."

The tone of the voice was threatening, and Mike thought it sounded familiar.

Now Mike heard anger in his grandmother's tone.

"I told you, she's not here."

"I don't believe you," the man said. "Who else is in this house?"

"Only my family," Anna replied.

"Let's just see about that!"

Mike could tell Anna was not afraid, but a great concern for her safety settled over him. Who were these men, and what were they doing here?

There was a scuffling sound. Mike edged along the darkened hallway, wanting to keep the element of surprise on his side.. He reached the doorway to the lighted room just as one of the men pushed his grandmother aside.

An icy rage began to build in him.

"Take your hands off her."

The men spun to look at him. The one with the scar spoke first.

"Is that you, Mike? It's me, Jack Cole. You remember me, I used to ride with your dad when you was a boy."

"I know you, Jack. Why are you pushing my grandmother around?"

"She's been hidin' a squaw that ran away," Stubs said derisively. "I knew from my time with Morgan that yer family wasn't a bunch of Indian lovers, so we came for the bitch. Yer granny says she ain't seen her, but we know better."

"What do you want with this woman you're looking for?" Mike asked.

"Friend of ours owns her, and wants her back."

"Well she's not here. Now you boys be on your way," Mike said. "I want you out of this house."

"Not 'til we search the rest of the place," Stubs growled.

"No. You're not doing that."

Mike felt his cold anger flash to white-hot rage.

"Don't think ya' can stop us, Mikey," Jack Cole said. "There's two of us and just you and an old woman. Why don't ya' step aside and make this easy on yourself?"

Now Mike's rage exploded. All rational thought left him as he bolted across the room and grabbed Stubs by the front of his dirty shirt. He became a whirling dervish as his momentum carried the two of them toward the door, which was still open. Throwing Stubs into the yard with anger-fueled strength, he turned to see what Jack was doing.

The man had twisted one of Anna's arms behind her back and he was pushing her toward the hallway that led to the back bedroom. With inhuman speed, Mike shot after them, and, slamming his hands onto Jack's shoulders, he jerked him away from Anna. He aimed a forceful punch at the man's face. The wrath behind the blow would have felled a mule, and Jack went down hard. Before he could gain his bearings and get up, Mike began dragging him toward the door. As he heaved him through it onto the lawn, he saw Stubs rise to his feet and reach into his belt for a pistol. Mike dove for the ground as the first shot whizzed past his head. Then the pistol seemed to jam and Stubbs was angrily shaking it, trying to get it to fire again. Mike's hand scrabbled in the grassy surface of the lawn, and closed around a loose brick in Anna's front walk. He tugged it loose, trailing little clods of dirt and grass. Time slowed, and his vision took on an unearthly clarity as he hurled this heavy missile. It sailed through the air for what seemed a very long time before it connected with Stubs' head. It made a terrible, clunking sound. Stubs expression was first shocked, then blank as he stood for a moment, then swayed and crashed to the ground.

Jack scrambled to get up from where he had landed, but Mike was on his feet, striking him with a sharp uppercut to the jaw. Jack fell again, laying still. In the grip of wrath, Mike grabbed up the brick again and raised it, determined to bash both their skulls in. Out of nowhere, the white owl flew between him and his adversaries. The sight of it brought him to his senses. Logical thought began to seep into his mind and he stopped in mid-swing, breathing hard. There was nothing to be gained from murdering these men when they could not defend themselves. They were only miserable tools of a greater evil. He looked around for the owl. It had disappeared.

Mike collected Stubs' gun where it had fallen and tucked it into the waistband of his jeans, then searched Jack for his. Anna and Velia both came outside. Mike handed the other gun to his mother, and took the length of clothesline rope his grandmother handed him. He dragged the two men together, and after tying their wrists and ankles, he sat their unconscious bodies up back to back, and ran several lengths of the rope around both of them, securely tying them together. Velia spoke quietly, as if trying to check whether Mike had regained control of his anger.

"Mike," she said, putting a hand on his shoulder. "I'm going to get Sheriff Lamborn now. He'll take care of these men."

Mike nodded, then he suddenly bent over, hands on knees, as a wave of dizziness clouded his vision. He stayed there as his breathing slowed and he calmed himself. Neither of the men moved.

"Well, Michael," Anna said with a chuckle, standing beside him. "Looks like y've a little of *Cúchulainn* in y'. That was a *grand* battle!"

Remembering the Irish legend of "The Hound of Ulster," his grandmother had told him many times when he was younger, Mike allowed himself a small smile. That she would see him as the seventeen year old Irish hero who defended Ulster single handed against vast armies amused him. Then he sobered, recalling that *Cúchulainn* also was known for his terrifying battle frenzy that caused him to become a contorted monster who could recognize neither friend nor enemy in the heat of battle.

He changed the subject.

"Grandmother," he began, "Why were these men here? Did you know anything about what they were trying to do?"

Anna nodded.

"I'm thinkin' they are working for Bart Knight. He was here earlier lookin' fer Little Moon, and probably fer Black Bird, too. He left when he learned Morgan's grandson was bein' born here today, probably because he's afraid of yer da'. I don't know where he was headed, but I've a feelin' he was on his way to Black Bird's house."

"Where's Little Moon?"

"She was here earlier t' be with Della. When I told her Bart had been here and might be after Black Bird, too, she rode fer home."

Dread seeped into Mike's heart, chilling him to the core. He turned his tormented gaze toward Anna.

"What shall I do? I can't leave Della, but they are my friends," he pleaded.

"Della is asleep. She will be fine. Go."

"Are you sure?"

"Go."

CHAPTER 29

▼

Mike ran to the livery barn. A quick search revealed that Willow's car was not there. In the corral, he caught one of the horses he had ridden in a few races for Morgan. He bridled it, and without bothering to saddle it, threw himself onto its bare back. He leaned into its mane as they raced up Lodge Grass Creek.

When he passed the entry to the Lorrah ranch, he urged the horse off the main road and onto one of the hidden trails that ran along the creek. He did not want Bart Knight to be aware of his approach. The shaded track was coated with damp leaves and moss, and the hoof beats of his galloping mount made almost no sound. When he reached the area near Black Bird's house, he stopped the horse, and slid off its back to approach on foot. He veered onto a secluded track that he and Black Bird had worn through the brush when they were boys visiting one another. At last, the log house came into view. Mike did not approach, trying to analyze what the situation might be for Black Bird and Little Moon. From where he hid, he could see both the house and the sweat lodge.

Steam was rising from the few openings in the cover of the little humped structure.

Black Bird must be having a sweat. Mike listened. He could hear his friend's voice, rising and falling in the prayer songs that he used in the sweat ceremony. From his secluded place, he heard another sound. A car was approaching from the direction of the lane. He heard it stop, and he heard the sound of footsteps from that direction. The person was trying to be quiet, but Mike had spent a lifetime perfecting his acute hearing for hunting and tracking. As whoever it was crossed the high runoff water of Lodge Grass Creek, there was no way to hide the splashing sounds.

Bart Knight came into Mike's view. At the same time, Black Bird emerged from the sweat lodge, clad only in the breechcloth he usually wore for the ritual. Bart's thin lips formed a smarmy leer. His eyes were a wasteland of vengeance and contempt.

"Well, if it ain't little Joe Black," he sneered. "Bet you thought I'd never find you."

Black Bird Shows face was stoic.

"I thought you would stop looking," he said.

"I never give up," Bart declared. "Especially not when I'm crossed by a stupid Injun."

"Now what will you do?" Black Bird asked, "Are you going to kill me? What good will that do?"

Bart couldn't resist being drawn into this question. He had waited a long time for this moment, and he wanted to make sure he had his say.

"I am going to kill you," he said. "And then I'm going to catch Agnes Little Moon and take her with me. She will pay for your sins and hers every day until she dies. No one double crosses me and gets away with it."

Bart licked his lips in an obscene way.

"I'm going to enjoy her in every way I want to," he said, watching Black Bird's face for a reaction. "And she's going to pretend to like it, too."

Mike felt the rage inflaming his spirit again. Why didn't Black Bird do something? He had to know that Bart had figured out Little Moon lived here. What was happening here? Something kept him from stepping out of his hiding place, but he was not sure what it was. Then he felt it. The cold reptilian thing in his chest twitched.

Black Bird was absolutely still for a long moment. Bart waited, but he was beginning to lose patience.

"Well, Injun," he hissed, "What do you think of that? You think that little whore of a squaw wouldn't give me everything I want?"

Still no answer from Black Bird.

Bart pulled a gun from his waistband and aimed it at Black Bird's head. He raised his voice.

"Answer me, ya' red bastard!"

Black Bird began to sing. The pitch was high and it sent a chill up Mike's back.

"Shut the hell up!" Bart shouted.

Black Bird sang on. The sound appeared to agitate Bart. Out of the corner of his eye, Mike saw a flash of white movement behind Bart. It was Little Moon on her horse. She slipped from the animal's back and moved silently on her moccasin clad feet. Mike did not know which direction she had come from, but he could see that she had ridden hard. Her hair swung in wild strands around her face, and her expression was fierce. Hate burned in her black eyes as she came toward the two men.

Black Bird did not look at her, and Mike was amazed at his discipline. Any quick glance would have given her away, but so far, Bart was not aware of her approach. Little Moon's movements were like those of a cougar as it stalked prey. Her motion was fluid and cautious, and she looked ready to spring at the man at any moment. Black Bird kept singing. Mike stared at the scene before him, knowing that whatever happened next would be bad.

Bart's gun hand began to shake as his face broke out in a sweat. The anger in his stance made it clear that he was on the verge of losing control. Mike saw his trigger finger begin to move and at the same time, he felt the first touch of a breeze move the air. A few leaves rustled in the trees behind Bart, and he spun around to see what the noise had been. He found himself face to face with Little Moon.

Surprise was replaced with cold triumph on his face as he recognized her.

"Well, Agnes," he mocked, "Have you come to your senses yet? You are mine, ya' know. I won ya' fair and square in that poker game at Hardin."

Little Moon stared at him, fury in her expression. She did not answer.

"Answer me, ya' little bitch!" Bart demanded, pointing the gun at her.

Black Bird kept singing, the pitch going even higher. Bart spun on his heels toward him.

"I told you to shut up!" he screeched.

His scream echoed for a moment, and the echo turned into another sound. First it was a distant moan made up of tiny sounds from the woods, the creek and the air. Mike knew what it was instantly, and it paralyzed him where he stood. The thing in his chest reacted, twisting, coiling, curling around and around itself, crushing his ability to breathe or to think.

When Bart turned his back on Little Moon, she wasted no time. She reached for a small scabbard that hung from her belt and pulled out a large, wicked looking knife, grasping its horn handle. Leaping at Bart's back, she slashed at him, cutting his arm. At the same moment, he squeezed off a shot, but it went wide of Black Bird's head, as Bart twisted to fight off the angry woman. He drew back his uninjured arm and punched Little Moon as hard as he could in her face. The first blow drew blood from her mouth, but did not stop her. She drove the knife into his leg, hard. He howled with pain, aimed the pistol at her and fired. She crumpled to the ground and lay still. Black Bird stopped singing and moved toward Bart at a speed that Mike could not comprehend. First he was standing in place, and suddenly, he had

Bart by the throat, holding him high off the ground like a rag doll. Bart made a gurgling sound, and his eyes began to roll back into his head.

Finally, Mike was able to move. He burst from the brush, pulling the gun from his jeans, and he shouted for Black Bird to let go of Bart.

Black Bird looked at Mike, gave Bart's limp form a rough shake, and threw the man to the ground. He moved quickly to gather up Little Moon's body, and ran, carrying her to the shelter of the porch. Mike stood over Bart with the gun trained on a spot right between his eyes.

The wind began to pick up, and the moaning came closer.

Bart gaped at Mike, his contorted face reflecting pain, fear and something else. He moved as if he might try to crawl away, but Mike gave him a kick that flattened him into the dirt. Leaves and bits of grass and twigs were spun off the ground and the wind increased. The moaning turned into a wail so piercing that Mike wanted to cover his ears. He was horrified. It was the Banshee. Was it coming for Little Moon?

"No!" he cried. "You can't take her! She has only begun to live!"

Then he saw the specter rise up out of the ground. His own bit of the horror expanded inside him in icy recognition of its parent. The Banshee itself was even more immense than he remembered, and seeing it in the daylight did nothing to diminish the awfulness of it. It stank of decay and death, and the ropes of smoke and dust and plant matter that spiraled lazily to give it shape were hideous. Where there should have been a face, there was only darkness, save the hellish glow of two red eyes. It threw back its head and shrieked so loudly that the air seemed to shatter. The parts of it that were skeletal arms were thrown back as if to take in all four of the souls there.

Mike made himself recall Moira's courage in the face of this terrible spirit, and he was determined to do no less. He stepped away from Bart and faced the monstrous heaving thing.

As he did so, he glanced down at Bart. The man was frozen in fear, staring at the Banshee with bulging terrified eyes. Then Mike saw it. Bart's leg was gushing blood where Little Moon had driven the knife into it. She had struck an artery, and his life was flowing out of him too fast for anyone to stop it. He slumped to the ground, eyes still staring, and his life ebbed out in a dark red pool that stained the rich soil beneath him.

The sinister, shadowy spirit that had inhabited his body sifted out of his mouth, and was drawn into the writhing folds of the Banshee. It emitted another unholy scream and then it was gone, a few leaves swirling in its wake. Bart Knight was dead.

When Mike turned his eyes toward the house, Black Bird Shows and Little Moon were no longer on the porch. He ran through the door and found Black Bird bent over the prostrate body of Little Moon. Black Bird was frantically cutting her clothing away from a bloody place on her chest, tears streaming freely down his face. Mike stared at her until he saw her take a breath. In an effort to do something to help, he sprinted outside to the well, where he pumped a full bucket of clear, cold water. As he did so, he looked up to see that Anna was on her way, her buggy careening with reckless speed across the creek crossing.

Before it stopped rolling, she swung down and carried her bag into the house. Mike followed her inside quickly, and saw her step in front of Black Bird Shows. She said a few words to him in Crow, and he moved to scrabble through his supplies on the shelves near the cooking area. Mike set the bucket of water down on a ledge, and Anna instructed him to pour some of it into a pot to be placed on the cookstove. She tossed a packet to him to mix into the water, and Black Bird added some other ingredients. The water turned a bright green, and the mixture thickened into a viscous paste. Anna issued another order to Black Bird and he rushed outside, returning immediately with a handful of dried moss. He mixed the concoction from the pot into the moss and kneaded it into a soft, moist clump. This he handed to Anna, who applied a portion of it to the area she had finished cleaning. She held it in place with the flat of her hand.

Black Bird looked desperately at Little Moon. Mike put a hand on his shoulder.

"Trust Grandmother," Mike said. "If anyone can help, she can."

The words were barely out of his mouth when Little Moon opened her eyes. She looked up at Anna, then at Black Bird. She smiled tremulously at him, and he reached for her hand as she lay there. Anna stepped back and he placed his other hand on the poultice, continuing to hold it in place. As Mike and Anna watched, the mixture hissed a bit, and steam rose from it. Little Moon winced, then breathed a sigh of relief. A few more minutes passed, and Anna reached out to move Black Bird's hand. She removed the moss and applied another piece of the clump. The results were the same, with steam rising. Anna continued this six or seven more times, until the mixture was completely used. At the fourth application, Anna brought her hand away. Cushioned in the used moss was a bullet, which had apparently been drawn out by the action of the herbal compress. She handed it to Black Bird Shows. It would make a powerful talisman.

When she peeled the last compress away, all that remained of the wound was a bright red scar on Little Moon's skin. Her patient sat up, and touched the spot carefully. Black Bird sat down heavily on the bed next to her, gasping for breath. He looked up at Anna.

"Again, you have given me a great gift, Missus Anna," he said. "I thought she was dead."

He looked at Little Moon with wonder. His eyes moved to Mike.

"And you, my friend, you have saved my life another time. No matter what happens in the future, I will always be dedicated to you and to your family. I will not leave them until the day comes when they no longer need me. Now, go to your wife and baby. We will visit you as soon as you are settled in the Dryhead."

Anna and Mike walked outside. Mike helped Anna into her buggy.

"What shall I do about that?" he asked her, indicating Bart's inert body.

"We'll be after tellin' the undertaker in town, and I'll be informin' him of what I saw." Anna said. "'Tis unlikely that anyone will challenge me story, but if they do, you be the best witness on Black Bird's behalf. Go to Della and your baby."

With a last glance at Black Bird's house, Mike walked to his horse, swung onto its back, and with a whisper, urged it into a gallop. There was much to do to ready his new family for their journey to the mountain, and his heart sang with the excitement of having them join him.

Once again, the awful cold thing next to his heart settled, and then slept.

The dreamers awakened again. All three of them exhaled expansively, as if they had been holding their collective breath inside their lungs throughout this part of their mutual observation. Colleen looked at Black Bird Shows. He looked smaller and weaker. Something about him appeared almost transparent in the early evening air.

"Black Bird," Colleen said, concern reflected in her voice. "I had no idea. Now I understand why you have remained so close to us all these years. What became of Little Moon?"

Black Bird gazed at her warmly, sadness touching only his eyes.

"We had three good years together. We visited your parents many times, and watched your brother learn to walk. He has a little pair of moccasins that Little Moon made for him, although I am sure he does not know where they came from. In her last winter, she tried to help a fawn out of the creek and she slipped into the water. She drowned before I found her. I gave her a tree burial near the house in the old Crow way, and mourned for many years afterward. Your father and mother helped me get through that dark time."

"I am so sorry," Colleen said. "It is easy to understand why you did not marry again, but it would have been good if you had your own children."

"I had the three of you. And I am clan uncle to a number of good young men. One of them is your friend, Thomas Sky Horse. He will assume my place when I am gone, so the young ones like Aisling will have a Crow guardian and teacher, too."

Aisling looked at him, eyes shining with her newfound knowledge.

"Mr. Black Bird," she said, "This is wonderful. You have made me see how my family history leads to me. I will work to learn from Mr. Sky Horse, but I hope you will teach me more, too."

Black Bird gave her a tired smile.

Indicating he wished to get to his feet, he accepted help from Andrew. In the standing position, he looked even smaller than when he had arrived at the camp. His head came only to Andrew's waist even though he stood very erect.

"I must go now," he sighed. "There is someone waiting for me."

He did not collect his things, but walked deliberately back in the direction from which he had come. As he moved, he began to fade from sight, and very shortly they could not see him at all. Above the spot where they had last had sight of him, a single raven circled, reverently riding the night sky in the light of the rising moon.

EPILOGUE

▼

At the end of the summer, Hugh came to the camp at Clear Spring to take Aisling home. In place of the sullen teenager he had left, he found a self-assured young woman. No rebellion, no distance. Serenity had settled over her like a shining cloak. She was ready to go, and went into the cabin to get her belongings.

As she strode away from him, he stood watching, almost speechless, next to Colleen.

"Who was that, and what have you done with my daughter?" he finally asked.

"Aisling has been a delight," Colleen said, "And she has been a very apt student."

"There's a lot more to it than that," Hugh declared. "It looked to me like she was going to be miserable all summer when I left her here."

Colleen laughed, but there were serious undertones when she replied.

"Black Bird Shows, your grandfather's best friend, spent some time with us right after she got here. He gave us the history of their friendship and of the Lorrah family heritage, much of it detail that I did not know, either. Aisling was riveted by every bit of it, and each thing she learned seemed to make her want more. By the time Black Bird Shows left us, she was completely committed to her place in the order of things."

Hugh pondered this. "It's funny," he said. "For me, it came so naturally. I was surrounded by Dad and Aunt Kathleen and you, and it just seemed like that was the way my life should be. I was fascinated by Dad's magic with word and image, and Aunt Kathleen is the very spirit of nature. She has a complete grasp of plants, animals, the seasons of the year and how to make all of us feel so cared for. And you, Aunt Colleen—it took me a while to understand, but you are the repository of all the family secrets. You collect memories and mysteries, and hold them for the rest of us."

Colleen looked at him thoughtfully.

"Well, I learned a lot this summer, too," she said. "Many of those memories and mysteries I knew nothing about. I had heard the family stories, but I never really had all the details. Black Bird Shows took me a lot further down that road."

"What happens for Aisling now?"

"She goes back to her life at home with you, Naima and her brothers. Let her have a normal teen age life. She should go to school, see her friends, and we must take care that she does not grow up too fast. Ultimately, the entire family legacy comes to rest with her. She will be a child of art, nature, and family magic. It is a fusion which must not be hurried."

"What about her summers with you?"

"Her desire to come here will grow each year. My friend, Thomas Sky Horse, has agreed to take over teaching her about the Crow. Before long, she will make a journey to Ireland, as well. There is much for her to discover there. It will all come as the time is right."

"It's a great responsibility," Hugh said. "Naima and I will do our best."

Colleen's laugh bubbled up again.

"That will be more than enough, Hugh."

After packing Aisling's things into the truck, Hugh hugged both his aunt and his uncle. There were other changes here. He couldn't be sure, but it seemed that Colleen and Andrew had grown even smaller over the summer, and there were a few more white strands in his aunt's hair. Both of them still looked very young for the years he knew they had lived.

When Hugh and Aisling descended from the mountain, Aisling was very talkative. Tales of her adventures in the meadows and canyons poured out of her, but she was not ready to relate the events that had come with the dreaming. There was no sign of the sullen, withdrawn girl he had driven here in the spring. She was more confident of her place in the family history. They stopped briefly at the ranch to see Sean and Lydia, who were equally surprised by the change in this remarkable girl.

Arriving at home, she bounded from the truck, gathered her things, and rushed into the house. Naima was waiting just inside the door, and Aisling threw her arms around her, dropping her duffle on the floor.

"I'm so glad to see you!" she cried to her startled mother.

She dug into her bag and produced a beautiful crystal from one of the caves on the mountain.

"When I found this, I thought of you right away, Mom. I hope you like it!"

Naima accepted it, and marveled at the rainbow of colors that danced within the stone.

Aisling had gifts for her brothers, too. She and Andrew had made slingshots and willow whistles for them. They were excited, racing to the back yard to play with their new possessions.

The next day, she went to see Jessica and Amy. They were delighted to see her, squealing their exclamations of welcome. For the briefest moment, Aisling wondered if they had moved from Jessica's room since she left. After the initial greetings, she asked how their summer had gone.

"Oh, it was *soooo borrring*!" Amy sighed petulantly, drawing out the words. "There was absolutely *nothing* to do, and we didn't go *anywhere*."

"I did get my hair streaked," Jessica said, pointing to make sure Aisling saw the rows of pink and green in her taffy colored hair. "And now I have a zit on my face that's not going to go away before school starts. I am *soooo* ticked off."

A tiny smile flitted across Aisling's lips. She reached into a pocket and pulled out a little paper packet.

"Here," she said with an enigmatic smile as she handed it to Jessica. "Mix a little of this in water and wash your face with it. I think you'll find it helpful."

Outside the window, two magpies watched from a window branch. Aisling spotted them behind her two friends, and she was sure she heard them laugh.

Printed in the United States
142148LV00001B/77/P

9 781440 123498